USA TODAY BESTSELLING AUTHOR

NIKKI ASH

You're worth the risk...

The Risk of Falling

The Risk of Falling Playlist

"Bad Habits" Ed Sheeran
"Leave Before You Love Me" Marshmello &
Jonas Brothers
"I don't Mind" Usher featuring Juicy J
"Strip that Down" Liam Payne featuring Quavo
"You can Get it All" Bow Wow
"Ballerina" Belly
"Dangerous" Kardinal Offishall featuring Akon
"I'm in Luv (wit a stripper)" T-Pain
"Come Get Her" Rae Sremmurd
"Hypnotized" Plies featuring Akon
"Bust it, Baby, Pt. 2 Plies featuring Ne-Yo
"Thinking Out Loud" Ed Sheeran
"You are the Reason" Calum Scott
"Obsessed" Mariah Carey
"I Wanna Love You" Akon featuring Snoop Dogg

Don't let the risk of falling keep you from flying.

-Unknown

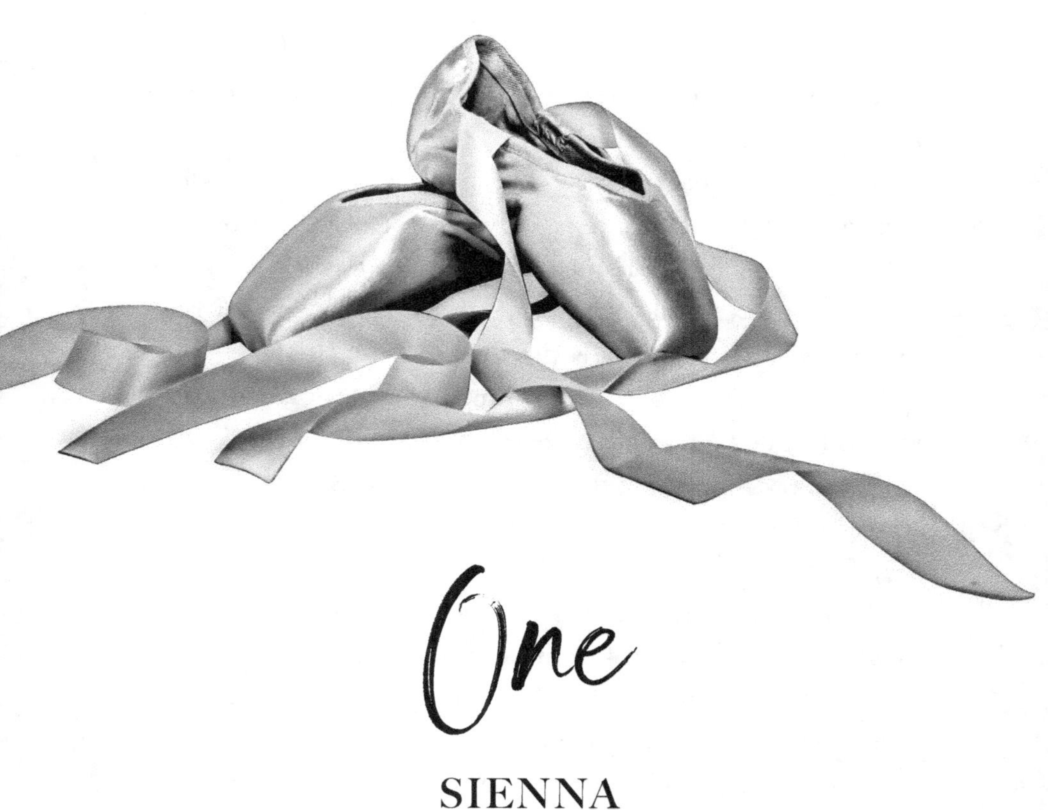

One

SIENNA

"Eliza Bardot, we need to go now!" I yell from the doorway, checking my phone, *again*. When I don't hear anything back, I shout in annoyance, "I'm going to be late for my shift. We need—"

"I'm right here." My sister huffs. "No need to use my government name. I was trying to find something to eat. I'm starved and today was pizza day at school." She mock gags. "There's nothing in the fridge," she whines, her sad eyes meeting mine. Guilt wraps around my heart and chokes it because she's right—the fridge is empty. It's been rough the past couple of months, ever since I lost my job. The place I was working at shut down, but thankfully, I've found another one that pays much better. I just need to get caught up and then we'll be okay again.

"I know," I tell her, softening my voice, since none of this is her fault. "But if we're late, I'm going to get fired, and then we won't have any money to eat. I'll get Ricco to make you something in the kitchen once we get to the club."

She grabs her backpack so she can do her homework while I perform, and we take off in my old beater of a car. It's not worth the insurance I'm required to pay on it, but it's a necessity since we live on the west side of Tesoro, in Booker Park, and I work on the east side, where the buses don't run.

"You're late!" Lincoln—my boss and the owner of Wanderlust—yells as I fly down the hallway past his office.

"I'm sorry," I shout back, not bothering to say it won't happen again. In the world I live in, it's better not to make promises I can't keep.

When I open the door to the dressing room, I'm hit with various smells, from flowery perfume to hair spray, to the burning of hair, as more than two dozen scantily clad women bustle around half-naked, getting ready for tonight.

"Sienna, you're on in five," Marina says, handing me my outfit for my performance.

"Can you do me a huge favor and order Ellie something to eat from the kitchen?" I pull out a twenty and try to hand it to her, but she waves me off.

"Go change. I'll get her fed."

"Thank you." I kiss her wrinkled cheek, grateful to have people in our life who care. Marina has been working in the entertainment industry since before I was even born. It's been years since she's been on stage, but she loves her job as house mom, and during the day, she teaches pole dance classes. She never had any children of her own, but she treats all of us like we're hers, including my little sister.

After changing into my outfit, I double check my makeup, and then go in search of Ellie.

She's where she always is—on the couch with her books spread out across the table in front of her.

"I gotta get on stage. Behave," I tell her, leaning down and giving her a kiss on the top of her head.

I pull back in time to see her dramatically roll her eyes. "I always behave, *Mom*." She glances up at me, her innocent green eyes meeting my blue, and my heart surges with love and protectiveness for my fourteen-year-old sister, wishing she were born into a different world, to a different mom, one who was capable of loving her. Then she wouldn't have to hang out at a gentleman's club all night while her older sister strips and gives strange men private shows and dances.

"I know you do," I tell her, trying not to choke up at the fact that my sister deserves better than this life, better than the hand she's been dealt. Despite the odds against her—geography and circumstance—my sister *is* well behaved. She gets straight A's, spends her free time at the dance studio, and never gets into any trouble. Most would use their crappy upbringing as an excuse to lash out and seek attention, but instead, it only makes Ellie that much more determined to succeed.

"Closer" by Nine Inch Nails starts, and I saunter onto the stage, mentally preparing for what I have to do. The second my hands land on the pole, I'm transported out of the club and into Lola's Dance Studio, where Ellie and I have studied dance our entire lives.

Instead of being dressed in black leather and lace with fuck me stilettos, I imagine I'm wearing a pretty pink leotard with a fluffy tutu and pointe shoes, my hair up in a tight bun.

Instead of dancing for men who are imagining all the ways they would fuck me if I let them, I pretend I'm at a dance recital or auditioning for a spot in a ballet company, performing for an audience who values my moves and grace.

It's been years since I've performed for a real audience, not since I quit dancing so I could get a job to pay the bills, Ellie's dance classes, and later, my college classes. Still, every time I get on stage, I'm taken back to the days when I was able to use dance as my escape—before the harsh reality of life shattered my dreams, knocking me to the ground and forcing me to crawl across the sharp shards left behind.

As I dance seductively, shedding each article of clothing until I'm completely naked, I'm taken away from here. Away from the ogling men, away from the smell of sex that permeates the air— far, far away.

And then the song ends, the lights go down, and I'm back in the present. At Wanderlust, I perform on a stage for money, three nights a week, just so my sister and I can barely skate by. While I pay the bills for the shitty apartment we're stuck in, our prostitute mom goes off fucking countless men in order to support her out-of-control drug addiction, as well as her pimp-slash-boyfriend's gambling problem—all in the name of love.

I quickly collect my clothes, then head backstage to put on a robe. Unlike most strip clubs, Wanderlust doesn't allow men to throw cash at the dancers. This is an exclusive members-only club for the obscenely wealthy. It has three levels: The bottom floor— underground—is a private sex club called Elite, where men and women can partake in various sexual acts while utilizing the club's carnal amenities. The ground floor is a high-class strip club and bar, which is where I work, and the top floor will be a restaurant called Impulse that's currently under construction.

We're paid a set amount per performance—each dancer performing two times per night—and then for every private show, we're paid a percentage of what is charged. Men can tip the dancers—which they do, *a lot*—and at the end of the night, it's split amongst the women working that shift. We can also provide *extras* in the private rooms, and a few of the dancers also choose to work the floor at Elite, providing a full range of services to that particular clientele. Between the dancing, the private shows, and the other options, many of the women who work here easily make in the high four figures per night.

After checking on my sister, who's practically inhaling her dinner, I change into my floor outfit—tiny, black leather booty shorts with a matching halter top that zips down the middle and dips low, showing off my naturally full-size D breasts. I pair the outfit with knee-high black leather combat boots and then make my way onto the floor.

Like every Friday night, as I walk around my assigned tables, I'm propositioned to partake in extras—to which I sweetly decline. Most of the regulars already know it's not going to happen, but a few newbies ask, unaware that aside from private dances and shows, I don't do any extras. It means less money, but I refuse to put a price on my self-worth.

When a group of businessmen walk in and the hostess says they've requested a private performance, I change, *again*, and then head back to the room they're holding their meeting in. Until I started working in this industry, I had no idea how common it is for men to hold business meetings in a gentleman's club. Oftentimes, they barely even notice me dancing. I'm more of a pretty backdrop that makes them feel powerful—I don't get it, but the truth is, I don't really understand men in general, and what little I do know, makes me wish I were attracted to women—it's a shame I'm not enticed by the female body in that way.

Marina once told me the annual membership fee here starts at seven figures. I can't even imagine having that kind of money to blow. But then again, the men who come here are worth millions, sometimes billions, so for them that fee is nothing more than a drop in the bucket.

The private show goes smoothly, and before I know it, I'm back on stage for my second performance of the night. Different outfit, song, and routine, but it's all the same—after a while, it all blurs together.

I'm about three-fourths through my routine when something—a spark, a zap of some sort—shoots through me, sending a shiver up my spine. It knocks me out of my escape and sends me flying back into the present. My gaze collides with a man, and for the first time in... I don't even know how long—if ever—my moves falter.

I can't see the color of his eyes from here, but the heat of his stare sears into me.

I want to look away—to avoid making eye contact—but I can't. It's as if he's holding me in place, his eyes locked with mine, demanding my undivided attention.

I continue my routine, knowing every move by heart, but I can't stop watching him, fully aware that his eyes never leave me. It's almost as if he and I are in a private room, and I'm dancing just for him. As I remove my bra and then bend, my legs spreading to tease the crowd before I take my panties off, I take in the man who's captured my attention.

He's standing by the bar, dressed in a typical power suit, sans tie, and even though he's completely clothed, I can tell he's built by the span of his broad shoulders and the way his shirt stretches across his chest. His jacket is unbuttoned and open, and his pants mold to his muscular thighs. His eyes are dark and piercing. He has a roman nose—slightly bent with a prominent curve—and his angular jaw is peppered with next-day stubble.

I imagine straddling him as I dance to "Rocket" by Beyonce, grinding against his groin. My fingers stroking the scruff on his face while his hands glide down my sides and land on the globes of my ass, massaging circles into my—

The lights come down, and I'm snapped out of my— *Holy shit*, was I just fantasizing about a member? I shake myself out of it as I scoop up my clothes—not even remembering when I got naked— and hastily make my exit.

I don't think about men, especially the members, and I *never* make eye contact. When I'm on that stage, when I'm giving them a lap dance, they don't exist. It's just me and the music. Yet, that man existed.

When I go to the dressing room to change back into my floor attire, I check on Ellie, who's asleep on the couch since it's after midnight, and then I ask Violet if I have any private room reservations.

"One," she says, glancing at her tablet. "Room four."

Two

MICAH

"WHO WAS THAT?"

"Who was what?" My brother glances around like he didn't just witness the most delectable, mesmerizing, fucking hypnotizing woman dancing on the stage. I guess when you're in the business he's in, you become desensitized to the women, to the dancing…

"The woman who was just on stage," I say, nodding in the direction she was a second ago, before the damn lights blacked out and she disappeared.

"A dancer," he says, being purposely obtuse.

"No shit," I growl, not in the mood for his crap. "I've never seen her here before."

"That's because you rarely come around and she's new. Was working at Pussycats until it closed down. A bunch of women came here wanting jobs. Most were trash, but as you can see, she's not." He smirks. Not because he's into her. My brother doesn't fuck where he eats. No, he's smirking because he knows what I know—I wasn't the only man getting hard from watching her on stage. She's not just sexy, she's fucking gorgeous…and real.

Most women in this industry are fake. Fake tits, fake face, fake tan, fake personality. I'm not knocking them. You do what you have to do to survive, to get ahead in this world, and a lot of men like that shit. But I prefer real. And that woman on stage was… All. Fucking. Real.

Those perfect tits with rose-dusted nipples. My mouth was practically watering at the thought of wrapping my lips around them. Sucking the hardened tips into my mouth.

Fuck.

And those luscious curves. The way she danced, swaying her hips to the beat, like she was one with the music. When she dropped to the floor and spread her legs, all I could think about was her riding my cock to that same rhythm. I've seen dozens of women naked, but not a single one has ever had that effect on me.

"I want her in a private room."

Lincoln chuckles and shakes his head. "She's not like that."

"What the fuck do you mean she's not like that? They're all like that." I've never been with any of the women here, but that doesn't mean I don't know what goes on. Lincoln might be the one who runs Wanderlust and Elite, but we co-own everything that's part of Alexander Enterprises.

"Not her," he says. "She only dances, does private shows, and will give the occasional lap dance, but that's it."

"You can't be fucking serious. Does she know how much money she could be making?" A woman like her could easily bring in five figures a night. Hell, I'd pay six if it meant she'd spread those creamy thighs and let me in.

"Trust me, I've tried," he says. "The guys are obsessed with her since she started here, some have offered to pay double…*triple* the going rate to get a room with her at Elite, but she won't do it."

My thoughts go back to the way our eyes connected, as if we

were the only ones in the room. The way I could feel the heat between us—even from afar. She might not be willing to give just anyone her body, but I'm not *just* anyone.

"We'll see about that," I say, standing and grabbing my drink. I swallow it in one go and set it down.

"Where are you going?" Lincoln asks.

"To book a private party for two."

Only when I walk over to Violet, I realize I never got the dancer's name. After Violet helps me out—and I learn her name is Sienna—I head back to room four and get comfortable. There are two hours left of Sienna's shift, and I've booked her for the entire time.

The music starts, and I couldn't tell you what song it is, only that it's upbeat and pulsates against the four walls of the room. The woman sings about wanting someone to give her more, and all I can think about is how much *more* I want to give this dancer, a woman I'm desperate to get to know.

A second later, Sienna appears on stage, dressed in a shimmery silver number and tall as fuck matching heels. When she gets to the center, she pulls the material off, exposing tight silver shorts and a sparkly bra. Her full breasts are spilling out of the cups and her flat stomach is on display. As my gaze descends, I notice her thighs are toned, and as she saunters over to the pole, I can see the muscular definition in her calves. I don't notice any piercings or tattoos on her skin. She's flawless, and fuck, if that doesn't make me want to leave my mark on her.

Her hands grip the pole and when she turns around, slowly bending over, my cock swells in my pants as I get a good look at her luscious ass that's on display, imagining her bending over and letting me take a bite out of her plump ass cheek.

I watch, completely enthralled, as she works the pole over. The strip club is Lincoln's area of expertise, but I've been in enough of them to know what good dancing looks like, and this woman knows what she's doing. She's sexy without appearing trashy.

Seductive without it screaming desperate. She gets lost in the music, lost in her moves.

When the song transitions to the next, she smoothly removes her bra and moves from the pole to the front of the stage. She's graceful like a ballerina, reminding me of the time my mom forced us to go see Swan Lake at the Metropolitan Opera House. It was boring as hell, and I'm pretty sure Lincoln and I both passed out halfway through it. But watching her reminds me of the way those dancers moved their bodies, with passion and rhythm. It doesn't matter that she's dancing in front of a stripper pole to some song laced with sexual innuendos or that she's topless. Her every move is threaded with elegance and grace.

I know the moment she finally *looks* at me because her eyes lock with mine, widening fractionally with recognition. The same spark from earlier ignites in her gaze, and it's clear that the chemistry I felt earlier wasn't one sided. But as quickly as it comes, she snuffs it out, her expression turning distant and cold.

Since I paid for a lap dance, she glides down the stairs that connect the stage to the floor and stops in front of me. Some women are willing to get completely naked for lap dances since they make more money, but Violet told me Sienna only does topless, and she doesn't allow touching. So, I sit back, drop my leg that was perched on my knee to the ground, and place my hands onto the arms of the chair, making it clear I'm ready and know the score.

She takes that as her cue and, turning around so her back is to me, swivels her hips seductively, shaking her ass from side to side. It takes everything in me not to grip her hips and pull her down to me, but I wouldn't disrespect her like that. The women here deserve to feel safe. But that doesn't stop me from trying to memorize every inch of her while she dances.

When she turns around, my eyes go to hers, searching for that heat, determined to light us aflame. Only she's not looking at me—she's looking through me—once again lost in her own world.

She might be dancing for me, but really, she's dancing for herself.

She dances in front of me for several seconds and then circles around my chair, stopping behind me. She leans in and slides her hands down my shoulders, along my chest and torso, stroking me seductively as she presses closer, her bare tits rubbing into my back. Her hands brush against either side of my groin, and if she were to move her hands a couple inches toward the middle, she'd feel just how turned on I am by her.

When her hair tickles the side of my face, I turn my head and inhale her scent. I don't know what it is… something floral I'm guessing, but it fits her perfectly. Sweet yet delicate. And then she backs up, taking her scent and hands with her. My fingers itch to grab her and pull her back toward me, but I sit still, letting her run the show.

She sashays toward me, then drops to her knees and rolls onto her back, spreading her legs up and out. The shorts she's wearing are so tiny, I get a glimpse of her cunt. It's not enough to satiate my appetite—it never will be until I'm tasting her essence on my tongue. But it's enough to cause my cock to thicken in my pants, damn near turning it to stone.

She parts her legs a bit farther then brings them back together, sitting up in front of me. And then she crawls… *motherfucking* crawls toward me, her tits hanging like the most beautiful, mouthwatering raindrops.

I assume she's going to climb into my lap, but instead, she dips her head and rolls forward, her legs coming up into a split before they wrap around my waist. With fluid ease, she uses my knees to pull herself up to where she's suddenly straddling me. It happens so quickly and smoothly, I have no time to mentally prepare for her body wrapping around mine. She reaches back with one hand and the other lands on my chest to steady herself.

And then she starts to move. Rolling her hips, grinding her warm cunt against me. I get a good look at her face. It's soft and feminine like the rest of her. Her eyes are bright blue like the color of a cloudless day. The light amidst a darkened world. Her makeup is natural, and her lips are shiny from the shimmery gloss she's wearing.

When she brings her other hand around to the front, I notice how they're small and delicate. Her nails are real and painted a light pink. Everything about her screams innocent, like she should be dancing at the Opera House instead of a strip club.

Her eyes meet mine momentarily before she backs off me and twirls around, giving me another view of that pert ass. Without thinking, I reach out to grab her hip, not wanting her to walk away, and in return, she swivels around and shakes her head, silently reminding me not to touch.

I sigh in frustration but remove my hand, and as a reward, she climbs back onto my lap, moving her body to the beat of the music. When she rises slightly, increasing the tempo of her movements, her luscious tits come into my line of vision. Her pink nipples are hard, and my mouth waters, begging me to suck them. I want nothing more than to taste her, touch her, feel her, and get fucking lost in her.

"What will it take?" I ask, leaning in slightly until our mouths are only inches apart.

She doesn't answer at first, so I assume she didn't hear me. I'm about to repeat myself when her eyes connect with mine, as she finally responds questionably, "What will what take?"

I draw in a sharp breath, the chemistry between us so hot, so intense, it's almost hard to breathe. I lean in closer, so close, I can feel her warm breath on my lips. "For you to give me *more*."

Still straddling my thighs, she slows her movements, the music continuing to play in the background. Her tongue glides slowly across the seam of her plump lips, and I home in on the way they glisten, desperate to lick them myself.

"There's nothing," she says, snapping me from my thoughts.
"What?"
"There's *nothing* you can offer me to give you *more*," she says,

climbing off my lap. She turns her back on me and saunters onto the stage, scooping up her bra and putting it on as she walks away. "Enjoy your night," she calls out over her shoulder, just before she disappears from my line of vision and the music abruptly comes to a halt. As I sit in my seat, with my cock still hard, I can't help but wonder who the hell this woman is and what it will take to make her mine.

One thing I've learned in this life is that everyone has a price. You just have to find out what it is and be able and willing to pay it. And since I'm a rich man, I'm more than capable of paying whatever the fuck her price is.

Three

SIENNA

It isn't until I'm out of the private room and back in the safety of the dressing room that I'm able to breathe again. I don't know what it is about that man that gets my blood flowing and my lady parts tingling, but that can't happen. I have a plan, goals that I've made to get my sister and me out of this hell hole of a life, and I'm only a year away from making it happen. I'm not about to let some ridiculously sexy man derail me. I can't afford distractions. Hell, I can't afford to even *think* about him. I don't know who he is, but hopefully, he now knows I can't be bought and will seek pleasure elsewhere because he won't be getting it from me, that's for damn sure—I witnessed firsthand my mom putting men before herself, and I refuse to follow in her footsteps.

Since I still have a little over an hour left of my shift, I change my outfit and help out on the floor until the club closes. I give two lap dances, which I'm grateful for, since I'm sure that asshole who wanted *more* will be pissed I wouldn't cave to his request and will likely take it out on my tip.

When the place is empty, I change back into my street clothes—a hoodie and sweats—and remove my makeup, not wanting to risk drawing attention to anyone in our neighborhood.

Once I'm ready to go, I say good night to the other women and wake up Ellie. As she staggers down the hall, half-asleep and mumbling about her bed, Lincoln comes out of his office and hands me an envelope.

"Thanks," I say with a laugh. "I was so busy trying to get miss sleepyhead over here out the door, I forgot to collect my tips." The manager on duty is the one who counts and gives us our tips, and usually that's Damon since he's the weekend manager. But since he recently got married and is on his honeymoon, Lincoln's been here more than usual—at least compared to how little I saw him when I first started a little over a month ago.

"Hey, Lincoln," Ellie says sweetly, a stark contrast to her grouchy demeanor only a few seconds ago. "How's the restaurant coming along?" I roll my eyes at her obvious crush on him. I told her once it's not happening, that he's a good decade older than her and she should focus her energy on the boys her age, but she just scoffed and said those boys were immature and she'd never date them.

"Hey Ellie," Lincoln says with a smile, ruffling her hair playfully. "It's coming along nicely. Working on the menu. How's school? You get that essay written?"

They discuss her writing assignment while Lincoln walks us to my car. Ellie loves dance and ballet, and she works hard to get good grades because her dream is to get into one of the top schools for the arts in the country, but she does struggle academically. And since I'm a math person, English is *not* my strong suit. Last week, she was struggling with an essay she had to write, and he spent hours helping her, which led to her newfound crush.

"I know you're all independent and shit," Lincoln says once

Ellie is in the passenger seat. "And this is a good area. But please have one of the security guys walk you out when I'm not here. If something happened to either of you, I'd be forced to kill whoever touched you, and I would *not* do well in prison. I'm too pretty for that place." He smirks, ending his statement with a joke, but that doesn't stop my heart from warming at the sentiment, unaccustomed to someone caring without a hidden agenda.

"Will do. And… thanks again for letting Ellie hang out while I work."

"Sienna," Lincoln says with a laugh. "You thank me every time you see me. It's not a big deal. She's a great kid, and you're a damn good employee."

"Well, still…thank you," I say again, unable to help myself as he opens the door and I slide in. "See you tomorrow night."

We get home and Ellie heads straight to bed. I shower and then sort my tips to figure out how much more I'll need to get caught up on the bills.

Only when I count the cash, my heart damn near stops. This can't be right. There's no way I made this much in tips. I think back to tonight. I did a private performance for that business meeting and a couple of lap dances. And then after my second performance I had… No. No way. There's no way he tipped that much after I told him no.

I grab my phone and send a text to Lincoln, telling him I think he messed up on my tips. All the girls have his number in case of an emergency. I assume since it's late, he won't see it and respond until tomorrow, but almost immediately, a text from him comes in:

LINCOLN

Too little or too much?

I type back:

SIERRA

Too much... way too much.

Not that I'm complaining, but we're talking thousands too much. And if he turns around and says he messed up and I need to pay it back, I'll be screwed if I have to return money that has already been spent.

LINCOLN

It's the right amount. Apparently, you made a big impression on someone tonight. Get some sleep.

SIERRA

Thanks. You, too.

I set my phone down and stare at the money. I want to refuse it, tell that guy that he can't buy me. That I'm not for sale. But at the same time, did he buy me if I refused him? I danced for him like I do for many guys. I didn't suck him or fuck him. I didn't give him my body in exchange for money. I gave him my time, just like I always do.

And this money will go a long way. It will mean paying for Ellie's dance classes for the next month in full and paying the rent without a late penalty. I can even pay the electric and water bill and have some money left over for next month. I already feel the pressure lifting off my chest. My head is finally above water, and I'm able to suck in oxygen without my lungs filling with liquid. For the first time in months, it feels as though I'm not drowning. Now I just need to stay afloat.

I should probably return the money to prove a point to him, but I don't even know who *he* is or if I'll ever see him again. Besides, I do have my pride. I also have a sister I need to take care of, and if he wants to hand over that much money thinking it will entice me into giving him *more*, he's in for a rude awakening. Because I'm not up for sale.

Four

SIENNA

"Time to get up, sleepy head!" I draw open the curtains and Ellie groans, pulling her covers over her head. It's early, seven in the morning, but thanks to that mystery man and his ridiculous tip, we're in the green for the moment, which means…

"Ellie, c'mon. I was thinking we could hit the farmers market and then make your favorite: Minestrone with meatballs. And afterward, we could go by Lola's to pick up that new leo you've been wanting."

This gets her attention. "Are you serious?" She gasps. "Meatball soup and a new leo?" Her brow furrows. "Is something wrong?" She flies up into a sitting position. "Are you dying?" Her eyes bug out. "Am I dying?"

"What?" I bark out a laugh. "No, nobody is dying, crazy."

"Then why the heck are we spending money we don't have?"

My chest tightens at her question. A fourteen-year-old shouldn't ever have to worry about money. She should be naturally selfish and lost in her own teenage world. But thanks to the shitty hand we were dealt, we were forced to grow up a lot quicker than other kids.

"Because for today, we're okay," I tell her honestly. "So, get your butt up and go get ready so we can head out." I know she's accepted my answer when a genuine smile spreads across her face and she jumps out of bed.

It's a beautiful morning, and we find tons of fruits and veggies at the farmers market. Ellie falls in love with a pretty summer dress, and I splurge, buying it for her. She's so shocked and happy, she throws her arms around me and tells me she loves me and how I'm the best sister ever.

At Lola's, she tries on the leo, and it fits perfectly, so I purchase it and pay for the next month of her classes.

"I'll see you girls on Monday," Grace says, handing Ellie her bag. Grace is Lola's daughter and the owner of the dance studio, who inherited the studio after her mom passed away two years ago.

Ellie takes a dance class three days a week, and I teach the beginner class two evenings a week in exchange for a discount toward Ellie's classes. Since I have school during the day, I make sure to plan my classes around Ellie's school and dance schedule, which allows me to be home with her.

Once we're home, we spend the next couple hours making her favorite soup. She always insists we make enough for leftovers, and today she's asked if we can bring Lincoln some to thank him for helping her with her essay.

We've just sat down to eat when the front door unlocks and then swings open, and our mom comes stumbling into the apartment.

"What the fuck is that smell?" she hisses. "It's stinking up the house."

Ellie visibly flinches. "It's soup, Mom," she says. "Are... are you hungry?"

"Not for that nasty shit," Mom spits, knocking over the lamp when her arm flails out and hits it. It crashes against the tile floor causing shards of ceramic to fly everywhere.

"Just fucking great," she slurs, clearly high…or drunk… or probably both. She rarely comes home anymore, choosing to crash at her boyfriend-slash-pimp's place, but when she does grace us with her presence, she's usually loaded.

"I need to go to bed. I'm fucking exhausted," she says. "It's been a long night. Phil is being an asshole again." Clearly, she has no real perception of time, and the thought that Phil is ever not an asshole, causes me to roll my eyes. I go back to eating, but then I stop when she adds, "The landlord raised the rent. You'll need to come up with an extra five hundred a month if you want to stay."

"What?" I gasp. "He can't raise it that much."

"He raised it two hundred. The other three hundred is for me allowing you to stay here." She smirks.

"I'm not giving you five hundred more a month for this shithole," I bark, pissed at the games she plays. Every time she and Phil fight, Mom comes home starting shit.

"You have any other options?" she asks, leaning against the wall since she's probably too fucked up to stand on her own. "Didn't think so."

She turns around and disappears, while Ellie sits there quietly, frowning down at her soup. I make the mistake of assuming she's out of earshot when I say to Ellie, "It's okay… One day soon, we're getting out of here."

"Oh really?" Mom snarks. "And where the fuck do you think you're going?" She storms back into the room and knocks my bowl of soup onto the floor. "You think you're so much better than me since you got that fancy fucking job at that fancy fucking strip club? If you don't like it here, move the fuck out!" She gets in my face, her rancid breath forcing me to hold mine. "Better yet… How about I kick you out?"

And here we go again… When my dad left, she would say she

couldn't look at me because I looked too much like him. I have his blue eyes and brown hair and pale complexion. I reminded her too much of him and all that she lost. But the more depressed she became, the more she used alcohol and narcotics to escape, and that led to her blaming me. I didn't behave myself enough. I required too much attention. I was a mistake, and he wasn't ready to be a dad. He didn't leave her—he left me. Somehow she's convinced herself that I'm the reason for her life falling apart, and because of that, she despises me.

"Mom, no! Please," Ellie cries.

"*Yes.*" Mom cackles. "We'll see how fancy you are living on the streets."

The truth is, with the amount I pay toward the bills and rent here, I could find a small place for me and Ellie and we'd be okay. Especially since our mom doesn't help with anything. With a year still left of college, it'd be rough like it is now, but we'd be safe and away from her.

But I can't do that because—

"And before you get any ideas," Mom says. "Eliza isn't going anywhere with you."

—the only reason I stay is because my sister is a minor, so our mom is her legal guardian. And since I'm a full-time college student and work as a stripper to pay my way through school, as well as the bills, no judge would ever grant me guardianship.

If I try to prove *she's* unfit, I run the risk of the state taking Ellie away from me, and I just can't take that chance. Instead, I stay here and put up with my mom's shit, so I can take care of my sister.

Next year, though, when I graduate, that's all going to change. I'm going to get myself a socially acceptable job and move us into a decent apartment. Since Ellie will be sixteen when I graduate, I can petition the court for guardianship, and they'll let her decide where she wants to live. Then our piece-of-shit mom can rot here all by herself.

Thankfully, Mom stumbles back to her room and slams the door behind her, ending her threats. She does this often, and tomorrow when she wakes up, she won't even remember this conversation. But that doesn't stop Ellie from looking at me with a pained expression etched into her features.

"I'm not going anywhere," I assure her. If it came down to it, I'd take her with me. Even if that means going on the run. I'd never leave her in this hellhole, *ever*.

I glance at the time and see it's getting late. "We need to leave soon."

"I'm going to need to borrow your sister," Lincoln says when we walk into the backdoor of Wanderlust.

"For what?" I ask skeptically, at the same time Ellie says, "Sure!"

Lincoln chuckles. "The chef I'm looking to hire is upstairs making an array of dishes for me to sample. I'd love a second opinion."

"I'm starved," Ellie lies, and I internally groan but don't say anything, not wanting to embarrass her.

"Okay, but I need her real quick. Can she meet you in a few minutes?"

"Sure," Lincoln says. "See you in a few," he says to Ellie.

"Oh, wait!" Ellie says, remembering the container in her hands. "This is for you. A thank you for helping me with my essay. It's homemade soup."

He takes it from her and lifts the lid, taking a whiff. "Smells good. You make this yourself?"

"Yep," she tells him with pride in her tone. "All you have to do is heat it up. It's delicious."

"Thanks," he says. "Meet me in my office when you're ready to go upstairs."

When we get in the dressing room, I pull Ellie to the side, making sure no one can hear what I have to say. "He's too old for you. You know that, right?" I've told her this before, but I feel like she's not listening.

Ellie's brows furrow. "Age is just a number."

Oh, Lord…

"Unless it's a number under eighteen. Then it's statutory rape."

Like the teenager she is, she rolls her eyes. "I'll be fifteen soon. Eighteen is only three years away."

I shake my head, making a mental note to have a chat with Lincoln. He's a good guy, and I'd like to believe he wouldn't cross that line, but I've come across enough sleazy men in my life—courtesy of our piece-of-shit mother—that I've stopped trusting in men altogether. So, while I'd like to believe that good, decent men do exist, when it comes to my little sister, I won't be taking any chances.

My thoughts go back to the night I walked into the house after my shift at Oswald's, the local twenty-four-hour diner I worked at throughout high school and my first year of college…

As I walk up to the front door of our apartment, I sigh in exhaustion. It's almost three in the morning and my shift sucked. I pull my keys out of my purse, ready to unlock the door, when I notice it isn't closed all the way.

A chill races up my spine. When I left at seven, Ellie was sitting at the desk in our room working on her homework. At nine, she texted me that she was going to bed. I hate leaving her alone, but since I'm in school full-time during the day, I have no choice but to work in the evenings. She's eleven years old, so technically she's okay to stay home by herself, but just because she can, doesn't mean she should.

I swing the door open, not bothering to be stealth. If our mom came home and left it open, she's probably passed out and won't wake up anyway. And if something's happened…

I swallow thickly, unable to finish my thought, and rush through the door and into the apartment. The sound of my sister screaming will forever haunt me.

I run down the hall and pull the man who's on top of Ellie off of her. Grabbing the closest item to me—a ceramic lamp—I smash it across his face, and he flies backward with a groan.

I expect him to go down like I've seen in the movies, but instead, he barks, "You fucking bitch!" and comes after me.

I fight him off the best I can, but he's stronger and bigger, so I don't stand a chance. He climbs on top of me and slaps me across the face— and just like in the movies, stars fill my vision.

He rips my shirt off my body, and even though I'm helpless to stop him from raping me, I fight back with all my strength, refusing to be a victim.

I'm so focused on him, I don't realize my sister has run out of the room and called the cops. I'm almost completely naked, my legs spread, when the man who's about to enter me is suddenly ripped away.

"Police!" the man barks. "You're under arrest."

Had I been a few minutes later, my sister would've been raped by a drugged out, piece-of- shit scumbag our mom brought home who was expecting to get laid. After she passed out from the drugs she took, he decided to go in search of someone else to get him off.

He was arrested and charged, and I thought maybe it would be our mom's wakeup call to get sober, since she was the reason both her daughters were almost raped. But instead, she simply disappeared for several months, showing up one day, high as a kite, as if nothing had happened.

After that night, I refused to leave my sister at home alone. So, I quit my job at the diner and got a job at Pussycats, where the manager agreed to let my sister hang out in the dressing room while I danced. It was all thanks to my high school best friend, Ingrid, who already worked at Pussycats and intervened on my behalf.

After Pussycats got shut down, several of the dancers went to Wanderlust in search of a job. Only a few got hired—me included—and thankfully, Lincoln agreed to let Ellie hang out in the back room while she ate and did her homework.

"Sienna, you're up first tonight," Marina says, bringing me

back to the present.

Dressed in an emerald number and white thigh high stiletto boots, I saunter onto the stage, ready to begin my first performance of the night.

Everything is going fine, my moves are on point. Until I feel eyes on me. I make the mistake of looking out into the crowd. And that's when I see him. The mystery man from last night. Watching my every move.

Five

MICAH

As Sienna dances once again on stage, teasing the men who are watching her, she looks as beautiful as she did last night. Her body grinds and sways in rhythm to the music, putting on a performance that will have the majority of the men in this club hard for her.

I overhear the guy next to me talk about how he's going to book a private show, and I chuckle, knowing it isn't going to happen. Because I've already booked her for the entire evening. Lincoln was pissed when he was told by the hostess what I'd done, saying I'm fucking with his business since Sienna is so popular. But Lincoln's not only my brother, he's also my best friend, so he knows better than anyone that when I'm determined, there's no trying to get in my way.

I get it from our father. While Lincoln works hard, he tends to play harder. Me, on the other hand… I'm more work, less play.

Which is why when he brought up the idea of a gentleman's club, I knew he was the perfect person to head it up. One of the most important things about running a successful business is knowing what one's strengths are and using them to the fullest.

Lincoln is the fun playboy. He manages the talent and other employees and oversees the day-to-day operation of all our clubs and hotels.

I'm the serious one. Which means, I handle the broader business side of shit.

Our father was a bit of both—at least until he met our mother and settled down—and then later handed over the reins to us when he had a stroke and our mother forced him to slow down.

The Alexanders own the majority of Tesoro and have been running this town for the past several decades. Most of the hotels and clubs belong to us. We own the marina where all import and export is handled. Not a single shipment gets in or out without our approval. Not a single business is opened without our consent. We have enough people in our pockets that we're a force to be reckoned with. The family every person in this town both respects and fears, and nobody dares to tell us no—until Sienna, that is.

Lincoln swears that's what has me coming back tonight. The chase. The determination to win, to get my way and have Sienna tell me yes. And maybe that's part of it. Up until now, when I want to get my dick wet, I snap my fingers and any number of women come begging.

Except her.

But what she doesn't know is that I don't give up that easily. And I'm not going to stop until I have her right where I want her—on her knees begging *me* to fuck her.

The song ends and Sienna scoops up her outfit then disappears behind the curtain, and I take that as my cue to head to the room where she'll be giving me a private performance.

I sit in the same chair I sat in last night, and she performs a similar routine to the one she performed for me before. Her outfit, music, and moves are different, but the outcome is the same—her gorgeous topless body dancing to the rhythm of the song.

When her eyes once again lock with mine, they widen in shock, then turn into thin slits, trying to convey her annoyance with my persistence.

But like the perfect performer she is, she doesn't break out of her routine. She saunters off the stage like she did last night and gives me a lap dance.

Only when she's grinding on me tonight, I lean in, our faces close, and visibly inhale her intoxicating scent, trying desperately to resist the urge to touch her.

"What are you doing?" she breathes, coming to a halt on my lap. "You can't—"

"—touch you? I know. But I can smell you…" Our eyes meet, and her breath catches. "I bet your cunt tastes the way you smell." I make it a point to lick my lips, drawing her attention to them. "Sweet with just a hint of spiciness. Intoxicating…" I lean in so close, our breaths are mingling. "Addicting…" Her lips part in a sensual sigh and her thighs, which are wrapped around my waist, tighten, telling me my words are affecting her.

But of course, nothing worth having ever comes easy, so I'm not surprised when instead of giving in, she says, "Off limits," and then climbs off my lap.

I watch as she stalks off—collecting her clothes along the way—and then disappears behind the curtain, leaving me wondering how many more times it will take before she finally gives in. This was only the second time, and I've already got her squirming in want. Another couple times and I have no doubt I'll have her on all fours, screaming my name while I pound into that perfect cunt from behind.

Before taking off, I stop by Lincoln's office, but he's not there, so I send him a text, asking where he is.

LINCOLN

MICAH

I'm about to take off when my phone rings.

"Micah, it's Pete," one of my contacts at the Tesoro police department says when I answer. "I have some information you might find valuable." In other words, he's expecting payment for whatever he's about to say. And I'll pay him because keeping the cops' pockets padded means keeping them on my side.

"Go ahead," I say, dropping into Lincoln's seat.

"Eduardo Gutierrez was found dead. Apparent heart attack," Pete says. "He was brought to Schneider, where an autopsy was performed off the record."

This gets my attention. The Gutierrezes are one of the most notorious crime families on the East Coast. While we own the majority of Tesoro, the Gutierrezes run the underworld, making their living off drugs, prostitution, and trafficking. We don't condone any of that shit, but because the Gutierrezes are a family you don't want to piss off, and our families go way back, we turn our cheek at the shit they do and, in return, they don't fuck with us.

"Schneider's reported foul play," Pete says.

"Any suspects?"

"I'm not sure, but word on the street is that his son is back."

There's a knock on the door, and my attention steers from Pete to the brown-haired, blue-eyed goddess walking in.

"What the hell are you doing in here?" she accuses.

"Thanks for the info," I say to Pete. "Keep me updated." I hang up without waiting for his response and give Sienna my full attention.

"Where's Lincoln?" she asks, glancing around the room with

wide eyes.

"Tasting food upstairs." I lean back in my brother's chair, clasping my hands behind my head. "But whatever you need, I'm sure I can help you..." I blatantly eye-fuck the hell out of her, causing her to glare my way. So damn sassy. I bet she'll be a hellcat in bed.

"Unless you're my *boss*, that's not possible."

I smirk, loving that she has no idea who I am—something that's rare. "Well, technically I do own this place." I shrug nonchalantly, lowering my arms and leaning over the desk.

"What?" she gasps. "What are you talking about? Lincoln..."

"Is my brother," I say, steepling my fingers. "And this club is owned by Alexander Enterprises, and since I'm Micah Alexander, part owner and CEO of Alexander Enterprises, that means I own this club and am *technically* your boss. So, what is it I can help you with?"

Several emotions flit through her features as she stares at me: shock, horror, a bit of curiosity. But when her eyes turn into thin slits and her lips purse together, I know she's settled on pissed.

"*Well*," she says, her hand going to her hip as she juts her chin out. "I came in here to tell my *boss* about the psychopath member who keeps returning, requests private shows, and then proceeds to harass me. But since you're my boss—" she glares daggers my way, and if looks alone could kill, I would be a dead man "—that will be a waste of time." She tilts her head to the side and smirks. "Speaking of which..." She steps closer, a gleam in her eye. "If you're my boss, wouldn't that mean you've been hitting on your employee?" She takes another step toward me and leans against the desk casually, crossing her arms over her chest like she's got this all figured out. "I'm pretty sure there's something in the employee handbook that says sexual harassment is not allowed. I could sue you."

I chuckle, turned on by her zero-fucks-given attitude. She either has no idea who I am—and by that I mean the weight my name holds and what I'm capable of—or she doesn't give a shit.

"What the hell are you laughing at?" she barks.

"Nothing." I shake my head.

"Tell me," she demands, and I'm pretty sure I catch her stomping a foot.

"You remind me of a Hellcat," I say honestly. "Gorgeous and sexy on the outside, with sleek lines and perfect, smooth curves. From afar, you assume that's all it is—beauty—but there's more to it than meets the eye—"

"I remind you of a cat?" she says, cutting me off. "And eww, you think they're sexy?"

She scrunches her nose up in disgust, and I bark out a laugh. "Not a cat. A Hellcat. It's a car."

"A car?" Her brows kiss her forehead.

"A Hellcat is one of the most insanely beautiful cars they make. It's full of raw power. Fierce and unstoppable. But you wouldn't know what it's capable of unless you get in and take it for a drive."

She swallows thickly. "And I remind you of this *car*? From the barely three interactions we've had."

"You do. I'm good at reading people. On the outside, you're beautiful, but underneath, I can see that raw fierceness trying to claw its way out. You're strong, but you don't want anyone to know because you're trying to blend in. Only you have no idea that you could never be a chameleon."

"Whatever." She scoffs, not wanting to accept the compliment. "I need to get back out there. I'm assuming you've booked a private show for after my performance?"

"I wasn't planning to," I deadpan, not wanting to admit that she totally had me pegged. "But since you brought it up, I'd hate to let you down." I smirk, clearly toying with her, and she rolls her eyes, turning her back on me and stomping out the door like the sexy, fiery Hellcat she is.

A few seconds later, Lincoln walks in, glancing behind him. "Is there a reason Sienna just stormed past me down the hall?" He looks at me and quirks a brow. "And why the hell are you sitting at my desk, bro? Get up."

"She's totally falling for me," I say, standing. "It's going to take a little more coaxing, but we'll be on the same page soon. I can feel it." I smile wide and waggle my brows, and Lincoln groans.

"I'm pretty sure sexually harassing my employee isn't the way to win her over. As a matter of fact, I'm almost positive the only way this is going to end is with a lawsuit."

I bark out a laugh for the second time tonight. "Funny… that's exactly what she said." I glance down at my watch. It's almost time for Sienna's second performance of the night, and since I'm still here, I might as well stay and watch. "I'd love to continue this, little bro," I say, patting his shoulder as I walk past him. "But I have a show to catch." And a woman to make mine.

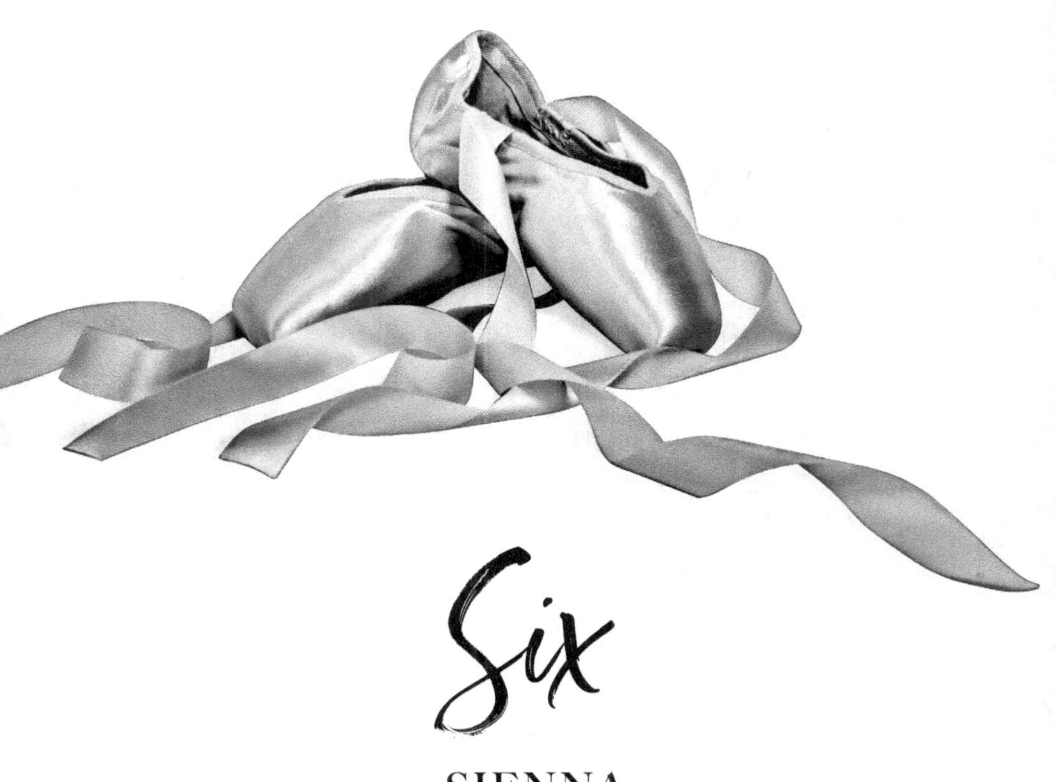

$\mathcal{S}$ix

SIENNA

HE'S IN THE AUDIENCE. THAT COCKY, INFURIATING, SEXY psycho stalker is in the audience once again watching me. After I learned he was Lincoln's brother, I asked Marina about him since she knows everything about everyone—not because I'm interested, but because if I want a fighting chance at beating him at whatever game he's playing, I need to know who I'm up against.

Unfortunately, what I learned was not good. Not only is he a sexy damn psycho, but he's Micah Alexander: the notorious, wealthy businessman whose family runs this town. I don't know why I never put two and two together, but now that I know who Lincoln's related to, it all makes sense.

According to Marina, Lincoln is the fun, playboy brother who everyone gets along with, making him the perfect front man to run a gentleman's club. His affable personality also translates well when it comes to handling all of the clubs, restaurants, and hotels that Alexander Enterprises owns and operates. Micah, however, has a personality that everyone seems to fear. He runs the business side of things with an iron fist and has the reputation of being a savage dressed in Armani. Nobody dares to fuck with him because he'll take you out in a heartbeat after first making an example of you.

When I told her about him showing up for my performances and booking private shows, her eyes went wide, and she said she's never known him to show any one woman special attention. Of course her suggestion was to milk him for all he's worth—she doesn't get why I refuse to sell my body for money—and once he's gotten his fill of me and my pockets are plenty padded, he'll move on.

But since that's not an option, I need to handle this differently. But the question is, how?

Micah clearly views my refusal as a challenge, so the only way to make him go away is for him to think he's won. But that would mean giving in and letting him fuck me, and that's *not* happening.

So, how the hell do I get him to go away without giving in to what he wants…? And then it hits me: What is the one thing men like Micah are afraid of? Commitment. And just like that, an idea forms in my head.

As I look out at the audience, locking eyes with the gorgeous, brown-eyed psycho, I can't help but smirk. Micah Alexander is playing a game he's convinced he'll win, but what he doesn't realize is that the rules have just changed, and I'm the only one holding the rule book. He'll catch on soon enough, but by then, it'll be *game fucking over*.

After I finish performing, I'm told by Violet that I'm booked, which doesn't surprise me since I knew it was coming. Micah is nothing if not predictable. Before heading to the room to get ready for the private show with my psycho stalker, I make sure to grab my sexiest outfit. It's a fitted, blood red, leather bodice that's cut low and wide, barely held together by three buttons in the middle of my breasts. Completing the outfit is a matching pair of tiny cheeky panties that reveal more than they actually cover. Once Micah learns the new rules, hopefully, he'll want to quit playing this game of his and move on to someone else.

Like the previous shows, he watches while I perform my routine, but tonight, I make it a point to dance extra sensual, swaying my hips a little harder, wanting it to hurt all the more when he realizes he's lost. When I move to the chair where he's sitting, I climb into his lap. His eyes never leave mine as I grind against his groin, teasing and toying with his body and emotions. Working him up higher and higher, so the fall that will soon come will be that much more devastating.

"Fuck, Hellcat," he murmurs, using the nickname he's apparently dubbed me with. "What's going on with you? Have you changed your mind?" His fingers twitch, wanting to touch but knowing he can't.

"Actually, I *have* been thinking," I purr, gliding my hands over the tops of his shoulders and down his hard chest, scratching my nails down his torso through the material of his shirt. His entire body shivers in response, and I smirk on the inside, knowing I've got the upper hand.

"Yeah?" he chokes out. "And what have you been thinking?"

"About how you want *more* from me." He swallows thickly and nods as my ass continues to rub along the bulge in his pants. "But there's something you should know before we take things any further," I say, licking my lips tauntingly.

"Tell me," he groans, thinking he's got me right where he wants me. He's so confident, his hands go to my hips, squeezing the sides.

Leaning in, I run my nose along his jawline and up to the shell of his ear, then I whisper the words I know are going to blow his game to bits. "I'm a virgin, and I'm not going to have sex until I fall in love and then get married."

His body stills, and his fingers that are gripping my flesh, tighten. I wait a second to face him, making sure my features are devoid of all emotion, and then I pull back, meeting his shocked gaze.

That's right… Game over, motherfucker.

Without waiting for him to say anything—because let's be real, there's nothing left to say—I climb off his lap and saunter back up the stage, feeling good about my win.

Before I disappear behind the curtain, I chance a glance back and see he's still sitting there, staring at me in utter shock.

"Have a good night," I quip. "It was lovely getting to know you." And with a wink that I can't help, I saunter off, knowing this will be the last I hear from Micah Alexander.

I learned years ago from watching my mom that if you give a man free milk, he doesn't need to buy the cow. Well, I'm not giving a man anything for free, and if he wants me, he'll be willing to buy the whole damn farm. Not that Micah will—because truthfully, that man can probably get as much free milk as he wants… just not from me.

I spend the rest of my shift on the floor, and I'd be lying if I said I didn't occasionally search for him. I knew spilling my truths would send him running, but a part of me was kind of hoping he was different.

Not because I'm attracted to him… I'm not—okay, fine, he's hot, whatever. Or because I want to be with him… I don't—this I'm standing firm on.

It's just that for my entire life, men have proven to be all the same, and it would've been nice if just once a man showed himself to be something other than a selfish pig.

Honestly, though, it's for the best because the last thing I need is to get tangled up with a man like Micah. That's just asking for trouble. I'm already struggling to stay afloat, barely able to make it through a day at a time. But every day, I move an inch closer to my goals—graduate, get a real job, and get Ellie the hell away from our mom. Getting mixed up with Micah would send me off course, straight into a fucking hurricane, and in those raging waters, I'd surely drown.

Once closing rolls around, I head back to grab Ellie, who's awake and reading a book—the girl is seriously the cutest book nerd.

"How was the food?" I ask as we walk to my car, accompanied by Rex, one of the bouncers at the club.

"So freaking delicious," she says, exaggerating her words. "And Lincoln said since I helped him pick out the items for the menu, once it opens, we can go eat dinner there at no charge."

I glance at her beaming face and mentally groan, wishing she wasn't crushing on a man who's over a decade older than her. Which leads to a tidal wave of guilt crashing into me because she wouldn't be in this position if it weren't for me working at a strip club and having to bring my teenage sister along with me. Anger with the strength of a tsunami surges through me at the thought of our lowlife mother, a druggy who can't take care of her own daughter, leaving me to take up that responsibility in her stead.

"Did you hear me?" Ellie asks, knocking me out of my spiraling thoughts.

"Huh?" When she sighs all dramatically, I apologize. "I was lost in my head."

"I was thinking for my birthday we could go to the movies," she says, batting her lashes. "They're doing an all-day Twilight marathon."

Her birthday is on Friday, which will mean taking off of work. Normally that would stress me out, but since Micah booked me in the private room three times this week—tipping like he has something to prove—money isn't an issue at the moment. I'm ahead bills-wise, and my sister deserves to have an amazing birthday. It's kind of last minute, but as long as I find someone to cover my shift, Lincoln shouldn't have a problem with me taking that night off.

"It's a birthday date," I tell her.

T HE NEXT SEVERAL DAYS FLY BY. I'M IN MY JUNIOR YEAR AND taking the core classes needed for my accounting degree, so, between going to school and studying like crazy, working at Lola's and finding time to hang out with Ellie, my days bleed together. And before I know it, it's Thursday night, and I'm back on stage at Wanderlust.

As I dance to "West Coast" by Lana Del Rey, moving my body in a sultry yet erotic way, I can't help but search for Micah. It's been five days since I last saw him, but I can't seem to shake him from my thoughts. When I walked out, he didn't say a word, didn't stop me, and that should've been enough to tell me all I needed to know—he was only after a quick fuck, and once he learned that wouldn't be happening, he let me walk away. But something in the back of my head keeps niggling at me. I've only conversed with Micah once, but he didn't seem like the type to let someone have the last word. Yet, as my eyes gloss over the various men, finding him noticeably absent, it's suddenly clear that Micah did have the last word after all.

I finish my performance and then locate Violet to find out if I have any private shows. When she lets me know that I have one, I change outfits and then head to the room. The music starts and I walk onto the stage. Until Micah, I would never look out at who was watching. The only way I could get through what I was doing—taking my clothes off for strange men—was to pretend, escape. But Micah fucked that all up because as I reach the center of the stage, my gaze goes straight to the table…to find *him* sitting there, one ankle perched over his knee, his hands resting on either side of the armrests, his heated stare searing straight through me.

Back before my dad took off, he and my mom were both dancers. So, I guess you could say that dancing is quite literally in my blood. I've been dancing ever since I learned to walk, and I could easily do my routines blindfolded. But when my gaze collides with Micah's, I stumble for the second time since I've met this man. My tall stilettos get caught on the wood, and I nearly hit the floor, only catching myself at the last second.

The song continues to play in the background, but I stop moving, my hands gripping the pole for support as if it's my lifeline. We stare at each other for several beats, and I wonder if I dreamt the conversation we had last week. Because why else would he be sitting in this room, paying for me to dance for him?

"What are you doing here?" I ask, getting straight to the point. When the corner of his mouth quirks into a cocky smirk, my blood boils. "Did you not hear what I said Saturday night? Or did you not understand?" I strut to the front of the stage and pop my hip out, my hand resting on it.

He cocks his head to the side, saying nothing, so I continue. "Let me spell it out for you. I'm a virgin. I won't be having sex with you, or anyone else, until I fall in love and marry. So, unless you plan to force me—"

He unfolds out of the chair and stalks toward me. Since the stage is only a couple feet above the floor, he jumps onto the stage with ease and steps into my personal space. "Go out with me."

"What?" I hiss in confusion because *what the fuck?* Did he seriously just ask me out?

"Go out with me," he repeats.

"Hello. I'm a—"

"—virgin," he finishes. "Yeah, I heard you loud and clear. But even virgins can go out on dates, right?"

"I'm not going to have sex with you," I tell him, releasing each word slowly so he fully comprehends.

A wolfish grin spreads across his too-damn-handsome-for-his-own-good face, and his eyes light up, looking like a delicious mixture of melted chocolate and caramel. "You will," he says, bridging the little bit of gap we had between us. "First comes love, then comes marriage... then comes me fucking you." A devilish smirk quirks at the corner of his mouth as he cages me in, pressing one hand against the wall next to my head, the other landing on the curve of my hip. "I can't convince you to fall in love with me and marry me without taking you out on a proper date, so first things first. Go out with me."

His words knock me back—figuratively and literally. On the inside, I'm struggling to catch my breath, but on the outside, I'm stone cold, my features devoid of all emotion. I refuse to let a man in. I know what they're capable of. How easy it is for them to reach in and grab your heart and yank it straight from your chest.

I was there the day my dad destroyed my mom's heart, leaving it battered and bruised and barely able to beat. Only functioning just enough to keep her alive while she wished it would just fucking stop.

And a year later, I thought maybe my mom was starting to heal…Until she found out she was pregnant, and the man she had fallen for didn't feel the same way in return. He took off, and as he drove away, he ran over what was left of her heart.

A few years after Ellie was born, she met Phil. Mom was so desperate for love and affection, for someone to take care of her, that it didn't take much for Phil to convince her to become his puppet. He fed her drugs and promised her the world, and in exchange, she gave herself over to him—and the thousands of men she's fucked because he's told her to. He's her pimp and her enabler. He feeds her addiction, and she makes him money.

When my dad took off to create a new family with another woman, my mom stopped parenting. But that doesn't mean she stopped teaching. And the biggest lesson I've learned from her is to be careful who you give your heart to. She gave hers to three different men and all three had a hand in destroying her. Little by little, they broke her down, until there was nothing left but a decimated heart that had once beat healthy and strong. I've had a front row seat to the utter carnage, and one day that crushed and battered heart will cease to beat altogether. Maybe then, she will finally be at peace.

When Micah squeezes my hip, I'm brought back to the present—him asking me on a date and me freaking the hell out.

"One, that's not how the song goes, and two, you're insane," I say, because who the fuck goes through all this trouble to get in a woman's pants?

"Eh." He quirks his head to the side. "That's neither here nor there. I want to take you out. Go out with me. One date."

"No." I dip under his arm and walk quickly across the stage, hoping he'll let me go like he did the last time. Only before I can make it out of the room, he wraps his strong hand around my bicep and twirls me around, pushing us back against another wall.

"Why not?" he asks, his mouth so close to mine I can smell the liquor on his breath. It's spicy with a hint of sweet. And as his tongue darts out, wetting his lips, I wonder if he tastes the same way.

No! No. No. No.

"I don't date," I say matter-of-factly. "So, let it go because you're just wasting your damn time. I'm not going to agree to go on a date with you, I'm sure as hell not going to marry you, and you're never getting in my pants."

This time, when I slip away from the wall and take off toward the door, Micah doesn't stop me. I'm so rattled from our encounter, I ask Marina if I can leave early, feigning illness. She agrees, and I tell her I'll see her Saturday night.

It's not until I'm out of the club and into the fresh night air that I feel like I can finally breathe again. Ellie asks if everything's okay, but I distract her by saying that I have a surprise for her. Her birthday begins at midnight, so I run by the store and grab a cake, and then we head to the docks down by the marina. At exactly midnight, I light the candles and sing happy birthday.

"Thank you, Sienna," Ellie says once we've devoured the mini cake. "I know you're not my mom, but you've been more of a mom to me than ours has ever been." She lays her head on my shoulder, and my heart fills with both pride and pain. "I love you," she murmurs, "and I don't know what I would do without you."

I kiss the side of her temple. "You'll never find out."

And just like that, I'm reminded of my goals—graduate, get a job, get Ellie away from here. Dating is not on that list, nor will it be any time soon. Ellie is my one and only priority.

Seven

SIENNA

"I could seriously watch those movies over and over again," Ellie says, as we walk out of the theater.

"And I'm sure it has nothing to do with you practically drooling over that wolf's abs," I joke.

"I mean, that's definitely part of it," she says. "But, also, I love the way Edward looks at Bella. The ways he's protective and devoted to her and would do anything in his power to make sure she's loved and safe." She shrugs. "Maybe if Mom had someone like that, she wouldn't be the way she is. Things wouldn't be the way they are."

"Maybe," I agree, wishing my sister would stay little and naïve for a little longer.

Her phone buzzes in her pocket and she pulls it out—it's an older model that a friend of mine gave me. It has a crack in the corner, but it works, and I like knowing she has one in case of an emergency.

When she frowns and then pockets it, it feels as though barbwire wraps around my heart and squeezes tightly because I know what has her sad.

"Mom's probably still asleep," I say.

Ellie stops in her place and spins around to face me, her harsh eyes connecting with mine. "You know I'm not a baby anymore, right? I haven't been one in years. I know she's a whore who cares more about herself than her kids and that you pay all the bills while she snorts what little she makes up her nose. You don't have to lie to defend her anymore."

Oh shit. Her words are so real, so raw, that I freeze, having no clue what to say, almost positive my mouth is opening and closing like a fish out of water.

And then she softens her features and takes my hand in hers. "I know exactly who our mom is, Sienna. But more than that, I know who *you* are, what you've done to protect me, to take care of me, and I'm sorry, but that bitch doesn't deserve your loyalty."

I should probably chide her for her language, but I'm too busy wondering when the hell my baby sister grew up. I don't know whether to be proud that her attitude is all in defense of me or ashamed that, despite my best efforts to protect and hide her from the harsh truths, she knows everything.

"Lenora might've given birth to me," she adds, "but you're the only *mom* I've ever had."

Pride. I'm going with pride.

"I just downloaded season one of Gilmore Girls." I waggle my brows, hoping it will convince Ellie to watch it with me.

"No way, it's still my birthday." She side eyes me. "Gossip—"

The front door swings open, and our mom flits inside with a

maniacal grin on her face.

"Oh, good, you're home!" Mom gushes. "Happy Birthday, baby!" She lifts her arms, letting several bags dangle in the air from various expensive stores. She drops them all into Ellie's lap and sits next to her, her eyes wide in excitement. "Go ahead, open them!"

Ellie glances at me in confusion but does as Mom says, opening the first bag. "Mom," she breathes, staring at the bright pink bag in horror. "Is this…?"

"A real Coach purse? Yes!" Mom bounces in her seat and claps her hands. "Every girl should own one. And I know how much you love pink."

Ellie hasn't loved pink since she was like five, but that's beside the point, because that purse had to have cost a few hundred dollars. And that's only one bag.

Ellie thanks her and opens up the next bag—an expensive pair of heels she'll never wear. Inside the next bag is another purse, the one after that has jewelry, and the one after that has a laptop.

When she opens the final gift—a brand new iPhone—Ellie shrieks in excitement, thanks Mom, and then runs off to our room to go put everything away and set up her new electronics.

"Mom," I say carefully once Ellie is gone. "How did you afford all those gifts?"

Her head whips around and she glares my way, already on the defense. "It's none of your damn business," she hisses. "You're always so fucking negative, and I'm sick of it." She stands and stalks over to me. I assume she's going to get in my face to argue, but instead, she reaches out and grabs a fistful of my hair, dragging me off the couch and toward the door.

"What the fuck!" I shout, my scalp stinging with pain. Because of the drugs, her body is frail and unfit, and it doesn't take much to shove her back, so she lets go. "Where the hell did you get that money? And don't lie to me because I'll be the one cleaning up the damn mess you've made, as usual."

"All you need to know is that I don't need shit from you anymore."

"Until you snort through whatever money you've magically come into," I scoff.

"You're such a judge-y little bitch. I've had enough of your shit. Get your things and get out, for good."

Seeing the fire in her eyes, I refrain from rolling my own. "Fine. Ellie," I call out. "Let's go." When Mom does this shit, we rent a motel for the night so she can calm down. By tomorrow morning, she'll be back to her usual non-existent, drugged-up self.

"No," Mom says. "Ellie isn't going anywhere with you."

"Yes, I am," Ellie says with a sigh, an overnight bag slung over her shoulder. We've done this so many times over the years, we keep a small bag packed at the ready. "Let's go, Sienna."

"Hey!" Mom reaches out and grabs Ellie's arm, making her squeak out in shock. "You're going to choose her over me? You're my daughter, not hers, and I can take care of you now."

"Are you serious?" Ellie asks incredulously. "Of course I'm choosing Sienna. I don't know what you did to get that money, but maybe you should use it to go to rehab. You came in here, throwing gifts at me, and for a second I forgot who you are, until you reminded me by kicking out the only real mom I've ever known."

Mom gasps as if she's been backhanded and then her eyes turn into thin slits. "Fine," she spits. "Leave… both of you! Get out and never come back. I don't need either of you. But don't come crying to me and begging for money when you're broke and homeless."

Since it's pointless to argue with her, we leave without saying another word. The drive to the motel is quiet, but instead of going to the shitty one I usually check us into, I make a left at the last second and pull up into a nicer resort we've seen a million times but could never afford to stay at.

"What are you doing?" Ellie asks.

"I've made decent money recently, and it's still your birthday.

I say we splurge and spend the weekend in style."

Ellie's green eyes light up. "Really?"

"Yeah, really." I lean over and kiss her cheek. "Happy Birthday, El."

After we check-in to the cheapest room they offer—which is insanely more expensive than I thought—we ooh and aah over the gorgeous two-bedroom suite and then spend the rest of the evening at the indoor heated pool. Since the motel we planned to stay at doesn't have a pool, I decided another splurge was warranted and purchased us swimsuits from the hotel's boutique.

The next morning, we go downstairs to check out the breakfast they offer. It's probably going to be as expensive as the room, but I want Ellie to have a good weekend, despite our mom almost ruining her birthday. She deserves to have good days. And my hope is that even though there are more bad than good, maybe the good will overshadow the bad.

"I'm sorry, ma'am," the hostess says. "This restaurant is reservation only, and we're booked solid. I recommend—"

"Actually, they're my *personal* guests," a masculine voice cuts in. When I glance up, I find Micah Alexander standing there in a power suit looking as gorgeous in the daylight as he does in the dark of the club.

"Miss Bardot, you're looking beautiful this morning," he croons, blatantly eye fucking me.

"Micah," I deadpan.

"Oh, Mr. Alexander," the hostess purrs. "I'm sorry, I didn't know. But regardless, there aren't any available tables." She pouts dramatically, and I have to hold back from snorting out a laugh.

"Very well. They can sit with me," Micah says, locking eyes with me. "That is, if you don't mind having breakfast with your future husband."

Ellie gasps, and I groan.

"I know you!" Ellie says. "You're Lincoln's brother, right?"

"I am," Micah says with a nod. "And you are...?"

"I'm Ellie," my sister says. "Sienna's sister. You called the night Lincoln was helping me write my essay in his office."

Micah grins wide, and a single dimple pops out of his left cheek—like he wasn't already gorgeous enough, God had to give him a fucking dimple. "He told me about that. It's nice to meet you. How did your essay turn out?"

"I got an A." Ellie beams.

The hostess clears her throat. "Mr. Alexander, would you like to be seated?"

"I would, and will you ladies be joining me?"

Before I can answer, Ellie says, "Yes! It's my birthday weekend, and Sienna brought me here for a special getaway."

Micah smiles warmly at her. "Happy Birthday. I'm honored you chose my hotel to celebrate your birthday."

I groan, again. Of course, Hotel Blu is his damn hotel.

We're seated at the table and a second later, Lincoln sits, glancing at Ellie and me in confusion. Then his eyes land on Micah and he chuckles.

"Sorry, we're crashing," I say to my *real* boss. "Micah invited us when we were told the restaurant was booked, and Ellie agreed."

"No worries," Lincoln says. "The breakfast here is delicious."

"Do you guys come here to eat often?" I ask, making conversation.

"We live in the penthouses on the top floor," Lincoln says, "so it's convenient."

"You live here?" Ellie gasps. "In a hotel?"

"This hotel actually has the option to purchase," Lincoln explains to her. "A lot of the guests own condos and will rent them out when they leave for the winter."

"That's so cool," Ellie says. "I wish I could live here. A pool, restaurant, and spa all at your disposal." She sighs dramatically. "I wish I were rich."

Lincoln and Micah both chuckle.

"Have you checked out the pool and spa yet?" Micah asks, his eyes landing on me.

"The pool, but not the spa," Ellie answers. "We want to get massages, but they don't have any appointments available."

I flinch and hold my breath, afraid of getting caught in my lie. The truth is, the services are too much money, and I've already splurged on the hotel and swimsuits. So, when Ellie asked, I told her nothing was available, not wanting to put a damper on our mini vacation.

"Hmm," Micah says. "I'll look into that for you. Are you here all weekend?"

"Yep," Ellie says. "Sienna has to go to work tonight, but we're staying until tomorrow."

"If you want..." Lincoln begins, but I'm already shaking my head.

"I need to work," I say quickly. I already missed last night, and with the added expense of the hotel this weekend, I need money coming in—especially if, by some chance, our mom really meant what she said and we're out on our asses.

Lincoln nods in understanding. Thankfully, the conversation is cut short when the waitress comes over to bring us glasses of ice water and then proceeds to take our drink order.

Of course, leave it to my sister to find an even worse topic to bring up.

"So, what's this about you being my sister's future husband?" she asks, after we've all ordered various types of coffees.

Lincoln snorts out a laugh, I stop myself from banging my head on the table, and Micah grins like a Cheshire cat.

"He was joking," I say, glaring at Micah, at the same time he says, "One day we're going to get married... as soon as she agrees to go on a date with me."

Ellie finds this amusing. "You haven't even gotten her to go on a date with you and you think you're going to convince her to marry you?" She shakes her head. "Good luck with that."

Micah's grin only grows wider as he leans in, pretending to

whisper. "Any pointers?"

"Nope," she says, popping the P. "She doesn't date. Ever. If it weren't for me coming across the porn she was watching once by mistake, I'd think she was a lesbian."

I'm drinking my water when she says this, and the liquid gets stuck in my throat as I choke on her words. I start coughing violently, so Micah reaches over and pats my back. His eyes, filled with mirth, connect with mine, and he whispers so no one can hear, "You know, if you let me take you out, you won't need porn anymore."

My breath hitches and I move away from his touch. "Hey, El, how about we don't share personal info with others, yeah?"

She tucks her lips in to hide her smile, and I know she did that shit on purpose to fuck with me. "Sorry, sis."

Once our coffees arrive and we order our food, Lincoln steers the conversation down a safer road, asking Ellie how her dance practice is going for her upcoming showcase. Excited that Lincoln remembered and always ready to talk dance, she tells everyone about her performance and how she wants to one day attend a college of the arts.

"What do you do with dance?" Lincoln asks curiously.

"Some people join a company, perform professionally." She glances at me. "Sienna was so good she was invited to join a company right out of high school."

The guys turn their attention on me, and I find myself suddenly flushed. "I thought you were an accounting major," Lincoln says.

"That's because dancing professionally doesn't pay very well," Ellie says, not knowing when to be quiet. "She needs a job that pays enough to cover the bills, since we'd be living on the streets if we left that up to our mom. She glances at me and smiles softly. "She's only working at your club so she can take care of me. She doesn't belong there, she's only doing it because of me."

And just like that, my sister is forgiven.

"I am *not* doing it because of you," I say, not at all okay with the misplaced guilt that's wrapped around her words.

"Yes, you are," she says, not caring that we're sitting with two men who are practically strangers and airing our dirty laundry out in front of them. "If it weren't for you having to take care of me, you'd be dancing right now—and not on a pole. And you wouldn't be stuck in college, majoring in something you don't even like." Her brow furrows and then she adds, "Is that why you never date? Because you're always with me?"

Oh, Jesus. This girl is killing me.

"Eliza," I hiss, my gaze swinging between her and the guys who are listening, trying to convey to her to stop. But of course, like the clueless teenager she is, she tilts her head to the side in confusion.

Thankfully, the food arrives, and she shuts up to eat. Lincoln and Micah make small talk over breakfast, and once our plates are cleared, I thank them for letting us crash. When I pull out some cash to give to Micah, not wanting to owe him anything, he shakes his head.

"Not happening, Hellcat."

"Hellcat?" Ellie asks, not missing a damn beat.

"It's an inside joke," Micah says with a smirk.

Of course his non answer has Ellie intrigued. "You guys have inside jokes? How well do you know each other?"

"Eliza Bardot, enough," I growl under my breath, making Micah and Lincoln laugh.

"What?" she asks. "The guy introduced himself as your future husband, has a pet name for you, and I don't even know how the two of you met."

"We met at the club," I explain. "He's *not* my future husband. I don't even like him, and that stupid name is his way of aggravating me."

Ellie grins like she was birthed straight from the devil. "Sounds like he likes you. Maybe you should go out with him."

"And now it's time to go," I say, standing. "Gentleman, it's been great. Thank you again for breakfast."

Eight

SIENNA

"Wʜᴀᴛ ᴛʜᴇ ʜᴇʟʟ ᴡᴀѕ ᴛʜᴀᴛ ᴀʙᴏᴜᴛ?" I ʜɪѕѕ, ᴘʀᴇѕѕɪɴɢ ᴛʜᴇ button for our floor when we enter the elevator.

"What?" she asks, sounding and looking like she genuinely doesn't get it. "I know you like Lincoln, who is still too old for you, by the way…" I give her a pointed glare. "But our money situation and why I'm working where I am isn't anyone's business. And my God, you told them I watch porn! And don't get me started on the way you were trying to play matchmaker. That was embarrassing."

Her face falls, her features showing a mixture of remorse and regret. "I… I didn't even think," she says. "I'm sorry. I was joking and talking, and I didn't mean to embarrass you. We always play around."

"Yeah, we do. But they're my bosses. That's different."

"He clearly likes you," Ellie points out. "Micah couldn't take his eyes off of you the entire time."

"Well, the feeling isn't mutual," I say, as we step off the elevator.

"You don't think he's cute?"

"Of course he is."

"And he's sweet. He invited us to breakfast."

"Yep," I say noncommittally, unlocking and opening the door to our room.

"You should go out with him."

"I don't have time to date, El."

"Because of me," she says. "Because you're too busy taking care of me. Which I get, but also, I'm fifteen now. It's okay to have your own life, too."

"Not because of you," I repeat. "Because—"

I stop in my tracks, my words freezing, when I see a dozen beautiful white and pink roses in a vase on the counter that weren't there before.

"Oh! So pretty!" Ellie bounces over and snatches up the card. "It has your name on it," she says.

I roll my eyes and open the envelope, pulling the card out and reading it...

Sienna, it was a wonderful surprise getting to have breakfast with you. I look forward to seeing you tonight. - Micah

Jesus, how the hell did he get this delivered so quickly? He must've done it when he was briefly on his phone.

"Oh! Another envelope. This one is addressed to me." Ellie rips it open and reads the card out loud...

"Thank you for staying at Hotel Blu. Enclosed you will find two complimentary day passes to the hotel's spa to celebrate your birthday. - Micah."

Ellie's eyes go wide. "He totally likes you." I open my mouth to argue but she continues before I can get a word in. "And he's nothing like the nasty assholes mom hangs out with. He's a good guy. Both he and Lincoln are. You seriously need to go out with him." She fans her face with the card. "But right now, we have a spa day to get to!"

"I GUESS I SHOULD SAY THANK YOU." I'M STRADDLING MICAH'S legs, my arms are wrapped around his neck, and my fingers are idly playing with his hair while a song is playing in the background. I'm supposed to be giving him a lap dance in this private room, but since he's holding me in place, his strong hands gripping the curves of my hips, it's more like we're sitting in an extremely intimate position. Especially since I'm topless and wearing only a tiny pair of panties that barely cover my lady parts.

"For what?" Micah breathes, his heated gaze searing into me.

"For the spa day. My entire body is relaxed and smooth and pretty."

Micah groans. "Any chance you'll let me feel the smooth and pretty parts?"

"Nope," I say. "And speaking of which..." I reach down and peel his hands off me. "No touching."

He rolls his eyes but obeys, lifting his arms behind his head. When he stretches back to relax, he shifts slightly, giving me a good feel of the hardness between his legs as it slides against my center.

A soft gasp escapes before I can prevent it, and Micah catches it, the corner of his lips curling into a knowing smirk.

"There's a cure for that built-up sexual tension," he murmurs. "Go out with me."

"Did you not hear my sister? I don't date."

"Why?"

Well, if that isn't a loaded question—one I have no desire to answer. I give him a half-truth instead. "Relationships require the time and attention I don't have."

He quirks a brow, waiting for the rest of the explanation, but since that's all I'm giving him, I start to move my body again to finish the lap dance. It's the least I can do since—if history is accurate—he'll be tipping very well afterward.

Surprisingly, Micah isn't in the audience for my second performance, nor does he book me for another private show. Before he started buying all of my time, I used to be booked solid, so I'm surprised when Violet tells me I have none booked for the evening. But the shock dies down when I get my tips for the night and see that Micah gave me enough for two performances. I should be annoyed that he basically bought himself a private dance even though he couldn't be here, but if he wants to waste his money to prevent me from dancing in another man's lap, I'm not going to look a gift horse in the mouth.

It's late when Ellie and I get back to the hotel room, so we both pass out right after we shower.

I'm not sure what time it is when I wake up, but when I open my eyes, the first thing I notice is that Ellie's awake and sitting in the chair by my bed, fidgeting like crazy and glancing at me like she's done something wrong.

"What's up?" I ask, rolling onto my side.

"I did something."

"Okay."

"I ran into Micah last night." Oh, jeez. This can't be good. "And I saw him go into Lincoln's office."

"Ellie, just say whatever the hell you did so I can fix it."

"That's just it. I don't want you to fix it. I wrote him a note, saying you wanted to go out with him and signed your name. Then I had Trixie give it to him on his way out."

"Ellie!" I bark, sitting up. "What the hell? Now I'm going to have to tell him what you did when he asks me out *again* and I say *no* again."

She swallows thickly, and I groan out loud. "What else did you do?"

"I wrote on the note that you're available today."

"Oh my God!"

"Just hear me out," she says, her eyes pleading. "I know part of the reason you never go out or date is because you won't leave me alone at our house… not since…" She trails off, unable to say the words—*not since we were both almost raped in our own home.* "But we're not there. We're here, in a safe hotel, where nobody can get to me. And I'm old enough to hang out by myself. I have homework to do, and I can order in room service. I won't go anywhere or—" Her words are cut off by a knock on the door, and her eyes go wide.

"Is that him?" I hiss.

She nods. "Yeah. I might've told him to pick you up at ten o'clock. You're usually up early, but you woke up late, and I overslept and…"

"Jesus." I scamper out of bed. "Go answer the door while I put on some clothes!"

She runs out of the room, closing the door behind her, and I dash into the bathroom to see how crazy I look. Not too bad since I showered and removed my makeup last night. I quickly wash my face and slip on a bra so I'm somewhat presentable when I let Micah know my sister is playing games and we're not actually going on a date.

But when I walk out into the main room and find him standing there dressed in a gray Henley and jeans, holding a bouquet of flowers, the words get stuck in my throat… because holy hell, how is it possible the man looks even more delicious dressed down than he does in his power suits?

And then he smiles—not the cocky, confident smirks I get at the club, but a genuine, almost boyish grin—and butterflies that have no business being anywhere near me flutter in my chest. And even though I have every reason not to go out with this man, suddenly I want to be a normal twenty-four-year-old being picked up for a date by a gorgeous man who's interested in me, consequences be damned.

"Not that I care what you wear out, but you don't exactly look like you're ready for our date," he says, cutting through my brain fog.

I glance down and groan. I'm wearing the t-shirt I wore to bed with tiny cotton boy shorts. I might've thought to put on a bra, but I forgot I'm not wearing any pants.

"Ummm..."

"We overslept," Ellie says. "If you can just give her a few minutes, she'll go get ready, and then you guys can be on your way."

Micah stares at me for a long moment, and I can see his features change when he comes to the realization that he's been had by the fifteen-year-old.

"You didn't write that note, did you?" His voice is uncharacteristically vulnerable, and the words drift into my chest and wrap around my heart, squeezing it tightly.

When I shake my head, he chuckles.

"What do you think?" he asks Ellie, who's standing to the side, gnawing on her bottom lip because she knows she's fucked up. "Should I give her an out or convince her to take pity on me and go out with me anyway?"

Ellie's eyes light up. "Pity date, for sure. I think once she's out, she'll have a good time."

Micah nods in agreement. "All right, pity date it is," he says. "Sienna..." He steps over to me, hitting me with the most pitiful puppy dog eyes I've ever seen. "It will absolutely devastate me if you don't go on this date with me. So, will you please take pity on me and go?"

I stare at him, knowing if I say yes, it's going to change everything. It goes against my rules, my plan. And I know that if I give in to him, if I let him suck me in, there's no going back. He's the type of man who gets what he wants and doesn't settle for anything less than everything. He doesn't just want a date with me. He wants to own me, possess me—my heart, my body, and everything in between. And there's a chance he's going to take it all, every part of me, and then destroy me, leaving me only a fraction of myself—just like my mother.

And for the first time, I understand why my mom allowed herself to get hurt by so many men. Why she continued to give herself over to them even though each one took a turn at destroying her.

Because despite knowing all that can go wrong, when a man looks at you the way Micah is looking at me right now, all common sense flies out the window, and you find yourself saying, "Yes, I'll go out with you."

Nine

MICAH

"You know what you did was wrong, right?" I say to Ellie once Sienna has disappeared into her room to get ready for our date.

"It was worth it," Ellie says, zero remorse in her words. "Sienna deserves to go out and have fun. She's always working and studying and dealing with our shitty mom. If I didn't do something, she'd be alone forever."

I chuckle at her dramatics. She's still young, but I appreciate the push.

"So what are your plans to make my sister fall in love with you?" she asks, not mincing her words.

"Brunch and a movie. If you want to join—"

"No way." She shakes her head in disgust. "I'm not playing third wheel on your date. Although—" a spark suddenly alights in her eyes "—if you want to get Lincoln to join, I'd be down for a double date." She waggles her brows suggestively, and I bark out a laugh.

"Not happening. When you're hungry, call for room service, and they'll put it on my tab."

"Thanks," she says with a smile. Then she steps toward me, her features turning serious. "Sienna's the way she is because our life has been a bit messed up. Our mom really is a piece of shit, and we've seen things we shouldn't see. So, if you're wanting to go out with her for the wrong reasons, let her go. She's been through enough."

I stare at this kid, who's wise beyond her years, and I know it's because what she's saying is true. They've been through some serious shit, and they've had to grow up fast. To a certain extent I get it because my dad brought us into the business at a young age, so I've seen some crazy shit myself. But by the way Ellie is looking at me, I have a feeling the things they've been through goes so much deeper.

I'm about to tell her she doesn't have to worry, that I have no intention of hurting her sister, when Sienna reappears, dressed in a pair of dark ripped jeans and a turquoise off-the-shoulder sweater with sandals on her feet. Her hair is up in a high ponytail, and her face is makeup free, except for a bit of gloss making her plump lips shiny.

"This is as good as it's going to get," she says with a shrug. "Didn't bring any dress up clothes, so I hope you didn't plan anything too extravagant."

"You look beautiful," I tell her, handing her the flowers I've been holding this entire time. "And don't worry—" I lean in and whisper so her sister can't hear "—you can be completely naked if you'd like for what I have planned." I shoot her a wink and she glares, making me laugh.

She's going to make me work for everything—every date, every smile, every laugh, every word—but that's okay because I'm wearing her down. I can feel it. Look at how far I've already come. In a short span of time, I went from paying for a lap dance to taking her out on a date. Soon, she'll be legally changing her last name to Alexander.

"You ready?" she asks, knocking me out of my thoughts.

"Yeah." I glance at her sister. "You sure you don't want to join?"

"Nope, I'm good. I'll just be here binging on Netflix and eating everything on the menu." She glances at her sister. "On Micah's tab, of course. He insisted."

Sienna gives her a faux glare. "Behave."

"Always, *Mom*," she says, taking the flowers from Sienna. "Now you two have fun, but don't do anything I wouldn't do. And if you do, remember 'No Glove, No—"

Sienna reaches out and covers her mouth. "Nope, you do not need to finish that statement." She releases her hand and says to me, "Let's go before I change my mind."

Ellie's cackling can be heard as we close the door behind us and head to the elevator. Since Lincoln and I live in the penthouses, our places are only accessible from the main elevator, so we have to take one down and then get on the other to go back up with my key card.

"Umm, what are we doing?" Sienna asks, glancing up at the numbers in confusion.

"Going up to my place," I say, as the elevator doors open and we step off onto my floor.

Her head whips around and she hits me with a hard glare. "Seriously? Can you get any more cliché? What part of I'm not going to have sex with you did you not understand?" she hisses.

The elevator door slides open, and I step out, but she doesn't follow. Instead, she stands there with her arms crossed over her chest, her nose pointed upward in a stubborn gesture.

"I'm not going in there with you. I knew this was a bad idea, but of course—"

Her words are cut off when I stalk back into the elevator and push her gently against the wall, having enough of her shit.

"Who hurt you?" I ask. "Who caused you to be so guarded? Is it just men you don't trust or people in general?" Her blue eyes widen, and she shakes her head, refusing to say a word.

"Jesus." I slam my palm against the wall, caging her in so our bodies are so close I can feel her warmth radiating off her, smell her feminine scent. Our eyes lock, and I watch as her features morph from fear to longing, to anger, to resigned. And I'm still staring at her when I see the light switch go off and her emotions shut down completely.

"I don't stand a chance, do I?" I whisper, reaching up with my other hand and trailing my knuckles down her cheek. "You don't even *know* me, yet you're so quick to make accusations and assumptions."

She swallows thickly, and her lids flutter closed for several seconds before she opens them back up, pain radiating in her eyes. "Can you blame me? Given the circumstances under which we met?"

"So, based on our unconventional start, you've already pushed me into the box with whoever hurt you and threw away the key. It doesn't really matter what I do, I'll never be able to claw my way out."

Her responding silence is deafening, yet I can hear the truth loud and clear. For the first time ever, I'm at such a loss. I've always gone after what I wanted, and as long as I was willing to put in the work, I would achieve what I was after.

Until Sienna.

Despite her trepidation, there's a part of her that wants me. At the very least, she's attracted to me. I can see it in her eyes when she's straddling my lap at the club, when she's dancing and looks out at the audience in search of me. But she's scared because she's been hurt. And for the first time in my life, I don't know how to fix it.

It would be a helluva lot easier to walk away, find a willing woman to spread her legs. I've been with dozens of women over the years. Women who would let me fuck them any way I want without question, who desire my company, who would marry me in a heartbeat.

Yet I can't get this stubborn, jaded, beautiful woman out of my head. It's become more than a sexual conquest. I want to get to know her. Hear her thoughts. Learn everything there is to know about her. With other women, I could never see anything beyond one night. But when I look at Sienna, I see late nights out together and lazy mornings spent in bed. I see family dinners. Weekend getaways. For the first time, I can see so much more… and it's with her.

So even though she's staring at me like she *expects* me to hurt and disappoint her, I'm not going to give up. I've helped make our family millions of dollars trusting my gut. Not every deal is black and white. Some require taking risks, making decisions nobody can understand but me. Oftentimes the numbers aren't there, but I can feel it in my soul that I'm making the right choice. And that's how I feel about Sienna.

"I didn't bring you up here to fuck you," I say, making sure my voice is calm. "Lincoln told me how protective you are of your sister, that you bring her to the club with you because you don't want to leave her alone, so I ordered brunch up to my room and thought afterward we could watch a movie in the theater. That way, we wouldn't have to leave the hotel in case she needs you at any time."

I can tell the moment my words sink in because her eyes turn soft and her body goes slack. "I…I didn't know," she mutters, her gaze dropping to the ground.

"You didn't ask," I say, pinching the tip of her chin and lifting it so she's forced to look at me. "The first night I saw you on stage I was immediately drawn to you. I've visited my brother a dozen times and not a single woman ever caught my attention like you did. I think about you all the damn time. But it's more than sexual. I want to get to know you… all of you. I want to know what you're thinking about when your brows furrow like this." I run my finger between her brows and along her nose. "What's going through that pretty head of yours when your nose scrunches up." I continue my descent to her pouty lips. "When your lips purse together, I wonder what's wrong and if there's anything I can do to make it better."

"I'm not that interesting," she murmurs.

"I beg to differ." I back up slightly and extend my hand. "I'm giving you a choice. If you take my hand, we can go to my place and spend some time together, getting to know one another. Or… you say the word and I take you back to your room and I'll leave you alone."

She stares at my hand for several seconds, and I think she's not going to take it, but then she shocks the hell out of me when she reaches out and places her hand in mine.

"This doesn't mean I trust you," she says, her voice hard. "And I'm definitely not going to sleep with you. But I felt it too… the chemistry, so I'm willing to see where this goes. But you should know that my priorities are my sister and my future. Everything else comes after, and you… you come last. I'm not trying to be mean, but it's just the way it has to be."

I can't help but smile at her admission. I should probably be offended, but instead, it only makes me want her that much more. She's clearly not had it easy, yet she's determined to stand on her own two feet and won't let anyone keep her down.

"Got it." I thread my fingers through hers and pull her out of the elevator and into the hall. "Now let's go eat. I'm starved, and since I can't have you *yet*, I'll have to settle for food."

Ten

SIENNA

THIS IS A BAD IDEA. I KNOW IT. I'VE SEEN WHAT LETTING A MAN in can do to a woman. But still, I said okay. As Micah leads me into his home, I keep telling myself that spending the morning with him doesn't have to mean anything. I'm not going to fall in love with him over a span of several hours. I'm not going to turn into my mom. I've watched her and learned from her mistakes, and I won't be making the same ones.

I expect his penthouse to look similar to the hotel room Ellie and I are staying in, so I'm taken aback when he opens the door to a gorgeously modern open floorplan with ceilings that look to be about fourteen-feet high. There's a state-of-the-art kitchen to the left with top-of-the-line appliances, a large living room to the right, and farther in the distance, I notice a glass staircase leading up to a second floor. The entire area is surrounded by floor to ceiling glass walls and… "Is that a pool?" I gasp, heading straight to the window that faces a wraparound infinity pool.

"Yeah," Micah says with a chuckle, as I press my hands against the glass. "My brother and I share the top floor, so we each have a corner unit. There's a privacy wall outside separating our places."

Nobody has a pool in New York unless they're stinking freaking rich. It's cold for months on end, which makes an outdoor pool useless.

"We can go in it after if you want," he adds.

"Maybe," I murmur noncommittally.

He nods and walks over to the table that's located just off the kitchen. There's a huge spread laid out: croissants, muffins, bagels, a fresh fruit and cheese platter, orange juice and champagne to make mimosas, and a carafe of delicious smelling coffee.

Micah lifts one of the silver tops where there's eggs underneath, still steaming hot. Another one reveals waffles, and the last one houses the best smelling bacon and sausage.

"Hungry?" he asks, pulling my chair out for me like a gentleman.

Before I can respond, my stomach growls, and we both laugh. "You can say that."

I make myself a mimosa, then pile on some waffles, eggs, bacon, and at the last second, tack on some fruit.

Micah takes a croissant and slices it open, then puts some eggs and bacon on it, creating a makeshift breakfast sandwich. "Egg, bacon, and cheese sandwiches are my favorite," he says, grabbing a slice of cheddar from the platter, slapping it on, and then taking a hearty bite.

I can't help the laugh that escapes past my lips as I watch him chow down.

"What?" he asks, once he's swallowed down a bite and has taken a sip of his coffee.

"Nothing, you just look so…normal." When he quirks a brow, silently asking what I'm talking about, I explain. "You're always in those expensive power suits and looking every bit the businessman.

Yet, here you are, dressed down and making yourself a sandwich. I guess I imagined brunch would equal fancy foods with caterers."

"We could do that too, if you want," he says nonchalantly, "but I prefer this. Out there..." He nods toward the window, exposing the beautiful city. "I have to be someone people wouldn't dare fuck with. In my home, I can simply be me. Suits are nice, but I prefer the jeans."

Wow, I never would've expected that type of response. It seems I really don't know anything about Micah aside from his obvious wealth, affluence in this town, and his unrelenting determination to date me.

"What's going through your head?" he asks, after taking another bite of food. "I can practically see the cogs turning."

"That I don't really know much about you," I admit, "but also that I'd like to get to know the *real* you, not the person that everyone else sees."

A smile spreads across his face, and that single dimple pops out, causing butterflies to attack my belly. "Good. Because I'd really like to get to know the *real* you, as well. Starting with... Romance or action?"

I go to say action, since I'm thinking he's referring to which movie we should watch, and up until now, romance was not my jam. But since I'm trying to get to know a guy and possibly enter a romantic relationship, I go with, "Romance."

He chuckles and shakes his head. "You're so full of shit."

"What?"

"What's the last romance movie you watched?"

"Umm... Twilight?"

He barks out a laugh. "With the sparkling vampires?"

"Yeah, it's Ellie's favorite," I say with a shrug.

"Let's try this again. Action or romance?"

"Action," I admit with a sigh. "But I could go for romance. Maybe it will teach me a thing or two," I mutter.

Micah laughs even harder, apparently finding my awkwardness

hilarious. "And what is it you're hoping it will teach you?"

"I don't know, like how to do this." I point back and forth between us. "I've never done this before, and the only men my mom has ever brought home are the kind who pay for sexual favors." The second the words are out of my mouth, I close my eyes and cringe, regretting my word vomit.

When I open my eyes, I expect to find pity in Micah's gaze, but instead, all I see is compassion. "We'll take this slow," he says. "The truth is, I've never done this either, but I know that I want a relationship like my parents have. They're in their fifties and still very much in love."

"You've never dated before?" I ask.

"Nope. I've been enjoying being a bachelor. Contrary to what you might believe, I'm not a manwhore by any means. I just wasn't looking to settle down yet."

"And now you are?"

"Yeah," he says contemplatively, his features turning serious. "My mom always said when I found the right woman I would know, and I think I've found her."

My heart picks up speed at his words, and I take a deep breath, trying not to let myself get too worked up. Men are good with pretty words. I've heard more than my fair share of men say pretty things to my mom before she fucked them. The problem was, after they had their way with her, those pretty words turned ugly.

"That doesn't sound very slow," I murmur, making him chuckle.

"Sorry," he says with a grin. "Sometimes I have a heavy foot."

When we finish eating, he takes me on a quick tour of his place, and it's even more gorgeous than I thought—complete with several bedrooms, bathrooms, a small gym, an office, and even a theater room.

"I thought when you said we were watching a movie, you meant your hotel had a theater."

"It does as well," he says, dropping onto the comfy, double

reclining, leather couch next to me. "But I had a mini one put in here for my personal use."

As I glance at the seat below me, wondering how many women he's fucked on this couch, he must sense my mood shift because he adds, "It's a great way to watch sports with friends."

"So, you've never fucked anyone in here?" I blurt out, curiously.

He turns my direction where his hazel eyes lock with mine. "I've never brought a woman here before. Living in a hotel means having access to rooms. This is my home, where I hope to one day live with my wife and kids. Hookups don't belong here."

And yet, he brought me here. My heart inflates in my chest at the notion that I'm the first woman he's brought to his home, but I quickly find a needle and pop it.

Stop it, Sienna! He's giving you pretty words. That's what men do.

"So… what movie are we watching?" I choke out, needing to change the subject.

He eyes me quizzically, and I can tell he wants to ask what I'm thinking, but he hands me the remote instead, and says, "Pick something while I grab us a couple of drinks and popcorn. What do you prefer to drink?"

"If you have sweet tea, I'll take that. If not, bottled water is good."

"Sweet tea is my favorite," he says with a grin. "Be right back."

I scroll through the movies and end up settling on Fast and the Furious. Since Micah's not back yet, I send a text to Ellie to check on her. She's quick to respond with,

ELLIE

Shouldn't you be busy on your date? If you're thinking about me, he must be doing something wrong.

I groan at her response, wishing she could go back to being ten again, when she was cute and sweet and didn't have a smart mouth. As a teenager, I didn't have time to get into trouble—I was too busy caring for my baby sister and working minimum wage jobs after school just to put some food on the table and to help pay the bills. But something tells me Ellie is going to give me a run for my money.

SIENNA

We're about to watch a movie. He's grabbing us snacks. And I'll never be too busy to check on you.

ELLIE

Yeah, yeah. Love you too, sis. Now go enjoy yourself.

When Micah returns with a huge bowl of buttery popcorn and two bottles of sweet tea, I take a bottle and the tub of popcorn from him and hand him the remote.

He presses a button on the couch that dims the lights and then clicks play. We watch the movie in silence for a good half an hour before Micah pauses it and turns toward me. "I think I messed up."

"Oh, how?" He hasn't done anything wrong as far as I can tell. He's been a complete gentleman all morning. The food was delicious, the movie is one of my favorites, and despite me accusing him of making plans for us to hang out at his place, once he explained his reasoning, his understanding of my need to keep my sister close was both thoughtful and appreciated.

"I wanted to get to know you, but it's kind of hard to do that without being able to talk. This might be the only chance I get. It was hard enough to get you to go on this date with me. I feel like I should take advantage of it."

"Okay," I say with a laugh. "What do you have in mind?"

Twenty minutes later, Micah is stepping out of his room, ready to get into the pool. He looks good in his powerful suits, sexy in jeans and a Henley, but in board shorts… Holy shit—this is by far my favorite look on him. He's solid everywhere, his chest and abs and *Jesus*, the V that dips low into his shorts, all look like they were airbrushed on. I suck my lips into my mouth, praying I'm not actually drooling, while wondering if he would think it's weird if I walked over and ran my fingers down his abs to see if they're actually real.

My eyes move to his arms. Since I've only ever seen him in long sleeve shirts, this is my first time seeing his bare arms. They're not only corded with muscle, but both forearms are covered in ink. With a suit on, he exudes power and money, but underneath, he looks like a sexy bad boy.

Not good, I tell myself, thinking about all the bad boys my mom has brought home. Bad boys equal trouble. They're good with pretty words… that lead to hurtful actions.

"Damn, you look gorgeous," he says, dragging his eyes down my body and knocking me out of my thoughts. Since I didn't have my suit with me, I ran down to my room and grabbed the one I bought in the boutique yesterday. Ellie was on the phone with her friend, eating a buffet of food she ordered from room service, and when I asked if she wanted to join us, she shooed me away.

"You've seen me naked several times," I scoff.

"That doesn't change the fact that you're gorgeous," he says.

The wraparound balcony is even bigger than it looks from the inside. It houses an outdoor kitchen and grill, a few lounge chairs, and a pool.

I ease my way into the pool and sigh as the cool water envelops my legs, then dive right in, plummeting under the water and not coming up until I get to the other side. When I push through the surface, I come face to face with a very wet Micah.

"Hey," he says, backing me up against the side of the pool.

"Hey," I say back.

He reaches out and tucks the wet hair that's clinging to my face behind my ear, and my breath hitches at his touch. This is exactly why I've made it a point not to date, not to be alone with a man—outside of work. It doesn't matter how smart a woman is, as soon as a man gives her that look, touches her like so, she turns into a puddle of stupid at his feet.

"Tell me something about you that no one knows," Micah says, caging me in with his strong arms.

"I don't want to be stupid," I admit without thinking.

"I think you're far from stupid. Aren't you majoring in accounting?"

"I might be book smart, but being here with you, letting you into my life, definitely makes me stupid."

"You haven't even begun to let me in," he says with a half-smile.

"Then maybe there's still hope for me yet."

"If you could do anything for the rest of your life, what would you do?"

"No way." I shake my head. "You have to answer, too. Tell me something about you no one knows."

He thinks for a second before he says, "My biological mom didn't want me, even threatened to have an abortion. My dad compensated her quite generously to carry me to term and then paid her another hefty sum to sign over her rights and disappear from my life forever.

"So, you and Lincoln aren't..."

He shakes his head. "No, everyone thinks we share the same mom. But the truth is, my dad met Lincoln's mom, Donna, when my bio mom was pregnant with me. They fell hard and fast, and she accepted me as her own after I was born." He smiles softly. "Everyone thinks she's my mom because she's always loved me the same as Lincoln, her own flesh and blood. She chose for me to be a part of her life when my own mom chose to discard me.

"Maybe that's the best kind of love," I say. "The kind where someone *chooses* to love you when they don't have to."

"As opposed to what?" he asks.

"Forced love. From my experience, when it's forced, it doesn't end well. My parents were both professional dancers who got pregnant with me by accident and were forced to marry. In the beginning, I think they tried to make it work. But dancing was more than a career to them, it was their dream. My mom had to give up that dream in order to care for me, and when my dad got injured and could no longer dance, things really started to unravel. My dad eventually left us, choosing to start another family, one he wanted. When my mom became pregnant with Ellie and her deadbeat dad skipped town, she was forced to care for two children on her own. Trapped and looking for an escape, she chose a path of drugs and prostitution and a string of men who were nothing more than a series of poor choices. Time and again, our mom has abandoned us, choosing that life over the children she is supposed to love."

"You love Ellie, and she loves you," he points out.

"True, but our love is tainted. You heard her at breakfast. She thinks she's a burden to me. That I'm giving up what I love to take care of her. What I want is for someone to *choose* to love me. To not see me as a burden or associate me with heartbreak. I want someone to look at me and think I'm the best part of their day. I want to feel a love that is pure and good and doesn't come with any strings attached. I don't know if that kind of love actually exists, but I want to believe in the fairytale."

"Yet, you refuse to date."

I chuckle at his truth. "It's not that I don't want to one day fall in love. It's just that right now, the only person I have room in my heart for is Ellie. She comes first. Our mom is a drug-addicted prostitute who gives all her money to her pimp. Ellie deserves the world, and I'm going to make sure she gets it, regardless of the odds against us."

Micah palms my cheek and tilts my face to look at him. "What if you had someone to carry the burden with you? Maybe then you'd have some more room in your heart to find your own love."

"I don't want to depend on anyone but myself," I admit. "My mom depended on my dad, and he eventually left us. Ellie's dad disappeared. Her pimp boyfriend promised to take care of her, but he preyed on her weakness instead. My mom wanted to be loved, and in the end, it's what broke her. I would be a fool if I didn't learn from her mistakes.

"Besides, I have work and school and Ellie. Once I graduate, I can get a job the state will approve of and petition the court for full custody of my sister. I need to get Ellie away from our mom, and I can't afford to risk falling in love before that happens because if it were to break me the way it broke my mom, who would Ellie have left? I can't risk it."

Micah nods in understanding, but I can see it in his face that he doesn't get it, which is precisely why I never should've agreed to go on this date with him. It doesn't matter how good looking he is, how strong the chemistry is between us. I can't afford to let him in.

"I appreciate your attempt at getting to know me," I tell him. "But I'm not in a place to be dating anyone. I think it's best if we end this date right now."

I dip under the water and swim away from him toward the steps. I'm out of the pool and grabbing a towel before he even makes it out of the water. By the time he joins me, I've gotten my towel wrapped around my body, my flip flops on my feet, and I'm heading inside to grab my clothes so I can leave.

I assume Micah is going to let me go, until I turn around and run right into his hard chest. His hands land on my hips, and he holds me tight, steadying me so I don't fall back. I glance up at him, ready to tell him I'm good, when his mouth descends on mine.

His strong yet soft lips curl around my own. He waits a beat, probably to see if I'm going to push him away, and when I don't, he takes that as his cue to deepen the kiss. Gliding his tongue across the seam of my lips, he coaxes them open and then slips his tongue inside while I stand frozen in place, experiencing my first kiss since high school.

Unlike the boy who kissed me back then—awkwardly and

sloppily—Micah kisses me with slow, methodical movements. He tastes like the perfect mix of sweet and salty from our snacks earlier, and I find myself wanting to kiss him back. My tongue tangles with his, and he sucks it into his mouth as he encircles his arm around my waist. He tugs me toward him, bringing our bodies flush, my hands landing on his muscular chest. Instinctively, I run the tips of my fingers up his hot, smooth flesh, until my arms are wrapped around his neck.

But it doesn't feel like enough. Not my arms around his neck, not his mouth fucking my own, not our bodies flush against one another, or his arms holding me tight. I need more.

I blame the next move on the oxytocin fogging my brain.

Parting my legs slightly, I trap Micah's muscular thigh between my legs and then grind my center against him, using him like my own personal pole. With only a thin layer of material covering my center, his hard leg pushes against my clit, and I let out a breathy moan.

And then he breaks the kiss…leaving me a panting, breathless mess.

"You feel that?" he murmurs against my lips, holding me close so our bodies are still connected. "That chemistry…" He pulls back slightly, his hazel eyes burning with desire. "You can continue to deny how much you want me, but the way your body, your mouth, *your fucking cunt* is practically begging for my touch proves that you crave me the way I desperately crave you."

He darts his tongue out and swipes it across my bottom lip before he bites down on it and tugs, causing an electrical current to shoot through me straight to my core.

"I bet if I stuck my fingers in you, you'd be soaked," he says, his voice deep with want. "But I'm not going to do that," he adds, backing up and breaking our connection. My body immediately goes cold, and I find myself moving toward him, wanting his warmth back.

But he shakes his head, stopping me in my place. "I feel it, how amazing it would be between us." He cups the side of my face and presses a chaste kiss to my lips. "But in the same way you want someone to *choose you*, Sienna, I want someone to *choose me*."

Eleven

SIENNA

"All right, ladies, we're going to finish class by working on some technique." The girls moan, and I have to stifle my laugh. When I was their age, I hated working on technique too, but dance isn't just about the fun stuff. You have to train as well.

The girls already know where this is going, so they head over to the barre. I run them through several positions, knowing each count by heart. I could teach this class in my sleep, which is probably a good thing, since my head isn't in it at all today.

It's still at Hotel Blu, at Micah's penthouse. Our date was a pleasant surprise—the brunch and movie and how he wanted to actually get to know me. When I spoke, he seemed to listen.

My thoughts go to the kiss…

The way our bodies aligned perfectly with one another, almost like we were meant to be. I bring my fingers up to my lips, remembering the way his mouth devoured mine. Afterward, he walked me back to my room, and with a chaste yet intimate kiss to the corner of my mouth, he told me he'd see me soon.

Class ends, and I tell the girls they did a wonderful job and I'll see them on Wednesday, and then I spend the next hour doing homework while Ellie finishes up her class.

"So, home?" Ellie asks once we're in my car.

"Yeah." Mom wasn't there when we went by the house earlier this morning so Ellie could get dressed for school and grab her backpack. More than likely, she's taken off again, so there's no reason to spend money unnecessarily on a hotel room when we can stay at the house for free. Since she's apparently gotten her hands on some money, chances are that Mom won't return for weeks, possibly months.

We stop at the store on the way home, and then, while Ellie is showering, I make us dinner. I'm stirring the chicken in the pan when there's a loud banging on the door followed by a masculine voice. "Open this fucking door!" Phil barks.

I set the spoon down and grab a knife, not wanting to be unprepared. I have no intention of letting him inside, but who knows what this asshole is capable of.

"Lenora's not here," I yell back at Phil, hoping he'll give up and leave.

"Open the fucking door!" he shouts again.

"Not—" I haven't finished my sentence when the door breaks open, pieces of wood flying every which way, and I stumble back before I get slammed by it.

"Where the fuck is she?" Phil growls, pushing past me. "That bitch is fucking dead."

"She's not here," I tell him, praying Ellie doesn't come out.

Phil swings mom's door open and stalks inside. He starts pulling drawers open and tossing everything everywhere, making a mess. I keep my mouth shut, not wanting to get on his bad side. Whatever he's looking for has nothing to do with me.

After he's checked her entire bedroom and bathroom, he moves on to Ellie's and my room, tearing everything apart.

When he grabs the bathroom handle and it doesn't open, he darts his gaze over to me. "Ellie's in there."

"Open the door!" he shouts.

"Fuck you!" Ellie yells back, letting her temper get the best of her.

"Ellie, please open it before he breaks it down," I say with a calmness I don't feel.

She swings the bathroom door open, and he barges in, checking to make sure our mom isn't hiding.

"Where is it?" he asks, storming out of the bathroom.

"Where is what?" I'm sure he's referring to the money she came into, but I figure it's better to play stupid since I really don't know where she or the money is. "She came home Friday and we got into a fight. I haven't seen her since then."

He bridges the gap between us and pushes me against the wall, his hand squeezing my face. I hold the knife tight in my hand, ready to stab him if necessary. "That bitch owes me," he says, confirming my suspicions, "and I always collect. If I find out you know where she is…"

"We don't know where she is," Ellie yells.

"El," I warn, not wanting her to put herself at risk. "I don't know where she is or what you're looking for, but as you can see, neither is here."

He releases me but doesn't move back. "You better hope she turns up," he says, his eyes locking with mine. His face is so close I can smell his rancid breath. "Your whore of a mother made a grave error, and if she doesn't fix it, I can't be held accountable for what happens next," he threatens, slamming his hand against the wall before stalking out.

As I watch him leave, several thoughts and emotions flit through my head: Anger that our mom has put us in danger—again. Fear that Phil's threat wasn't an empty one and the possible ramifications of him not tracking down my mom. Exhaustion, since I seriously wish I could lie down and take a long ass nap. And desperation—because all I want is to give Ellie a safe and stable home. Why must that be so difficult?

My phone dings in my pocket and when I pull it out, I find a text from unknown:

UNKNOWN

Hey beautiful, how was your day?

I know instantly that it's from Micah. When he asked for my number, I caved in a moment of weakness and gave it to him. And then, like a lust-struck teenager, I spent the next twenty-four hours checking my phone for a text from him.

UNKNOWN

<picture of the pool overlooking the sunset and city> Wish you were here with me.

My thoughts go back to Sunday and how it was so easy to get lost in him, in the moment. The way he looked at me and listened to me and wanted to get to know me. And when he kissed me, I felt like I was in a fairytale, getting swept off my feet by my very own Prince Charming.

"Sienna," Ellie whispers, causing me to look up from my phone to where she's standing in the hallway. Her arms are wrapped around her body in a protective gesture. She's scared. And rightfully so. Because in the world Ellie and I live in, fairytales are nothing more than make-believe stories giving false hope to people just like us.

My brain flashes back to Micah's words after he ended the kiss: *In the same way you want someone to choose you, Sienna, I want someone to choose me.*

I've been thinking about what he said, what he wants. Even considered giving him a real chance. Ellie told me I deserved to find love and happiness, and for a moment, I allowed myself to believe I could somehow possibly have it.

But as much as the thought of choosing Micah gets my heart racing a little faster, deep down, I know I can't choose him. I just don't have any room in my life for Micah—not right now, anyway. My primary focus needs to be on Ellie and keeping her safe, which means I need to figure out where she and I will be sleeping tonight because clearly, we can't stay here.

SIENNA

I'm sorry, Micah. I made a mistake going on that date with you and giving you my number. Please don't text me again. Goodbye.

"Go pack a bag," I say to Ellie, pocketing my phone. "We're going to the motel tonight."

Twelve

MICAH

"To thirty-two years of marriage. May the years to follow be just as amazing." Lincoln holds up his flute filled with champagne, and we all raise ours, clinking our glasses together.

We're at The Kitchen, an upscale restaurant that's located in downtown Tesoro, celebrating our parents' anniversary.

"Thank you," Mom says, leaning over and kissing Lincoln's cheek. "Maybe one day we'll be toasting to one of your engagements..."

She side eyes me, and Lincoln snorts out a laugh. To mom, hitting thirty is apparently a signal that it's time to settle down—especially since Dad was thirty when the two of them first met. And since I'm almost thirty-three, she thinks it's way past time I exchange my bachelorhood status for a long-term, committed relationship. Lincoln's twenty-nine, so he still has a little bit of time before Mom starts to get on his case.

"Never know," Lincoln says with a smirk. "Micah's been obsessing over a dancer at Wanderlust. Maybe you'll get to plan his wedding sooner than you think. Or be a character witness when she files harassment charges against him."

Both my parents' eyes swing over to me, but before either can start in on the third degree, a masculine voice speaks first. "Good evening."

We all glance up and find none other than Eleazar Gutierrez standing at our table with a beautiful woman on his arm.

"Mr. Gutierrez," Dad says, standing to shake his hand. He's the son of Eduardo Gutierrez, the crime boss who recently died from a heart attack. "I didn't know you were back. Had I known, my boys and I would've come to your home to personally extend our condolences." Lincoln and I follow our father and stand, shaking Eleazar's hand.

"Thank you," Eleazar says. "We only just got in a few days ago." He gestures toward the woman on his arm. "This is my wife, Arielle."

"Lovely to meet you," Mom says, giving the woman a two cheek kiss out of respect.

"I didn't hear anything about a funeral," Dad says, making conversation.

"Dad didn't want one. He'll be cremated and brought back to Mexico with me."

"How long are you in town for?" Mom asks. "We would love to have you over for dinner." The truth is, my parents would like nothing less, but while we own the majority of Tesoro, the Gutierrezes run the underworld, and their family is not one to be fucked with. We've been coexisting for decades because our families go way back, but they're sleazy and dirty, and with their prostitution and trafficking rings, they make us look like boy scouts.

"Hopefully, not too long," Arielle says with a strong Spanish accent, pouting at Eleazar.

Eleazar visibly glares at his wife then smiles at my mom. "Thank you for the invite. Can I let you know? I have a few loose ends to tie up that will need my attention. You know how it is…" He glances at Dad. "Business before pleasure."

"All too well," Dad agrees.

"It's an open invitation," Mom adds.

After a few more minutes of chatting, Eleazar and Arielle say goodbye and we sit back down. I was hoping with the interruption my mom wouldn't remember the topic of conversation, but when her eyes meet mine and she says, "Now tell me about this dancer," I know I'm not in luck.

LINCOLN

stalker: a person who harasses or persecutes someone with unwanted and obsessive attention.

LINCOLN

an idea or thought that continually preoccupies or intrudes on a person's mind.

LINCOLN

<insert company handbook>

"If you send me one more stupid fucking text, I'm going to shoot you." I glare up at my brother from my phone.

"Just figured I'd lay it all out for you." He smirks. "Did you click on the handbook? I highlighted the important parts."

I reach out and grab the marble coaster on his coffee table and chuck it at him. He ducks and it hits the wall behind him.

"Jesus, fuck!" he barks. "You could've taken my head off with that thing."

"Consider that your warning."

"So much anger," he mutters. "Maybe if you got laid…"

"How about you worry about your own damn—"

My words are cut off when I see a certain brunette pass by the office, heading in the direction of the back door.

I hop up to follow her out and Lincoln chuckles. "Careful, you're quickly crossing from obsessing to stalking. Might want to read those definitions I sent you."

I give him a one finger response to his asinine remark as I head out the backdoor so I can talk to Sienna about the bullshit text she sent me the other night. I could've texted her back, but I figured it would be best to discuss it in person.

When I swing the door open and glance around, I spot her piece of shit car but not her. My eyes trail the area, knowing damn well I saw her come out here, when a noise catches my attention.

The first thing I notice is two guys, dressed in all black, standing with their backs to me, facing the brick wall. Even from behind, I can tell neither work for us, which immediately has me on alert. But what has me pulling out my gun is the fact that they're not just staring at the wall, they're actually cornering someone—and the flash of silver sequins confirms that the person they're cornering is Sienna.

With my gun in one hand and my cell phone in the other, I quickly shoot a one-handed 911 text to Lincoln. He'll know from those digits that he needs to get his ass out here immediately and bring backup.

"Back the fuck up," I say in a low voice.

The guys spin around, and I instantly memorize their features— black hair, black eyes, light skin, tattoos covering both their arms.

"This ain't your business," one guy says, his accent thick.

I raise my gun and point it at him. "Do you know whose property you're on?"

"We just need the girl," the other guy says, avoiding my question.

"The girl is on our property," Lincoln says, joining me, along with Rex and Oscar. "That makes her ours. Which means, if you're trying to take her, you're taking from us."

"I'm gonna ask you again," I say. "Do you know whose property you're on?"

"Like I said..." the first guy starts to say, but before he can finish his sentence, I stalk over to him and raise my gun to his forehead.

His friend curses under his breath while he swallows thickly, lifting his hands up in surrender.

"Hellcat," I toss out, my eyes never leaving these assholes. "Go with Oscar inside."

Sienna scrambles around us and runs inside. Once I know she's safe, I nod toward the two guys. "Check them."

Rex does as I say, removing a knife from one guy and a gun from the other. He pulls out their wallets and reads their names out loud.

"Josue Gamez," he says, referring to the guy my brother is holding a gun on. "And Manuel Ortega."

"Who do you work for?" I ask Manuel, pressing the barrel of the gun against his forehead.

When he juts out his chin defiantly, I know he's about to play hardball. And since this isn't the place for shit to get messy, it's time to take this conversation somewhere more private. I pull out my phone and text Ricardo—one of my most trusted men, who has been with me for years. He's savage as fuck and knows how torture information out of someone. I've never not seen him be successful.

Twenty minutes later, Josue and Manuel are tied to chairs in the middle of our warehouse while, little by little, Ricardo cuts into their skin every time I ask a question and they refuse to answer.

"Who are you working for?" I ask them.

When neither answer, I nod toward Ricardo to take it up a notch. He digs his knife into the meaty part of Josue's leg, and he curses. I can tell he's getting close to his breaking point, so I nod again, and he digs deeper.

"Fuck! We're not working for anyone!" he hisses.

"Again," I say.

Ricardo digs so deep that a chunk of his flesh is exposed, causing him to scream out like a little girl, "Gutierrez!"

"Nice try, he's dead."

Ricardo lifts the knife and Josue shrieks, "Not him! His son. Eleazar."

My hackles rise. Why the fuck would Eleazar be after Sienna?

And then Josue answers my silent thought. "He's got a bounty on her head. I don't know why, but whoever delivers that chick, dead or alive, will get a million-dollar pay day."

Lincoln's eyes meet mine, silently thinking the same thing as me... *What the fuck?* I pull my gun out and shoot both of the guys in their foreheads, killing them instantly.

Generally, we try to stay away from unnecessary violence since it's bad for business and a mess to clean up, but there's no way I'm chancing either of these assholes going after Sienna again or reporting her whereabouts to Eleazar.

"Call for a cleanup," I tell our guys, knowing they'll handle it.

"Any idea what the fuck Eleazar wants with Sienna?" Lincoln asks as we walk back to his car, since we left my vehicle at the club and drove here together. "And why doesn't he care if she's handed over dead or alive?"

"No idea, but until we figure it out, we need to get Sienna and her sister hidden. Who the hell knows how many people are searching for her?"

When someone as powerful as Gutierrez puts a hit out on someone, people come running. Not just for the money, but also for the respect. If you're the one who brings him who he wants, he'll owe you, and people take that shit seriously.

As we leave the warehouse and head back to the club, I pull out my cell to make a call. "Oscar," I say when he answers the phone.

"I need you to get Sienna and her sister ready to go. I'll be there in five minutes to pick them up."

"Boss, they already left," he says.

"What the fuck do you mean they left?"

"I tried to—"

"Never mind," I bark. "I'll deal with you later."

I hang up on him and slam my fist into the glovebox. "Fuck, any chance you know where she lives?"

"I know she's from Booker Park, but I'd have to get her address from my office."

When we pull up to Wanderlust, Lincoln runs in to grab the address, while I hop into my car and start driving toward Booker Park, hitting Sienna's name on my phone to call her. The neighborhood is only about fifteen minutes away, but at the speed I'm going, I'll get there in half the time.

"Micah," Sienna breathes over the Bluetooth, the fear in her voice clenching my heart like a vise.

"Where are you?"

"Pulling up to our house." Fuck, the last place she should be going is to her house.

"Sienna, listen, you can't go—"

"Shit, my phone's going to die," she says, distracted and not paying attention to me.

"Sienna!"

"Ellie, grab the—" Her words are cutoff by the sound of a blood-curling scream that has me pressing my foot on the pedal harder.

"Sienna!"

"Oh, my God," she gasps. "He's dead."

Thirteen

SIENNA

The place has been destroyed. Cushions slashed. Glass shattered. The few pictures I hung on the wall to try to make it a home have been smashed.

But that's not what has my heart pounding behind my rib cage. On the floor is Phil, lying in the middle of the glass coffee table with a jagged piece of glass sticking out of his chest.

"Holy shit," Ellie murmurs. "He's dead. Does that mean mom…?"

I snap my head up and glance around. Is she dead too? Is she the one who killed him?

"Fuck," a masculine voice curses, making Ellie and me jump.

We spin around to find Micah standing in the doorway, assessing the situation.

"Do you know him?" he asks, walking inside.

"He was our mom's boyfriend and pimp," Ellie answers first.

"All right, let's go," he says, reaching for us.

"I didn't…" I shake my head. "We didn't… We found him like this."

He nods. "We need to get you out of here."

"Wait," Ellie cries. "I need to know if Mom is here somewhere…" *dead.* She can't say the word, but I know what's going through her head.

Micah looks like he wants to argue, but when he sees the tears gliding down Ellie's face, he nods in understanding. "Don't move, either of you." He pins us both with a hard look and then takes off down the hall. A few minutes later, he reappears, shaking his head. "There's no one else here. Let's go."

"What about my stuff?" Ellie asks.

"Whatever you need can be replaced," Micah snaps, clearly losing his patience. "Whoever killed this guy will be back to clean it up. We gotta go."

He ushers Ellie and me gently out the door, then he grabs my wrist when I start to head toward my car. "You're staying with me until this gets sorted."

"What? No," I argue. "We'll get a room at the motel and—"

Micah pinches my chin and forces me to look at him. "Your independence is something I find extremely attractive about you, but now is not the time to debate the issue. I know you don't have all the facts yet, but please trust me when I tell you that you and your sister aren't safe."

I open my mouth to argue, but before I can, Ellie's hand lands on my arm, and my eyes meet her panicked, scared green eyes. "Please," she whispers, and that's all I need for my stubbornness to dissipate. Ellie comes first, and if she needs to go with Micah to feel safe, that's what we'll do. Even if the thought of going with him equally terrifies me.

The ride to Micah's penthouse is filled with him barking orders to someone on the phone while Ellie and I remain quiet. When we arrive at the hotel, instead of pulling up to the front, he drives down a small side road that leads to what looks like a private garage that can only be accessed with the clicker he has clipped to his visor.

Two men are waiting for us, and he must feel me go immediately on alert because his hand lands on my thigh, squeezing it in a calming gesture. I try not to pay attention to the fact that my body does just that—calms.

"That's Ricardo and Bruno," he says. "They're two of my men. I trust them and you can as well. This hotel is secure, and no one can access my personal elevator, but they're going to be standing guard just as an extra layer of protection."

Standing guard? Why is he making it sound like…?

Oh, my God. The men who were cornering me. Seeing Phil dead fogged my brain. I had assumed they were just rapist assholes trying to take advantage of a woman alone in a dark parking lot. But what if the two incidents are somehow connected? What if whoever killed Phil came there to kill us? What if we were the targets?

Goose bumps spread along my flesh, my blood running cold at the thought that we could've ended up like Phil if we had been home.

"How much danger are we in?" I whisper.

Micah goes to get out without answering me, but I grab ahold of his bicep and lock eyes with him. "Whoever killed Phil… Was he… Do you think… he was trying to get to us?"

Micah swallows thickly, and for a split second, I see a hint of sympathy in his features, telling me all I need to know—this is exactly what he thinks.

"We'll talk once we're inside," he says.

Once we've entered his penthouse, Micah sets the alarm, and I feel like I'm able to take my first breath in hours. I'm still freaking out, but now that we're here, I know we did the right thing by trusting Micah to keep us safe. We're dozens of floors up with a private elevator and extra security protecting us.

Ellie is safe.

Micah hands Ellie and me each a bottled water and guides us over to the living room, gesturing for us to have a seat. Ellie sits in the corner, bringing her legs up to her chest in a protective manner, and I sit next to her, reaching over and rubbing her shin, trying to reassure her that everything is going to be okay even though I have no idea if that's true.

"There's a bounty on your head," Micah says, sitting on the coffee table across from me.

"What the hell does that mean?" I ask.

"Like the show?" Ellie squeaks. "Like where people who are wanted get tracked down and whoever finds them gets a reward?"

"What?" I hiss, my gaze flitting from Ellie to Micah.

"Exactly like that," Micah confirms.

"Somebody wants us? Who? Why?" I ask, my hands starting to shake.

"I don't know about Ellie," he says, glancing at my sister. "But I have it on good authority that there is a million-dollar bounty on your head. Those guys at the club were after you for the money."

"We have to run," I breathe, ready to bolt.

"No, you have to stay right the fuck here," Micah says, his tone authoritative yet calm at the same time. "Ever heard of the Gutierrez family?"

"No," my sister and I say at the same time.

"They're one of the most powerful crime families in New York, maybe even on the East Coast. They deal in drugs, trafficking, and prostitution—"

"Our mom's a prostitute," Ellie says.

And then it hits me... "Mom came home for Ellie's birthday with bags of expensive gifts. I asked her where she got the money to pay for all of it, and she flipped out on me. Phil showed up on Monday looking for her, tore the place apart, saying she owes him. Could whoever killed him... whoever is after us... be looking for whatever she has? Oh, God, do they think we have the money?

Because we don't."

"It's a possibility," Micah says. "I'm going to find out, but until this gets figured out, you're both going to stay here. With a million dollars on your head… and possibly your sister's, you can't risk leaving."

I just finished my finals this week, but… "Ellie has exams… and dance." Micah glares at me and I flinch, realizing how dumb I sound. "I'm sorry." I shake my head.

"I can get my teachers to let me take them online," Ellie says, standing. "And there will be other showcases." Her voice is strong, her head held high, but I know deep down she's bummed. She's worked hard in dance, and once again, our shitty mom has taken something from her. She should be pissed and upset, lashing out, but she won't because she's a good kid who knows the score, who learned early on that life isn't always fair.

"I'm assuming there's a room in this mini mansion for me to shower and sleep in?" she says, covering her true feelings with sass.

"El," I groan.

Micah chuckles. "Upstairs, first door on the right there is a guestroom with an en suite bathroom. I'm having one of my guys pick up some clothes for both of you. I'll have Sienna bring them up to you once they arrive. But until then, there's a robe you can use in the bathroom."

"Thanks," Ellie says. She leans in and kisses my cheek. "We'll get through this, sis," she says softly. "We always do."

I nod, trying to remain strong for her. "Of course we will," I say, pulling her into a hug.

"I've worked so hard trying to provide her with a normal life," I say to Micah once she's gone. "And yet again, Lenora did something to fuck it up. It might not be confirmed yet, but whatever is going on, I'm positive she's at the heart of it."

"Lenora is your mom?"

"Yeah. The woman is a disease, hell-bent on destroying

everything and everyone around her."

Micah leans in and palms my face. His thumb swipes gently across the tears I didn't realize had fallen. "She's why you're scared," he says, moving from the table to the couch and pulling me into his arms.

"She's why I have to focus on my goals. So I can get Ellie and me far away and safe. I'm the only person in this world Ellie can count on, and it's my job to protect her." I swallow thickly, trying to tamper down the lump of emotion in my throat. I don't know what Lenora has gotten herself mixed up in this time, but I can feel it...this is different, scarier. All I know for sure is that whatever it is, it's really, really bad, and somehow she's managed to drag me, and possibly Ellie, down with her.

Micah wraps his arm around my shoulders and guides my head to his chest. I should push him away, but his strong, comforting hold has me sighing into him. "I know it's hard for you to let people in," he says, tipping my chin to look up at him, "but sometimes things are too much to handle on our own. We all need someone to lean on, to be there for us, to help us through the rough patches. I have my parents and brother...a handful of men I trust. Who do you have, Sienna? Who is there looking out for you?"

I can't help but choke out a sob at his question because the truth is... "I don't have anyone," I admit, a puddle of tears filling my lids and blurring my vision. The only person I have is Ellie, but it's my job to look out for her, not the other way around.

"That's where you're wrong," Micah says. "You have me." He dips his face and kisses my forehead. "You just have to trust me enough to let me in, and I promise I will do everything in my power to make sure you and your sister are safe and happy."

"Why?" It might seem like a stupid question, but the fact is, I met this guy at a strip club, a place men go for an easy, good time. And entangling himself with me would be anything but easy.

"I told you already," he says, tucking a few strands of hair behind my ear. "There's something about you that has me wanting more. I can't explain it, but I think about you all the time." He chuckles darkly. "My brother thinks I'm obsessed, accused me of being a stalker." He shrugs, clearly not giving a shit about that accusation, and despite what's going on outside of these walls, I find myself laughing.

"I can admit that I was sexually attracted to you from the start. Can you blame me, though? You're fucking gorgeous." My cheeks heat up at his words. "But it's more than that now. I want to get to know you. You can't deny there's chemistry between us, we felt it on our date, and I want to see where things go. I understand your priority is your sister, and that only makes you more attractive in my eyes because family is everything to me."

He grips the curves of my hips and pulls me onto his lap so I'm straddling his muscular thighs. "Let me in, Hellcat. Give me a chance to show you that you don't have to go through this life alone. It's okay to find love and be loved. It doesn't make you weak...it makes you human."

I know what he's asking shouldn't be a big deal. People offer up their hearts to love all the time. But he hasn't lived the life I have. He hasn't suffered the consequences of trusting the wrong men, and he hasn't witnessed the devastation and destruction they leave behind in the aftermath.

"I..." I begin, but Micah shakes his head and presses his fingers to my lips.

"Before you say you can't, just think about it, please. Give me a chance to show you. You're here for the foreseeable future anyway, right? Let that wall you've built come down for a little bit and know that my bigger wall is protecting you both."

He leans in and presses a soft kiss to the corner of my mouth just as his phone pings with an incoming text. "My guy's here with the clothes. Let me grab them and then I'll show you to your room so you can shower today off and get some rest."

He lifts me off his lap and I follow him to retrieve the clothes. He types in a code, then opens the door. "Here ya go, Boss," the guy says, handing him two large bags from a store that should be closed at this time of night. "I got everything on the list, and Sara said if you need anything else to let her know."

"Thanks," Micah says, before closing the door.

He leads me up the stairs, past the door he told Ellie is her temporary room, to the one right next to hers. "You can stay here," he says, opening the door. "It has its own bathroom as well. As you might recall from the last time you were here, farther down the hall is the library and gym. My room and office are downstairs, near the theater room. Laundry room is attached to the kitchen. I'll give you and Ellie a more thorough tour tomorrow."

"You don't want me to sleep in your room?" I blurt out. I thought for sure he would try to trick me into sleeping with him. He's made his desire for me more than clear.

"I told you before," he says, framing my face with the hand that's not holding the bags. "The way you want someone to choose you, I want the same. I would never force you to do anything you're not comfortable doing, Sienna. When you sleep with me, share a bed with me, it will be because you want to, not because I tricked or forced you into it."

His words are like the heat of the sun shining down and melting away a layer of ice that formed around my heart. "Thank you," I murmur, lifting onto my tiptoes and kissing his cheek. "For not only giving me a choice, but for protecting Ellie and me." I take the bags from him. "Good night."

After showering and getting dressed in clothes that somehow are magically my size, I take Ellie's clothes over to her room.

"Thanks," she says, opening the door so I can come in. I plop on the bed while she changes in front of me, not caring if I see her naked. The girl has zero insecurities when it comes to her body.

"I'm in the room next door if you need anything."

"Any chance that's Micah's room?" she asks, playfully waggling her brows.

"It's not."

She sifts through the bag and pulls out a swimsuit. "Oh, nice. Guy's got good taste. Think he'll let me head to the pool downstairs?"

"Don't need to. He has one here."

Her eyes bug out. "You seriously need to get with this guy. Can you imagine living here? It's like a castle… he's the king and you could be his queen." She drops into the reading chair in the corner. "I bet Lincoln's mini-mansion is just as nice."

"Something you'll never find out since he's much too old for you," I remind her. "And anyway, money and materialistic possessions are not reasons to be with someone. You can't let those things define your life." I lock eyes with her. "Mom has been chasing love for all the wrong reasons, and yet, she still has nothing—not even us. Don't you want to have a different life than hers?

"Of course I do," Ellie scoffs. She averts her gaze, glancing down at her lap. "But Mom's a druggy always looking for her next fix. Phil is her dealer. He hurts her. Lincoln and Micah are different. They're safe and protective. Micah saved us tonight. I don't think he would hurt us. And besides, he likes you. I see the way he looks at you. It's different…" She sniffles and her eyes flit toward the ceiling as she tries not to cry. "Maybe if Mom would've landed someone like Micah instead of Phil things would've been different. Maybe she would be clean and happy and in love.

"Is it so bad that I want you to find love and be happy? You've put your life on hold for me, taking care of everything that mom doesn't. You deserve it. The castle, the king…You deserve it all. We both do," she whispers.

"El…" I choke out as it hits me just how quickly my sister has had to grow up. She might only be fifteen, but because of the life we've been thrust into, she's been forced to grow up faster than other kids. I thought her crush on Lincoln was nothing more than a teenage crush, but now I see it…her need to feel safe, to have a stable, loving home. As much as I try to shield her from the bad, what I'm doing is just a temporary Band-Aid being placed over an open bullet wound.

I open my arms so she can come to me, and when she does, I hold her tight. "I know it's scary right now, but we'll get through this." I don't comment on what she said about Lincoln and Micah because she's not wrong. I felt it when Micah held me earlier. The safeness, the stability, the feeling of not being so alone.

Maybe it's like Micah said: *Sometimes things are too much to handle on our own. We all need someone to lean on, to be there for us, to help us through the rough patches.*

"Do you think she's okay?" Ellie murmurs, her face tucked into my chest.

"I don't know," I tell her honestly. "She's a fighter."

"A part of me wishes she were dead," she admits. "But another part of me just wishes she could go back to being our mom again," she adds.

"Me too," I agree. "Me too."

Fourteen

MICAH

"Is that bacon I smell?" Ellie asks, descending the stairs, dressed in a pair of pajamas, her hair up in a messy knot on top of her head.

"And coffee," Sienna adds, dramatically sniffing the air. Like her sister, she's still in her pajamas with her messy hair pulled on top of her head.

They're both rubbing their eyes as they stumble down the stairs, the scent of breakfast seeming to guide their movements.

Ellie plops down at the table first and snatches up a piece of bacon, while Sienna goes straight for the coffee, taking a huge sip and then sighing as she drops into another chair.

With Sienna's mix of brown and blond hair, creamy complexion, and bright blue eyes, she doesn't look the least bit related to her sister, Ellie, who has darker brown hair, olive skin, and emerald eyes. But as I watch them sip their coffees, butter their pastries, and munch on the crispy bacon, their mannerisms are very similar even if their appearances are different. Sienna has basically raised her sister, and while Ellie has a bit more sass to her—my guess is because even though Sienna might disagree, she's done a good job of providing a loving, stable home that's allowed Ellie to spread her wings—it's obvious they're close.

"Thanks for breakfast," Ellie mumbles around her bite of food.

"Any time," I tell her, taking a sip of my coffee. "There's a phone in the kitchen. Dial two-one-four and it will take you to room service. They'll deliver whatever you'd like and charge it to my account."

"Thank you," Sienna says, her eyes finally meeting mine. With caffeine now coursing through her veins, she looks more awake.

"They charge you at your own hotel?" Ellie asks.

"That's how business works," I say with a shake of my head. "Every item must be accounted for. Otherwise, the numbers won't add up. I don't own the hotel, Alexander Enterprises does."

Ellie nods in understanding.

"So, what's on the agenda?" Sienna asks.

"I was thinking the pool then the spa," Ellie answers. "Unless we can't leave here. Then the pool and a movie in the theater room. Wait, can the masseuses come here?" Her face lights up in excitement, and I laugh as Sienna glares her way.

"It's best to lay low this weekend," I tell her. "Let me see what I can do."

"Don't you have exams to study for?" Sienna says, sounding like a mom. The thought has me imagining her one day pregnant with my baby. The two of us filling this house with lots of kids, turning it into a home. She would make a damn good mother. She's kind and loving, selfless and strong, and fiercely protective of her sister.

I should probably be concerned at my train of thought, but it doesn't shock me in the slightest. Since the moment I laid eyes on Sienna, my feelings on relationships, marriage, and commitment have done a complete one-eighty. My dad always said that meeting Donna was a game changer. That the moment he met her he knew his life would never be the same. He could be cold and ruthless when it came to business, but the second he laid eyes on her, everything in him softened. I didn't get it, not until I met Sienna.

"Fine," Ellie says, bringing me back into the moment, "but after I study, I'm hitting the pool. Weekends are meant for relaxing, and since you can't go to work all weekend, you should join me."

Sienna's eyes widen, as if just remembering what day it is. Typically, she would've been working tonight and tomorrow night. But due to their current situation, that's no longer possible. No work equates to zero money coming in.

"Whatever you're thinking, stop," I say, reaching over and squeezing her hand. "I got you. Your safety comes first."

"I know but..." She releases a harsh breath and shakes her head. "Never mind."

"No, not never mind. Talk to me."

She stares at me for a long moment, as if she's warring with herself, trying to decide if she should keep that wall up or lower it enough to let me in. I sit quietly, waiting while she decides.

Then she sighs, her shoulders drop, and her eyes meet mine as she finally starts talking. I take that as a win—she's actually opening up and letting me in.

"I need to pay for my summer classes. I paid for Ellie's dance, thinking I would use my earnings from this week and next to pay for them, but now..." She shakes her head. "I can call and see if it's not too late for me to take out a loan for this semester."

"How much is it?" I ask.

"What? No, I can't let you—"

"Baby," I murmur, gently massaging the top of her hand. "Stop shutting me out. Let me help."

She lets out a shaky breath. "Okay, but I'll pay you back. Once we sort this all out and I can go back to work, I promise I'll pay you back."

There's no way in hell I'm letting her give me a cent, but I don't tell her that. My phone rings, and when I see it's Ricardo, I answer it.

"Boss," he says. "I've got an update."

Last night I had him and Bruno watch Sienna's place to see what would happen. About twenty minutes after we left, two guys showed up and burned the place to the ground. Then they torched her car and took off. When they told me what happened, I had them follow the two guys, hoping they would eventually lead us to the person who was responsible.

"Go on," I say, keeping it simple so I don't alert the girls. I need to figure out how to tell them that their home and vehicle, along with everything else they own, is all fucking gone. But before I do that, I need to get to the bottom of the situation. The asshole last night blamed Eleazar, but before I go off making accusations, I need more proof than that.

"They went home last night, but this morning, they went straight to Gutierrez's residence."

Fuck. If that's not proof, I don't know what is.

"And there's more," he adds.

"Go on."

"I spoke to my contact who confirmed the bounty on Sienna's head."

I met Ricardo several years back when he was working the streets. I was in Booker Park dealing with a situation that had gone bad and shit got real, very quickly. Had he not had my back, I'd be buried six feet under.

"And what about the other one?" I ask, silently referring to Ellie.

The girls eat quietly, both of them shooting nervous glances my way, and I vow to do whatever I have to do to make sure they're both safe and taken care of.

"He said Gutierrez made it clear it's only for Sienna. His guess is that since her sister is barely more than a kid, he's leaving her out of it."

"Any idea why?"

"It appears that their mom is the one who killed Eduardo." *What the fuck?* "Word on the street is that she went there to fuck him and ended up drugging him instead. Gave him a heart attack that killed him. She also stole some drugs and a bit of money. Not surprisingly, Eleazer plans to make an example out of her. If whores think they can get away with that shit, it'll mess with the order of hierarchy. Since she's nowhere to be found, he's put a hit out for her daughter. Blood for blood."

Fuck, this is worse than I thought.

"Thanks. Keep me updated."

"What's going on?" Sienna asks before I've even pocketed my phone. "And please, don't lie to me."

I wasn't going to lie to her, but I also wasn't planning to tell her anything just yet. There's so much to all of this, I don't know where the hell to begin.

So I go with the least fucked up information first, hoping it will distract her from asking more questions until I can get this all sorted.

"Your house and car were torched."

"What?" Both girls gasp.

"All of our stuff is gone?" Ellie shrieks. "What about my clothes and shoes and…"

"Our pictures," Sienna whispers. "And my car? How will I get another one?" Tears fill her eyes. "Why?"

I go with the simplest answer. "To cover up killing Phil. It's the easiest way to cover up a murder."

"We're homeless," Sienna murmurs.

"Hey," I say, dragging her chair over and pulling her into my arms. "You guys are not homeless." I glance at Ellie. "It sucks that everything is gone, but you both are alive and safe here. I know the photos can't be replaced, but the clothes and car and other shit can be."

They both nod in agreement, but I can tell they're devastated and in shock. They didn't have much to begin with, and the little bit they did have is now all gone.

"Did you find out why they're after me?" Sienna asks.

"My guy has a theory, but I'll need to confirm it."

Normally this is when Sienna would argue, but she's too shaken by the loss of her home and vehicle, so she simply nods without argument instead.

"I'm going to take a shower," Sienna mutters, standing.

"I'm still kind of tired," Ellie says.

Both girls head upstairs, and I'm left feeling helpless. Up until now, I've never been in a situation before when I wasn't completely in control.

Speaking of which...I head into my office, which is soundproof, and I call the one person who has any control over this situation.

"Gutierrez," Eleazar says, when he answers my call.

"It's Micah Alexander."

"Micah, to what do I owe this phone call?"

"I need to speak to you about an important matter. I was hoping we could meet soon."

"I'm dealing with a few things at the moment, but how about Monday? Come to my place...Nine A.M."

"Will do. Thanks."

We hang up, and I glance at the time and see it's eight o'clock. This is when I usually leave for the office, but I don't think leaving Sienna and Ellie alone is the best idea. So, I pull out my phone and let my assistant know I won't be in until Tuesday and to only call if it's important.

She responds, asking if I'm okay since I never take that much time off, and I let her know I'm dealing with some personal shit and to clear my schedule.

I don't want the girls leaving since Sienna has a bounty on her damn head, but I need to do something to cheer them up, and as long as they're with me and my guards in this hotel, they'll be safe. So I decide to text the spa manager and schedule appointments for Sienna and Ellie for this morning, and then I put a call into my personal shopper, letting her know I need more of everything delivered, including a few cocktail dresses. Once she's confirmed she's on it, I make a reservation at the rooftop restaurant for tonight and invite my parents and Lincoln.

It's probably too soon for the whole meet-the-parents situation, but my mom is great about comforting others, and I know once I tell them what's going on, they'll be more than willing to meet us for dinner. Sienna might not think she has anyone, but she has me, which means she has a lot of people in her corner without even realizing it.

After I speak to my brother and parents, catching them up on everything, I head upstairs to try to cheer up the two women who have me feeling all sorts of shit I've never felt before.

I stop at Ellie's room first and knock since she's not in the shower.

"Come in," she says softly, not sounding at all like her usual sassy self.

When I open the door, I find her sitting on the bed, typing on her laptop. It looks expensive and new, and if I had to guess, it was probably one of the gifts her mom gave her.

"Spa appointment in one hour," I say, stepping inside.

"Thanks," she says, smiling half-heartedly. "I was just emailing my teachers so I can take my finals online."

I glance back to make sure Sienna isn't near before I say, "I know I can't replace everything you lost, but if there's anything in particular that can be replaced, please tell me, and I'll get it for you and your sister. We both know Sienna won't say shit, so I need you to speak up, please."

"Truthfully, we really didn't have all that much. I think it just sucks realizing it's possible to have even less."

"We'll get this sorted," I tell her. "I have an appointment with someone on Monday, but until then, I need you and your sister to lay low to ensure your safety."

The girls spend the morning at the spa—after I have to practically drag Sienna there—and when they return, I have clothes, shoes, undergarments, and toiletries in their respective rooms waiting for them.

"This was so sweet of you," Sienna says, closing the distance between us. "I don't know how I'll ever repay you for your generosity."

"Well, I can think of one way," I say with a smirk. When she rolls her eyes, thinking I'm referring to sex, I add, "Wear that dress without complaint." I jut my chin toward the simple black dress that's hanging on the corner of the mirror.

"Where in the world would I wear that?"

"To dinner with me...and my family."

Her eyes widen. "Micah," she hisses, but I cut her off by pressing my mouth to hers for a quick, chaste kiss. Her lips are soft, and she smells like roses, thanks to the oils the spa uses.

"Okay," she breathes when I end the kiss.

"Thank you."

She shakes her head and scoffs.

"What?" I ask, confused.

"You're thanking me for agreeing to go to dinner with you and your family when I'm the one who should be thanking you for everything you've done for me and my sister. You brought Ellie and me into your home after I was almost attacked and then insisted we stay when our apartment was torched, leaving us homeless. On top of that, you paid for a spa day to cheer us up and bought us a shit ton of clothes and other stuff...Oh, and you even offered to pay for my classes." Tears fill her eyes, and I encircle my arms around her, having a feeling all the pent-up stress is about to boil over.

"This is why I tried to give you an out over and over again," she chokes out. "You wanted to have sex in a private room and look what you got instead." She snorts out a humorless laugh, and I lift her chin, needing her to look at me.

"What I wanted...what I *want* is you. Anyway I can have you. And your *mess of a life* hasn't changed that."

"But don't you see?" she says. "My shitty circumstances took your choice away. What were you going to do? Leave us to die?"

"Everyone has a choice. I could've rented you a hotel room, or hell, I could've given you cash to go to a motel. I could've said fuck that, they're not my problem, and turned my back. I'm choosing to have you and your sister here. I want to get to know you, Hellcat, and before all this shit went down you were on board as well."

"I was," she admits. "It just feels selfish, putting me and you before Ellie's safety, or putting you on the backburner..."

"There are no placeholders," I say, kissing her tear-stained lips. "We're all in this together. You can have it all if you'd just lower those walls you've erected and let me in all the way. I know what's happening between us is fast, but I can't deny what I feel...what I *know* you feel too."

I sear my gaze into hers, willing her to accept that there's something between us that's worth exploring. To stop holding me at a distance and to let me stand by her side. To stop trying to go through this life alone when we can go through it together.

"I do," she breathes. "I do feel it, and it scares the shit out of me." She releases a harsh breath, her eyes fluttering closed and then open. "Okay, I'll let you in. But we need to take things slow."

"Slow," I agree, mentally fist bumping the air because she's actually giving in and giving us a chance. "We can take things as slow as you want."

Fifteen

SIENNA

"Oh, look at you," Donna gushes. "You're even more beautiful than Micah described." Micah and Lincoln's mom pulls me into a warm embrace, and I can't help returning it. Lenora has never been motherly, but when my grandmother was alive, this is how she'd hug me whenever she came to visit.

Donna is a beautiful woman with dark brown eyes and shoulder-length brown hair that has honey-colored highlights mixed in. She's clearly had some work done like most wealthy women, but it's tasteful and makes her look a good decade younger than her age.

"And you must be Ellie," Donna says, pulling back and taking my sister into her arms. "I've heard all about you," she adds with a twinkle in her eye, telling me either Micah or Lincoln has filled her in on my sassy teenage sister.

"It's nice to meet you," Ellie says politely. She's dressed in a floral, knee-length dress that makes her look sweet and innocent—which is exactly the look we were going for—it's bad enough I'm a stripper at the club their sons own. (And yes, I'm well aware it sounds ridiculous that they would judge me for working at the establishment their children own, but double standards are a thing for a reason.)

"It's lovely to meet you," Micah's dad, Michael, says, leaning over and giving both me and Ellie a chaste kiss to our cheeks. When he smiles gently at me, he reminds me of Micah, especially when a single dimple pops out, identical to his son's. His face is a bit scruffier with grey hairs speckled throughout, but I have no doubt this is what Micah will look like when he's older.

"Sorry I'm late," Lincoln says, strolling in. "The favorite has arrived. We can eat now."

Donna laughs and gives him a hug, then we all find our seats. Since Micah doesn't want to risk me going out in public, we're eating dinner in a private room at The Lounge, one of the restaurants in the hotel.

I sit in between Ellie and Micah, and Donna and Michael sit on the other side with Lincoln sitting across from Ellie. I say a prayer that she doesn't spend the meal drooling over him, but to be on the safe side, I lean slightly forward to make eye contact with Ellie, who just rolls her eyes, knowing exactly what I'm silently trying to convey without having to say a word.

"So, Sienna," Donna says, "I heard you're a dancer."

I still in my spot. Apparently, we're going to lay all the cards out on the table now without any sort of small talk.

But before I can open my mouth to confirm what she already knows—that I'm a stripper at Wanderlust—she adds, "I drag my husband to see the ballet everywhere we travel, but I would have to say Milan and London are my favorites."

"Sienna's an amazing dancer," Ellie jumps in. "She was accepted to New York University, Julliard, Dominican University, all with a full scholarship," she gushes. "And on top of that, she was invited to join several dance companies, including the American Dance Company."

"That's amazing," Donna says. "My body could never move like that." Her eyes comically widen and she giggles. "But I love watching the ballet."

"I'm going to New York University," Ellie says. "I haven't gotten in yet, but I will."

"That's a great goal," Donna says with a smile. "And will you dance for a company?"

"No, I don't want a career as a professional dancer—that was our mom's dream. When she got pregnant, she lost both her dream and her job. Sienna's dad was injured...same thing, no job. Our dream is to open our own dance studio one day. Right, Sienna?"

Ellie glances my way and I nod, refusing to let the tears that are burning behind my lids fall. I'm happy that my sister has goals and that she loves me enough to want to open a studio together, but she's too young to understand that it would take years to get the money needed to open a studio. My goal is to get Ellie to college. And once she's a little older, she'll be able to understand how loans and business actually work.

"It'll happen," Micah leans over and says, his hand squeezing the top of my pantyhose-covered thigh. I'm wearing a cute lilac, off-the-shoulder mini dress that lands a few inches above my knees when I'm standing, but once I sat down it rode up several inches.

"What?" I murmur, distracted by the way his thumb is now massaging circles into my flesh.

"Opening your own dance studio. One day it'll happen."

I swallow thickly, realizing that while I thought I was doing a decent job of hiding my pain, Micah could see right through me. I'm not used to anyone paying such close attention to my words and actions, reading my thoughts and feelings.

The rest of the meal goes smoothly. We flit from one topic to the next, and not once does either of Micah's parents say or imply a single negative thing about Ellie or me. By the time we're finishing up coffee and dessert and Lincoln is saying he needs to head to the club—and how he's looking forward to the manager returning from his honeymoon so he can have his social life back—Donna is making Ellie and me promise we'll get together soon for lunch.

"It's weird being home on a Friday night," I say to Micah once we're back at his place. Ellie has already excused herself to her room, probably anxious to gossip with her friends on the phone. "I'm so used to working I don't even know what to do with myself."

Micah chuckles. "What would you be doing if you didn't have to work and you weren't stuck here?"

I think for a moment, then laugh. "I don't know. I've been working pretty much every weekend since I turned fifteen." Whether it was at the diner or the strip club, both of those places brought in the most money on the weekends, so the tips were really good. "And if I'm not working, I'm studying or taking care of Ellie." I start school on Monday, but with everything going on, I switched my in-school classes to online, which works out for the best since I really didn't want to leave Ellie alone.

"Pretend," Micah says, leaning against the island and tugging on the front of my dress so I'm rubber banded into him. "Close your eyes." I do as he says. "It's Friday night and you can do whatever you want. Where are you and what are you doing?"

An image pops into my head, and I share it with Micah as I visualize it. "I'm out with my friends, drinking." Mind you, I've lost touch with the majority of my friends, most of whom have been living it up while I've been working two jobs, going to school, and caring for my teenage sister. "We've gotten dressed up, complete with full-on makeup, and we're downtown club hopping, dancing...just for fun. We're drinking and laughing and having a good time." I open my eyes to find Micah looking at me with a soft smile splayed across his face.

"Well, we can't leave here, so the club is out, but..." He walks over to a cabinet and pulls out a bottle of liquor and then presses something on the wall. Music instantly starts playing, the sound of Ed Sheeran singing about having conversations with strangers filling the space. "We're dressed up, we have music and alcohol…" He scoops the arm that's not holding the bottle around my waist and pulls me into him. "And if it means I get to touch you, I'm down for dancing."

"You're crazy," I say, trying to sound serious, only the giggle that escapes past my lips tells him otherwise.

He releases me and grabs two shot glasses, then he takes my hand in his and guides us outside by the pool—the music continuing to play even out here.

Setting the glasses down, he opens the bottle and pours us each a double shot and hands me one.

"Should we toast?" I half joke.

"Would you toast at the club?" he asks.

I nod. "To good liquor, good music, and—"

"Great fucking company," Micah finishes for me.

We throw our shots back and then he pours us another…and then another. After my insides are nice and warm, he pulls me into his arms and I go willingly, snaking my arms around his neck. The song playing is upbeat, similar to what you'd hear at any club, and I let myself go, rubbing my body against Micah's like I would if we were actually there and out on the dance floor having fun.

It should feel awkward since it's only the two of us and we're not actually at a club, but it doesn't. With the busy city below us, and the twinkling stars above, it simply feels nice. It feels good to let loose and have a moment where nothing else exists—not the strip club or my mom or the bounty on my head. I'm just a twenty-four-year-old woman having a good time with a guy I'm attracted to.

When I twirl around, giving him my back, his hands glide up my sides as I back up and grind my ass against his groin. I can't help but notice he's hard…very hard.

I reach out and grab the bottle from the outdoor kitchen island, pour us each a messy shot, then down mine before handing him his. He throws it back, then sets it down.

Gripping the curve of my hip, he turns me back around and pushes me against the wall. My fingers trail up his muscular torso and pecks, while he pushes my legs apart, his knee finding my center.

Our eyes meet, our gazes clash, and then our mouths collide. This kiss isn't gentle like the last time. It's filled with passion and lust and want. Our tongues stroke and swirl around one another. His hand palms the side of my face, deepening the kiss. I suck on his tongue, getting drunk off his taste, as his hands glide down my body until he's palming the globes of my ass.

With our mouths connected, he lifts me into his arms, my legs circling around his waist, and walks us over to the island, setting me down. We continue to kiss, taste, devour each other, but it's not enough. I want...no, I *need* more.

I push myself forward and grind my center against the bulge in his pants, creating the best kind of friction. I've kissed guys before, but I've never gone any further than that. Micah backs up slightly, and for a second, I assume he doesn't want to take things any further, but then he spreads my thighs and slides his fingers under my dress and over my pantyhose. He rubs his finger along my center, and when he touches my clit—even through the material of my pantyhose and panties—it feels so good, I let out a loud moan that he swallows down with a plundering kiss.

"You want me to make you feel good?" he murmurs against my lips.

"Yes," I breathe.

"You sure?" he asks, pulling back slightly. I wonder why he's asking, until he says, "We've been drinking, Hellcat. I don't want to do anything you'll regret once you're sober." And just like that, my heart swells in my chest that he cares enough to ask, to make sure.

"I'm sure," I tell him, nowhere near drunk enough to regret any decision I make. "Please make me feel good."

"You got it," he says, then his mouth is back on mine—tasting, licking, devouring. His fingers press into me, but the material he encounters halts his access. And before I can lift so he can remove them, he rips a hole into my pantyhose, shoves my panties to the side, and pushes his fingers into me. I'm so wet, they slide right in.

"Fuck, you're so tight," he mutters. "One day, after we're married, I'm going to fuck this tight cunt, baby, stretch it out and mold it to the size of my cock. But until then, I'll be gentle."

His words should probably scare me. I mean the guy's talking about marriage...*marriage!* But my brain is too caught up on the part about him fucking me, and my body is lost to the way he's curling his fingers inside of me and rubbing my vaginal walls. I've used small dildos and vibrators to get off plenty of times, but none of them have ever made me feel like this.

His thumb pushes against my clit, and it's my undoing. My walls clench around his fingers, my legs shake, and when his mouth crashes down on mine, swallowing my moans, stars— bright and colorful—explode behind my lids as I come harder than I've ever come in my life.

He doesn't stop coaxing every ounce of pleasure from my body until I gently push him back, my sex sensitive, my body satiated.

When I open my eyes, I find him smiling softly at me.

"What?" I murmur, still trying to catch my breath.

"You look so beautiful when you come." He leans forward and presses his lips to mine, and I sigh into him, not wanting the moment to end.

Without thought, I reach between us and squeeze his hard length, making it clear what I want. He groans into my mouth and I—

"Oh, shit! My bad."

Ellie's voice has Micah pulling back and spinning around. I wonder why he's standing in front of me until I realize my dress is up around my waist. Shit! I pull it down quickly and close my legs, pushing him forward slightly.

"Sorry about that," Ellie says with a knowing smirk.

Oh. My. God. How could I forget that Micah and I weren't alone? I wasn't lying when I said I wasn't drunk enough to regret any decisions I made tonight, but I obviously drank enough to forget that my fifteen-year-old sister was here.

"I was just going to ask if you guys wanted to watch a movie with me, but please"—she grins like a Cheshire cat, and I want to die—"carry on."

"A movie sounds great," I say, my voice squeaking at the end.

"Yeah," Micah agrees. "Let me just..." He clears his throat. "I just need to take a quick shower and then I'll meet you guys in the theater room."

He takes off inside, and I feel bad that he's totally going to have to rub one out since I got him all worked up and then left him hanging. I'm torn between following after Micah, staying to talk to Ellie about what she just walked in on, and running to my room to hide.

"Poor guy," Ellie says. "He looked like he was in pain."

"Ellie!" I hiss.

"What? I'm fifteen not five. I know what a guy looks like when he's been cockblocked. Maybe you should... I don't know... go help him out."

"Eliza Bardot! Not another word."

"Fine, fine." She raises her hands. "But for what it's worth, I'm happy for you."

Her comment catches me off guard. "Happy for me?"

"Yeah," she says with a smile. "Micah is a good guy. I thought for sure you'd push him away, but I'm glad you came to your senses and are giving him a chance. You deserve to be happy."

My throat clogs with emotion and tears burn behind my lids. "Thank you." I jump off the counter and walk over to her, wrapping my arms around her for a hug. "You know you'll always come first, though, right?" I need her to know that regardless of me seeing where things go with Micah, she'll always be my priority. She might be cool with us dating, but I still need her to know, she'll always come first.

"Well, duh," she says, laughing lightly. "But in three years I'm leaving for college, so it makes me happy to know you won't be alone. I mean, I won't be far, only in the city." She shrugs. "But I'll be living in a dorm and won't see you every day."

Oh, this child...when the hell did she grow up?

"C'mon, sweet girl, let's go watch that movie."

"Or you can join Micah in the shower and help him out."

Oh, this girl...I'm going to kill her. Or..."I think it's time we have the talk."

"What talk?" she asks, pulling back and eyeing me suspiciously.

"The sex talk."

"SIGH, I'LL NEVER GET TIRED OF WATCHING THIS MOVIE," ELLIE says, when the credits for Twilight start to rise to the top of the screen.

When she picked the movie and Micah agreed to watch it—despite me trying to convince him otherwise—I figured we were in for a boring two hours. But little did I know that watching a movie with Micah would be anything but boring.

He plopped onto the couch, dropping a blanket over us, and spent the entire movie feeling on me. Touching me just enough to turn me on but steering clear of the parts that would send me soaring. Halfway through the movie, I was so turned on I had to excuse myself to use the bathroom because I was so freaking wet. And when I returned, the sexy quirk of his lips told me he knew exactly what he was doing to me.

I wanted to get him back, to rub on him to the point where he'd be just as turned on and uncomfortable as he'd made me, but I fought the urge to do so. I knew I couldn't finish what I started, and I'd already left him hanging once today thanks to Ellie interrupting us.

"What's on the agenda for tomorrow?" Ellie asks, as we head out of the theater and toward the stairs. It's late and I'm beyond exhausted. How has it only been twenty-four hours since our lives imploded? In that short span of time, I was nearly attacked, we found Phil dead in our apartment, and after taking temporary refuge in Micah's penthouse, we learned that our home and car had been torched, leaving us with nothing. To top things off, there's a million-dollar bounty on my head!

"Nothing," I tell her. "We have to lay low."

"We can still do stuff," she says with a pout. "What about a pool day? We could order some floats for the pool and buy stuff to make fruity drinks and get pool snacks. It would be fun!" She glances at Micah, hopeful, and he chuckles.

"Sounds good. Make a list and I'll have everything on it delivered tomorrow morning."

I mock glare at him, and he shrugs. "It's okay to say no to her, you know," I tell him.

"No it's not," Ellie disagrees, stopping in front of her door. "Okay, well, it's been fun, but I'm just gonna go to bed now with my earbuds in my ears...They're noise canceling, so I can't hear anything." She shoots us an exaggerated wink and I groan. "So, if you guys wanted to...I don't know...pick up where you left off, you won't be interrupted."

Micah chuckles and looks at me with a smirk. "That's not happening," I say to him, reaching up and giving him a kiss on his cheek. "Good night." I glance at Ellie. "Both of you."

"Sorry, man," she says to Micah as she opens her door. "I tried."

Sixteen

MICAH

"I think you're starting to burn. I could put some sunscreen on you if you want." I run my finger down Sienna's arm, and she slowly turns her face toward me, popping one eye open to glare at me. We've spent the day at the pool, just as Ellie wanted, complete with fruity drinks—virgin for Ellie, alcoholic for Sienna, and scotch for me—and plenty of food to snack on. I can't remember the last time I've lounged anywhere all day, let alone by the pool, but I can see the appeal. Despite my phone blowing up, I've fielded the majority of the calls to my assistant or replied that I would be back in the office Tuesday. It's nice to just...relax.

"Something tells me you're only using that as an excuse to rub on me." She rolls to her side, and I do the same. We're lying in the double lounger while Ellie floats around in an oversized donut, listening to her music that's blasting in her earbuds.

"That's definitely part of it," I admit, reaching out and grabbing the globe of her ass so I can tug her closer to me.

"I was thinking about you last night," she murmurs, dragging the tip of her pink-polished nail down my shirtless chest. The entire day has been the best and worst form of torture. From the tiny—and I mean fucking tiny—string bikini she's sporting, to the way she's been not-so-innocently touching me all day. Playfully feeding me during lunch, hanging onto me while we lounge in the pool, and snuggling up into my side while we took a nap on the lounge chairs earlier this afternoon.

"What were you thinking about?" I ask, nipping at her finger when she drags it up to my face and runs it along the seam of my lips.

"I feel bad that I got off and you were left...unsatisfied." She glances up at me through her lashes and my stomach knots at how much I want this woman. I've only known Sienna for a short time, but she's quickly begun to mean so much to me. Before her, settling down wasn't on my radar, but now, I can't stop thinking about what it would be like to have her as my wife, to bear my children, to live with me here. I love sharing my home with her and Ellie. It's only been a couple of days, but I already dread the thought of them moving out once everything is resolved.

"Watching and hearing you as you came all over my fingers was plenty satisfying," I tell her honestly. Sure, I look forward to the day when I can bury my cock into her tight cunt and be with her completely, but until then, I'll take her anyway I can have her. I love that she's a virgin...that she's waiting for someone worthy of both her heart and body before giving that part of herself away.

But I imagine much of her trepidation stems from her mom's indiscriminate behavior as it pertains to men, having witnessed firsthand the ensuing fallout when you give of yourself too freely. I hate how it's negatively affected her, but despite her circumstances, she's proven herself to be so damn strong, and she's raising her sister to be the same way. I have no doubt they could take the world by storm if given the chance. And my hope—*my goal*—is to be there every step of the way, cheering them on as they do it.

"Still," she says softly, so her sister can't overhear. "Maybe tonight, once Ellie's asleep, I can sneak into your room so we can finish what we started."

"I'm sunburned and hungry," Ellie yells, making Sienna and I separate. "I'm going to take a shower. Feel free to carry on."

Sienna rolls her eyes. "Actually, I think I'm kind of hungry too. After I shower, we'll figure out what we're going to do for dinner."

"Damn, smells good." After taking a shower and then spending some time in my office to handle a few time-sensitive matters, I came out looking for the girls and found the table set up with food from one of the hotel restaurants. Candles were lit and music was playing in the background, creating a romantic ambiance.

"Oh, hell yes, I'm starved," Sienna moans, plopping into a seat that has a covered plate of food in front of it. She lifts the lid. "This smells delicious." She leans in and inhales deeply. "What is this?"

I sit across from her and lift the cover of my plate. "Crab and lobster stuffed shrimp. It's from Shells, one of the restaurants in the hotel."

Sienna takes a bite and moans, and even though it's in response to the food, my dick still takes notice since it sounds a whole lot like the sound she made when I got her off last night by the pool.

While we eat, we make casual conversation about school, work, Ellie's dance, and how nice my parents are. I've lived here for the past four years, yet it's the first time I've ever had dinner at this table with a woman. It's nice...natural. But then again, everything regarding Sienna feels genuine, not forced. Having her here just feels *right*. Anytime I imagined a woman moving in, I'd freak out, picturing them taking over the place, their shit being everywhere, and being forced to pay attention to them when I needed to focus on business. But with Sienna, I find myself wanting that. I was only working in my office for less than an hour when I stopped what I was doing to go in search of her.

When we're both stuffed, she leans back and sighs. "That was freaking good. Thank you. Keep it up and you just might convince me that you're husband material after all." She winks playfully and I chuckle. But then, something hits me...

"Wait, I didn't order this food."

She glances around. "You didn't do this? The food, the candles... the music?"

"No..."

We stare at each other for several seconds before we both say "Ellie" at the same time.

"That girl." Sienna shakes her head.

"Hey, you can't be too mad. The food was good, the ambience was on point, and I got the chance to enjoy a nice meal with you."

"I know, but she shouldn't be sticking her nose where it doesn't belong." She gets up and walks toward the stairs, and I follow after. "Ellie! You can come out now."

When it remains quiet, aside from the music, Sienna's features morph into concern. "Eliza!" Nothing.

She glances back at me and then ascends the stairs, two at a time. She swings open Ellie's door and finds the room empty. While she checks the bathroom, I'm already pulling my phone out and clicking on my security system app.

Fuck. She opened the door twice. Not good. I click on the camera and rewind and sure enough, she's accepting the food brought up by the restaurant and then heads out a few minutes later.

Not good. Not fucking good at all.

"Oh my God," Sienna cries, glancing at my phone. "She left? How did I just enjoy an entire meal without realizing my sister was gone? This is exactly why I told you I can't date. She has to be my priority. What if someone takes her?"

As I'm dialing security, the alarm sounds, indicating my front door has been opened. A second later, Ellie's voice rings out. "You better be careful. The last time I snuck up on them they were—

"Yo, Bro," Lincoln yells, cutting Ellie off. Sienna and I both rush to the top of the stairs and find Lincoln and Ellie in the doorway. "Missing something?" he asks, pushing Ellie inside the foyer.

"Oh, thank God!" Sienna flies down the stairs and pulls her sister into a hug. "Where were you?" Before Ellie can answer, she turns toward Lincoln and asks, "Where did you find her?"

"She convinced Bruno to let her into my place," Lincoln says dryly. "I was in the shower getting ready to go to the club. Came out and she was sitting on my couch."

"Ellie!" Sienna hisses.

"What?" Ellie scoffs. "It's not like I was naked or anything. I was just trying to give you two some quiet time to make up for walking in on you guys last night."

Lincoln chuckles. "I gotta run."

"Thank you," Sienna says. "I'm so sorry. This won't happen again."

"It's all good," Lincoln says with a small grin. He reaches out and ruffles Ellie's hair playfully, which has her glaring his way. "Try to stay out of trouble, kid."

"I'm not a kid," Ellie yells as he closes the door behind him.

"Yes, you are," Sienna says with a glare. "And now you're a grounded kid. Phone." She extends her hand and Ellie gasps.

"Seriously?"

"Seriously," Sienna says in a stern voice, reminding me of my mom when she would punish us.

Ellie rolls her eyes but drops it into her sister's palm. "Try to do something nice and end up grounded. So ridiculous," she mumbles, as she stomps up the stairs. A few seconds later, her door clicks shut, and it's just Sienna and me, alone again.

"I'm sorry," she says with a sigh. "I'll try to keep her under control while we're here."

"Hey." I snake my arm around her waist and pull her into me. "I think your sister is pretty fucking awesome. I mean, she's the reason I finally got to take you out on a date. She's clearly team Micah." I shrug, and Sienna snorts out a laugh. "Besides, with Ellie in her room for the night, I get to have you all to myself." I press my lips to hers, loving that I can do that and she won't push me away.

"Nice try," she says dryly. "But my dear sister never ate dinner. Which means, she'll be coming out at some point, bored and complaining that she's starved, and I'll be damned if she catches me in a compromising position *again*."

Seventeen

MICAH

"Micah."

My lids snap open, and I sit up quickly, instinctually reaching for the gun I keep in my bedside table. But when my eyes adjust, I find Sienna standing in the doorway. She's wearing a tiny pink silk tank top and even tinier matching shorts, the light from somewhere outside of my room making her glow like a goddamn angel.

"What's wrong?" I ask, trying and failing to ignore the way her pebbled nipples are poking through the thin material of her top.

"Nothing," she says, her voice cracking. "I was just..." She sucks her bottom lip into her mouth, and I'm momentarily distracted. Between being half-asleep and her looking like a walking wet dream, it takes me a second to focus. But once I do, I get the impression she's nervous about something.

"Come here." I nod toward my bed for her to join me. Clearly she needs to talk to me, otherwise, she wouldn't be coming into my room at—I tap the screen on my phone—two in the morning.

She closes the door behind her, and the room goes dark with only the lights from the city peeking in through the slats. "What's going on?" I ask, once she's seated on the edge of my bed. "Is Ellie okay?"

"Yeah, yeah. Everything's fine. Ellie's asleep."

"Okay, then—"

My words get stuck in my throat when she reaches out and palms my cock. It's soft since I was asleep, but with her squeezing it, it wakes up instantly.

"I was hoping we could pick up where we left off," she says softly, releasing me and crawling onto the bed. My legs are already spread, and she settles between them. "I've never done this before. Well, I did once… kind of… to my high school boyfriend. He shoved my head down and then I threw up in my mouth. I broke up with him right after."

Not exactly the visual I want in my head, but I like that she's honest with me. That she feels she can talk to me about the hard shit.

"You don't have to do this," I tell her, needing her to know that she always has a choice. I've accepted we're going at her pace, and I'm okay with that because I believe the wait will be worth the reward. *And the reward is Sienna being mine forever.*

"I know," she says, "but I want to. Until you, I never trusted someone enough to be intimate with them, but you've proven to be trustworthy. The few guys I've dated never put me first, but when we were out by the pool, your only focus was on my pleasure, and now I want to focus on yours."

She reaches for the waistband of my sweats and pulls them down along with my boxer briefs. Then she looks at my cock, assessing it. It's at half-mast and laying against my stomach. I shift myself upward so I can watch her easier. She follows my movements, her tongue peeking out and running along the seam of her lips like she's hungry for me. She glances up at me momentarily, her blue eyes hooded with lust, and then drops her eyes back down as she wraps her fingers around my shaft. At her touch, it starts to swell, and when she dips her head and licks the tip, it grows even bigger and harder.

She licks me several times like it's a fucking lollipop and then opens her mouth wide, taking me all the way in until her nose is nestled in the neatly trimmed pubes that surround my cock.

I know she wants to give me pleasure, but I can't help it when I reach out and tweak one of her nipples through the thin material of her tank. They're there and hard and begging to be touched. Sienna groans around my hard shaft causing my hips to buck slightly in response.

"Shit, sorry," I murmur, not wanting her to think I'm just like that self-absorbed pubescent boy she dated all those years ago.

She sucks harder in response, taking my sac between her delicate fingers and massaging it, clearly knowing what she's doing.

I lift her by her ponytail and her mouth pops off my dick. "Where did you learn to suck cock?" I ask, because if she's fucking with me and is actually experienced, we're going to have a damn problem. I've seen women pull that bullshit, thinking it's cute and sexy and will turn a guy on, but I didn't take Sienna for someone who would play those kinds of games.

"I...I've listened to the women at Wanderlust talk...and...I've watched some porn." She sucks her bottom lip into her mouth, then releases it. "Does it feel good, what I'm doing?"

"So damn good," I tell her. Then, because her swollen lips are like a damn beacon, I pull her up my body and kiss her hard, needing to taste her, not giving a shit that her mouth was just wrapped around my dick.

"I wasn't done yet," she murmurs against my mouth. She backs up and lifts my shirt over my head, then presses her warm, soft lips to my collarbone. She works her way back down, trailing fiery kisses all over my flesh, paying special attention to the happy trail that leads to my dick.

When she's back to where she started, she goes to town on my cock, sucking and licking and massaging my ballsac, never letting up. It's not long before I'm warning her that I'm about to come, but she only takes me deeper, sucks harder, causing me to swear to fucking Christ as I come down her throat harder than I've ever come in my life. It takes everything in me not to beg this woman to marry me right here, right now. Because after experiencing her mouth around my cock, I can't even imagine what it will feel like when I get to fuck her tight little cunt.

"WHILE I'M GONE, I NEED YOU BOTH TO STAY HERE." I GLANCE at Ellie. "If you leave, I can't protect you."

I have an early meeting with Eleazar, and I have no idea how it's going to go, but what I do know is that he's not touching a hair on Sienna or Ellie's head. I don't care what it fucking takes, I'll make sure to protect them.

"I'm scared," Sienna admits, and I pull her into my arms, rubbing her back and neck comfortingly. After Sienna gave me a mind-blowing orgasm, I made her come twice before we fell asleep. It was the third time I've fallen asleep and woken up with a woman in my bed. The first two times I was a bit younger, and I freaked out both times. But as I watched Sienna snuggled into my side, her head resting in the crook of my arm, there was no freaking out because I knew I wanted this—wanted her—for the rest of my life. And I'll do everything in my power to keep both her and her sister safe.

"I have two guys standing outside, and I'm going to set the alarm when—"

"Not for us," Sienna says. "For you."

I stop my movements and stare at her, momentarily taken

aback. In the life we live, I'm used to the danger, to the risk that comes with doing the type of business we do...work with the type of people we work with. Aside from my mom, I've never let another woman get close enough to worry about me.

"I'm going to be just fine," I assure her. "I'm going to talk to the guy who's put the bounty on your head and clear everything up." I kiss the corner of her mouth. "Don't worry. Go swimming, lay out by the pool with your sister, watch a movie. I'll be back soon."

Twenty minutes later, I'm standing in what was once Eduardo's office, shaking hands with his son, Eleazar. "What can I do for you?" he asks, offering me a drink.

Not wanting to offend him, I nod and thank him for the drink purely out of respect. "I'm here to speak to you about a personal matter."

He raises a single brow, gesturing for me to continue. Growing up, Eleazar and I went to the same private school, hung out with the same circle of people. We were friends. But just after graduation, his brother was killed, and Eleazar left unexpectedly to take over his part of the family business in Mexico. Soon after, he met his wife and never returned...until now.

"It's been brought to my attention that you have a bounty on Sienna Bardot's head."

Eleazar takes a sip of his drink and sits, setting the glass down and clasping his hands together in front of him. "Her whore of a mother killed my father, stole his money and drugs."

"I've heard, but she shouldn't be held responsible for her mother's actions."

"Blood for blood," he says simply.

"So, it's only Sienna you're after?"

He chuckles. "If you're asking if I've put a bounty on the child's head, no. Children are off limits, even for monsters such as myself." He smirks, and I sigh in relief.

I take a sip of my drink and set it down, then lean forward, locking eyes with Eleazar. "Your father died owing me a debt, and

I'm here to collect."

⚜

EIGHTEEN YEARS AGO

"I GOTTA GO. IF I'M NOT HOME BY DINNER, MY MOM'S GONNA kill me." I jump on my bike and take off down the street toward our house. As I'm crossing the street, I notice two men grabbing a woman, her body flailing in an effort to get away. When I look closer, I see it's not just any woman. It's Marta Gutierrez, the wife of Eduardo Gutierrez, one of the most dangerous crime bosses in Tesoro. Because he does business with my dad, we've had dinner with them a few times, and I'm also friends with Eleazar, their son.

I don't know what possesses me to do it, but instead of minding my own business like my dad taught me to do, I follow the car that leads to a dark alley where they drag Marta Gutierrez out. She's kicking and screaming, so one of the guys slaps her across the face. "Shut the fuck up, bitch. Save the screaming for when I'm fucking your ass."

I should probably call my dad, ask him what I should do, but something tells me this woman won't be alive long enough to save if I don't act soon.

I watch as one of the guys turns around to make a phone call. Then I make my move. With the baseball bat I was still carrying after playing ball at the park with my friends, I come up behind the guy and hit him across the head with it. He falls to the ground, and I quickly grab his gun, aim it at his head, and pull the trigger. Then I aim for the other guy and do the same. My dad taught us how to shoot a gun at a very young age, so I have no problem taking out both guys. Assuming it's over, I'm about to lower the gun when the door they were dragging Marta toward swings open and a guy steps outside to see what's going on. Before he can wield his weapon, I fire the gun, hitting him directly between the eyes.

"C'mon, let's go," I say to Marta, pulling her into the car. I grab the keys from the dead guy, and we take off to her house.

When we arrive, she insists I come in. When she tells Mr. Gutierrez what happened—that had I not shown up when I did, they would've raped and killed her—he shakes my hand and says, "I owe you, son. One debt to be repaid any time, no questions asked."

"You saved my *mom's* life. And you think it's equivalent to saving that bitch's life?" Eleazar spits. I ignore him calling Sienna a bitch since it wouldn't do anyone any good to start a war over name calling.

"You seem to have taken a special interest in this girl. Who is she to you?" he asks. "Your wife? Your lover? Your daughter?"

When I shake my head, he shrugs as if that's all he needs to know. "That deal was done with my father, not me. And maybe I would consider honoring it if she was someone of any real significance, but she's *no one*. She's not worthy of being spared." He shakes his head. "I'm sorry, Micah, but no deal. She and her mother are dead."

Because I'm not on a suicide mission, I stand and shake his hand, thanking him for his time. I head out knowing exactly what I need to do, certain that Sienna isn't going to be happy about it at all.

Before I go home, I stop by my parents' place to talk to my dad. He's been the man I've looked up to my entire life, and I trust his opinion. I already know what I'm planning to do, but I still want to hear what he thinks.

"Son, nice of you to stop by," Dad says. "Business or pleasure?"

"A bit of both," I say with a light laugh.

"Can you bring us some fresh pastries and coffee, please?" Dad asks Adeline, the woman who's been running the house for the past thirty years. She cooks, cleans, and when Lincoln and I were younger, she was like a nanny to us, making sure we were taken care of when Mom and Dad were busy.

"Of course," she says with a smile.

He gestures for me to have a seat on the couch in his office, and we make light conversation until after the food and drinks have arrived and we're left alone.

"I'm going to ask Sienna to marry me."

Dad chokes on his coffee. "Don't you think it's a little soon for that? I know you care for her but—"

"I'm in love with her," I admit. "And if I don't marry her, Gutierrez is going to kill her. I can't let that happen."

"That's a lot of info in one sentence. I think you're going to need to start from the beginning."

I explain how quickly I've come to care about Sienna and how I know she's the one. I can feel it in my heart and soul. When we kiss and touch, the way I crave her all the time. I tell him all about the life she and Ellie have had to endure. And then I go on to explain what her mom has done and how it's fallen down into Sienna's lap.

"And you believe by marrying her it will stop Eleazar from killing her?"

"I believe it's my only shot. He practically told me as much. If I go to him with a marriage certificate, I think he'll agree to call off the bounty. His father owed me a debt, and while Eleazar won't be happy about it, I trust he'll call it even."

"And what about Sienna's mother?"

"I don't give a fuck about that woman. She made her choices and fuck her for running and leaving her daughters to deal with the fallout. From what Sienna and her sister have said, she's done nothing but hurt them their entire lives. It ends now."

Dad nods in understanding. "You know you always have your mother's and my support."

After talking with my dad, I call my mom into his office and tell her what needs to be done. She hates that Sienna is going to be forced to do something she doesn't want, but she understands that it's our only shot at saving her life.

"I would love to help plan the wedding," Mom offers.

"It'll have to be quick. I can't chance someone getting to her before we're married and Eleazar *hopefully* agrees to call off the bounty. I'm thinking this weekend...maybe Friday?"

"We can make it happen."

"And what if Eleazar doesn't agree?" Dad asks the question I've been thinking about since the solution came to me.

"Then I'll find another way," I tell him. *Even if it means I have to end his life.* Any enemy of Sienna's is an enemy of mine, and I won't stop until she's safe.

Eighteen

SIENNA

"No. No. No. No. This is *not* how it's supposed to go." I back away from Micah as tears fill my lids.

"How what is supposed to go?" he asks gently, looking at me like I'm a rabid animal ready to attack. When he got home, I could tell something was wrong. His hair was a mess like he'd been running his fingers through it repeatedly, and the look on his face was as if someone had died. When his eyes met mine, I could see the sympathy and sorrow in his gaze. I thought he was going to tell me I needed to pay back the money or run. What I didn't expect was that he was going to tell me that the only solution is to get married.

"Falling in love," I choke out, answering his question. "I was supposed to wait. I have goals. Get my sister and me out of this hellhole and get her off to college before that happens."

"Falling in love?" he asks, trying to follow along with my

hysteria.

"Yes! I'm not supposed to make the same mistakes my mom made," I cry out. "I'm supposed to meet a man who *chooses* to be with me, who *chooses* to love me and marry me." My sobs increase and the tears blur my vision. "He'll wear a sharp black tux, and I'll wear a beautiful white dress, and when he says, 'I do' it'll be because he loves me and wants me and *chooses* to spend forever with me… not because it's the only way to save my life."

Micah steps toward me carefully and I shake my head, not wanting him near me. "You said you wouldn't force me. You said you wanted it to be my choice! You lied."

"I *am* choosing you," he argues, bridging the gap between us. He palms the sides of my face and wipes the tears that are sliding down my cheeks. "I love you, Sienna. I've fallen so fucking hard for you. This isn't how I wanted to say the words. It's not how I wanted this all to go. But I swear to you… this is me, *choosing you*." He kisses my lips softly, and for some reason. it only makes me cry harder. "I'm choosing to save you, Hellcat. Please, let me save you."

"No." I shake my head. "No. Choosing to save me isn't choosing me. We're supposed to date and then get engaged and then get married. Because we want to, not because we need to."

Unable to be in this room with him a moment longer, yet knowing I can't leave, I do the only thing I can do and run upstairs to my room, slamming the door behind me.

I've only barely fallen onto my bed when the door opens behind me. "Sienna, it's me," Ellie says, her voice unnaturally soft. She climbs onto the bed with me and guides my head into her lap. For several minutes, she strokes my hair, attempting to calm me. And it works…until she speaks.

"I don't want you to die." Her words are said with such raw emotion that goose bumps spread across my flesh. "I've never had a dad, and you're as close to a mom as I've ever had. If you die, I'll have no one. So, if marrying Micah will keep you alive, I really think you should consider it. I know that makes me sound selfish but..."

Her voice trails off, not needing to finish her sentence, and I lay with my head in her lap thinking about what she's said. What she needs. And I know deep down that I don't have a choice. And that right there is the whole crux of the problem.

All I've ever wanted in my life is to have a choice, to *be* someone's choice. And by marrying Micah—despite having feelings for him, despite being attracted to him—both of our choices are being taken away from us.

He can say he's choosing me but he's doing so under duress. He's not choosing to spend the rest of his life with me, to stand at the altar and vow to love me forever. He's simply *choosing* not to let me die. My heart deflates at the thought.

The truth is, I've enjoyed spending time with Micah, even thought maybe there was a chance something between us was developing. The circumstances weren't ideal recently, but our first date was real, filled with only pure intentions. Micah claimed to want to get to know me on more than just a sexual level, and for the first time, the possibility of finding love left me feeling hopeful. But now everything feels tainted. I'll always wonder if Micah marrying me is out of obligation or if he's truly making the decision because he wants to be with me.

But at the end of the day, the only thing that matters is keeping Ellie safe. And in order to do that, I have to be alive. Bottom line... There never really was a choice at all. I have to marry Micah.

"How long?"

Micah glances up from his laptop and quirks a brow.

"How long do we need to stay married?" I clarify, walking further into his office.

"For a while," he says. "At least until you're off Gutierrez's radar or his men find your mom."

"Okay, I'll do it. I'll marry you."

He juts his chin, silently beckoning me to come closer, but I'm too raw at the moment to be near him, so I shake my head. "I'm not feeling well. I think I'm just gonna go to bed early. Can we discuss the specifics tomorrow?"

He frowns, and I can tell he wants to say something—but really, what is there to say? After a few seconds of him staring at me, warring with how to handle this situation, he simply nods and says, "I'll see what Ellie wants for dinner and order something extra in case you're hungry later."

I thank Micah and head up to my room, feeling like shit because he doesn't hesitate to take care of me even though I'm upset and sounding ungrateful. I cuddle into the soft blankets and go to sleep, cursing my mother to hell for tainting everything good in my life.

"WHY AM I PUTTING THIS ON?" I ASK, AS I EYE THE CREAM-colored, floral print dress that's set out before me. It's a knee-length wrap dress that will look absolutely stunning paired with the champagne Christian Louboutin heels that accompany it.

"Because I said so," Ellie smarts. "And once you're done, I'm going to curl your hair and do your make up, so you don't look like your puppy was run over by a truck." Her eyes suddenly light up. "Oh! Do you think you could convince Micah to get us a puppy?" For a moment, she looks so young and innocent, reminding me of a normal teenager who has zero cares in the world. "What kind would you want? A big one or a small one? Do hotels allow dogs?" She shakes her head. "Doesn't matter. Micah owns the place. He makes the rules. I'd want a small one, all cute and cuddly that I could put in my purse and carry around."

"Does Micah look like the kind of guy who likes puppies?" I

ask, unsure why I'm even discussing this with her. My sister has a way of absorbing you into a conversation before you even realize what is happening.

"That man would give you anything, including a puppy," she deadpans. "Now, up! Get that dress on. We need to get going."

I sigh, not having the energy to argue with her. I have no idea what she's up to, but at this point, it doesn't even matter. For all I know, this is my wedding dress and I'm about to get married.

Of course, the dress and shoes fit perfectly, and once Ellie's done playing fairy Godmother, I look like a princess, ready for the ball.

When we get downstairs, I find Micah standing in the living room, staring down at his phone. Ellie clears her throat and he looks up, his gaze landing on me. His eyes immediately heat with molten lust, warming my insides from his look alone.

"You look perfect," he says, pocketing his phone and sauntering toward the stairs. He's dressed in an all-black suit, but his tie is burgundy, the same color as the flowers on my dress. His hair is neatly styled, and his face is sporting the perfect amount of stubble. He's beautiful. That's the only way to describe him. Sure, he's masculine, has that dangerous vibe going on, sporting arms adorned with intricate tattoos, but he's also really fucking beautiful.

I meet him at the bottom of the stairs, and he leans in and gently kisses the corner of my mouth. He smells intoxicating—the perfect mix of fresh and masculine—and it takes everything in me not to beg him to let me inhale his scent for a few more seconds.

Tucking my arm into the crook of his, he guides us to the front door when I realize we're leaving without Ellie. "Is she okay being here alone?" I look back at her. "And what about dinner?"

Ellie rolls her eyes. "I'll be just fine here. And I won't leave. I only went to Lincoln's because he lives on the same floor, and I knew I'd be safe there. Plus, I have exams I need to study for and take since it's my last week of school. If I get hungry, I'll order room service. So go, have fun. Stop worrying so much."

It doesn't surprise me when we end up at a restaurant in the hotel since Micah won't chance me leaving the property. We enter through the back and end up in a private room. Unlike the last time we ate here with his parents, the table is only set for two, and there are gorgeous roses in the center with candles glowing on each side. Soft music plays in the background just loud enough to create the vibe without it being overbearing.

Like the gentleman he is, Micah pulls out my chair before taking the seat adjacent to me. Once our drinks have been delivered and we've placed our food orders, Micah shifts toward me, his eyes meeting mine. "I was going to wait until the end of the meal to do this, but the tension between us has me wanting to talk to you now."

I know what he means. We went from us flirting and kissing and making out, to me hiding in my room and crying at the thought of marrying him.

"What is it you'd like to talk about?" I ask, sounding more formal than intended.

Micah reaches out and takes my hand in his and then brings it up to his lips, giving it a gentle kiss that acts as a key starting the engine to my heart. A simple kiss shouldn't cause such a disturbance in my body, yet it does.

"The moment I saw you on that stage at Wanderlust, I knew I had to have you in every way possible. I know that sounds crazy and a tad bit stalkerish," he says with a chuckle, "but it's the truth. I've only known you for a short time, but I'm attracted to everything about you. The way you're passionate for dance, how hard of a worker you are. Your determination to come up in a world that's hell-bent on keeping you down. The unconditional love you have for your sister and the way you selflessly put her first every day."

He squeezes my hand, and I choke up at the way he sees me. Nobody has ever *really* seen me before... not like that, not until

Micah.

"I love how determined you are, which is not to be confused with stubbornness. It's simply that you have goals and dreams and expectations that you are hell-bent on achieving. You want so much out of life and you're willing to fight for it. You could've easily slept with the members of Wanderlust and made a shit ton of money, and nobody would've faulted or judged you for it, but you refuse to go against the bar you've set for yourself."

"I don't want to be like her," I murmur.

Micah smiles and palms the side of my face. "Hellcat, I don't know your mom, but from what I do know, you couldn't be like her if you tried." He presses a soft kiss to my lips, and I sigh into him. I might not be happy with the situation, but I can't ignore the way I feel when I'm around him. The way his touch lights up my body and his words spark such emotion in my heart.

He reaches into the pocket of his jacket and pulls out a black velvet box. My pulse quickens, knowing what that is.

"In the short amount of time I've gotten to know you, I've fallen hard," he says, his gaze searing into me. "I've fallen in love with you, Sienna."

My breath hitches at his words and tears pool in my lids. "I... I—"

"Shh," he says calmly. "I know, you're not there yet. And the situation doesn't help. You've had so many choices taken from you and I hate that, but I need you to understand that while we're getting married sooner than planned..."

"It was never planned," I choke out.

Micah chuckles. "Trust me, Hellcat, marrying you is part of every single one of my plans." Tears track down my cheeks and Micah gently wipes them away. "This is my choice," he says. "Nobody is forcing me to do anything. I'm choosing you. And if you agree to marry me, I'll keep choosing you every day for the rest of our lives if you let me."

"But you said you wanted me to choose you, too," I remind

him. During our first date at his penthouse, he told me that this was a sentiment we both shared.

"I know," he says, his voice turning solemn, "and my hope is that one day you will. But right now, your safety comes first. In order for you to fall in love with me, you need to be alive, and us getting married seems to be the only way to ensure you stay that way.

He pops open the box, exposing a beautiful diamond ring. "I want to give you the world, Sienna. Starting with me in a black tux and you in a white dress. And I promise that when I say, 'I do,' it's because I love you and want you and desire nothing more than to spend forever showing you just how much."

A sob escapes past my lips at his admission, at the fact that he's always listening, absorbing, taking in what I say. I hate that I'm being forced into this, that even if one day I do fall in love with Micah—which, at this point, he's making it damn near impossible not to—it will always feel marred. Still, I can't deny that Micah cares about me, that his feelings for me are genuine. He's made those feelings and his intentions clear from the first time we met and he's never, not once, faltered from them.

The scrape of Micah's chair being pushed back catches my attention. And then he's down on one knee, looking up at me with the ring between his fingers and hope in his eyes. "Sienna Bardot, will you do me the honor of becoming my wife?"

My first instinct should be to say no, to tell him I need to think about this, ask more questions, consider if there are any other options, but my heart takes over before my head can respond, and I blurt out, "Yes, I'll marry you."

As Micah slides the ring onto my finger, I think about how I always pictured this moment. Although I'm not in love with Micah, I can't deny how much I've come to care about him in such a short amount of time. Nor do I doubt the love I feel radiating off of him. Despite this marriage being forced upon me, I know that Micah is a good man, and he'll make a good husband. He's made it a point to put me first from the beginning, and every day he shows me how much he cares. I might not be doing things the way I imagined, but he's right, I'm not following in my mom's footsteps. If anything, I'm stepping out of her shadow and moving toward a better future, leaving her destructive path far behind us for good.

Once the ring is on my finger, he pulls me onto my feet and into his arms. "I know this isn't how you envisioned your engagement," he says, knowing exactly what I'm thinking, yet again. "But if you give us a real chance, I think you could be happy."

"It's not that," I say with a choked sob. "I was happy getting to know you. Going on dates with you. I just..." Fresh tears fill my eyes as I try to explain what I'm feeling. "I just wanted to do things the right way. For once, I wanted some control over my life. To not suffer from the bad choices thrust upon me by our mom. Even now, she has managed to tarnish and sully everything, and I just wanted one thing to feel pure and clean and right."

Micah nods in understanding. "I know, and I'm sorry, but I'll do everything I can to make sure you never regret this."

Nineteen

SIENNA

"You look stunning," Donna coos. "Like a queen. I'm so honored to have you as my daughter-in-law." She pulls me into her arms carefully, mindful not to ruin my hair and makeup, and murmurs, "I've always wanted a daughter," and my emotions get the better of me.

Today is my wedding day. It's been three days since Micah proposed. When we returned home from dinner, we were greeted by his family and my sister. They congratulated us on our engagement, and I felt bad, thinking that everyone is under the impression this is real, until Micah told me they're all aware of what's going on. I was shocked that they were welcoming me with open arms, knowing what they know, but it also warmed my heart because it's clear that Micah's family is close, and I'm thankful to have them in my corner.

The next few days were spent with Micah working, Ellie

taking her finals—she's officially done with her ninth-grade year—and Donna helping me with the wedding arrangements. Since I couldn't leave the hotel, everything and everyone came to me. And in only a few short days, all of the wedding plans were set.

"And you," she says to Ellie, who's donning a beautiful maid-of-honor dress. "This will make you family as well." She hugs Ellie. "If you need anything, I'm always here."

Since the wedding needs to be kept private to ensure that the asshole who's after me doesn't find out, only Micah's family and Ellie are attending the wedding. I told Micah we didn't need to dress up or have a formal ceremony. All we needed was a marriage certificate to show that guy Eleazar as proof of our nuptials. Then, hopefully, he'll stop coming after me as a favor to Micah.

But Micah insisted on having as much of a traditional wedding as possible, complete with the black tux and white dress.

"Thank you," I say to Donna. Having people in our corner isn't something Ellie and I are used to. Micah's mom didn't have to embrace us, but she has, so it really means a lot to me.

Donna scoffs. "No need to thank me. I swore my son would die a bachelor until he met you. Seeing him in love makes me so happy. That's all a parent wants, for their children to fall in love and be happy."

Ellie and I glance at each other, and I know she's thinking what I'm thinking: our mother couldn't care less if we ever find love or happiness.

When I step into the space where the ceremony is being held, Micah is talking to his brother who's standing beside him as his best man. But the moment he sees me, it's as if everyone else disappears. Micah's full attention goes to me, and as I walk toward him, I see only him. He's beyond handsome in his tux, with his hair freshly cut, and his face cleanly shaven.

But what has my attention is the way this man looks at me. When Micah asked me to marry him, he confessed that he's fallen in love with me. I wanted to tell him it's too soon, that he doesn't know what he's talking about, but as I watch him watching me, the look in his eyes can't be misconstrued as anything other than love.

Our vows are standard repeat after me, and once we both say them, the officiant pronounces us husband and wife. Then Micah kisses me. And it's in that moment—when his soft yet strong lips meld with mine—that I realize how much I've missed him this past week. I was starting to get used to his touches and kisses, but he stopped it all to give me the space I needed in order to come to terms with what was about to happen. Yet before this marriage idea was thrust upon us, we were slowly getting to know each other, and I was beginning to fall. I don't know where our future lies as husband and wife, but what I do know is that I want to continue moving forward with Micah to see where things go from here.

After the service has concluded, we move to a private room where champagne and dinner is served. I've just finished eating when Micah stands and extends his hand. "May I have this dance, wife?"

It's only then that I realize a song has started to play and Micah is waiting for my response. I take his proffered hand, silently accepting his request for our first dance as a married couple. This wonderful man has thought of everything, determined to give me the most memorable wedding possible, despite the circumstances.

With my hand in his, he guides me to an open area and encircles his arms around my waist. As we dance, with my arms around his neck, I take in the lyrics and wonder if Micah picked out this song himself or if he had someone else choose it for him.

But then his lips brush against my ear and he whispers the words, clearly knowing the song, and warmth spreads through my body. As he continues to relay the words about climbing mountains and swimming oceans just to be with me, I lay my head against his chest wondering what I've done to deserve a man like Micah Alexander.

"When I heard this song, I knew it was the one," he says, answering my earlier question. "You're my reason, Sienna." He taps my chin and raises it to look at him. "I've spent years focusing on work, helping to take Alexander Enterprises to the next level. I thought my life was complete until you and your sister appeared, and I realized just how lonely I really was. How regimented my life had become. I love you and marrying you today will always be one of the best decisions of my life."

Without waiting for me to say anything back, he kisses me with such passion it feels as though I'm syphoning every ounce of love from his body into mine. The kiss ends too soon, and when we separate, he must see the want in my eyes because he chuckles. "It's good to know you want me almost as much as I want you."

Once the song is over, Micah shocks me by suddenly announcing that it's time for us to go. When I glance at Ellie, Donna smiles knowingly. "Don't worry. She'll be fine. I'm staying with her tonight." She winks playfully. "Enjoy your wedding night."

Oh, shit. My wedding night.

I've been so preoccupied with the actual wedding and the reality of getting married, I didn't even consider there would be a wedding night.

We thank everyone for being here, and I tell Ellie to behave. Then Micah guides us up to a room that isn't his penthouse. The suite is similar to the room Ellie and I had stayed in, but it's even more luxurious.

Micah takes the champagne that's being chilled in a bucket and pops it open, pouring us each a glass and then handing me a flute. "To finding love," he says. I nod in understanding, knowing that he's referring to himself and hoping one day I'll find it too.

After taking a few sips, he sets his glass down and I do the same, my nerves suddenly electric. I'm assuming this is the part where we consummate our marriage, where I finally have sex for the first time.

My mind races to think about the specifics: What am I wearing under this dress? Did I shave everywhere? Shit! I'm not on birth control. Did he bring condoms with him?

A million questions and thoughts are flying through my head when Micah takes the side of my face in his strong hand. "Breathe, Sienna. I'm not going to force you to do anything you're not ready for."

"What? What do you mean?"

"The fear is practically radiating off of you at the thought of having sex with me. Don't worry, that's not why I brought you here." He hands me a manila envelope, and I take it in shock.

That's not why he brought me here? He's not planning to have sex with me? I don't understand.

"What's this?" I ask in confusion, my head spinning.

"I guess it's kind of a wedding present." He scrubs the side of his face, looking nervous. Why is he nervous?

I open the envelope and pull the papers out, skimming the text. Initially, I assume it's a prenup, which would make sense since Micah is wealthy. I, on the other hand, bring nothing to this marriage but issues. He has every right to protect himself.

But then I see the words: **Decree of Divorce**

"Are these divorce papers?" I choke out. I flip to the end and see Micah's signature. "Did you marry me and file for divorce on the same day?"

"I'm not divorcing you," he says softly. "These papers were drawn up for *you*. My hope is that you'll fall in love with me and never use them. But you said you feel forced, that the choice to marry has been taken from you. Yes, we married out of necessity in order to save your life, but I don't ever want you to feel trapped in our marriage. I told you before that I want you to choose me the way I'm choosing you."

"You chose to *save me*," I mutter.

"I've said it before and I'll continue to say it," he replies, setting the papers down and pulling us onto the couch and me into his lap. "I chose to marry you because I'm in love with you, and I see an entire future with you. Sure, the circumstances sped up the timeline." He smirks. "But I told you at Wanderlust, I want it all with you. The love, the marriage... Hell, if you're willing, someday I'd like nothing more than to have you pregnant with my babies." He sucks his bottom lip into his mouth and glances down at my belly, heat filling his gaze.

And suddenly, I can picture it: going to bed and waking up together, creating a family together. The dinners, birthdays, holidays. Everything I've ever wanted but refused to believe I could have is now at my fingertips.

"But I'm getting a little ahead of myself," he adds, looking back up at me. "I want this marriage to work, and if you give us a real chance, I'll show you just how good it can be. I can only hope that one day you'll be telling me that you love me, too. But I want you to know that with me, you *always* have a choice. So..." He nods toward the papers sitting on the table. "I had divorce papers drawn up. Once you're safe, you can file them at any time. My signature is already on them."

Most women would be deeply offended if their husbands gave them divorce papers on their wedding night, but I understand exactly why Micah did it, and the gesture has me falling harder for him.

"Thank you," I say, wrapping my arms around his neck.

"You're thanking me for divorce papers?" he half-jokes.

"I'm thanking you for making me feel a little less trapped."

I lean in and kiss the corner of his mouth first, then the other corner. When I glide my lips to meet his, my insides tighten with need, and I tell myself I can do this. I can have sex with my husband. I might not love him yet, but I hope with time, I will. And if anyone has a chance of winning my heart, it's definitely Micah.

But sex is suddenly off the table when he breaks the kiss and lifts me off his lap, setting me onto my feet.

"What are you doing?" I ask, confused as to why he would stop our kiss.

"As much as I love kissing you, having you in my lap wearing that sexy wedding dress is absolute torture." He chuckles lightly. "Especially since we won't be having sex tonight."

"Wait, what? We're not having sex?"

"Oh, we're going to have sex," he says with a smirk. "But no, it won't be tonight. When we finally do, it's going to be because you choose to, not because you were forced into a marriage meant to save your life.

"I don't understand," I say in shock. "If you didn't plan to have sex with me, why did you get us this room?"

"You said you wouldn't be having sex until you were in love and married. I can't help the marriage part, but I can help the love part. Starting tonight, I'm going to do everything in my power to get you to fall in love with me, but the sex won't happen until you say so. As for the room..." He shrugs. "Just because we aren't having sex doesn't mean we can't enjoy our wedding night together." He pulls me toward him, and I go willingly. "I packed us bathing suits. What do you say we take that champagne outside and enjoy the hot tub?" He waggles his brows, and I swear I fall again.

Hell, at this rate, if I keep falling like I am, I'm going to hit the ground in no time. And I'll have to hope that Micah is there to catch me.

"The hot tub sounds good."

"Your clothes are in the luggage placed in the master bedroom along with mine, but if you want to sleep separately, that's fine. The suite has three bedrooms."

Of course it is. Because he's the most understanding and patient man I've ever met. "What do you want?" I ask. When he raises a brow, I clarify. "I wasn't sure if you would want me in the same room as you, in your bed, knowing we aren't having sex."

"Being with you is more than sex. Sleeping next to you, holding you, kissing you. I want you any way I can have you, and when you're ready, I'll be here." He takes my hand and guides us into the room. "Turn around."

I do as he says, and he carefully undoes each button along my back until the dress is parting ways down the middle. I consider taking it to the bathroom to change, but since he is my husband and we've been intimate, I figure *what the hell*, and I let the dress fall to the floor, leaving me in only my lacy white bra and panty set. They're nothing special since I didn't even consider buying a bridal set, but you wouldn't know that by the way Micah is staring at me in the mirror with heat in his gaze.

"Sorry, should I go change in the—"

"No," he says, spinning me around. "I can handle seeing my wife like this. Is it torture? Yes. But it's the best kind. Because one day, this…" He drags the tip of his finger down the center of my breasts and torso, stopping just below my belly button. "*You* will be all mine, in every fucking way."

I swallow thickly as liquid heat flows through my body, ending at the center between my legs. I've never wanted a man the way I want Micah, never allowed myself to want anyone like I do him. For a split second, I consider throwing my rules out the window and begging him to fuck me, to show me what it's like to be with someone in the most intimate way, but I take a deep breath and push the thought away. I refuse to be like my mom. When I have sex, we'll both be in love. But until then, there's nothing wrong with being with him in other ways, right?

As if he can read my thoughts, Micah grins knowingly. "Go change, and I'll meet you outside."

After changing into my bikini, I head out to the hot tub and find Micah already there in board shorts, sans shirt. His muscular chest and torso are on display, and I imagine licking my way down each hard ridge.

He drops into the bubbling water, the bottom half of his body disappearing, and he extends his hand for me to join him. I take it, allowing him to lift and set me on his lap so I'm straddling his thighs. The water is warm, and it feels good, relaxing my muscles.

"Did you have a good day?" he asks after a few minutes of silence, a hint of uncertainty in his tone.

"The wedding was beautiful. Thank you for doing everything you could to make it as perfect as possible." I wrap my arms around his neck, and his shoulders visibly sag in relief.

"I would do anything for you," he murmurs. "You're my wife in every sense of the word, and from this day forward, you come first. Always."

The way he says it, so matter of fact, sends goose bumps across my flesh. I've never come first to anyone, not until Micah. I don't know how to respond to his confession, so I lean down and kiss him, trying to convey without words how much that means to me. Knowing I have someone I can trust in my corner. It's something most people take for granted. Something I've never had. It's always been me against the world, standing front and center, protecting Ellie.

Micah reaches around and gently fists the back of my head, deepening the kiss, and I moan into his mouth, wanting more. He tastes sweet like the champagne, and I suck on his tongue as I grind down on the bulge between his legs, hitting the sweet spot between my own.

It doesn't take long before the best kind of pleasure is ripping through my body and pulsing in my veins. Micah holds me tight, kissing me hard, as I ride out my orgasm.

"It's addicting," I admit softly, making him chuckle.

"It's why the world revolves around sex. We connect through it, fight for it, fight over it. Hell, some of the greatest wars were because of beautiful women." He smirks.

"If it feels this good without having actual sex, I can't even begin to imagine how it will feel when I actually do," I say absentmindedly, as I run my hand down Micah's torso to where he's still hard. "Lift up."

It takes him a second to understand what I'm saying, but once he does, he lifts his body onto the edge of the hot tub so he's no longer sitting in the water, and I'm situated between his legs. If my husband can't get laid on our wedding night, the least I can do is get him off with my mouth. The last time I gave him a blowjob, he enjoyed it so much, he thought I'd lied about my inexperience.

Getting onto my knees, I pull the waistband of his shorts down and watch as his cock springs to attention, the swollen head begging for me to put my mouth on it. I thought giving head would be gross. My mom used to bitch about it all the time, but with Micah, I enjoyed it. Not only does he taste good, but knowing that I'm the reason for his pleasure is such an aphrodisiac.

I use my mouth and hand to work him over—tasting, licking, sucking—until he's moaning my name and coming down my throat. And then he's pulling me into his lap, kissing me, devouring me. He carries me back inside to the bathroom where he gives me another orgasm on the counter, this time with his mouth.

Once we're both rinsed and dried off separately—since I'm not ready for that kind of intimacy yet—he takes me to bed, refusing to let us get dressed. He pulls me into his arms, our warm, naked bodies entwined, and then he kisses me softly as he runs his fingers through my hair. Soon after, my body becomes limp, and my eyes flutter closed.

"I love you, Hellcat," he murmurs, as I slowly drift off to sleep, feeling things I never thought I'd feel—safe and cherished and loved.

Twenty

MICAH

"You on your way to see Gutierrez?" Lincoln asks over Bluetooth.

"Yeah. Figured it'd be best to get it over with. He's either going to accept it or we're going to end up in a war."

When I woke up this morning with Sienna's body wrapped around mine for the third morning in a row, I knew I needed to get this shit handled. Until we know where we stand, we're at an impasse. She and Ellie can't leave the hotel, and as much as I love having Sienna all to myself, she deserves to live her life. And my hope is that once things calm down and she doesn't feel like her back is against the wall, she'll give us a real chance, one that isn't overshadowed by all the bullshit.

"Fuck," Lincoln breathes. "I know you care about this woman but going to war with Eleazar would mean—"

"I don't give a shit what it would mean," I bark, cutting him off.

I meant it when I told Sienna she comes first. I'll do everything in my power to ensure she's safe and out of harm's way, even if that means going up against the dirtiest underground crime boss. The Alexanders might be cleaner, have more legit businesses, but we're also wealthier and have more clout in this town. I'm trying to handle the situation without a bloodbath. But if that's what it takes…

"All right, all right." He sighs. "Let me know how it goes. You know I got your back no matter what."

"Thanks."

We hang up just as I pull up to the guard gate at Gutierrez's home. It's risky coming here without clearing it with Eleazar first, but if I attempt to arrange another meeting, he'd definitely know something is up.

After getting my info, the guard lets me know Eleazar is home and will see me. I walk through his house and into his office, and without so much as a hello, I slap the marriage certificate on his desk.

He reads over it, shakes his head, and chuckles. "This girl must really mean something to you," he says, his accent heavy. There are several beats of silence as Eleazar contemplates his decision. "Fine, we're even. I won't touch her, but the mom is dead."

"I don't give a fuck about that bitch. So the bounty…?"

"I'll have it removed today. Just to be on the safe side, I would have your new bride wait a few days before she ventures out… Just in case someone doesn't get the message." He smirks, and I ball my fists, holding myself back from punching him in his face since that wouldn't end well. Besides, I've already gotten him to agree. Sienna is free.

I extend my hand and Eleazar shakes it, but before he releases my hand, he says, "Just remember that I'm doing this favor because she's your wife. If that ever changes, I can't help what happens."

Without responding, I grab our marriage certificate off Eleazar's desk and walk out the door. His threat doesn't matter because if I have it my way, Sienna will be my wife for the rest of our lives. I just need to get her on board.

On the way home, I stop to pick up coffee and breakfast for Ellie and Sienna, along with a dozen roses for my new bride. I've never been the romantic type, but she makes me want to do all kinds of things I hadn't wanted to do before.

"For me?" she asks, when I hand them to her. The smile that spreads across her face as she sticks her nose into the bouquet to sniff them has me wanting to buy her every goddamn flower on the planet. "What are they for?" she asks, hugging them to her chest.

"We're celebrating." I wrap my hand around the back of her nape and pull her face to me. "You're free, Hellcat. The bounty is being lifted as we speak."

"What?" she breathes. "Seriously?"

"Yep."

Sienna drops the roses onto the table and jumps into my arms, her legs encircling my waist. She peppers kisses all over my face and then crushes her mouth against mine. "Thank you," she murmurs. "I don't know what I would've done without you."

"You don't ever have to find out," I say, kissing her back.

"Does that mean we can leave this penthouse now?" Ellie asks, her question making me tense up. I didn't consider that they'd want to leave once they were safe. I assumed they would continue living here. Give me a chance to get Sienna to fall in love with me and choose to stay with me. If they're not living here, it will be harder, but it won't stop me from trying to make my wife love me in return.

"You need to give it a few days so word can spread but then, yeah," I choke out. "You guys are free to leave. I know money is tight right now since you haven't been able to work, but I can pay for whatever place you find."

"Wait, what?" Ellie says. "We're leaving? Like moving out?" She glances at Sienna in confusion, who looks at me.

"Isn't that what you just asked?" I say, confused myself.

"No," Ellie scoffs. "I just want to leave this building. I missed my dance competition last weekend, but I'd like to go to the studio and see how everyone did." She looks at Sienna. "We're not moving out, are we? I like it here."

I stay quiet, not wanting to sway Sienna either way. She was already forced into marriage. She doesn't need me trying to force her to live here as well.

"Do we have to stay here?" Sienna asks. "In order for it to look real?"

I could try to tell her that it's safer to live here because it looks more legit. But in our world, a lot of couples don't live together. Hell, Eduardo Gutierrez had several mistresses while he was married, and his wife lived in a completely separate home than he did for years.

"No, you can live anywhere you want. We just need to remain married."

She nods and nibbles on the corner of her lips for several seconds before she finally speaks. "I'd like to stay living here if you're okay with that... On one condition."

"Anything," I blurt out, shocked that she's willing to stay. That has to mean something, right? That she's wanting to try, that she wants more than a fake marriage of convenience?

"I want to continue to work..."

Okay, so she wants to be independent. That doesn't surprise me. This is definitely something I can—

"...at Wanderlust."

Fuck. I should've seen this coming.

"I like my job there. I enjoy dancing plus I make good money. I want to make sure that if something happens between us I'll be able to take care of myself and Ellie."

As my wife, everything that's mine is hers, but I refrain from telling her this because I know it isn't just about the money. It's about her not wanting to depend on me by earning her own way.

Unfortunately, anywhere else she works won't pay her what she makes at Wanderlust. It's going to damn near kill me to watch her get on that fucking stage and take her clothes off for other men, but I won't force her to quit. I met her at the club and there's no shame in what she does there.

"Friday," I say. "You can go back to work then." I glance at Ellie. "And you can go back to the dance studio. By that time, the word should be out. But I want you driving something safe," I say to Sienna. "I have a shit ton of cars. You can drive one of them. Ellie already has an updated phone, so I'm getting you one as well, and I'm putting both of you on my plan."

"Okay," Sienna agrees. "I can live with all that."

After Ellie runs up the stairs to let her friends know she'll see them in a few days, I tug Sienna close to me. "One more thing," I murmur. "Until you tell me otherwise, you're mine. Other guys can look, they can dream, hell, they can even fantasize." I lick the seam of her lips and she shudders in response. "But nobody is touching you but me."

Twenty-One

MICAH

"I can't believe you're letting your wife work here," Lincoln snickers. It's Friday night and, as agreed upon, Sienna is back to work, which means, I'm here to watch her. The past few days have been good. She and Ellie have been hanging out, and Sienna started her online classes, so she let me get her a laptop. When I get home from work, we eat and hang out, and instead of sleeping in her own room, she's been continuing to sleep in mine without me having to ask. Her clothes are still in her room, but every night when Ellie excuses herself to go to bed, Sienna crawls into my bed. We spend hours talking and kissing, which leads to getting each other off, before she wraps herself around me and falls asleep in my arms.

"She needs to feel in control." I shrug. "If she needs to dance naked for a room full of men to do that, who am I to say no. Besides, she agreed not to give any private dances."

Lincoln whistles, shaking his head. "You're a stronger man than I am. I would've yanked her ass off that stage and—"

His words are cut off by a knock on the door, followed by Marina, our house mom, entering through the partial opening with Ellie trailing closely behind.

"Mr. Alexander," Marina says curtly. "We have a bit of a problem. It seems Miss Bardot has taken it upon herself to work here. Security caught her delivering drinks and asking the members if they needed anything."

At her statement, I turn around to look at Ellie, who doesn't look the least bit apologetic or embarrassed.

"What the hell do you mean, if they needed anything?" I bark. "You're fifteen years old. There's nothing you got that they should want."

"Not like that." Ellie huffs.

"You can go," Lincoln says to Marina. "We'll handle it from here. Thanks."

"Wait, where's Sienna?" I watched her on stage earlier, so she's not due to go back on for a few more hours.

"She's performing for a private party," Marina says, before making her exit.

"Explain," I say to Ellie, once it's just the three of us.

"I need a job," she says simply. "So... I offered to deliver drinks so the ladies can focus on giving lap dances, and in exchange, I would get a cut of their tips." She shrugs like it's no big deal, and I have to give it to her, it'd be a solid plan if Lincoln weren't hell-bent on making sure this club is run correctly—and that includes not having an underage girl serving alcohol.

"Don't fifteen-year-olds get jobs at the grocery store bagging?" Lincoln asks.

"Did you bag groceries when you were fifteen?" Ellie sasses.

"Well, no," he says, looking slightly perplexed by the teenager. "But that's different. We were learning to run the family business."

"Well, my sister works here, *and* she's married to him..." She points at me. "So technically, this is the family business."

I cough to cover my laughter, and Lincoln glares my way, silently telling me to handle this. I should let this continue just to fuck with him, but I don't, since I need to get back out to the main area soon to watch my wife dance.

"What do you need money for?" I ask Ellie.

"Dance camp. It needs to be paid this week, and since Sienna wasn't able to work because our mom's a bitch who likes to fuck her over every chance she gets, there's no way I can ask her for the money. I figured if I could deliver drinks or something, I could earn enough cash to go."

"Is Sienna okay with you going to dance camp?"

"Of course. Dance is my life," she says matter-of-factly. "This camp is for the elite and it's my first time being invited. They've offered me a partial scholarship, and if I could just do something around here, I would be able to come up with the rest." She glances at Lincoln. "I'll do whatever you need."

"Send me the info and I'll pay for it." I expect her to be excited, so I'm confused when she looks uneasy. "What?"

"It's just...Sienna told me to stop taking things from you because if it doesn't work out it'll be more she has to pay back."

Fuck. Looks like I have more work to do than I thought.

"It is going to work out, and if it doesn't, you guys don't owe me shit. I promise. Send me the info and I'll pay for it. When does it start?"

"I leave next week."

"It's not here?"

"Nope! It's in New York City! It's going to be amazing!!"

"You paid for her dance camp?"

Sienna and I are in a private room where she's grinding her ass against my groin while I glide my hands up and down the sides of her thighs. The music is pumping, though I couldn't tell you what's playing. My only focus is on my sexy wife who somehow looks even more beautiful when she's frowning. She had several private parties this evening, so when I saw an opening in her schedule following her second dance, I booked her for the rest of the night. And then I told the hostess I want to book her every night she's on the schedule. She wants to dance on stage? Fine. But the private shows will only be for me.

"This just happened like twenty minutes ago." I chuckle. "How the hell did you already find out?" When Ellie sent the link over to me, I saw I was able to pay online, so I did.

"I got a confirmation email," she says, encircling her arms around my neck.

"Your sister deserves to go to camp. She's a good kid and wants to spend her summer dancing. She was trying to earn her own money by working the floor here."

Sienna's eyes widen, clearly having not known that little fact.

"I wasn't about to let my sister-in-law miss out on a huge opportunity over money, especially when I have more than I'll ever be able to spend."

Her features soften, and I tighten my grip on her hips. "You're mine, Hellcat, which makes your sister mine to take care of by default. And I'll do whatever I can to ensure you're both taken care of...always."

She presses a soft kiss to the side of my neck, and I sigh into her, inhaling her fresh, floral scent. "Thank you," she murmurs, peppering kisses along my flesh and across my jawline. When she gets to my mouth, she licks across the seam of my lips. "You might not have noticed, but I'm not good at accepting help..." I chuckle at her dry humor. "But I really do appreciate it."

Her mouth descends on mine and her thighs tighten around me. She's dressed in a tiny top and bottoms that leave damn near nothing to the imagination, and I want nothing more than to lay her ass out on the couch and devour her. So I do just that.

I carry her over to the leather couch and lay her on her back, taking a moment to look at her. Her head is propped up against the arm of the couch, and her creamy legs are slightly spread, beckoning me to slide between them. Fuck, what I wouldn't give to rip those tiny excuse for shorts off her body and fuck her into tomorrow.

Patience, I remind myself. In time, she'll trust me enough to let her guard down, and then her heart will be open and ready for the taking. Tonight was definitely a step in the right direction. I was expecting her to freak out and insist on paying me back, but instead, she accepted my help and even thanked me.

Sienna watches with hooded eyes as I climb between her legs and trail fiery kisses along her heated flesh, starting at the juncture of her neck and working my way down, stopping at her top and unlacing it so it opens to expose her perfect perky tits.

Before Sienna, being with a woman was always about getting off. Like most people, I enjoy sex. But I never paid attention to the small details, like the way Sienna's nose has a light smattering of freckles that darken when she's in the sun. Or the beauty mark on the top of her left breast. Or how when she's turned on, goose bumps prickle her skin, and her flesh gets overheated.

I love watching her facial expressions. When she's happy and sad and frustrated. But most of all, I love watching the way she looks at me when she wants me.

"Micah," she groans. "What are you doing?"

"Looking at you," I say honestly. "I can't believe you're mine."

Her cheeks tint pink, and I love that no matter how badass she comes across, when I say something sweet, she gets shy with me, momentarily letting down her wall.

I kiss her beauty mark and then suckle each of her nipples. She squirms, clearly turned on and wanting more. I move lower, kissing down her middle and stopping at her navel, swirling my tongue around it. I kiss each of her hip bones and then slide her shorts down her legs, tossing them to the side. Her cunt is trimmed neatly, and when I spread her thighs wider, it's glistening with need.

I lean over and press a kiss to the hood of her pussy, and she groans, her fingers delving into my hair, silently begging me for more. Always wanting more.

I dip lower, separate her pink lips, and lick up her center slowly, inhaling and tasting her essence. Everything about Sienna has become an addiction. Her words, her touch, her mouth, her body, her pussy. I can't get enough.

Lifting her thighs, I lick from bottom to top, and her moans grow louder. When I do it again, my tongue brushing against the sensitive spot between her pussy and ass, she starts to pant, her fingers tightening their hold on my hair.

"You like that, Hellcat?" I murmur. She moans in response, so I do it again and again. "One day, after I ruin this tight cunt, I'm going to claim your ass."

I look up at her and instead of seeing fear, want is shining in her gorgeous blue eyes. She wants me as much as I want her. She's just determined not to follow in her bitch of a mother's footsteps, so she holds back, not wanting to make the same mistakes. And I can respect that, but soon she's going to see that she and I are not a fucking mistake. And when she does, I'm going to claim and devour every inch of her, leaving nothing untouched, including her heart and soul.

I lick her until she's falling apart at the seams, and then I thrust two fingers in, bringing her to a second orgasm. By the time I'm done, she's come all over my face, my fingers, and the leather couch. Her lids are heavy, and her entire body is languid. She strokes my hair as I pepper small kisses over her flesh, and within minutes, her eyes are closed and she's snoring softly.

I could wake her up since her shift isn't over, but I don't. Instead, I text Marina to let her know Sienna's off the clock for the remainder of her shift and tell her to keep Ellie in the dressing room until we come get her. I gently reposition myself to watch her sleep, and I know without a doubt, I could spend the rest of my life simply watching her.

A couple of hours later, we get home and Ellie goes straight to bed, exhausted. Sienna always showers after work, so I turn the water on to let it heat up. Then I help her out of her clothes since she's practically dead on her feet from the multiple orgasms I gave her earlier.

"In you go," I tell her, guiding her into the bathroom.

"Mmm," she moans when she steps in and the steamy water hits her body. "Join me."

I stop in my place and glance at her, unsure if I'm hearing her wrong. Yeah, we've done shit, but we've yet to do anything as intimate as shower together. Hell, thinking about it, I don't think I've ever showered with a woman.

"You sure?" I ask, just to be certain.

"Uh-huh."

Not wanting her to change her mind, I quickly undress and then step into the shower that's big enough to fit four people easily. She's still standing under the spray, letting the water rain down on her. When she feels my presence, she opens her eyes and drags her gaze down my body.

I'm not hard, but even soft, I know I have nothing to be embarrassed of, so I own that shit and grab the soap, squirting some onto the loofah. I start to wash my body when Sienna steps toward me and takes it out of my hand.

I stand still, watching as she scrubs my arms and chest and torso. By the time she gets to my cock, it's no longer soft. It's hard as a steel beam, and if it could talk, it'd be begging her to touch it. Luckily, she doesn't need to be begged because without me—or my dick—saying a word, she drops to her knees and takes it into her mouth.

I push the wet strands of her hair out of her face so I can watch as she takes me down her throat. It doesn't take long before I'm ready to explode. I know she doesn't mind swallowing, but since we're in the shower and it'll be easy cleanup, I fist the back of her hair and pull her off my cock just in time to come all over her chest. When she stands, I can't help palming her tits and massaging my cum into her flesh. I want to own this woman in every way possible. To mark her and make her mine. Being my wife isn't enough. I want her to love me and crave me the way I do her. I want her to let me in and trust me. I want to give her the entire world. I want to fill her with my seed and knock her up, create a family and a life with her.

As if she can sense my thoughts, she asks, "What's going through your head?"

I pull her into my arms and kiss her lips. "I was just thinking about how much I love you." Despite knowing she won't say the words back, every chance I can, I tell Sienna exactly how I feel about her. I need her to know that my feelings are real, and I'm in this marriage for the long haul. At first she looked a bit uncomfortable, but now she simply smiles softly and kisses me back.

When we're in bed—with Sienna's body splayed out across mine—I run my fingers through her hair, and she sighs deeper into me, feeling safe and content.

"I think it's possible," she murmurs after a few minutes.

"What?" I ask, unsure what she's talking about.

"To fall in love with you. I didn't think it was possible, but now...I think it is."

Twenty-Two

SIENNA

"It's so quiet," Micah says, coming out of his office. "How long is she gone for, again?" He leans against the wall and pouts while I continue to type my paper for one of my online classes. "She at least pays attention to me."

I outwardly laugh at how adorable he is when he's not being paid attention to, but inside, my heart swells that the man I'm falling for doesn't just love me and crave my attention, but he also cares about my sister and genuinely enjoys her company.

Before we dropped Ellie off for dance camp, he took her shopping to make sure she had everything she could want or need. He also gave her a credit card so she would have money in case she wants or needs anything else. Then he made her promise to call and text daily. After she left, Micah told me he's having one of his men guard her surreptitiously. Even though Gutierrez has called off the bounty and Ellie was never on his radar, Micah isn't taking any chances. Watching him with her showed me the type of man he is and what a good dad he'll be one day. The thought of having kids always scared the hell out of me, but seeing Micah in pseudo-dad mode has me seeing things in a different light, one filled with possibilities.

The following night, he insisted on driving me to work, and he has been doing so every night since, watching me dance and then booking me the remainder of the evening. We spend the time talking and getting to know each other more—with some delicious orgasms mixed in—and once we're home, we shower together and then fall asleep in each other's arms. He doesn't know it, but he's slowly knocking down my wall brick by brick, and pretty soon that wall—which has done a damn good job of guarding my heart—will be nothing more than rubble on the ground.

"She's only been gone four days," I point out. "And I pay plenty of attention to you."

"Only when I'm making you come," he smarts, smirking like the damn devil he is. "We should go out and do something."

"Like what?" I click save on my document and close my laptop since it's clear I'm not going to get anymore work done right now.

It's Monday morning, but since my classes are online, I spent all day yesterday working on my assignments to stay ahead. Since dance season is over and Grace takes over the summer program, I don't have any classes to teach, either. That leaves my week completely open, aside from Thursday through Saturday nights when I work at Wanderlust.

"I don't know." He sighs. "But it's a beautiful day out and we're wasting it cooped up inside. I'm bored."

I throw my head back with a laugh. "Did Micah Alexander, millionaire, CEO businessman, and king of Tesoro just say he's bored? Don't you have like a gazillion businesses to run?"

"Eh, they practically run themselves. I want to do something fun."

"Okay, so go do something fun."

"With you."

"I'm not fun. I'm the opposite of fun. I'm boring. I work and go to school and raise Ellie."

"Well, Ellie isn't here, and your classes are online, and based on the amount of work you've been doing, I'd bet you're ahead." I open my mouth to argue, but before I can get a word out, he adds, "And you don't have work until Thursday." He walks over and plops down on the couch next to me. "C'mon, let's do something fun. Anything you want." He bats his lashes at me playfully, and I shake my head at his antics.

"Anything?" I joke.

"You name it, and we'll do it. If you could do anything, go anywhere, where would it be? What does fun look like to Sienna Alexander?"

I think for a moment, refusing to acknowledge that he just referred to my last name as his, and then tell him exactly what I would do, knowing there's no way it's going to happen. "I would fly to London and attend the Royal Ballet at the Royal Opera House in Covent Garden."

His jaw drops and he stares at me like I've grown a second head. "That's what you would do? Go watch the fucking ballet? Of all the things to do in this world, you would go watch a boring ass show where people dance to a story that nobody even understands." There's no heat or accusation in his tone, more shock than anything.

"Yep. You asked, and I answered."

He nods slowly, then says, "All right. Let's do it." Standing, he pulls his phone out of his pocket while I'm still trying to register what he just said.

"Wait, what?" I stand as well.

"You want to go to London to see men in tights dance with swans...let's go. Go pack a bag."

"What?" I say again. "We can't just go to London."

"Of course we can," he says, completely nonchalant like we're discussing going to a drive-thru fast-food restaurant and not to another freaking country across the pond.

"Actually, we can't. One, I don't have a passport..." And now that I'm thinking about it... "Or a birth certificate, or social security card. All of our important documents were lost in the fire. And even if I did have all that, I still have to work on Thursday."

Micah glances up from his phone. "Challenge accepted."

LESSON NUMBER ONE TO REMEMBER: WHEN YOU TELL MICAH Alexander something can't be done, he will prove you wrong.

Case in point: we're about to land at Heathrow airport in London, and I have my brand-new passport in hand, ready to show customs. The flight was long, but thanks to Micah's luxurious private plane, we slept through it in a bed—yes, the man's company has a plane with an actual bed that's bigger than the apartment I lived in before it was burned down.

"This is insane," I tell Micah, nervously tapping my foot on the floor as the plane lands, but really, deep down, I'm so freaking excited because holy shit! We're in London! When I was growing up, my dream was to join a traveling dance company, which would've meant dancing here. That's a dream no longer possible, but getting to see a show here is beyond amazing.

"I meant what I said," Micah tells me, leaning over and kissing the shell of my ear. "Whatever it is you want, whatever you need, I'll make it happen."

At his words, a bolt of emotion shoots through my veins and straight to my heart. It's not about him giving me whatever I want. To be honest, there isn't a lot that I want or need—a safe home for Ellie and me, a job that pays the bills, and my mom to drop off the face of the earth. Those are my top priorities. It's that for the first time in my life, I have someone who cares enough to *want* to give me those things. It's as if he thrives on me being happy. I've felt alone for so long, and now, I have someone by my side, who listens and cares.

Since we slept during the flight, we're both wide awake when we arrive, so Micah surprises me by spending the day showing me around London. We visit all the touristy attractions like the London Eye, Big Ben, and the London Bridge. He's obviously seen it all already, but rather than appearing bored, he seems to enjoy watching me gush over all the sights. He takes pictures of me, and with me, and joins in my excitement and happiness.

And when I mention how I would've tried to get Harry Potter tour tickets had I known we were coming here, he assures me that we'll come back, but next time with Ellie, since she loves Harry potter just as much as I do.

I had assumed it would be a quick turn-around trip to see the ballet, but Micah said the show we're seeing isn't until Wednesday, so we spend the next two days sightseeing and having a blast. The food is divine, the city is magical, and my husband is so much fun to be around. He might be a serious businessman to everyone else, but with me, he's funny, playful, attentive, and affectionate.

Tonight, we're attending the ballet, and it's also our last night here. Since I have to work tomorrow evening, we're heading back home first thing in the morning.

When I step out of the room in the gorgeous floral print, tiered, silk gown by Marchesa that Micah surprised me with, I feel like a princess in a fairy tale, once again. Growing up the way I did, I'd come to believe that fairy tales are nothing more than fantastical stories giving false hope to people just like me. But now I'm starting to believe that fairy tales can come true. That it's possible for me to find my very own Prince Charming, to fall in love and live happily ever after.

The thought both scares and excites me.

"Jesus," Micah says when he sees me. "You look stunning, Hellcat."

He's dressed in a sharp suit that somehow is even sexier than the usual suits he wears, his hair is gelled in that messy look only men can get away with, and his face is sporting some sexy five-day stubble that burned the inside of my thighs last night when he ate me for dessert and made me come several times.

He steps toward me and kisses the corner of my mouth, careful not to ruin my lipstick, and I inhale his fresh, masculine scent. I don't know what it is about the cologne he wears, but every time I smell it, I instantly relax, like just the scent of him alone calms me.

"For you." He reveals a black box and opens it, exposing an exquisite chain in white gold or maybe platinum. Hanging from the chain is a simple, yet elegant, ballet slipper.

When I glance up at him in question, he smiles softly. "You once told me it was your dream to dance but that life got in the way. This is to remind you of your dream. It may not be for a traveling ballet company, but one day you will dance again the way you were meant to.

He removes the necklace from the box and gestures for me to turn around. As I turn, I lift my hair, and Micah clasps the chain around my neck. When the charm falls onto my chest, I glance down at it, my emotions getting the best of me.

"Thank you," I choke out, turning back around to look at him. "Thank you for everything you've done for me and for Ellie." I sniffle loudly, trying and failing to hold it together, and he gently swipes a tear from my cheek. "But also… thank you for loving me even when I tried to push you away."

"You never have to thank me for that," he says. "Loving you is the easiest thing I've ever done."

Once I've gotten a handle on my emotions and have touched up my makeup, Micah takes us to an upscale restaurant before we make our way over to the Royal Opera House. Dinner is delicious, and the show is breathtakingly beautiful. I laugh and I cry, and the entire time, Micah holds my hand and listens to me talk about the details of the performance.

When it's over, we head back to the hotel so we can get some sleep before our flight the next day. As I sit on the bed undoing the straps of my heels, I watch Micah shrug his suit jacket off his shoulders and loosen his tie. As I do, I can't help but imagine us both getting completely undressed and then him laying me out on the bed so he can make love to me. But I quickly shake off the thought because as much as I want Micah and have grown to like him, I'm not in love with him.

Sure, my heart beats quicker when he's around.

And yes, butterflies have taken up permanent residence in my belly every time he's near.

And yeah, he's thoughtful and caring and puts me and Ellie before everything else.

And when he smiles at me, it feels like he's looking straight into my soul.

And when we're together, his focus is solely on me, like we're the only two people in the entire world.

And when he's kissing me and touching me, it's as though he knows my body better than I do.

And when we finish and he makes it a point to carry me to the shower to clean me up, I feel cherished and treasured.

And when we go to bed, and I wrap myself around him, he holds me tight, making me feel safer than I've ever felt in my life.

But love? No. It's not love. It can't be.

Micah turns around, his tie hanging loose around his neck, his shirt partly unbuttoned to expose a small spatter of chest hair. He smiles softly at me, and then suddenly it hits me like a train going at full speed with no brakes… Holy shit, it's happened. He warned me it would, but I didn't want to believe it. But he was right. I've fallen in love with him. *I'm in love with Micah Alexander!*

"What?" he asks, as he continues to unbutton his shirt.

When I don't say anything, unsure of what the hell to even say, he walks over and kneels in front of me. "Hellcat, what's wrong?"

As I consider how to word what I need to say, my fingers go to the ballet slipper charm that Micah gave me. Patiently, he waits for me to gather my thoughts.

"When I was a little girl, my dream was to dance. I lived and breathed it, and it was all I wanted. And when I got older and learned it wouldn't be possible, I was so devastated that I stopped dreaming. I stopped living. I went into survival mode. I picked a major that would ensure I could take care of Ellie, I got a job that paid the bills and my schooling. The only future I allowed myself to see was one where Ellie and I were out of that hellhole and away from our mom. These past several years have been rough. I've struggled every day to keep a roof over our heads and food in our bellies. I couldn't afford to dream. Not about my future and definitely not about love...until you."

Micah's eyes shine with hope, and my heart swells in response. "I've fallen in love with you," I tell him. "It wasn't supposed to happen, it wasn't part of the plan, but I did anyway. And as much as I hate that our marriage was forced upon us, I don't regret becoming your wife. I love you, Micah, and I want to be with you...in every way."

Micah's quiet for several seconds, and I worry I've made a mistake, that maybe he changed his mind or that his feelings have changed. It doesn't make sense since he literally told me tonight he loves me, but your brain doesn't always think clearly when it's in freak-out mode.

But then the most beautiful smile spreads across his face, and he flashes me that sexy dimple. The warmth I feel wraps around my frosty heart, heating it up.

"It happened sooner than I thought," he says.

"What?" I choke out.

"I thought it would take at least two, maybe three months for you to get on the same page as me, but it only took..." His eyes rise to the ceiling before returning his gaze to me. "Six weeks. It took six weeks for you to fall in love with me."

"What?" I gasp, mentally doing the math. "That's it?" I shake my head. "No, that can't be right. It's too soon." Nobody falls in love that quickly. That's the shit my mom does, not me.

"Hey, stop," he commands. "There's no timeline on falling in love. And you are not your mother." Oh shit, did I say that out loud?

"I don't need to hear your thoughts to know what you're thinking," he says, creepily responding to another thought I didn't say out loud. "Maybe we didn't do shit in the socially acceptable order, but there's nothing wrong with how we're doing it."

I take a deep breath, knowing he's right. This isn't like my mom or her situation. What Micah and I are building is real. In the middle of the darkness, I met a caring, selfless, amazing man who shined his light on me, refusing to let me stumble alone in the dark any longer. He's everything that is right in this world, and I won't allow my mom to ruin what I feel for him. She's taken enough from me, and I won't let her take him too.

"You're right," I say, palming the side of his face. "It doesn't matter how long it's taken. I know what my heart feels. I love you, and I want to consummate our marriage, but more than that, I want you to make me yours."

Twenty-Three

SIENNA

"Are you sure?" he asks. "I need you to be completely certain because there's no going back. Once I'm inside you, I'm never going to want to leave. A lot of things can be undone, but not this."

A giggle at his words escapes past my lips, and he frowns, probably thinking I've lost my mind. "Sorry, but I was picturing you burrowing inside me like an animal hibernating in the winter."

His lips quirk into a boyish grin. "Hellcat, I've tasted that sweet pussy, and I wouldn't mind burrowing in it all winter."

I bark out a laugh as his grin widens. "I was being serious, and you spoiled it!" I pout. "Now the moment is ruined." His smile drops, and I laugh again.

"I can fix the mood," he says, standing and giving me a kiss. "You get undressed and put this on." He walks over to the robe that's hanging on the back of the door and hands it to me. "Give me a few minutes." He kisses me again and then disappears into the bathroom.

Just as I'm securing the knot on the belt of my robe, Micah opens the door wearing a matching robe and gestures for me to join him.

The bathroom lights are dimmed, and a couple of candles have been lit. The large Jacuzzi tub has been filled with water and bubbles, and soft music is playing in the background.

"I was thinking we could take a bath together."

"You want to take a bath?" I repeat like a dumbass.

"Yeah. I love taking baths." He shrugs. "They always relax me."

"You want to take a bath instead of having sex?" I ask, since I've apparently lost my filter.

Micah chuckles. "Of course I want to have sex," he says, grabbing the knot of my robe and tugging me toward him. "But it should happen naturally. I would like to take a bath with you, relax and talk. And if it happens afterward, great. If not, then it will happen eventually."

And just like that, I fall for my husband even harder. Only now, I'm not as scared to fall because I know he'll be there to catch me when I do.

"Okay, then a bath sounds good," I say, unknotting my belt and shrugging out of my robe. I don't miss the way his eyes heat with molten desire as I walk over to the tub with a little extra sway to my hips. He might want to play the gentleman and not jump my bones the second I tell him I'm ready, but that doesn't mean I have to be a lady. I've experienced the way he works his tongue and fingers, and I'm ready to find out if he works his cock just as expertly.

I step into the steaming hot water and sigh at how good it feels and then wait for Micah to join me. He disrobes, and my mouth waters at the sight of him. Hard chest, ripped abs, and a thick, long cock that's standing at attention, practically begging to be inside of me.

He climbs in and sits behind me, and I settle between his muscular thighs. Once we're situated, I lean back and sigh into him, loving the feel of his hard body pressed against mine. We sit in comfortable silence for a few minutes while Micah strokes a finger up and down my arms, and I revel in the calmness.

"What are you thinking about?" he asks, when I absentmindedly reach behind me with one arm to play with his hair. With my arm up, he strokes the curve of my breast and then moves to my nipple, circling the areola. I let out a soft moan and push my chest out slightly, silently telling him not to stop.

"Us," I finally say. "How calm it is when I'm with you. For so long it felt like my life was a rollercoaster, going so fast I couldn't catch my breath, with loops and turns and flips that never allowed me to get comfortable. But since I've moved in with you, I feel calm, and I really like that."

"Good," he says, leaning forward and placing an open-mouthed kiss to the crook of my neck. "That's exactly what I want. You calm and happy." His large hand covers my breast, and he massages it for a moment before he pinches my nipple, making me squirm in my spot.

When he continues to tease me and it's clear he's not going to take things further, I decide to take matters into my own hands. It's like buying a chocolate bar and then placing it on the counter to stare at and not eat. Micah is mine. I love him and I want him, so why the hell am I just staring at him instead of devouring him?

Taking his hand in mine, I bring it down and spread my thighs so his fingers can easily brush against my clit. I tilt my head slightly as he suckles on my heated flesh. He works me up higher and higher until I'm coming all over his fingers. My legs shake, the water sloshes over the sides, and my body loosens, sated and happy.

Once I've come down from my orgasm, I twist around in my spot, maneuvering myself so I'm still between Micah's thighs.

Then I reach over and release the plug for the water, so it goes down enough that his cock is on display.

"What are you doing?" he asks curiously.

"Checking things out."

I get onto my knees and slide downward, wrapping my fingers around his shaft and sucking the mushroom head into my mouth. I lick and suck his dick until I know he's good and hard and ready. Then I stop, glancing up at him.

When I raise myself up, using the side of the tub to steady myself, Micah gives me a confused look. But before he can ask or figure out what I'm doing, I grab ahold of his shaft, lift up, and then guide myself onto him.

"Whoa," he says, catching on as my pussy sucks in the head of his cock. "I was thinking we'd do it in a bed…or…" More of me wraps around his shaft, stretching me little by little, and it must be too much for him because he doesn't finish whatever he was about to say. Instead, his hands grip the curves of my hips, and he looks me in the eyes. "Is this what you want? For me to fuck your virgin cunt right here in this tub?"

"Yes," I moan, loving his dirty words.

"Go ahead," he murmurs, leaning forward so our mouths are so close I can feel his sweet, warm breath. "Sit on my cock."

I do as he says, slowly lowering myself. The farther down I go, the more my walls stretch to accommodate him. When I'm almost all the way down, it begins to burn and sting. I wince, feeling the pain I knew to expect when having sex for the very first time.

"That's it, wife," Micah says, his hazel eyes locked with mine. "Keep going. All the way down. Give me that fucking cherry."

His filthy words cause me to clench around him, and he groans in response. "Fuck, Hellcat, you're so goddamn tight. You're going to choke the hell out of my cock."

With a deep breath, I lower myself the rest of the way down, crying out as Micah's cock tears through my virginity. When I'm completely stuffed full of him, he fuses his mouth to mine and takes over. Holding the curves of my hips, he slowly makes love to me from the bottom. With every languid thrust, the pain slowly morphs into pleasure. Then, something tightens inside of me. It's unlike anything I've ever felt. A building of some sort.

"That's it," Micah says. "I can feel you, baby, you're about to come. Don't fight it." He swivels my hips in just the right way, and like a rubber band being stretched too far, I snap. My entire body detonates, my eyes close, and stars flash behind my lids when I come harder than I've ever come in my life.

My head lulls forward onto Micah's shoulder as I sink farther down onto his shaft, unable to hold myself up any longer. My legs are shaking and feel like Jell-O. My heart is racing behind my rib cage.

We sit like this for I don't know how long—me trying to catch my breath, while Micah runs the tips of his fingers up and down my back in a loving way—until the water turns cold and the chill in the air causes goose bumps to prick my skin.

With my legs less shaky, I lift my head and attempt to stand. As I slide off Micah's semi-hard shaft, the pain from earlier comes back slightly, and when our bodies separate, he glances down between us, his entire body going rigid.

"What?" I ask. The little bit of water that's left is tinted pink, but that's to be expected since I just lost my virginity. I read that not all women bleed, but some do, and the amount of blood can vary.

When he doesn't say anything, I start to freak out. "Micah, what's wrong?"

"Sienna." Chills run up my spine at the way he says my name. "I need to ask you something, and I need you to stay calm. Okay?"

"Stay calm?" I hiss. "You can't tell a woman to stay calm and expect her to stay calm. What's wrong?"

"Before I ask, I need you to know that whatever your answer is, we'll deal with it together."

"Micah!" I screech. "Just fucking—"

"Are you on birth control?"

"What?" I shake my head, confused by the direction of the conversation. "Why would I be on birth control? I'm not even having sex." He quirks a brow and looks back down between us.

"You know what I mean. I wasn't having sex... up until a few minutes ago. So there was no reason for me to be on—" And then like a wrecking ball, it hits me. "Oh my God, Micah..."

"Baby, stay calm."

"Stay calm?" I stand and scramble out of the tub, and Micah follows. "Stay calm?" I grab my robe from earlier and wrap it around me. "How the fuck am I supposed to stay calm? We just had sex without protection... and I'm not on birth control."

"Sienna."

"Oh my God. I'm pregnant." My hand goes to my belly, and deep down, I know I'm acting like a crazy person, but right now, I'm not thinking clearly. "I'm pregnant." I look at Micah. "What are we going to do?" I cry. "I did this. You wanted to wait, but no, I had to take control, and now look what I did! I knocked myself up."

Micah snorts out a laugh, earning himself a glare. "What do I do?"

"You have two options," he says, way too calmly for a man who's about to become a dad. "One, we get you the morning-after pill."

"Here? In London? Is that even possible? And won't it be in British?"

He laughs again but quickly schools his features. "British is just an accent," he says. "I think you're having a panic attack. Let's take a shower, get cleaned up, and then we can talk. Okay?"

We go through the motions of showering and getting ready for bed, and the entire time my head is spinning. Once we're settled in for the night and Micah is holding me, I start to finally calm down and think more clearly.

"I'm sorry," I murmur into his chest. "I wasn't thinking."

"Stop," he says softly. I feel his lips press a kiss to the crown of my head, and instantly, my body relaxes. "If you don't want to take the next day pill here, we can get it once we arrive home. But if that's not something you want to put into your body, that's okay, too."

"I could be pregnant," I mutter.

"You could, and if you are, we'll cross that bridge when we have to." He tucks my wet strands of hair behind my ear and tilts my chin so I can look at him. "*If* you're pregnant, whether you choose to keep the baby or not, I'll be right there by your side. Whatever you decide, I'll support you."

"What if I want to keep the baby?"

"Then we'll turn a room into a nursery. I'd bet you'd be even sexier swollen with my baby in you."

For a moment, I imagine what it would be like, being pregnant... having a baby. But it's so hard to picture it. "I never thought about having kids," I admit.

"No? You don't want any kids?" he asks, zero judgement in his tone.

"It's not that I don't want kids. I just never allowed myself to think about it one way or another. My life was consumed with taking care of Ellie and trying to make ends meet so we wouldn't end up homeless."

"That makes sense."

"What about you?" I ask. "Do you want kids?"

"I wouldn't say no to a little blue-eyed mini you running around. All full of sass and charisma. Or, a little boy who has your freckles."

He runs his finger along the curve of my nose to where my freckles are. Unlike before, I'm able to picture it. The pregnancy, the babies...creating a loving home. I would make sure it's nothing like the home I was raised in. My child would be loved and cherished and protected. But even though I'm in a better place, I'm not ready for that responsibility yet.

"I think I'd like to have kids someday," I admit out loud. "But not yet. Not with Ellie still at risk with my mom out there somewhere. First, I need to graduate so I can apply for guardianship of my sister. It's the only way I can keep her safe from Lenora, who still has Eleazar's men out hunting for her.

"And we should be married for a while first. We don't want to rush into something and regret it. My mom getting pregnant is what drove my parents apart, and when she got pregnant with Ellie, it only made things worse. I don't want that to happen to us.

"This is all too new. We need to spend time together, get to know each other better. We have to plan and make sure it's at the right time." I take a deep breath. "When we get back, I'm going to get on birth control to ensure no accidents happen."

"Whatever you want to do is fine by me," Micah says, wrapping his arms around me tightly. "But just remember, you are not your mom, and we are not your parents. If you end up pregnant, it's not going to tear us apart. That baby will be loved and cherished every day of his or her life."

He strokes my back, and as my eyes close and I drift to sleep, an image pops into my head of a beautiful, hazel-eyed little boy with a dimple identical to Micah's...laughing, smiling, happy.

I want to believe him, but I saw what a surprise pregnancy did to my parents, and I don't want to risk it. Having a baby isn't worth losing the love and happiness I feel right now.

Twenty-Four

MICAH

> Good news! I got my period, so I'm going in today to get the shot.

I chuckle at her text and send her a quick one back:

> Does that mean I get to come in my wife any time I want?

I hit send and glance back up at the marketing team who is presenting their ideas for the upcoming opening of a new restaurant. I should be focused on what they're saying, but these days, my wife seems to be the only person who can hold my attention.

It's been a week since we returned from our trip, and Sienna has been worried about being pregnant. She didn't want to take the morning-after pill, so we agreed to wait it out. Due to the stress of the situation, we haven't had sex since the one and only time. I've been counting down the days until we would know one way or another, eager to get back inside my wife. One time in her tight little cunt and she's already got me addicted. Which shouldn't surprise me since I'm addicted to everything regarding her.

HELLCAT

Yeah, once my period is over and the shot has kicked in.

MICAH

There are other things we can do in the meantime...

Did I mention I've really missed being with my wife? A little blood won't stop me.

HELLCAT

Eww...I'm on my period!

MICAH

I'm okay with getting my redwings.

HELLCAT

I DON'T WANT TO KNOW WHAT THAT MEANS.

HELLCAT

OMG! I looked it up.

MICAH

Or, I could claim your ass.

She doesn't respond right away, and I assume she's going to leave me hanging until my phone indicates an incoming text.

HELLCAT

Will it hurt?

Hmm...That wasn't a no. I was only half-joking, but I can definitely work with this.

MICAH

A little, but I'll make it good, I promise.

HELLCAT

That's what my high school boyfriend told me when he was begging to take my virginity.

I bark out a laugh and everyone's gaze swings over to me. As I quickly scan their features, I realize they're waiting for my feedback. I trust my team, and really, this meeting was more of a formality, so I stand and button my suit jacket, ready to get home to my wife. "Everything looks great. We can go ahead and move forward."

They sigh in relief, and I take off, stopping at the store to pick Sienna up some flowers and chocolates and then swing by the sushi place she loves. It's Tuesday night, which means, I get my wife all to myself since she's not working.

When I walk through the door, she's curled up on the couch watching some girly show she loves. She sits up when she sees me, and when she spots the flowers and huge box of chocolates, a beautiful smile spreads across her face.

"You spoil me," she says, taking and smelling the flowers before setting them down and ripping into the chocolates.

"I love you." I press a kiss to her forehead and then head into the kitchen. "I got us sushi for dinner."

"Mmm, you really do love me." She comes up behind me and wraps her arms around my middle, laying her head against my back. "Thank you."

I turn around and pull her into my arms. "You don't have to thank me for feeding you. How are you feeling? There's Tylenol in the cabinet."

"I'm good. I actually don't have bad periods. No cramps and the bleeding is never too heavy. I'm one of the lucky ones."

"Well, in that case." I waggle my brows playfully and she smacks my chest.

"Sorry, buddy. You will not be getting any wings tonight. But..." She trails off and smirks. "I did look up anal sex and I'd be down for trying that. At least if you come in my ass, I won't risk getting knocked up."

And just like that, I fall even more in love with my wife.

I DON'T END UP CLAIMING HER ASS. AFTER WE EAT DINNER AND she devours half the box of chocolates, we cuddle on the couch, watching one of her shows, and Sienna passes out. I turn the television off and then carry her to bed before I head to my office to get some work done.

I'm working on the books when the sound of feet padding across the wood floor sound, followed by my sexy wife entering my office, dressed in only my shirt.

She heads straight for me, sliding into my lap and nuzzling her face into my chest. "I missed you in bed," she rasps. "Are you almost done?" She presses a kiss on my neck and whatever I was working on is done for the night. All these years I never knew what I was missing until I found Sienna. Now, I can't imagine not having her here, in my home, in my bed, in my arms.

"I'm done," I tell her, closing out of what I was working on and then standing with her in my arms. She wraps her legs around my waist and holds on to my neck, while I walk us back to bed.

My brother fucks with me daily, telling me I've gone soft, that he never imagined I'd let a woman control me the way Sienna does, but nothing he says bothers me because I'm okay with it, knowing I get to wake up and go to bed with her in my arms.

Spend my life with her.

When I lay her out in the middle of the bed, she grins up at me, not looking the least bit tired. "I was thinking...if you're up for it, we can try out what we talked about earlier."

"And what was that?" I ask, playing stupid as I hover above her, my arms caging her in.

"You know..."

"Mmm." I edge downward and stop at her tiny cotton underwear. "I believe there was talk about wings." I press a kiss on the top of her mound through the material.

"No way." She giggles, trying to pull me up. "I meant you fucking my ass."

"Oh, *that*." I smirk and then kiss her. "You sure you're up for that?" I lift my shirt over her head and pull a nipple between my lips, sucking on it.

"Yes," she breathes.

I swirl my tongue around her areola and then move to the other one, giving it attention as well.

Turned on and in need, Sienna's breathing increases as I suck and lave at her breast and then dip a finger into her underwear. When she tries to stop me, I shake my head and gently slap her hand away. "Let me do what I want," I murmur against her lips. She gives in, her hand instead going to my sweats, pulling them down so she can stroke my cock. I grab the bottle of lube out of my drawer and squirt a little onto my fingers. I use it to massage her clit, and within minutes, she's writhing under me, screaming out her release.

Without waiting for her to come down, I flip her onto her stomach and shove her underwear down her legs.

"Give me that ass, Hellcat," I say, giving her perfect round ass cheeks a playful slap.

She immediately lifts, and I bend over and take a bite out of her cheek, making her shriek in surprise.

"You sure you want my fat cock in here?" I ask, spreading her cheeks and running the tip of my finger along her puckered hole.

"Yes," she moans, wiggling her ass teasingly. She twists her head around slightly and looks back at me. "I trust you."

Her words are like a vise to my heart, wrapping tightly around it and making it hard to breathe. For most people, trust comes easy, but for Sienna, her telling me she trusts me is huge. That wall she was using to keep everyone out—including me—has been lowered, and I'll do everything in my power to make sure she never regrets it.

I grab more lube and squirt it between her cheeks, then push a finger into her tight hole. She moans, telling me it feels good, so I add another digit, working her up, stretching her out. Once she's begging for more, I lather a shit ton of lube on my shaft and then slowly enter her. Inch by inch, I watch as her perfect ass swallows my cock.

When I'm halfway in, I ask how she's doing, and she rasps to keep going, so I do, not stopping until my entire shaft is inside her ass.

"Fuck, baby. You should see how good your ass looks with my cock in it," I say, as I slowly slide back out, exhaling harshly and praying I don't blow my load yet.

"Micah, I love you, but if you don't make this good, I'm never letting you back inside my ass again."

I chuckle and start to move in and out of her. She's too tight, her ass too goddamn sexy, and I know I won't last long. So, I reach around and find her clit, and as I fuck her tight little hole, she starts to meet me thrust for thrust, moaning and begging me to fuck her harder. It's such a fucking turn on the way she loves to take control.

She finds her climax first, and then I allow myself to let go as well, coming deep and hard in her ass. When she drops onto the bed, her legs giving way, my cock slides out of her ass and I'm able to get a quick glimpse of my cum leaking out of her. Fuck, I could spend my life with this woman. Around her, with her, in her. I can't get enough.

"I think I need a shower," she whines, half asleep.

"You definitely need a shower," I say, rolling her over and lifting her into my arms. "Thank you, baby." I kiss her and when I pull back, she gives me an odd look.

"Did you just thank me for butt sex?"

"No." I chuckle. "I thanked you for trusting me."

"So, you're really going to watch every one of her shows?" Lincoln asks, as I watch Sienna perform on stage.

"Yep. It's not like I have anything else going on since my wife insists on spending three nights a week working here."

We've been married for two months, and Sunday we're leaving for the city to celebrate. We'll also be attending Ellie's end-of-dance-camp showcase, which happens to fall on the very last day of our trip. But first...I get to enjoy one uninterrupted week with my wife—no clothing required.

Sienna's performance comes to an end, and I get up to head to the private room where I'll get my nightly dance. She no longer lets me book her for hours at a time, but since she stopped performing private shows for other men, she spends her time either on stage or serving drinks.

The music starts and the lights dim, and then my gorgeous wife appears on the stage. It doesn't matter how many times I watch her dance, it never gets old, and each time I'm just as mesmerized and turned on as the last.

When the show ends, she saunters down to where I'm sitting and straddles my thighs, and I love that I get to touch her whenever the fuck I want.

"I booked our room for the week," I tell her, as she peppers kisses along my jaw. She's no longer performing, but my wife loves to be affectionate. Maybe it's the honeymoon phase, but the past couple months—ever since she got on birth control—I've spent more time in her than not. We've fucked in every damn room, on every surface of our home at least twice. I imagine it'll be a little harder once Ellie is home, but that just means we'll have to get creative.

"I can't wait to see my sister," she says, lifting her head and looking at me. "The summer has flown by. She's had such a good time. Thank you for making sure she could go."

She presses her lips to mine and then her tongue slides inside my mouth. When I suck on it, she moans, grinding down on me. "Fuck me, Micah," she breathes, and since she doesn't have to tell me twice, I do just that.

Lifting her, I carry her over to the couch and lay her out. After removing her clothes, I trail kisses all over her body and then eat her sweet pussy until she's coming all over my mouth. And then I'm lifting one of her legs over my shoulder and sliding inside her. She grabs my nape and pulls my face to hers, kissing me while I fuck her, both of our bodies pulsing with adrenaline as we chase our pleasure.

Sienna falls first, squeezing the fuck out of my cock and taking me straight over the edge with her.

When we've both caught our breath, she shocks the hell out of me when she says, "I'm going to quit working at Wanderlust."

I pop my head up to look at her. "Really? Was the sex that mind blowing?"

She laughs. "No...I mean, yes. It's always amazing. I just...it's time. Ellie will be returning home soon, and if I work nights, she'll either have to come with me or stay home all alone. Besides, if all goes well, I'll have enough credits to graduate in December."

"With a degree you don't love," I add. We've had a lot of conversations about this, and I've told her she should do what she loves: Dance. But she insists on wanting a job that looks good on paper since she's planning to apply for guardianship of Ellie now that it's been over two months and Lenora is still missing.

With her gone, Sienna should have no problem becoming Ellie's guardian. But to be on the safe side, I've insisted she let me hire the best attorney.

"Actually, I was thinking about that too," she says, shocking me for the second time tonight. "I'm going to ask Grace if I can pick up some more classes at Lola's."

"Yeah?"

"Yeah," she says with a smile. "Being a dance teacher pays well, and the judge will see I can provide a stable home, especially since we're married."

"Whatever you want to do is fine with me," I tell her, pulling out. She stays right where she is, knowing the drill. I grab a wet washcloth from the bathroom and come back so I can clean her up. Once she's halfway decent, she pads to the bathroom to finish cleaning up.

"I told Lincoln tonight. I offered to give him two weeks, but he said it's all good, so tonight was my last night."

Bastard. He didn't say a damn word to me. "You have no idea how happy this makes me," I tell her, lifting her into my arms.

"Because you hate me dancing?"

"No." I shake my head. "Because now I get you every damn night, including the weekends. Let's get the fuck out of here," I say, kissing the curve of her neck. "I'm ready to start our vacation early."

Twenty-Five

MICAH

"WHAT THE HELL DO YOU MEAN THEY'VE RAISED THEIR ASKING price? I thought the contract was locked in?" I'm standing outside on the terrace of The W, staring down at the bustling city. Unlike in Tesoro, Manhattan is overcrowded and never sleeps. I enjoy coming to the city, but I don't think I could live anywhere but Tesoro. The cars honk and people yell, and at least three people on bikes almost get hit.

"There was some miscommunication and…"

A feminine throat clears from behind me, and I turn around, coming face to face with my gorgeous wife. She's dressed in what appears to be bridal lingerie—an arousing blend of white lace, innocence, and seduction—and tall, very sexy heels. Her hair is down in waves and her lips are glossy. When she said she was going to go to the bathroom to freshen up after we arrived, I thought she meant brush her teeth.

George, my legal department manager, continues to speak, but I couldn't tell you what the hell he's saying because I'm too entranced by the woman in front of me.

"George, I'm going to have to call you back," I say, and then hang up without waiting for him to respond. Pocketing my phone, I stalk back inside.

"Where did you get that?" I ask. When we packed for our trip, I didn't see it, and she rarely goes anywhere other than to work and home. Not that she can't go wherever the hell she pleases, but I'm just wondering how she got it, and where I need to shop to buy her more.

"I ordered it," she says, running her hands down her body. "I was thinking about our wedding night and how it should've went down, and since we're in a hotel room, just the two of us, I thought we could have a do-over." With a seductive sway to her hips, she closes the distance between us, and flashes me a coy smile while her fingers work to unbutton my shirt.

Fuck, this woman.

She slides her hands under the material of my shirt and removes it from my body then presses a soft kiss to my pec before swirling her tongue around my nipple. I stand in place, watching as she kisses her way down my chest and torso, stopping just above my navel.

While glancing up at me through her lashes, she presses an open-mouthed kiss to the bulge in my pants, then backs up slightly. "But first," she says, "I have something to give you."

She reaches into the cup of her bra and pulls out a… "Is that a ring?" I ask in confusion.

"It's a men's wedding band." She stands back and extends her hand so I can get a better look at it. It's all black with tiny black diamonds going around the center of the band. Sienna takes my left hand in hers and slides the band I'm currently wearing off my finger. Since she wasn't thrilled about being forced into marriage, I didn't want to bug her about the details. She was already having a hard enough time planning the wedding with my mom. So, I went to the store and picked up a simple band to wear.

"The day we said I do, I wasn't in a good place, but since then, things have changed," she says. "I love you, and I want to be married to you for real." She places the ring she's holding between her fingers. "I had it engraved." I take it from her and read the words that are inscribed inside: *I'll always choose you.*

"I choose you, Micah. I choose us...forever." She slides the ring onto my finger, and my heart swells in my chest with so much love for this woman, I can't think straight.

"One more thing," she says, walking over to where her luggage is. She pulls out an envelope and brings it back over to me. I immediately recognize it as the divorce papers I gave her on our wedding night. "I don't need or want these." She pulls the papers out and rips them in half, and I have never been as turned on as I am right now. "Now," she says, tossing them to the side. "Make love to me, husband. The way it should've happened on our wedding night."

Fisting the back of her hair, I crush my mouth to hers, tasting and devouring, as I walk us to the bed. When we reach it, I reluctantly stop kissing her so I can lift her onto the mattress.

When she's lying in the center, looking like a goddamn fallen angel, I take a moment to memorize everything about her. And then I make love to my wife, bringing her to orgasm several times before sinking inside her to find our joint release. Not that what we've been doing for the past several weeks isn't making love, but this time, I go slow, worshipping every inch of her just like I would've done on our wedding night.

"Thank you" I murmur once we're both cleaned up and she's lying in my arms, her body draped over mine, "for choosing me the way I choose you."

"Oh my God, you guys are totally in love," Ellie squeals. "I knew it would happen!" She throws her arms around Sienna and then me. "Welcome to the family, big bro. Now that you're really married to my sister, you're stuck with me, too."

Sienna groans, and I chuckle. "I'm okay with that, kid." I ruffle Ellie's hair, and she swats my hand away, rolling her eyes.

"I'm fifteen. That's hardly a kid." She scoffs.

"The show was fabulous, and you did amazing," Sienna says, changing the subject. "I'm so proud of you."

"Yep," I agree. "I didn't even sleep through it." I hand her the flowers Sienna and I picked up and Ellie takes them, thanking me.

"So, I know school starts in a couple of weeks," she says, as we walk to the car. "But there's something I want to talk to you about." She glances between Sienna and me nervously, a trait that Ellie doesn't usually sport.

"Okay," Sienna says, stopping at the car but not getting in.

"So, there's this school of the arts and the headmaster attended the camp and offered me a spot. I could possibly get a partial scholarship, but it would mean you having to drive me to and from school every day because they don't offer transportation. At least until I get my own license."

"What's the name of the school?" Sienna asks.

"Anderson School of the Arts," Ellie says, and Sienna's eyes go wide.

"They offered you a spot?" Sienna breathes. "That's huge."

"I know." Ellie grins, practically bouncing on her toes.

"And expensive," Sienna adds. "Even with a partial scholarship, it would be—"

"Handled," I say. Sienna and Ellie both look at me. "I'm not saying you can go because that's ultimately up to Sienna, but if she decides it's okay, we'll pay for the tuition, and I can arrange for a driver to drop you off and pick you up."

"Seriously?" Ellie shrieks. "Can I go, please?" She fists her hands in a prayer-like manner and begs.

"We'll see," Sienna says sternly, brooking no room for argument. "Micah offering is very generous, but he isn't aware of how expensive the school is. He and I will talk about it later and then let you know what we decide."

"Ugh, is this what it's like having two parents?" Ellie grumbles. "I think Micah should make all the decisions if that's the case."

Sienna chuckles. "Oh yeah? Hey, Micah, Ellie likes this boy and wants to go on a date with—"

"Hell no," I bark, not letting her finish that asinine statement. Dance school, I can handle. Dating, fuck that. "I was fifteen and know exactly how boys act at that age," I say to Ellie. "Focus on dancing."

"I WAS THINKING..."

"Does your head hurt?"

I glare at Sienna, who laughs, thinking she's cute. I mean, she is, but that's beside the point. "I was thinking," I say again. "I could buy you a dance studio, and then you could do what you love."

We're in bed, both of us naked and glistening with sweat. Sienna's eyes are hooded over from the two orgasms I gave her, and my dick couldn't get up if I begged it to. This is how it is every night after Ellie goes to bed. We talk and fuck and then fall asleep spent.

When Sienna doesn't respond, I roll over to get a better look at her and find her staring up at the ceiling with tears in her eyes. "Hey, did I say something wrong?" I ask, pulling her into my side.

"No," she chokes out. "You're perfect. It's just...I love dancing, but sometimes it's hard because my love of it stems from my parents. They were dancers. It's how they met. They fell in love dancing together. But once my dad was injured, and my mom got pregnant with me, everything slowly fell apart. Sometimes, I think

I hold on to dancing because I couldn't hold on to my parents."

I squeeze her hip, so she knows I'm listening, encouraging her to continue. "I want to hate my mom," she says softly. "After everything she's put us through, she deserves for me to hate her. But I can't because I can still remember the woman she used to be. I was young, but I can still remember her happy…before her broken heart destroyed her."

She lifts up on her elbows, looking at me, and I edge higher so we're more comfortable. "Ellie once said that maybe if our mom would've met a man like you, her heart wouldn't have broken the way it did. I didn't get it at the time, but now I do because every day, you put me together. If you broke my heart the way my dad—"

"It's never happening," I tell her. "I can't predict the future, but I know I will *never* break you."

She nods, but I can see a bit of hesitation in her features. I get it because heartbreak is all she's ever known, but over time, she'll see I mean it.

"I used to wish for her to disappear or die," she says, after a few minutes of silence. "But now that I know what it's like to be in love and can imagine what it would feel like to have my heart broken, I wish she'd get help. It's probably too late, but…yeah, I hope one day she gets the help she needs."

I wrap my arms tightly around her and kiss her soft lips. "And that's why I love you, Hellcat. Because despite the fact that that woman has hurt you, you still wish her well. You have a huge fucking heart, and out of all the men you could choose to give your heart to, I'm so grateful that you chose to give your heart to me." I kiss the tip of her nose and then her forehead. "And I promise, I will do whatever it takes to protect it."

"Thank you," she murmurs, laying her head back down on my shoulder. "I'll think about the dance studio. I appreciate the offer, but I'm not sure if dancing is in my future. Right now, my only goals are to graduate and get guardianship of Ellie."

Speaking of which…"You know you could apply now, right?"

She pops her head up. "What do you mean? I haven't graduated yet."

"You're married to me. What's mine is yours. And your mom has been gone for months. No judge is going to deny you guardianship of Ellie. As a matter of fact, it's probably a good idea for you to apply now before the state finds out her mom has gone AWOL. You've already been raising her for years. At this point, it's just about making it legal."

"I don't even know where to begin…"

"If you knew you could get approved, would you want to pursue it?"

"Hell yes," she says. "Knowing Ellie is safe and can't be taken away from me would mean everything to me."

"Then I'll make sure it happens."

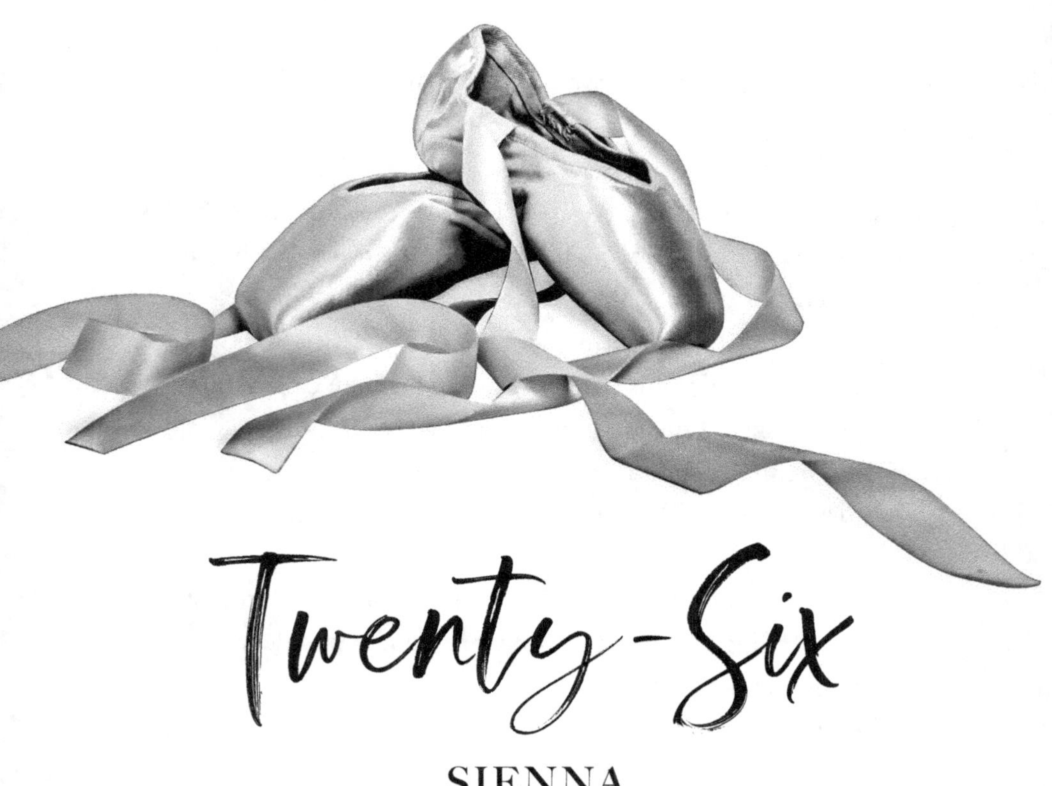

Twenty-Six

SIENNA

"By next week, I need the name of the professional you'll be shadowing. Thirty hours is required." The professor nods, indicating we've been dismissed, and I quickly jot down what I need to do in my planner, so I don't forget.

"I'd be okay with you shadowing me," a masculine voice says, making me practically fall out of my seat. When I spin around, I find Micah standing there, dressed to the nines in his CEO bad boy suit and grinning at me. With the threat gone, thanks to Micah, I'm back to being able to take classes on campus instead of online.

"What are you doing here?" I ask, jumping out of my seat and wrapping my arms around him.

"I thought I would surprise my wife by taking her to lunch. Your classes are done for the day, right?"

"Yeah." I peck his lips, loving that he knows my schedule. "Let me just grab my stuff." I shove my laptop and planner into my bag, and then with my hand laced in Micah's, we head out.

"I meant what I said," he affirms, as we walk. "If you need someone to shadow, I'd love to help you." He pulls me into his side and his voice lowers. "I could even give you some hands-on experience."

I snort out a laugh at his adorable banter but stop when I imagine him shoving his papers to the side so he can lay me out across his desk and fuck me seven ways to Sunday.

"You're thinking about it, aren't you?" he asks, his lips quirking into a devilish smirk. "Me bending you over my desk and fucking you."

"Actually, I was imagining you laying me out on the top of the desk but bending me over it would work, too." I waggle my brows at him, and he barks out a laugh.

"Do you want to eat on campus or meet somewhere?" I ask since we came in separate vehicles.

"I already had someone grab your car so you can ride with me."

"Damn, am I that much of a sure thing?" I joke.

"No, but I think I'm wearing on you."

"Yeah, you are," I agree as he opens the door for me so I can get in.

"This impromptu lunch date actually has another purpose," he says, once we're sitting in a Greek restaurant we love, devouring our gyros. "We have a meeting afterward with Oliver Stein, a family law attorney who's good friends with my dad. I explained our situation, and he believes it should be an open-and-shut case. He needs some information from you, though, before he can file.

It doesn't go over my head that he says *our* situation. It shouldn't be that big of a deal, it's only a simple three-letter word, but when you've been going at life on your own for as long as I have, the use of that word coming out of his mouth is like a direct link to my heart.

Reaching across the table, I throw my arms around Micah and

lay a big, fat kiss on his cheek. "Have I told you today how much I love you?"

"This morning, right after I made you come in the shower," he says, with a smirk. "But you can tell me as often as you like."

The meeting with the attorney goes smoothly. He assures me that applying for guardianship of Ellie will be simple, especially since I'm her only living relative aside from our mom, who has been missing for months. Once he has the papers drawn up and I come back in to sign them, he'll file them immediately.

"My assistant texted that she needs me to approve something. Apparently there was a mix-up and it's time sensitive. Do you mind if I run to my office really quick?" Micah asks on our drive home.

"Is this your way of turning that sex on the desk fantasy into the real thing?"

"No," he says with a laugh. "But we can definitely make it happen if you want."

Alexander Enterprises is a ten-story corporate building located downtown. With their name etched in large, mirror letters at the top for all to see, the building screams luxurious without being over the top. I've seen the building a million times over the years, but I never thought twice about it. Now, that name is also mine.

As Micah strides through security and into reception, speaking to people with authority and demanding answers regarding whatever got messed up, I can't help comparing this man—who is sure of his place in the world and doesn't take no for an answer—to the man I've grown to love. This side of Micah I'm witnessing right now is the same man I first met at the club, the one who was cocky enough to believe he could snap his fingers and I'd do whatever he wanted. But when that didn't work, he showed me another side of himself—the vulnerable side that told me he was looking for more than just sex. It's weird seeing him like this, but I also love that he saves all his softness for me.

Taking my hand in his, Micah guides us into his office so he can sign the papers, and while he does so, I take an opportunity to explore his workspace. It's as lavish as the rest of the building. Clean and modern with expensive looking furniture and a view most would die for. Yet, there's nothing personal, no photographs, nothing that denotes that this is even his office, a place where he spends most of his day working. And now that I think about it, his home is exactly the same way.

But when I step around his desk, my heart swells at the sight of the two photographs placed right next to his laptop. One is of the two of us from our trip to London. There was a photographer outside the theater offering to take pictures of the guests. He handed Micah a card afterward and he must've ordered this one and had it printed. The other is a photo taken at our wedding with the two of us in the center, surrounded by his parents, brother, and Ellie.

"What?" he asks when I've been standing here pensive for a few minutes.

"Your home doesn't have any personal touches. No pictures or knickknacks. Nothing that screams you. Neither does your office."

Micah turns his chair and grips the curve of my hip, dragging me over to him so I'm situated between his legs and leaning against the desk. "First of all, it's not my home, it's *our* home. And I've honestly never thought about it. When it was built, I hired an interior decorator to handle it all. Before you and Ellie came to live with me, I rarely spent any time there. It wasn't until you two moved in that it even felt like a home."

Once again, his words wrap around my heart like a warm comfy blanket on a chilly night. "I like the sound of that," I admit. "A home. I always tried to provide as much stability for Ellie as I could, but we never had a home… until now."

"I'm glad you both feel safe and comfortable there," he says. "If you want to add pictures or decorate, that's fine with me. If Ellie wants to paint her room and make it more girly or whatever, I'm completely okay with that. It's your home as much as it's mine."

"Thank you," I say, leaning forward to kiss him. "Now, how about we lock that door and test out this desk. Add our own personal touches?"

"Sounds like a fucking plan."

"So, remember a few weeks ago when you *jokingly* said I couldn't date," Ellie says to Micah. It's Friday night and she's dressed, ready to go out.

"No," Micah deadpans, making me laugh. We're lounging on the couch with my feet in his lap as I watch One Tree Hill and he does some work from his phone. "I remember saying hell no, you can't date, and nothing about it was spoken jokingly."

"Micah." Ellie groans. "There's this guy at school. He's in a few of my classes, and he's asked me out for a *study* date."

I already knew about this since my sister texted me the second it happened, and of course, I told her she could go as long as I meet him first. The problem is, he's on his way over to pick her up—he's sixteen and drives—and there's no way he's getting past Micah's security without him knowing about it, which means, she needs him to approve the kid to come up.

"No," he repeats, deadly serious, which only makes me laugh harder, and in turn, has him glaring at me.

"Babe," I say, rubbing his arm. "Ellie is going out tonight, and he's already on his way to pick her up." Just as I finish my sentence, there's a knock on the door.

"He's here," Ellie whisper-yells. "Please, please be cool," she begs Micah, whose jaw ticks. "Remember, it's a *study* date, so not a real date."

"Does it have the word date in it?" Micah volleys. "Then it's a real damn date."

Ignoring Micah, she rushes over to the door and swings it open, but standing on the other side is Lincoln, Micah's brother, not Ellie's date. "Oh, it's you," she says, sighing in disappointment. Me, on the hand...I mentally rejoice because her hanging out with someone else might mean she's finally moving past her crush on Lincoln.

Only I've apparently thought this too soon because as he walks in, the look in her eyes tells me she's definitely still sporting that crush.

"What's up?" Lincoln asks.

"Ellie is about to go on a study date," I say, ignoring the way Ellie is glaring daggers my way.

"Really?" Lincoln says. "Aren't you only fifteen? Should she even be allowed to date?" His second question is aimed at Micah and me.

"Of course I can date," Ellie hisses as the security system chimes. "But it's not a *date* date. It's a study date. We're going to get coffee and work on a project for school."

She rushes over and answers it. "There's a Jameson Reynolds here," security states. "Says he's here to pick up Eliza."

"Tell him to go the fuck away," Micah yells, making Lincoln laugh.

"Ignore him," Ellie says. "Please let him up."

Lincoln grabs Micah and him beers from the fridge and then drops into a seat just as Ellie glances my way, silently begging me to save her. Even if this is not technically a real date, it's still a first for Ellie, who deserves to finally act and feel like a normal teenager. I pat Micah's leg and say, "Please behave. This is important to her," and then glare Lincoln's way so he knows I'm talking to him as well.

"Fine," they both mutter, sounding more like children than grown men.

Jameson is a tall and lanky brown-haired, blue-eyed cutie. He's polite when he introduces himself and mentions that he's going to the school of arts that Ellie attends for music.

"He has the best voice," Ellie gushes, making Jameson blush.

"And where are you going?" Micah asks, even though Ellie already told us.

"To Coffee Grind to work on a project," Jameson says. "Then, maybe to hang out with some friends after."

"What kind of car do you drive?" Lincoln asks.

"A GTR."

"That's a pretty badass car," Micah adds. "How fast have you gone in it?"

I hold my breath, realizing it's a trap, but luckily, Jameson doesn't fall for it. "I don't speed," he says, his voice cracking.

The guys take turns interrogating poor Jameson, and as embarrassing as it is for Ellie, I love that we have people in our life who care. For too long it has just been us against the world. But now, we have family.

When it seems the kid has passed whatever test they've given him, Micah sighs and says, "You can wait for her outside." Jameson wishes us a good night and walks out the door.

"What was that for?" Ellie hisses.

"You have your phone on you?" Micah asks, standing and walking over to her.

Ellie nods.

"And money?"

Another nod.

He pulls a credit card out of his wallet and hands it to her. "This is in case of an emergency."

She takes it from him and mutters, "Thank you."

"If you need anything, I mean anything at all, you call us," he says to her. "He might seem cool and have a decent car, but he's still a teenage boy. Don't let him talk you into doing anything you don't want to do."

Ellie's eyes well up, and I worry Micah's pushed her too far. But then she throws her arms around him and hugs him tightly.

Micah pats her head, and a lump of emotion fills my throat.

"Behave," he says to her. "And remember, if you're ever in a situation and need us to pick you up, we're here. You won't be in trouble. We'd rather you call us and be safe than have something bad happen because you're afraid to tell us."

"Thank you," she says, pulling away and wiping her tears. "I've always wondered what it would feel like to have a dad." She glances at me. "I guess it's not so bad." With those words, she's out the door, leaving us all speechless.

My phone goes off a few minutes later, and I grab it, worried it's her already, but it's Micah's mom, Donna.

DONNA

Micah never lets us celebrate his birthday. Any chance you can convince him to let us celebrate this year? (And yes, I'm trying to get you to use the wife card. LOL)

I laugh at her text and then it hits me... "When is your birthday?"

"What?" Micah asks at the same time Lincoln barks out a laugh.

"How are we married, and we don't know when each other's birthdays are?"

"Speak for yourself." Micah scoffs. "Yours is April 3rd."

"Of course you know when it is...You're like a professional stalker!"

Lincoln laughs again and I glare at him. "And on that note," he says, standing. "I'm out of here."

"Did you come by for a reason?" Micah asks him.

"I wanted to talk about the restaurant's grand opening, but we can talk later." He glances at me and grins. "His birthday is next Saturday. Let me know where the party is."

"Your birthday is next week, and you didn't tell me?" I pout.

"It's not a big deal." He shrugs. "I'll be thirty-three. I'm practically an old man. That's hardly anything to celebrate."

"But you're such a sexy old man," I joke, snaking my arms

around his neck. "Can we throw a party?" I ask, batting my lashes.

"You already know I can't say no to you," he groans, capturing my bottom lip between his teeth and tugging playfully. "I say we take advantage of the fact that we have the house to ourselves. I'm thinking kitchen island. I don't think I've fucked you on it yet."

"I don't know," I say, keeping my voice serious. "Are you sure an old man such as yourself can handle fucking me on the kitchen island?"

"Oh, I'll show you what this old man is capable of," he growls. Picking me up and carrying me over to the island, he proceeds to show me *exactly* what he's capable of—twice!

Twenty-Seven

MICAH

"Happy Birthday, baby. Make a wish and blow out the candles," Sienna says, grinning from ear to ear.

"I already have everything I could ever want," I tell her, not giving a shit that the fifty people gathered to celebrate my birthday can hear me sounding like a damn sap.

Everyone sighs and Sienna scrunches her nose in embarrassment. "Just blow out the damn candles," she says, playfully nudging my shoulder.

"Or, I can do it," Ellie cuts in. "I could always use an extra wish." She smirks like the teenage brat she is, and Sienna rolls her eyes.

"Go for it," I tell her.

Ellie doesn't waste any time closing her eyes and then blowing out my candles. Everyone claps and then the caterer appears to cut and serve the cake. The party is being held in a private room at the hotel. There's an open bar, a four-course dinner, cake, and a dance floor where I've spent the majority of the evening dancing with Sienna.

"Here, have a bite," Sienna says, forking a piece and putting it up to my mouth. "Good?" she asks once I've chewed and swallowed.

"It's my favorite." Chocolate with whipped cream and strawberries.

She takes a bite and moans. "So good. Too bad we didn't get to have cake at our wedding. I saw in a movie once that the bride and groom are supposed to feed each other." She forks another bite and feeds it to me. "She starts off giving him a bite and then ends up smashing it in his face." She giggles and I pull her into my arms.

"You even think about smashing that cake in my face, and I'll take the rest of it home, cover you in it, and eat it off your body."

"Is that supposed to be a threat?" She laughs. "You can eat food off me any time you want." With another piece on her fork, she teasingly brings it up to her lips, making a show out of slowly sliding it into her mouth. She moans, sounding a lot like when I make her come, causing my dick to swell in my pants.

"I think it's time to go," I rasp. "Someone promised me a birthday blowjob, and I'm ready to collect."

It was how she convinced me to go along with this birthday party bullshit. *If you're a good birthday boy and let us throw you a party, afterward, I'll give you the birthday BJ of your life.* And how the fuck could I say no to that?

Sienna cackles and shakes her head, but I see the glint in her eye. She's ready to go as much as I am. "Okay, fine," she concedes. "You've done good. We can start saying our goodbyes so we can go upstairs and I can give you your birthday gifts."

It takes way too fucking long to get away, but once we're back at our place, the wait is well worth it when Sienna walks out of the bathroom wearing some sexy lingerie I've never seen her in.

Ellie asked if she could spend the night at a friend's house after the party, so we have the place all to ourselves.

She clicks the wireless remote to the sound system that connects to our devices via Bluetooth and some chick starts to sing about some guy being obsessed with her. I chuckle, knowing this was intentional. My wife loves to poke fun at the way we started—my obsession for her. And she isn't wrong. If anything, that obsession has only increased over time.

With a sway to her hips that she knows turns me on, she saunters toward me, pushing me back onto the edge of the bed once she's reached me.

She wastes no time stripping me down to nothing before she goes to town on my cock, giving me the best damn blowjob of my life. Before long, I'm shooting my cum down her perfect, slim throat, gripping her to me as she swallows. Once she's drained me of every last drop, she sits back and licks her lips, flashing me a shy but satisfied grin. Quickly, I turn the tables, and Sienna is taken by surprise when I splay her out on the bed and feast on her until she's screaming out in pleasure.

When we've both come multiple times and she can barely keep her eyes open, we rinse off and climb into bed. Just as she does every night, she drapes herself across my body like the best kind of blanket and nuzzles her face into my neck.

"Did you have a good birthday?" she asks, her voice raspy with sleep.

I run my fingers through her hair, knowing it will put her to sleep quickly and murmur, "The fucking best." Dipping down slightly, I kiss the crown of her head, inhaling her floral scent that I'm addicted to.

I don't know when we fall asleep, but at some point, something wakes me up. I glance around and find Sienna still curled up into my side. And then my phone lights up.

I grab it and see a text from Oscar:

OSCAR

Was dealing with a shipment and heard Sienna's mom was spotted. Grabbed her before she was brought to Gutierrez. Figured I'd let you decide what to do with your mother-in-law. I've got her at the warehouse. And FYI: she's a crazy fucking bitch, so good luck with that.

The text was sent a couple minutes ago, and I also have a missed call. This must be what woke me up. I text back that I'll meet him at the warehouse and then carefully remove Sienna from my side. She groans softly but stays asleep.

As I get dressed, I think about what I want to happen regarding her mom. I should call Gutierrez and tell him I have her. Feed her ass to the wolves. But as I pocket my phone and keys, Sienna's words come back to me: *I hope one day she gets the help she needs.*

Fuck, Lincoln is right. I really have turned soft.

"I don't need rehab!" Lenora hisses. "What I need is for my daughter to tell me why the fuck my home was burned to the ground."

When I told her I would take her to Sienna, I lied, but she went along with it, thinking she was being taken to her daughter. Until she saw the sign for the drug rehab facility.

"You don't have a fucking house because you screwed with Gutierrez," I bark, at my wit's end with this drug-addled woman. "You killed and you stole and then they came after you, and when they couldn't get to you, they went after Sienna. They killed your druggy pimp and were going to kill your daughter." This has Lenora stopping in her place and finally paying attention.

"They burned your place down, and I moved your daughters in with me to keep them safe. Gutierrez is still after you, and he won't stop until you're dead. So, you have two choices here...You can either go to rehab, get clean, and I can help you disappear, or I can drop you off at his doorstep. Which one will it be?"

"Wait," she says, her brow furrowed. "How is he after me if he's dead?"

"Not him, his son," I explain. "Eleazar Gutierrez came back from Mexico to extract revenge on his father's killer."

"Eleazar...it can't be." She glances up at me. "Eleazar Sanchez?"

Almost nobody refers to him with his mother's maiden name. I only know it because we were close at one time. Whenever he didn't want someone to know the family he was linked to, he would use his mother's last name. "Eleazar Sanchez Gutierrez," I correct.

"Okay, I'll go to rehab," she says, scrambling out of the car. I have no idea why she's suddenly changed her mind, but I don't give a shit. She's going to rehab—that's all that matters.

"WHERE WERE YOU?" SIENNA ASKS WHEN I WALK THROUGH the door a couple of hours later. "Everything okay?"

"Yeah." I kiss the top of her head and consider telling her the truth, but I don't want to get her hopes up. The woman in admitting told me that Lenora can check herself out at any time, and unfortunately most do. "I had some business to deal with. What do you want to do today?"

"I was thinking a picnic. Ellie is spending the day at her friend's. We can go by the deli on the corner and pack a lunch and take it to the park."

"That sounds like the perfect way to spend our day."

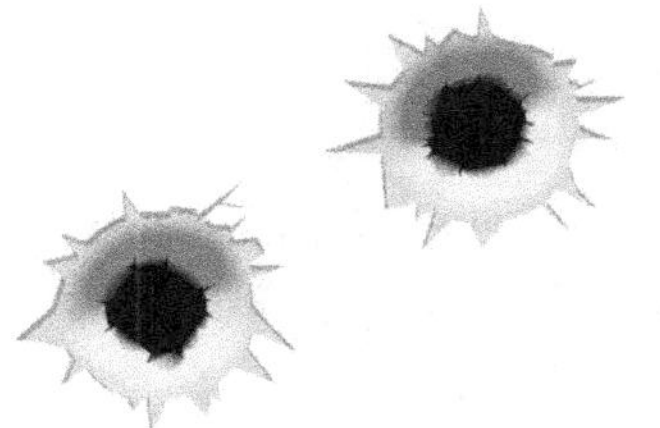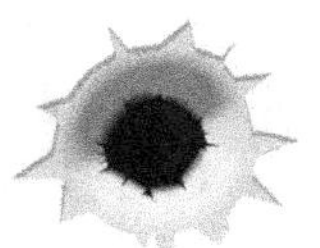

Twenty-Eight

ELEAZAR GUTIERREZ

"Boss, there's a woman here to see you. She fits the description of the woman who killed your father."

I drop my fork onto my plate and glance at my wife, who quirks a brow. Could it be that easy? Could the woman who killed my father be handing herself over on a silver platter? If she thinks she can convince me to spare her life, just as I did for her daughter, she couldn't be more wrong.

"Bring her around back to the holding cell," I say, not wanting her to taint this home more than it already is, thanks to her. This is where she stole and killed my father, and I won't allow her back in here again.

"After this, can we please go?" my wife whines. "I've already missed two appointments." We've been trying for years to have children, but we haven't been blessed yet. She's suffered four miscarriages, and now she can't seem to get pregnant at all. The only doctor she trusts is back home in Mexico.

"Yes, you can start packing," I tell her as I stand. "We'll leave this afternoon."

I've already gotten a handle on the business. The only thing keeping me here was the hope of finding this bitch so I could end her life the way she ended my father's. Now that she's resurfaced, once I put a bullet in her head, my business in this town will be concluded.

"Why have you come back here?" I ask the strung-out whore when I enter the holding cell. The question is born out of curiosity more than anything else. Her brown hair is greasy, and her clothes are tattered. The report said she's in her early forties, but this woman looks like she's at least a decade older.

"You don't remember me, do you?" she asks, smiling like she's in on a secret I know nothing about.

"I know you're the bitch who drugged, stole from, and killed my father." Reminding myself what she did has my temperature rising. I pull my gun out from its holder and aim it at her head, ready to blow her brains out. I considered torturing her, but now I just want her gone.

She shakes her head and grins wider—crazy bitch. "Sixteen years ago at Gloria's. Your eighteenth birthday."

It takes a second, but once I wrack my brain, I vaguely recall the night she's talking about. "What about it?" I ask, removing the safety, ready to end the whore's life.

"You won't kill me," she says smugly.

"And why the fuck not?"

"Because I have something you want..."

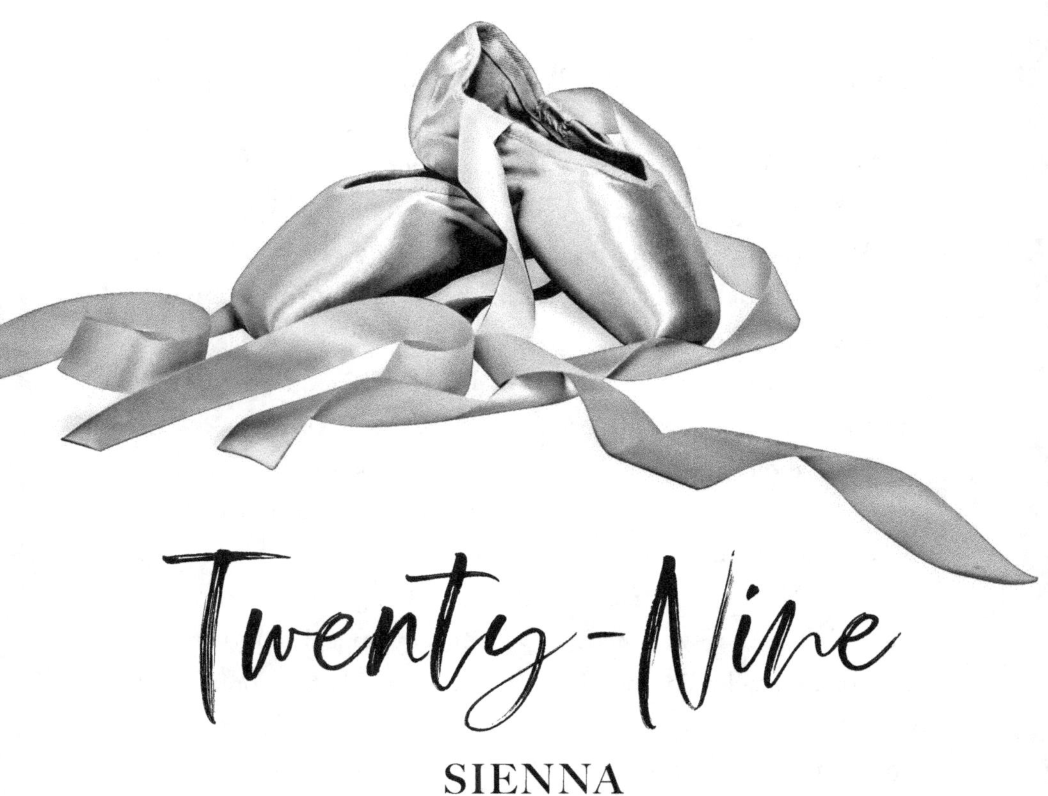

Twenty-Nine

SIENNA

"I CAN'T BELIEVE SHE'S DEAD," I SAY, AS WE STARE AT THE URN that holds Lenora's ashes.

"It was inevitable," Ellie murmurs. "Maybe now she can finally be at peace."

"When did you get so wise?" I ask, wrapping my arm around her. When the police department notified Micah that our mom was found dead—a single gunshot to her heart—they said they didn't have any suspects, but I didn't expect they would. Not after Micah confessed he tried to save her by bringing her to rehab, only for her to run once he left.

I don't know what was going through her head, but whatever it was, it cost Lenora her life. Micah asked if we wanted to hold a service for our mom, but Ellie and I decided against it. We have her ashes in the urn and knowing she's finally at peace is enough for us. We should probably be sadder than what we are, but it's been a long time coming, and I think we were both waiting for the day it finally happened. She made her choices, Micah tried to get her help, and her ending was completely her own undoing.

"I've learned it from you," Ellie says, leaning into me.

"At least now with her being declared dead, we should be able to get guardianship of you quicker," I say, trying to spin what's happened into a positive.

Ellie glances up at me and nods. "I agree. Once I know no one can take me from you, I'll feel a lot better."

"How about some lunch?" Micah asks. "You've been holed up in here for a few days now. Let me take you both out to eat."

"Sounds good," Ellie and I say at the same time. She took a couple of days off from school and will be going back on Monday. She didn't feel it was necessary, but I'm concerned that our emotional detachment over Lenora's death is only temporary, and once the numbness wears off, she might break down and need some time to work through her feelings.

"Sienna Alexander," a gentleman says when we step outside the building. Because it's a beautiful day out, Micah suggested we walk to the restaurant to get some fresh air.

"That's me."

"You've been served." He thrusts an envelope at me and then adds, "Please sign here."

I scribble my signature on the line and then he nods and takes off.

I glance at Micah, confused, and then open the envelope. When I pull the papers out, I skim the words over and over again. "No," I gasp. "This can't be true."

"What is it?" Micah asks, as I stumble toward him, needing his comfort. This can't be happening. It doesn't make sense.

"Paternity test for Ellie?" Micah says, reading the papers.

"For me?" Ellie asks. "Who?"

"Eleazar Gutierrez," Micah answers.

"The man who wanted Sienna dead?" Ellie shakes her head. "I

don't understand."

"According to these papers, he has reason to believe that you're his daughter. He's seeking a paternity test and full custody of you."

"What?" she shrieks. "Can he even do that?"

"He's claiming to be your only living parent."

"Oh, God." I pull Ellie into my arms while still being held by Micah. "We're not going to let him do this." I glance up at Micah. "Right? I can't lose my sister to a fucking crime boss. He's dangerous. Look what he's already done. He tried to have me killed, and we both know he's the one responsible for murdering our mom. Who the hell knows what else he's capable of?"

"We'll figure it out," he says, but the worry in his eyes has me on edge. Micah is rich and powerful, and his name alone holds a lot of weight in this town, but if there's one man who could give him a run for his money, it's Eleazer Gutierrez. And then it hits me...

"Eleazar..." I back up and look at Ellie. "Eliza." Her eyes go wide. "That bitch knew the name of your sperm donor this entire time and never told us." I asked her so many times over the years and she refused to tell me, swearing he wasn't worth remembering. She was a damn liar.

"We can't stay here," I blurt out. "We have to run. Get as far away from him as possible."

"Sienna," Micah says, reaching for me. "Running isn't the answer."

"Why? Because it would mean leaving you?" I hiss, averting his touch. "I told you I didn't have room in my life for anyone but Ellie, but you didn't listen, and now," I choke out. "We have to go. We can't stay here. I can't risk him taking her."

Micah grabs me and pulls me into his arms, refusing to let me go. "I promise we'll do whatever it takes to keep him away from Ellie, but he already knows about her, and even with my money and resources, she's on his radar. He won't stop looking until he finds her."

His words have my blood turning cold. This can't be happening. I thought with our mom dead, we would finally have a chance at a safe, normal life, but I should've known it wouldn't be that easy. Everywhere we turn, there's always someone trying to bring us down.

"Sienna," Ellie says softly. "Please don't push Micah away. He loves you, and no matter what happens, you deserve to be loved."

"Hey," Micah says to Ellie. "Your sister isn't the only one who deserves love. You do, too. And as much of a pain in the ass as you are at times, this place wouldn't be the same without you." He pulls Ellie into a side hug and kisses her temple. "I love you, kiddo."

"I love you, too," Ellie chokes out. "And I love my school and my life and my friends. For the first time, I'm safe and happy and we have a home. I don't want to leave. I don't want to run." She glances at Micah. "Set up a meeting with Eleazar. I want to speak to him."

"What? No way," I snap. "No, the man is dangerous!"

"And he's my bio dad," she says. "He's not going to hurt me. If he wanted to do that, he could've come after me, but instead, he filed for custody. Please," she says to Micah, "I want to speak to him."

Micah nods. "I'll make it happen."

Thirty

MICAH

"We had a deal." I drop the papers onto Eleazar's desk, and he leans back, casually lacing his fingers behind his head.

"And I honored it," he says. "Is your wife's heart still beating?"

"What will it take for you to leave Ellie alone?"

"Did you know that Arielle and I have been trying to have a baby for the past six years?" he says, ignoring my question. "Rounds of IVF, four miscarriages...The doctors aren't sure if we'll ever have a baby of our own."

"That sucks," I deadpan. "But in case you aren't aware, Ellie isn't a fucking baby."

"No, but she's my blood." He leans in toward me. "I need an heir. Would've preferred a boy, but she'll do. I can always marry her off..."

"She's not fucking cattle!" I bark. "You can't barter with her life."

He shrugs. "Everyone serves a purpose. You'd do better to go along with this. I won't keep her sister from her. She'll have to move to Mexico with me, but she can visit."

As I stare at him for several seconds, knowing he's dead fucking serious and nothing I say or do is going to sway him any other way, it hits me like a freight train at max speed—there's only one way to protect Sienna and Ellie.

"You're leaving."

"What?" Sienna gasps.

"No!" Ellie cries.

"You don't have a choice. Eleazar is not going to stop until he has you. And he doesn't just want custody. He wants to own you."

"Let me talk to him," Ellie begs, while Sienna stands frozen in her place, tears welling in her eyes because she understands the implications of what I'm saying: This is the end for us.

"It's not happening, El. There is no talking to him. You guys have to run now. I have the money and resources to make you disappear, but it has to be before Eleazar realizes what's happening."

"Micah," Sienna sobs, but she doesn't argue because I promised to protect them, and she knows that's exactly what I'm doing.

"Go pack a bag. Make sure you have all the essentials since you won't be able to stop for anything."

"No!" Ellie barks. "I'm not running."

I step up to her and put a hand on her shoulder. "Yes, you will run. Your sister has fought tooth and nail to keep you safe, and I'll be damned if all of that's for nothing. You are her entire world, and the only way to protect you from Eleazar's clutches is by running."

"What about you?" Ellie asks softly. "Will you come with us?"

I glance toward Sienna, whose tears track down her cheeks even harder. "No, I have to stay here. I have my parents and brother. I need to keep an eye on things, keep my ear to the ground for what Eleazar is planning."

Ellie's eyes flit between her sister and me. "But what about Sienna?"

"I love your sister with all of my being. That will never change." I lock eyes with Sienna, needing her to not only hear the words but feel them. "But sometimes you have to love someone enough to let them go."

"Oh, fuck that!" Ellie hisses. "That's so cliché. When you love someone, you fight. You don't let them go."

"You do when you're saving their life," Sienna says, her voice broken. "I couldn't live without you, El. And I don't ever want to find out."

"So, let me talk to him. I can make this right. I'm his daughter, which has to mean something."

"Yeah, it means he feels he has control over you and your future, and the only way to keep you from being caught under his thumb is for you to get as far away from him as possible," I tell her. "Now, please go pack a bag. I have arrangements to make. We'll plan for you guys to leave tonight."

I'm on the phone, working with a friend of mine who's a retired Marshall and has dealt with his fair share of witness protection cases, when Sienna walks in and goes straight to me, settling in my lap.

"Rodriquez, someone just walked in. Look into what we talked about, and I'll call you back soon."

I hang up just as Sienna situates herself so that her thighs spread across mine, straddling me. "Are you all packed?" I ask, trying to remain strong for my wife.

"Yeah," she breathes, nuzzling her face into my neck. I feel her breathe me in, and I get choked up, knowing she's trying to memorize my scent because this is the last time she'll see me, smell me, feel me.

"I love you, Hellcat," I tell her, inhaling her floral scent. "Never forget that."

"I know," she chokes out. "You've showed me every day that we've been together, but never more so than today."

Slowly, she lifts up to look at me, and the sight of her splotchy, tear-stained face has me wanting to run away with her. But I can't do that. If I want to keep Sienna and Ellie safe, I need to stay behind to keep an eye on Eleazar. When he finds out they're gone, he's going to flip his shit. Hell, there's a chance he's going to come after me, but that's another reason why I have to stay. I can't risk him going after my brother or parents.

"I will love you forever," I tell her, framing her face. "We won't be able to talk, but just know that I will always be thinking about you. You are my beginning and my end. You are my life. And I'm so lucky to have had this time with you."

Sienna's sobs deepen, and I hate that my words are hurting her. So, I kiss her instead, hoping to convey everything I feel. The moment our mouths fuse, we attack each other with frenzy, both of us knowing this will be the last time we're together like this. It feels like only yesterday when I made love to my wife for the very first time, yet it feels like we've known each other forever. When I'm with Sienna, time seems to stand still.

But as I lay her out on my desk and remove her clothes, it feels like time is suddenly moving too quickly. The clock is ticking. Our time is limited.

Once we're both naked, I start with her mouth and move to her jaw, then to her neck and collarbone, kissing and memorizing every inch of her, trying to get in a lifetime's worth of touches. When I get to her pussy, I stick my nose between her pink folds, inhaling her essence, wondering how the fuck I'm supposed to live without her.

I lick and devour her, bringing her close to the precipice and then pulling her back, not wanting the moment to end. When she begs for release, I give in and take her over the edge.

And then I'm inside her, right where I belong, where I wish I could spend the rest of my life. With one hand digging into the curve of her hip and the other holding her face, I make love to my wife, hoping months, hell, years from now, she'll look back and remember how much I loved her.

As we both find our release, she chokes out my name, and I crush my mouth to hers, needing us to be connected in every way possible. How ironic is it that I waited over thirty years to find the woman I want to spend my life with, and now I have to let her go after only a few short months.

"Micah, I can't do this," Sienna cries. When I separate our bodies and pull her into my arms, I don't give a shit that my cum is dripping out of her and likely all over my clothes.

"You can," I murmur into her ear. "You can for Ellie. She comes first. Maybe one day..." I trail off, stopping myself, not wanting to give either of us false hope.

"Thank you for loving me," she says softly, kissing my neck. "For not giving up on me and tearing down my walls. Before you, I didn't know what it felt like to be in love, but you showed me more love in these past few months than I've felt in my entire life."

"Loving you is as easy as breathing," I tell her, not for the first time.

We stay like this for several minutes, and then, because we don't want the moment to end, I put my shirt on her and carry her to our bathroom where we shower together. We stand under the water until it turns cold and then for a little while after that.

When we can't delay the inevitable any longer, I tell her I'm going to touch base with my contact, and she tells me she's going to check on Ellie.

I'm on the phone when Sienna tears into my office, horror etched in her features. "She's gone," she stammers. "Ellie's gone."

Thirty-One

SIENNA

It's been over three days since Ellie walked out the door. During which time I've gone from hating myself for being too consumed by Micah to notice her leaving, to being pissed at my sister because she's not a damn baby and knows better, to hating myself for being pissed at her because being pissed at her won't bring her home.

Micah and his team of men were able to confirm she went to see Eleazar. The cameras showed her leaving the penthouse, going down the elevator, and stepping outside the building, and Micah's contact at the PD was able to get her on camera getting into a taxi that dropped her off at Eleazar's front gate.

Micah has reached out to Eleazar, but he's not responding, and his guard on duty said he's not accepting any visitors. He had her phone tracked, but it was a dead end, so it's probably been destroyed. Eleazar might be a piece of shit, but his family didn't get to where they are by being dumb.

"Here, try to swallow a bit of ginger ale," Donna says, rubbing my back. I'm currently situated with my body wrapped around the porcelain bowl wondering how I'm still throwing up when there's no way there's anything left in my body.

"Thank you," I tell her, sitting back against the cool tile wall. "The stress of Ellie missing is really getting to me."

Donna purses her lips, and I can see it in her features that she's about to say something I'm not going to like. "Do you think it's possible that your sickness isn't due to stress?"

"Like what?" I ask, sipping the warm drink.

"Like, maybe...you're pregnant."

Without even having to think about it, I say, "No, I'm on birth control. Maybe I have a flu bug or something, though."

She nods but doesn't look convinced. She's been with me the past three days, holding my hair back, patting my neck with cool washcloths, all while Micah works around the clock to find Ellie.

"Okay, well, I brought this." She pulls a pregnancy test out of her purse and sets it on the counter.

"I'm not—"

"I know," she says, "but just in case, it's here if you want to take it." She pulls me into her arms and hugs me tightly. "Micah is going to get Ellie back. I just know it. There's nothing that boy wants that he doesn't get when he's motivated." I chuckle at that, knowing what she's saying to be true.

"I'm going to the store to pick up some things and then I'll be back later with dinner. Do you need anything?"

"No, thank you."

"Okay, rest. I know it's easier said than done, but your sister needs you healthy."

After she leaves, I stare at the test on the counter, wondering if there's any truth to what she said. I think back to the last time I got my period. It was a few months ago, before I got on birth control, but my periods have never been regular, so I didn't think anything of it.

Is it possible? I guess there's only one way to find out.

PREGNANT

THE BOLD CAPITAL LETTERS FILL THE SCREEN ON NOT ONE, NOT two, but three tests. I'm pregnant. I did everything I was supposed to do and still ended up pregnant.

I stare at myself in the mirror, my hand going to my still flat belly. There's a baby in there. I can't see it or feel it. But it's in there. A baby that Micah and I created. A baby who will need love and attention, who will need to be nurtured and cared for. There's so much that can go wrong. A million ways we can mess up this baby's life.

You are nothing like your mother.

I repeat the words, trying to stop myself from getting in my own head, but what I need is for Micah to hold me, to tell me everything will be okay. He's my safe place. My strength. He'll know what to do, what to say. He'll make it better.

This is literally the worst timing, but that seems to be the theme of my life.

I call his phone, but it goes straight to voicemail. So I call again—voicemail. I'm about to send him a text when my phone lights up with an incoming call from unknown.

"Hello."

"Sienna." Only my name is spoken, but the way it's said sends chills racing up my spine.

"Who's this?"

"I have your sister. If you want her back in one piece, I suggest you come get her. This is her only chance at escaping."

"Who are you?"

"You won't get another chance to save her. She'll be waiting for you at Tesoro Park. Come alone so you don't draw attention."

The line goes dead, and I race toward Micah's office where he keeps his car keys, grabbing the ones I use when I need to drive somewhere. As I run out the door, his security tries to stop me, but I demand they move, desperate to get to my sister. I don't know who that was on the phone, but it doesn't matter. My sister needs me.

As I drive to Tesoro Park, I try calling Micah once more, and this time he answers. "I'm going to get Ellie," I cry out, the second I hear his voice.

"What do you mean you're going to get Ellie? Sienna, where are you?"

"I'm going to get her," I repeat. "Some woman is helping her escape. I have to pick her up from Tesoro Park."

"Sienna, baby. I need you to calm down. You can't go alone. Give me a few minutes and we'll figure this out. I have guys working on—"

"I can't," I say, cutting him off. "She's going to be waiting for me. The woman said it's her only chance. I have to go get her now."

"Fuck," he curses. "I don't like this, Hellcat."

"I have to," I choke out. "She needs me."

"Okay, I'm tracking you now. As soon as you have her, you need to drive toward the edge of town. I'm going to stay on the phone with you and start heading that way, and then we'll figure out what to do next."

"Okay, thank you," I tell him, as I arrive at my destination and pull into the empty parking lot. There's a playground nearby, but nobody is there. I spot an SUV at the end of the road and drive toward it, my heart pounding in my chest.

"Sienna, do you see her?" Micah asks.

"Not yet, but there's an SUV."

"I don't like this," he murmurs.

The door to the SUV opens and a woman gets out. I don't recognize her, but with her jet-black hair and pale skin, she looks to be Hispanic.

"I think the woman who called me is walking over. I'm going to get out and talk to her. I don't see Ellie anywhere."

"Stay on the phone with me!" Micah barks, as I open my door.

I'm not paying attention to my surroundings, too focused on the woman, so I don't realize what's happening until it's too late. Someone comes up from behind me and snatches my phone out of my hand, sending it flying, while my hands are pulled together and tied.

"What are you doing?" I yell at the woman, who stands there in her tight black dress and stilettos, her blood red lips curled in an evil smirk. "Where's my sister?"

"Don't worry, dear, you're going to see her soon," she says, with a thick accent.

"You said you were helping her escape!"

"I lied," she says, nonchalantly.

I'm dragged down the street to the SUV, where another man opens the trunk and shoves me in. I kick and scream, but it's useless.

What feels like forever later, I'm lifted out and forced into what looks like some sort of basement.

"Sienna!" Ellie shrieks, flinging herself at me just as the door slams shut. "I'm so sorry," she cries, and goes about untying my hands. "I never should've went to see him. I'm so sorry." Tears stream down her cheeks. "I'm so sorry. I'm so—"

"Shh, it's okay," I tell her, wrapping my arms around her shaking body. "It's okay. Who is she?" I ask, rubbing my hands up and down her arms, trying to calm her.

"Eleazer's wife," she cries, burrowing herself into me as she apologizes over and over for going to him when she should've listened to us and stayed.

"It's okay," I murmur. "Micah knows something is wrong.

He'll get us out of here."

I move to let go of Ellie so I can check the place out, but she clings to me, refusing to let go. I hold her tight, repeating to her that everything is going to be okay.

When she's finally calmed down, I gently break away and survey the empty, dingy room, trying to open the only window that's shining light in. Of course it doesn't budge, and neither do the doors.

When a weird smell wafts in the air, my stomach roils, and I have no choice but to run to the corner to throw up. Since I haven't eaten anything, it's a mixture of acid and liquid.

"Are you okay?" Ellie whispers. When I glance at her, I notice her bloodshot eyes and the dark circles underneath. Her hair's greasy, and the tank top she's wearing is dirty and ripped. She looks like she's been to hell and back.

"Yeah, something smells rancid."

"Like death," she agrees, her vacant gaze glancing around the room.

"Hey, El, did anyone—"

Before I can finish my question, I'm retching again. This goes on for several minutes until my body finally gives me a moment to take a breather.

"What's wrong?" Ellie asks, when I become too lightheaded to remain standing and situate myself on the nasty basement floor.

"I'm pregnant." I close my eyes and lay my head against the rough wall. "I only just found out."

"What?" Ellie gasps. "No... No. No. No." She shakes her head, fresh tears sliding down her face. "I did this. This is all my fault. I went to go see him and now—"

"Hey, stop it. You couldn't have known. But don't worry, Micah will find us and get us out of here."

"No, you don't get it. She's going to kill us," Ellie mutters. "She—"

"Well, aren't you observant?" The woman from earlier says, as she walks into the room, followed by the guy who helped throw me into the trunk. "You are nothing but a stupid *bastarda* born from a whore." She steps into our space and reaches for Ellie, fisting her hair. "You don't deserve anything, and I'm going to ensure you never get a dime."

I don't know who this woman is, but her words and actions have me jumping up to protect my sister. "Don't you dare speak to my sister like that," I say, getting in her face and forcing her to release Ellie.

"Back up," the guard says, stepping into my personal space. "Or I'll have to teach you some manners, the same way I taught your—"

"Leave her alone!" Ellie shrieks. "Don't you touch her!"

"Looks like you haven't learned your lesson," the man says.

"I've had enough!" the woman barks. "Sit down and shut up!" The woman shoves me back, and I stumble, tripping over my own feet and falling to the floor. When my back hits the harsh ground, the wind is knocked from my lungs.

Just as I'm glancing up, I see a foot coming toward my stomach. I curl into myself like a shrimp, attempting to protect my baby, but before she makes contact, a loud gunshot rings out.

I pop my head up and see Ellie holding a gun and the woman on the floor, blood pooling around her body.

"What the fuck did you do?" the guard barks. He snatches the gun from a shocked Ellie and points it at her.

"Enough!" a loud voice rings out, forcing our attention toward the man who's walked in brandishing his own weapon. "Give me that gun." The guard nods once and hands it over.

The men speak in Spanish for several seconds, and I have no clue what they're saying, but whatever it is, it can't be good because the man who just walked in glares at Ellie.

"First, your whore of a mother kills my father. Now my daughter, my own flesh and blood, kills my wife. I should shoot you dead. But since I still need you, I've come up with a much better option…"

He moves the gun a foot to the right and aims it at me.

"Wait, please," Ellie screams. "It's not her fault. I did this. I killed Arielle. She kidnapped me from the room you put me in and…" As Ellie rambles on, begging him not to kill me, I stare down the barrel of the gun, my life flashing before me. But it's not my past I see. It's the future I'll never have. My belly swelling with a baby, Micah doting on me, putting together a nursery. The baby's first ultrasound, her first cries, first steps, first words. Picnics at the park. Watching Ellie graduate. Making love to my husband.

My fingers splay out across my belly, and my eyes close, wanting the last things I see and think about to be happy. A second gunshot rings out, and as I accept my fate, I pray that death finds me quickly.

Thirty-Two

MICAH

WHILE MY WIFE WAS CALLING ME, *NEEDING ME*, I HAD NO IDEA that a tower was down for maintenance, and my phone was getting zero signal. Then, when it rang, and Sienna was freaking out, I could barely understand a goddamn word of what she was saying. But when she screamed, I heard and felt that shit in my fucking soul.

The second the line went quiet, I knew she was no longer with her phone, and I pulled up the tracker I have on her—which is a tiny chip in the ballet slipper charm I gave her. I never thought I'd need to use it, but better to be safe than sorry.

I was already with Lincoln and our team of men figuring out how to locate Ellie, so when I knew Sienna had been taken, we suited up and took off after her. It didn't take long to track her to the Gutierrez's warehouse. Since they weren't expecting us, we had the element of surprise on our side and were able to easily take them out.

Finding Sienna and Ellie was easy because all we had to do was follow the raised voices. But when we got there, we realized that shit had already hit the fan. Eleazar's wife was on the floor bleeding out, while Eleazar was pointing a gun at my wife and Ellie was begging him not to kill her. Without thought, I put several bullets in him, and Lincoln took out his guard. My wife was in danger, and I meant what I said. She comes first, always.

With Eleazar and his wife dead, I had my men clean up while Lincoln and I got Sienna and Ellie out. Both were trembling and crying, obviously traumatized by what they had witnessed. I don't know who killed Arielle, but even when it's deserved, taking someone's life is never easy.

Now we're back at the penthouse. Sienna is curled up in my lap, and Ellie is still holding onto Lincoln. Both of them are still shaking and crying softly, and if I could kill the assholes who did this to them all over again, I would.

"Hey, Linc," I say, "Someone should probably go to the warehouse." Because there's nobody left in the Gutierrez family, there won't be anyone to retaliate, but we need to double check that all our tracks are covered to safeguard us against the cops.

He nods and starts to sit up, but Ellie latches on tighter, whimpering. "Please don't leave me," she murmurs.

"I'll go," Rex offers. "Bruno has already spoken to the cops, so everything has been handled."

"Thank you," I tell him. "Keep me updated."

"I need to go to the bathroom," Sienna murmurs, sniffling back her tears.

When Sienna is gone, Ellie turns to look at me, and all I can see is devastation and fear in her eyes. I'm confused as to why she's still fearful since the threat has been removed. Then, in a trembling voice, she asks, "Am I...Am I going to go to jail?"

It takes me a second to wrap my head around her question before it hits me..."You're the one who shot Arielle?"

"She went after Sienna," she chokes out. "Was going to kick her...I couldn't let her hurt the baby."

"Micah," Sienna breathes.

I turn my attention toward where my wife is slumped over, her arms wrapped around her waist, her face way too damn pale.

"Hellcat, what's wrong?" I ask, going over to her.

Tears fill her lids and then spill over. "I'm bleeding."

What? "Where?" I drag my eyes down her body, trying to find where she's hurt, but I don't see any blood. "Where are you hurt?" I ask, getting worried. She seemed okay when I carried her to the car. Shaken up, yeah, but not injured.

"The baby," she murmurs, and Ellie's words that I didn't have time to absorb, immediately click.

Sienna's pregnant, and Arielle was going to kick her in the stomach, so Ellie shot her.

Fuck.

"You're pregnant?" I ask softly, palming her cheek and wiping the falling tears.

She nods. "I found out today. I tried to call you," she says, fresh tears sliding down her face, and my heart cracks. She needed me and I wasn't fucking there. Dammit.

"I went to pee and there was blood. I...I don't know what to do." She looks up at me, silently begging for me to make this right, but I have no idea how. So, I do the only thing I can think of. I call my mom, who advises me to take Sienna to the hospital, which is exactly what I do.

I offer for Lincoln to stay with Ellie, but she insists she wants to be there with her sister, and I get it. They've both been through a traumatic ordeal, and now her sister might be losing her baby that she only just found out about.

"I'll drive," Lincoln offers, so I can sit in the back with my wife. I hold her the entire way, praying that everything's okay.

Fortunately for us, it's a slow night at the hospital, so Sienna is seen right away. Since only one person can go back with her,

Lincoln stays with Ellie in the waiting room. The nurse asks Sienna a bunch of questions and then attaches a band with a barcode and all of her pertinent info to her wrist. We're taken to a private room where she's given a gown to put on while we wait for her to be seen.

Once she's dressed, she sits up on the bed and her eyes meet mine. "I didn't want to get pregnant," she says quietly, liquid emotion filling her lids. "But now..." she chokes out, shaking her head, and I cut across the room to pull her into my arms. I hold her tight while she silently cries into my chest for several minutes before she speaks again. "I want our baby," she admits. "When I thought I was going to die, I saw it...our baby, our family. I could never really picture it before, but in that moment, it was all so clear. I felt so much happiness. Then, just as quickly, it was gone."

I want to tell her everything is going to be okay, but since I don't know if that's true, I tell her the only truth I do know. "I love you, Sienna, and no matter what happens, we'll get through it together." She nods into my chest and snuggles closer.

"Good afternoon," the doctor says. "I'm Dr. Peterson. Are you Sienna?"

"I am," she says, sitting up and wiping her eyes.

"Can you tell me what's going on?"

She explains to the doctor that she's been sick, but she had passed it off as stress since she's on birth control. When my mom suggested that she might be pregnant, she took three separate tests, all of which came out positive. But then later, she found blood on the tissue when she went to pee.

"All right, I'm going to have the nurse take your blood to run some tests. How far along do you think you are?"

"I don't know," she admits. "I haven't gotten my period in a while, and they're always so irregular."

"Based on the urine sample you gave when you arrived, there is a high enough level of hCG to indicate you're pregnant. The spotting you noticed can mean several things, so rather than make assumptions, I'm going to run some blood tests and put in for an ultrasound."

After a nurse comes by and takes several tubes of blood, a woman comes in to take Sienna to the ultrasound. "You don't have to get up. I'll wheel your bed there," she says, with a soft smile. I notice the name on her tag reads Madeline.

"Can he come with me?" Sienna asks nervously, as if there's even the smallest chance that I would let her out of my sight. We have no idea what we're going to see, and there's no way I'm leaving her alone with a stranger, even if Madeline does seem friendly enough.

"Of course," she says.

When we arrive, the room is dark, and the tech explains she's setting up the equipment. Since Sienna's not sure how far along she is, she tells us she's going to do a transvaginal ultrasound. I stay by Sienna's side, holding her hand and massaging circles with my thumb, trying to reassure her that I'm here and that everything's going to be okay, one way or another.

The tech is quiet for several seconds, moving the instrument around inside of her and clicking buttons on the screen. My heart drops, thinking there must be something wrong. I can't tell what's on the screen, but it's grey and grainy and it doesn't look like there's a baby in there. Then again, I'm not sure what it is I should be seeing this early in the pregnancy.

A few moments later, a loud *whoosh, whoosh, whoosh* fills the quiet room, and Sienna gasps. "Is that my baby's heartbeat?"

"Yep, it sure is. And it's strong, too. Based on the measurements, you're roughly five weeks."

Holy shit, Sienna is five weeks pregnant. Despite her being on birth control, it seems fate had other plans.

Sienna squeezes my hand and glances up at me, her eyes glassy with emotion. "We're having a baby," she murmurs softly.

"Yeah, we are," I agree, leaning over and kissing her forehead.

The tech walks us through the ultrasound, while taking

pictures for the doctor. She can't give us any information as to why Sienna was bleeding, but she says once the doctor has a look at the photos, he can tell us more.

After the ultrasound is finished, Sienna is wheeled back to the room, and we're told that the doctor will be in soon to go over all the results.

We wait in silence, unsure what to say. We saw our baby, heard the heartbeat, but that doesn't change the fact that Sienna was bleeding.

A little while later, the doctor returns and informs us that we have no need for concern. Everything looks good, including the bloodwork. "As for the bleeding, it's common in the beginning of a pregnancy due to implantation." He goes on to explain in more detail what the ultrasound showed, and once he's done, he says, "I'm going to discharge you and recommend a few days of bed rest and then a follow-up with your OB-GYN."

When he walks out, Sienna glances down at her flat stomach. "I can't believe there's a baby in there." I snort at how adorable she is. "Only your sperm would be so potent that even birth control can't stop them." She mock glares, and I bark out a laugh.

"You know you love my super sperm," I joke, waggling my eyes.

"This baby is going to be loved," Sienna says after a moment of silence.

"Damn right," I agree, already thinking of everything my wife is going to need during the next nine months. Then, after the baby comes...Fuck, there's so much to do and buy. "Let's get you home and into bed. Are you hungry? Thirsty? We should probably order more pillows so you're comfortable. And we need to find an OB-GYN. How are you feeling? I know the doctor said—"

"Micah," Sienna says with a laugh. "Breathe."

I don't know why she's laughing. I was being serious. "You better use the ride home to mentally prepare yourself, Hellcat," I warn her. She might be Miss Independent, but she's now pregnant with my baby, and that changes everything.

"For what?" she asks, obviously confused.

"The next nine months. You're carrying our baby. And it's my job to make sure you're taken care of and comfortable. You thought I was crazy when we first met...You haven't seen anything yet."

"Are you sure?" Ellie asks, her nose scrunched up in confusion.

"Yes, ma'am. Mr. Gutierrez put a rush on the paternity test and had me come over as soon as the results confirmed that you are his biological child. He asked me to amend his will to where if something should happen to him, you and his wife would split everything fifty-fifty. But because they both passed away, the entire estate goes to you as his only living relative. Since you aren't eighteen yet, I'll remain the executor of the estate until your eighteenth birthday."

It's been a week since Eleazar and his wife were pronounced dead—burned in an electrical fire at his warehouse. A couple of days afterward, Norman Eisenburg requested a meeting with Ellie. He's the Gutierrez family's attorney, and when he told me that he needed to meet with Ellie for the reading of the will, I damn near choked on my coffee.

"I don't want it," she says softly, her voice cracking with emotion. She's been like this ever since we rescued her and Sienna from the warehouse. Quiet, withdrawn. I told Sienna I thought her sister needed to see someone. She killed a person, and that's not an easy thing to live with, but Ellie refused, saying she just needs time.

Mr. Eisenburg looks at her like she's crazy, but before he can get a word in, I put my hand on Ellie's shoulder. "Right now, your emotions are all over the place. Before you make any rash decisions, why don't you sit on it for a little while? Regardless of how you feel about Eleazar Gutierrez, you are his blood, which means everything he left to you is rightfully yours."

"It's blood money," she mutters. "He was a criminal. Everyone who worked for him were disgusting criminals."

"Miss, if I may say something," the gentleman says gently. "The estate and assets are estimated at two hundred million dollars. If you don't want to partake in the *family business*"—he raises his brows to make it clear he's referring to the illegal aspects of it all—"you can simply sell off and walk away from the parts you don't want. But the rest of the money and investments are all clean."

Ellie swallows thickly. "Two hundred million?"

Mr. Eisenburg nods slowly.

"So, could I sell everything and keep the money?"

"Absolutely, you can," I tell her. "Mr. Eisenburg has to approve it all, but I don't think that will be a problem. And I can help you every step of the way."

She lets out a sigh. "Okay, then that's what I want to do. But anything of his that came from dirty money, I want to donate."

"You got it."

"Umm, Mr. Eisenburg, how soon can I purchase something? Like something kind of expensive?"

He quirks a brow. "It will depend on the amount, of course, but the papers will be processed with the courts later today, and by the end of the week, you will have access to everything."

When we're back in my car and heading home, Ellie says, "Can you stop somewhere for me, please?"

"Sure, where?"

"Lola's Dance Studio."

Thirty-Three

SIENNA

"You what?" I exclaim from bed. The doctor recommended a few days of bed rest, but Micah insisted I stay put for a week. Surprisingly, I didn't argue. I think between the traumatic events with Eleazar and learning I'm pregnant, then fearing I'd lost the baby, I needed some time to rest.

For the first few days, Ellie stayed home as well, but then she returned to school, saying she didn't want to fall behind.

"My sperm donor left everything to me," Ellie says, tears filling her eyes. She's been extremely emotional since everything happened. Micah suggested I take her to see someone, but she begged me not to, saying she just needs time.

I glance from Ellie to Micah in shock. "Is she for real?"

"Yep, she was left the entire Gutierrez estate," he confirms with a shrug.

"Wait, does that mean she's like some mob princess?" I shriek, starting to freak out. "Oh my God, is she in the mob?"

"No," Micah says with a laugh, which has me glaring his way. "The guy was corrupt, but like any smart businessman, he also had plenty of legal assets. His estate will be broken down and dismantled. Any dirty money will get donated at Ellie's request, and the legal money will go into a trust account that she'll have full access to once she turns eighteen. Until then, anything she chooses to purchase has to go through the executor of the estate, Norman Eisenburg, who seems like a decent guy."

"And I've already decided on the first thing I'm going to purchase with my money," Ellie adds, raw emotion laced in every word. "Lola's Dance Studio. Grace said she's thinking about selling it, and I want to buy it for you. You love to dance, and your dream was always to do just that."

"Oh, El," I rasp. "But not just for me, right? You've always said you're going to go to school locally and live at home. We could run it together."

Ellie smiles sadly, and not for the first time, it feels like something is off, but I can't figure out what, and she's not talking. "Yeah, maybe," she says noncommittally. "But for now, I just want this to be yours. You've given me so much, and I want to give this to you." She lays a hand gently on my belly. "And who knows? Maybe this little boy or girl will love dance as much as we do."

I choke up, my hormones getting the better of me. "Thank you." I wrap her into my arms and hug her tightly. "I love you, El."

"I love you, too," she says, standing. "I have a bunch of homework I need to get caught up on, so I'm going to go do that."

Once we're alone, Micah takes up the spot where Ellie was just sitting. "How are you feeling?"

"Emotional," I joke, making us both laugh. "I just can't believe how much our life has changed in such a short amount of time."

"For the good?" Micah confirms.

"Definitely. For so long, I felt like we were forced into a life neither one of us asked for. Until you came along, I was scared of falling in love, but you reminded me every step of the way that the risk is worth the reward."

"And what's the reward?" he asks, even though he knows damn well what it is. He just wants to hear me say it.

"The reward is love."

Epilogue

MICAH

"I can't find my pink leo!" Ellie shouts from somewhere in the house.

"Blue leo!" London, our almost two-year-old-daughter, adds.

"I haven't seen either one," Sienna yells from somewhere. "And I can't find London's ballet slippers. If anyone sees them, let me know."

It's official. My once bachelor pad has been overrun by women. And not just women—ballerinas.

I walk upstairs to London's room first and find her flinging her leotards all over the place, making a mess. Leaning against the door, I clear my throat to get her attention, and the second she sees me, her entire face lights up.

"Daddy!" She stops what she's doing and runs straight for me. She giggles as I lift her into my arms and over my head, pulling a move she loves from the dancing movie she watches repeatedly.

Then she spreads her arms out wide and juts her legs out like she's a professional. When I bring her back down, she wraps her arms around me and kisses my cheek. "Blue leo?" she asks, her bright blue eyes—identical to her mother's—alight with hope.

"I don't know where it is, sweetheart. How about you put on another one?" Her eyes immediately dim, and I regret my words, knowing that wasn't the right thing to say. Like her mother and aunt, my daughter takes dancing seriously, and that includes wearing the leo she wants.

"Blue one." She pouts, wiggling for me to set her down. She runs back to where she's destroying her drawers, so I head out to find my wife next.

She's in the laundry room, sifting through the clothes, and I take a moment to watch her. Today, she's wearing a tight tank top and black leggings that show off every perfect curve. Her hair is up in a messy knot on the top of her head, and though I can't see her face, I would bet it's makeup free, aside from some of that glossy shit she wears on her lips that always gets all over mine when I kiss her.

When she feels me watching her, her head snaps up. "Hey, you're home," she says with a huff, blowing the unruly strands of hair out of her face.

"I am." I pull her into my arms and give her a kiss that's far too short for my liking, but I'll kiss her longer tonight once we're in bed. "How's my baby mama doing?"

"Feeling like a beached whale," she says with a laugh. As if the baby can hear her, her belly erupts with kicks that I can feel since her front is pressed against mine. We weren't planning to get pregnant so soon after she had London, but once again, fate had other plans. We're excited to welcome this baby into the world soon, and London is excited to be a big sister.

"I told you to take some time off," I say, even though I know she won't listen. She's due in a couple of weeks, but that doesn't stop her from dancing and teaching classes at the studio. She did the same thing when she was pregnant with London—I literally had to pick her up from the studio when her water broke.

"I think this is my last week," she says with a pout. "I spoke to Carmen, and she's agreed to take over my classes. I'm tired, and she can use the hours."

"Has anyone seen my pink leo?" Ellie asks, poking her head inside the laundry room. "I'm going to be late to class."

"Maybe use a different one for today until you can find that one?" I suggest.

Ellie's reaction is the same as London's, so I close my mouth and start searching for a pink and blue leo in the pile of clean laundry, mentally noting to hire someone to come in to organize this place as soon as possible. Three girls in one house is insane, and if my guess is correct, another will soon be added to the mix.

"Mommy, blue leo?" London asks, joining us in the laundry room.

"I'm look—" Sienna's eyes go wide. "Oh, God."

"My blue leo?" London asks, hopeful.

Sienna looks down, and I follow her line of vison.

"Mommy, you go pee pee on the floor," London says. "Gross! Use the toilet!"

"Oh, shit," Ellie hisses. "You're having the baby."

Pink and blue leos forgotten, Ellie scoops London up while I help Sienna to the car. The ride to the hospital is quick, and so is her labor. Within a couple of hours, our newborn is delivered. Just as we had done with London, we chose not to learn the baby's gender ahead of time, so we wait for the doctor to announce it.

"Congratulations, it's a healthy girl."

They clean up the baby a little and then place her on Sienna's chest so she can hold her. She kisses the top of our daughter's head and glances up at me, tears shining in her eyes. "You ready for another girl?" she chokes out, her voice filled with emotion.

Images of the clothes and shoes and hormones that have overtaken my home flash before my eyes, and I can't help but smile. "I wouldn't have it any other way."

SIENNA

"THERE'S SOMETHING I NEED TO TELL YOU," ELLIE SAYS SLOWLY, and I can already tell by her tone it's not going to be good. I thought that once everything settled down and we were safe and no longer struggling to make ends meet, it would strengthen our relationship, but for some reason, Ellie's shut me out. There's something that's eating away at her, but when I ask, she plasters on a smile and tells me everything is fine.

She still goes to school and dances, but she doesn't hang out with any of her friends or show any interest in dating. And she rarely spends any time at the studio. She says it's because she's busy with school and her senior showcase, but something feels off. I try to chalk it up to her being a hormonal teenager, but deep down, I think there's more to it. I just can't figure out what it is, and Ellie won't speak to me about it.

"Okay, what's up?" I say, taking Brooklyn off my breast. Since London was named after the city where I fell in love with Micah, we thought it was only right to name Brooklyn after the city where we renewed our vows.

"I've received my acceptance letters for college, and I've decided I'm going to California School of the Arts."

"California?" I say, confused. "But...I thought you were going to stay local."

"Mommy!" London yells, running in and jumping on the bed. "I give baby kiss." She leans over and kisses Brooklyn's head.

"We can talk later," Ellie says, but I shake my head.

"No, don't go, please. You always said you wanted to go to New York."

"I know," she says softly, "but I think California is a better fit."

"It's five hours away by plane," I choke out, letting my emotions get the better of me. "We've never been that far away from each other." Tears blur my vision, and I know I'm being unfair. Ellie deserves to go to whatever school she wants, but there seems to be something else driving her decision.

"You leaving me?" London asks, looking at Ellie. Despite Ellie keeping everyone at arm's length, she's a damn good aunt to London. Our daughter worships her and is not going to take it well if she moves across the country.

"Oh, London Bridge," Ellie says, silently begging for me to understand. "I'm going to be back all the time, I promise. And you'll come visit me."

"But I miss you," London murmurs. "I no want you to go."

"We'll see her a lot," I say, forcing a smile on my face.

"I no like it." London pouts, making Ellie do the same.

"London, stop," I say gently. "This is amazing news." I give Ellie a hug. "You've worked hard and deserve this. She'll be okay. We'll all be okay."

MICAH

FOUR YEARS LATER

"Good job, ladies. You looked so in sync today."

I watch from the back of the room as my wife praises the students in her class. A couple of the girls ask her questions about an upcoming performance, and she answers them with patience and smiles before telling them to have a good night and that she'll see them next class.

Since she doesn't know I'm here, once everyone is gone, she turns on the music and walks over to the barre to stretch. Inside this studio, she's in her element, and the outside world doesn't exist. I hate that she's unaware of her surroundings, but I know it's because she feels safe. It took a long time for her to feel that way, but she knows that I'll always make certain that she and our kids are secure.

When she lifts her foot onto the barre and bends forward, I step out from behind the wall. Her head lifts and our eyes lock in the mirror.

"What are you doing here?" she asks.

"Kids are spending the night with my parents." My mom and dad are hands-on grandparents. With Lincoln still refusing to settle down, London and Brooklyn are their only grandkids, and therefore, they are extremely spoiled by my parents.

"Hmm." A twinkle alights in her eyes as she bends slightly forward again, her gaze never leaving mine. I step toward her, bridging the gap between us until I'm standing directly behind her. She lowers her leg, then lifts the other, stretching it out. When she has both feet back on the floor, I settle my hands on her hips and pull her back against my front, my fingers stretching across her swollen belly. Six months pregnant. Ever since she told me this will be the last one, I find myself wanting to touch her even more, wanting to memorize the way her gorgeous body grows and changes when she's carrying our babies. Because it's our last child, once again, we've chosen to let the gender be a surprise.

With her hair up in a tight bun, I have perfect access to her slim neck. I lean in and place a soft kiss to her heated flesh, and a shiver visibly runs through her body.

I relish how my wife still reacts to me, even after all these years. My dad once told me that the key to a good marriage is to never stop dating your wife and to never, ever get complacent. If you show her your love every day, she'll gladly give you her heart in return. Our days can be crazy, filled with two rambunctious little girls, our careers, and simply life in general, but we always make sure to find time to be with each other.

"Put your hands on the barre," I command gently. She does as

I say, and her pert ass juts out slightly. Reaching around, I pull the front of her sports bra down, exposing her breasts. I tweak and pinch her rosy nipples, and she moans in pleasure, her body squirming in want.

My wife loves to be fucked, and I love to be inside her. She's wearing leggings today without a leo, so it makes it easy to tug both the material and her underwear down her legs, leaving her ass on display.

"Micah, please," she moans, then I give it a good, hard slap, the sound ringing out in the room.

"Patience, Hellcat," I tell her, as I spread her legs and then tease her pussy. She's wet, her juices coating my fingers, so I shove two inside her, causing her moans to get louder, competing with the music that's playing.

She lets go of the barre, wanting to take over, but I give her a stern look. "Hands back on the barre," I say, my demand only making her that much wetter.

I fingerfuck her good and hard until her cunt's tightening around me and she's coming all over my hand. Without giving her a chance to come down, I undo my pants, lift her ass slightly, and plunge into her from behind, mindful not to jostle her too vigorously. After all, she's carrying precious cargo.

"Yes," she cries out, meeting me thrust for thrust. "Right there."

I hit her sweet spot over and over again, and all too soon, she's coming for a second time, this time taking me along with her.

While still inside her, I lean over and kiss the top of her shoulder. "I love you."

She glances at my reflection in the mirror, a small, satiated smile on her lips. "I love you."

We clean up in the bathroom where she changes into her street clothes. As we're heading out, her phone goes off and she glances at it, frowning.

"The kids?" I ask.

"Ellie."

I sigh, knowing this won't be good. Over the past several years, while our marriage has grown stronger, her relationship with her sister has slowly deteriorated. It started the day Ellie saved Sienna and our unborn baby and has only continued to worsen, especially once she moved across the country for school.

She rarely comes home, and it's usually only when Sienna guilt-trips her into it. She tried to give her sister space, but Ellie is more than just a sister to her. Sienna views her as a mother would her daughter, and it breaks her heart that the girl she dedicated herself to care for and protect has completely shut her out.

But not wanting to upset Ellie, Sienna has stopped saying anything. She plasters on a smile and takes whatever her sister is willing to give her.

"What'd she say?"

"She's not coming home." She looks up at me with tears in her eyes. "She's decided to stay in California for the summer after she graduates." A sob rips through her. "I've officially lost my sister."

"It's just the summer, Hellcat. You haven't lost your sister."

"No." She shakes her head, sniffling. "I know Ellie. The summer is just her way of easing us into it. Next, it will be just until the new year, and then, before we know it, she'll be living there for the rest of her life."

ONE WEEK LATER

"Do you really think it's wise to go visit Sienna's sister without her?" my dad asks, as I press the button for the elevator in the building where Ellie lives.

"Ellie won't talk to Sienna, and Sienna is too emotional to talk to her. We had hoped that once her sister graduated and moved home, they'd finally have a chance to work things out, since Ellie asked for time, which Sienna reluctantly gave her. Enough is enough. I'm not going to have my wife crying every day. I'm going to get to the bottom of this shit, so we can get our family back together."

The elevator doors open, so I hang up with my dad since I'll likely lose service anyway. I press the number for Ellie's floor, and once the car arrives, I step out, heading straight for her door. I'm lifting my hand to knock, but before my fist touches the surface, the door flies open, and I come face to face with Ellie. The first thing I notice is her shocked expression, her green eyes wide with surprise. Since she wasn't expecting me, I find her reaction understandable.

But then she backs up slightly, her features morphing into something else—fear, maybe?—and that allows me to take all of her in. My gaze skates downward, assessing her, making sure she's okay. It's warm in California, so she's dressed in a tank top and cotton shorts. Nothing unusual there. But as my eyes ascend back to her face, something catches my attention.

A bump. I would recognize it anywhere, since my wife has sported the same one three times now. It's not big, but with her tank being so tight, it really accentuates it. Makes it stand out. My eyes meet hers and she instantly sees that I know.

"Are you pregnant?"

She swallows anxiously as her hand goes to her protruding belly, telling me all I need to know. She's pregnant. And she wasn't planning for us to know.

A Risk Worth Taking

A Risk Worth Taking Playlist

2Step – Ed Sheeran
Numb – Marshmello & Khalid
Crush – David Archuleta
The Heart Wants What It Wants – Selena Gomez
Over My Head – The Fray
Numb Little Bug – Em Beihold
There's No Way – Lauv
When You're Gone – Shawn Mendez
Beautiful Mistakes – Maroon 5 & Megan Thee Stallion
Thank God – Kane Brown & Katelyn Brown

I don't think anyone is ever ready,
but when someone makes you feel alive again,
it's kind of worth the risk.

– Nikki Rowe

One

ELLIE
PRESENT

"Stop! Please...Please don't do this..." I kick my feet out, aiming for his dick, but as I'm about to connect, I'm flipped onto my stomach like a rag doll, my elbows barely catching me before my chin hits the concrete.

He shoves my shorts down my legs, my underwear next.

I squirm, trying to get away, but a pair of hands hold me down while another pushes my thighs apart.

"Please," I beg, refusing to lie here and take it. "Please don't—"

"Ellie, what the fuck? Ellie!"

The sound of my name, combined with the shaking of my shoulders, has my eyes snapping open and scanning the room as I gasp for air.

"You okay?" Tim asks.

I glance around and remember where I am: in my condo, on

my bed, half naked with my boyfriend of two months. We were working our way toward having sex, until...

"Ellie," Tim says again. "Are you—?"

"No," I choke out, shoving him off me. He momentarily loses his balance but quickly catches himself before he falls backward onto the floor.

While tucking my breasts back into my bra, I scramble off the bed and snag my shirt off the ground, throwing it over my head, all while feeling Tim's eyes on me. Following me. Trying to figure me out.

He won't, though. None of them ever do. Because I never let them get close enough.

"El," he finally says, the pity in his tone making me flinch. He hasn't the first clue what I've been through, but it doesn't take a genius to realize I'm a broken mess that no one can piece back together.

"Please leave," I tell him, my tone flat even to my own ears.

"What?" he asks, confused as to where this is going—or not going.

"I want you to leave. We're done," I say, having yet to meet his gaze. It's easier this way. I don't have to see the hurt or confusion in his eyes.

When the heat of his body wraps around mine from behind, his hands seeking to comfort me, I recoil, not wanting any part of him touching me.

It's clear he's not going to leave without putting up a fight. Most women probably love a man who will fight for their relationship. I probably would too if I wanted him to fight for us...But I don't.

"I said we're done. Please leave." I turn to face him, my gaze meeting his, so he understands I'm serious.

He stares at me for a long moment and then shakes his head. "I should've known better. Mark said you were a coldhearted bitch, but I didn't listen." I cringe slightly at his harsh words but don't argue, because while calling me a bitch is rude, he isn't wrong, and I did waste two months of his life.

With a huff, he swipes his shirt off the floor, yanks it on, and walks out the door.

I wait until the front door slams before I slide to the floor. My tears are barely halfway down my face when my best friend is barging through my door and on the floor next to me, holding me tightly in her arms.

"Another flashback," she says with a sigh—not asking, because she already knows the answer. We've been roommates for the past three and a half years, and she knows more about me than anyone.

"I tried," I rasp, knowing that's not exactly true and hoping she won't call me out on my white lie.

Of course, Raelyn isn't having it. "No, you didn't. You had a flashback and kicked him out."

"I'm not ready," I repeat the same three words I say every time I'm looking to end things with a guy right before we have sex.

"You're never going to be ready if you don't stay with anyone long enough to let them in. Trust takes time, El."

"I gave him two months," I remind her. "There's no sense in wasting any more of his time if I know I'll never be able to trust him." This isn't the first instance where Tim tried to round second base and I pushed him away. However, today, when the flashback hit hard, I knew it was a lost cause. And since Tim is a twenty-one-year-old red-blooded college student who thinks with his dick, I didn't see any reason to delay the inevitable. By this weekend he'll be balls deep in another woman, and next weekend he won't even remember my name.

"El," Raelyn sighs. "You don't trust anyone. You keep everyone at arm's length."

"That's not true," I scoff, resenting her blanket statement. "I trust you and Sienna."

"You trust us to a certain extent, but not even Sienna knows everything..." I shudder at the thought of my older sister, who raised me like her own, knowing *everything*. The sadness, the disappointment, the guilt...Nope, not happening.

"And yeah, I know what happened," Raelyn adds, "but only because we've been roommates for years and I never stopped pushing you to open up and let me in. Except if we're being honest..." She sits back, her gorgeous brown eyes meeting my emerald ones. "I probably don't know the full extent of what you're dealing with."

"I don't want my sister to worry." Raelyn opens her mouth to argue, but I shake my head. "She will, Rae, and I don't want her to. And as for you, you know enough." Enough to understand why I am the way I am without the sort of gory details no one else should have to live with.

"You know I think you're wrong," she says, not for the first time. Whenever I try to take things to the next level with a guy and have flashbacks, freak out, and send him packing, we have this same conversation. "I think you should tell her. It's affecting your relationship, and you're hurting her worse by shutting her out."

"I know," I mutter, hating that the person I love the most in the world is the person I can't stand to be around. Not because of anything she did. No, Sienna Alexander is perfect. She's the perfect sister, the perfect mom, the perfect wife.

It's me.

I'm the broken one.

And if she knew why, she'd blame herself. Then she'd try to fix me, and I'm not sure I can be fixed, which would only cause her more pain.

"I just need to figure my shit out. It all unraveled so fast." I went from having a close-knit relationship with my sister to escaping to California to get away from her, only going home to New York when absolutely necessary.

"Well, you have five months until we graduate, and unless you've changed your mind, you'll be right back where you started," she reminds me. "Regardless, I wasn't talking about Sienna and me when I said you keep everyone at arm's length. I was talking about men." She side-eyes me. "You claim you need to trust a guy in order to be with him, but you don't let anyone get close enough to build up that trust."

"That's not true," I balk.

"Really? Who do you trust?"

Two

ELLIE
THE PAST

"Ugh, I hate writing essays." I slump on the couch, crossing my arms over my chest. "It's not like I'm going to need to write essays when I'm dancing."

"Sometimes in life we have to do things we don't want to do so we can do the things we want to do," Marina says as she stitches a pair of booty shorts one of the dancers ripped. It's Friday night and I'm at Wanderlust, the gentleman's club where my sister works. There's no shame in her job, because it not only pays enough for her schooling, as well as my dance lessons, but also the bills our piece of shit mom is responsible for. Marina is the club's house mom, and in the short time I've known her, she's always treated me like her own.

"I just don't know how to start it," I whine. "Once I get going, it's—"

A loud knock cuts my words off, followed by Marina yelling for whoever it is to come in.

"Everyone decent?" the club owner, Lincoln, asks as he walks in and straight over to Marina.

Everyone is not decent. I glance around and find two women topless, one completely naked. Each perking up at the sight of him, hoping he'll take notice.

I don't blame them. He's good-looking with his hazel eyes, prominent nose, and scruffy angular jaw. Add in his height, probably a little over six foot, the way he wears those designer suits—he clearly works out—plus the fact he's stupid rich, and he might as well be Prince Charming.

"I'm placing an order," he tells Marina, not giving a single woman even the slightest bit of attention. From what I've heard, Lincoln rarely spends much time here, but his manager is on his honeymoon, so he's filling in for him.

I tune him and Marina out and focus on my essay, but when I read over the prompt again, I get frustrated and groan. "Writing sucks."

"Whatcha writing?" I glance up and find Lincoln standing in front of me, looking at my paper.

"That's the problem. I'm *not* writing. This stupid essay is due Monday, and I haven't even started it."

He picks up the prompts and as he's reading over them, Candy walks by, still topless, and rubs up against him. His gaze lands on her for a beat before he looks back at me. "You're Sienna's little sister, right?"

I nod.

"It's probably hard to focus in here. Why don't we go to my office, and I can help you there?" He glances at Marina. "Let Sienna know Eliza is with me."

"You can call me Ellie," I say, standing and gathering my stuff.

Lincoln walks me over to his office and takes a seat behind the desk, motioning for me to sit in the plump, leather visitor seat.

I notice he leaves the door open, and he explains, "I have an open-door policy. If I'm here, the door is open, and everyone knows they can come to me for anything." He sets the paper down. "Now, the key to writing a good essay is to understand what it's asking you to do."

He spends the next several minutes walking me through how to break the prompt apart and outline, something my teacher never went over with us. By the time he's done, I understand what I need to do.

"Now, you have to—" His phone rings and he raises a finger, silently telling me to give him a moment. "What's up, big bro?" I don't know who his brother is, although I've heard from the women talking that they're close. His name is Micah, and while Lincoln is all smiles, Micah is apparently a brooding asshole—at least that's how the women describe him.

They talk for a few minutes about the restaurant Lincoln's opening. From what I've gathered, the building has three levels: the bottom floor is an underground sex club called Elite, the ground floor is a strip club and bar, which is where my sister works, and the top floor will be a restaurant called Impulse. They're still in the building stages, according to Sienna.

When he hangs up, he glances at my paper and mock glares. "You got nothing done."

"I think I have trouble focusing," I admit. "I can memorize any dance number, but when it comes to reading and writing, I struggle."

"You're a dancer?" he asks.

"Yep, dancing is my life. Not dancing like stripping, though," I'm quick to clarify.

"Obviously," he says with a laugh. "So, what do you do—ballet?"

"All types, really. My sister and I started dancing before we could walk," I joke. "My plan is to get into NYU and go to school for dance therapy. It's always been my safe place, and I'd love to teach it one day with my sister. Help other people find their safe place through dance like I did." I shrug. "Maybe we could even open our own studio. Who knows. But in order to get into NYU, I need the grades, especially if I'm going to apply for a scholarship."

There's no way Sienna can afford my tuition, nor would I ask that of her, which means I have less than three years left to get the grades I need to get in and hope for an academic or dance scholarship of some sort. I'll get some financial aid since we're poor as hell, but it won't be enough—honestly, it's never enough.

"You've got this," Lincoln says, his hazel eyes meeting mine. "And if you need any help with your schoolwork, I'm always here. Don't tell my brother, but I'm the smart one in the family." He winks playfully, causing butterflies to swarm in my belly.

We work on my essay for another hour or so, and when we finish, he walks me back to the dressing room. This is the first time I've been around a man who doesn't look at me like I was a prize lamb at the county fair.

Growing up in a home with a drug-addicted prostitute for a mom, I've come across my fair share of men, none of which are bothered that I'm underage. Pussy is pussy to them, and virgin pussy only makes them want me that much more.

I've never met a gentleman like Lincoln. He kept the door open, was respectful, and he didn't make a single crude comment the entire time. As I watch him speak to Marina, before he glances back at me and smiles softly, I can't help but wonder what it would be like to be with a man like Lincoln. My assumption has always been that all the women here flirt with him because he's rich and hot, only now I realize it may be more than that. They see what I didn't see before: the safety, security, comfort. Things girls like me don't have the luxury of getting.

"I'M GOING TO NEED TO BORROW YOUR SISTER," LINCOLN SAYS

when we walk through the back door of Wanderlust.

"For what?" Sienna asks skeptically, at the same time I say, "Sure!"

It's been almost two weeks since Lincoln helped with my essay, and I've only seen him a handful of times since. But during each interaction he's nice and sweet. He talks to me like I'm his equal, not like I'm a little kid or a piece of meat. I like him, and even though I know I'm too young for him right now, one day I won't be. I read an article online that says the way to a man's heart is through friendship, so that's what I'm going to do. Unlike the women who throw themselves at him, I'm going to befriend him, and once I'm old enough, it will be easy to convince him to be with me.

Lincoln chuckles. "The chef I'm looking to hire is upstairs making an array of dishes for me to sample. I'd love a second opinion."

"I'm starved," I shamelessly lie. Sienna and I literally just ate dinner before we came here. But I want more time with Lincoln. How can we develop a friendship without spending time together?

"Okay, but I need her real quick," Sienna says, thankfully not calling me out on my little white lie. "Can she meet you in a few minutes?"

"No problem," Lincoln says. "See you in a few." He graces me with a soft smile that makes my belly tighten.

"Oh, wait!" I say, holding out the container in my hands. "This is for you. A thank you for helping me with my essay. It's homemade soup." Occasionally, when we have the money for the ingredients, I make meatball minestrone. It's Sienna's favorite— mine too—and we can eat the leftovers for days.

Lincoln takes it from me and lifts the lid. "Smells amazing. You made this yourself?"

"Yep," I tell him, imagining that one day, when we're together, I'll make meatballs for him. Men love food, and I'm a great cook. "All you have to do is heat it up. It's delicious."

"Thanks," he says. "Meet me in my office when you're ready to go upstairs."

When we get in the dressing room, Sienna pulls me to the side, glancing around to make sure no one can hear what she's about to say. "He's too old for you. You know that, right?"

She's sounding like a broken record. When I mentioned to her how he helped me with my essay, I made the mistake of also saying he's nice and I like him. He's different from the men our mom brings home to fuck. And he's way more mature than the guys at school.

"Age is just a number," I counter stubbornly. It's not like I expect him to be with me now. I'm aware that at my age, he doesn't see me like that—hence my goal to form a friendship with him.

"Unless it's a number under eighteen," Sienna says with a stern face. "Then, it's statutory rape."

At her words, I roll my eyes because Lincoln isn't that type of guy, and I wouldn't risk hitting on him right now. I need to be smart about things if I want him to give us a real chance one day. "I'll be fifteen soon. Eighteen is only three years away."

I looked it up, and as long as I'm eighteen, we can be together.

And once I'm legal, all bets are off.

Three

ELLIE
THE PAST

"Ellie...what are you doing down here?"

I glance up and wipe my eyes when I see Lincoln standing in front of me in the corner of the hotel lobby.

"I wasn't ready to go home yet," I admit with a sniffle. "Bad night."

He sits next to me on the bench and asks, "What's wrong?" Then waits patiently for me to answer.

So much has happened recently. My mom stole money and drugs from a client and took off, leaving Sienna and me to deal with the fallout—the fallout being our home and car getting torched and a million-dollar bounty on Sienna's head. Lincoln's brother, Micah, saved the day by marrying my sister and moving us into his penthouse, which is in the hotel he and Lincoln own.

I left for the summer to attend dance camp—thanks to Micah

paying for it—and came back to find my sister and her husband madly in love.

Micah paid for me to start at a new school—a fancy school of the arts—where I thought I was making friends, only to learn tonight that several of them have been talking shit about me behind my back.

"Was it that guy you went on a date with?" Lincoln eventually asks.

"It wasn't a date." He and Micah called it that because it's Friday night and Jameson picked me up. Lincoln lives next door to Micah and was over when Jameson showed up. "It was just supposed to be a study date," I tell him softly. "We were assigned a project and he asked if I wanted to work on it with him. Turns out, it was just a way for him to try to get in my pants."

Lincoln visibly tenses up next to me, looking around as if the asshole would still be here.

"I don't know where he is. We were supposed to go to the coffee shop, but instead he took me to a party. He offered me a drink, and when I told him I thought we were supposed to be working on our projects, he told me to lighten up. Said he thought a girl from *Booker Park* would be more fun."

Booker Park is where Sienna and I are from. A small, lower income neighborhood in Tesoro. "I thought when we moved in with Micah, we were leaving that part of our life behind," I admit. "But I guess the saying is true. You can take the girl out of the ghetto but—"

"Stop," Lincoln demands. "That's not who you are. You're Eliza Bardot. A damn good student, an amazing dancer, and you're a good person. I saw how hard you were pushing for your sister to find her happiness with my brother. You're a good sister, El. Fuck that kid."

His words spark a flame in me. He sees me, like really sees me. Despite where I came from and who my mom is, Lincoln Alexander sees *me*.

"He thought because I was from Booker Park, I'd be easy." I shrug. "Then he got pissed when I refused to do anything with him, so I got an Uber and got out of there." I sniffle back my tears as I stare at a couple stepping up to the elevator, hands intertwined, love in their eyes. "What if I'm destined to follow in my mom's footsteps?" She spent most of her life begging for men's attention and love, only to be treated like trash. Eventually, I think she just accepted it.

"That's bullshit," Lincoln says. "Look at Sienna. She found love and they're happy as hell, on cloud nine. Both are good to each other and for each other. You are *not* your mother." His eyes meet mine. "She made shitty choices. You're smarter than that. And one day, you'll meet a man who's worthy of you. The fact that you walked away from that asshole speaks volumes of the person you are." He rests his hand on mine and pats it gently. It's only meant as a friendly gesture, but that doesn't stop the butterflies from swarming in my chest. His touch is warm and comforting, and I would do anything to keep it forever. "You have your entire life ahead of you. Don't let one dumbass bring you down."

SHE'S DEAD. MY MOM IS DEAD. SHOT IN THE HEART BY ELEAZAR Gutierrez, one of the deadliest crime bosses on the East Coast. And he's filed a petition stating that I'm his daughter. She should've told me. Warned me. Instead, she must've told him. Because he knows and wants me as his own. Sienna and Micah said they'll get this sorted out, but I don't see how.

"Figured I'd find you here," Lincoln says, taking a seat next to me. I'm sitting in the garden on the roof of the hotel, a quiet place I go to when I need to collect my thoughts. Lincoln's come across me here a few times and has dubbed it my place. The only people that have access to it are Lincoln and Micah since only their elevator goes up here. After the first time he found me up here, the entire place was renovated with new couches, tables, and flowers—like my own little sanctuary where I can just sit and think and be alone. He never mentioned it, but I know it was him.

"I thought when she died, I'd finally be safe," I admit out loud as I swipe away a traitorous tear. "When I was eleven, she brought a man home to fuck. Got too high and passed out and he tried to rape me. Sienna saved me and, in turn, was almost raped herself. But I called the cops like she taught me to do, and the guy was arrested. You'd think that would've been an eye opener for my mom. Nope," I say with a humorless laugh. "She disappeared for months, and the next time we saw her, she was high and fucking some guy on the couch."

I glance at Lincoln and find his entire body tense, his jaw clenched in anger. I reach out and pat his hand. "You don't have to be angry on my behalf. It's just the cards we were dealt. Lenora was a shit mother and destroyed everyone and everything in her wake. So, I guess it makes sense that even in her death she would put her daughter at risk."

"He's not going anywhere near you," Lincoln says, his voice steady and calm, so sure of his words. I wish I could be as confident as he is. "Micah, Sienna, and I won't let it happen."

"Stop! Please…Please don't do this…" I kick my feet out, aiming for his dick, but before I can connect, I'm flipped onto my stomach like a ragdoll, my elbows just barely catching me before my chin hits the concrete.

My shorts are shoved down my legs, my underwear next.

I squirm, trying to get away, but a pair of hands hold me down while another pushes my thighs apart.

"Please," I beg, knowing it won't do any good but refusing to lie here and take it. "Please don't—"

I close my eyes and try to mentally block out what's about

to happen. I did this. I fucked up. Eleazer was coming after my family, threatening to take me. He was going to get custody of me, thanks to paying off a judge. Sienna and I were going to have to run, and she was going to have to leave Micah behind.

I couldn't let her do that. She's been through so much. She's worked so hard to take care of me, and she's finally found her happiness. I couldn't be the person to take that away from her. I thought I could talk to him, make him see reason. And maybe I could've, except I didn't have all the facts.

Eleazar's wife, Arielle, has been having trouble getting pregnant and carrying to term. Several rounds of IVF and just as many miscarriages has Eleazar desperate for an heir—me. She's jealous and heartbroken that she can't give him the only thing he wants—a baby.

When I showed up to talk to Eleazar and learned that his plan was to use me as a pawn, I knew I messed up. Especially once he stuck me in a room and said I wouldn't be going anywhere until this all got sorted. At the time, I thought that was the worst that could happen, until Arielle showed up. She told me she was taking me to Eleazar, but she lied. Instead, she took me to a warehouse and said as soon as she gets Sienna, we would both be killed.

Tying up loose ends, she called it.

She left me with the guards and told them they could do whatever they pleased since I'd be dead soon anyway.

Sienna begged me not to go talk to him.

Micah said he'd handle it.

I didn't listen.

I left without them knowing, thinking I could fix it.

But now, I'm broken.

"Sienna!" I yell, throwing myself at my sister. I notice her hands are tied behind her back, so I quickly untie the rope to release her. "I'm so sorry," I cry. "I never should've gone to see him. I'm so sorry." Tears race down my face, hating myself for not listening to my sister when she told me not to go to him. "I'm so sorry. I'm so—"

"Shh, it's okay," she coos, wrapping her arms around me. It only makes me hate myself that much more because she's always so forgiving. It doesn't matter what I do, she loves me unconditionally. "It's okay."

She rubs her hands up and down my arms trying to calm me, but I can't be calmed. The visions of what the men did to me, what they took from me, are in the forefront of my mind. I can still feel them—

"Who is she?" Sienna asks, knocking me from my thoughts.

"Eleazer's wife," I tell her.

I spend the next several minutes apologizing for what I've done—what I've gotten us into—while she assures me it's all going to be okay because Micah will get us out.

After a while, she gets up to check out the room, trying to open the single window. It doesn't budge. I already tried.

I'm lost in my own head when out of nowhere, Sienna runs to the corner and throws up.

"Are you okay?" I whisper, praying the guards don't come in. When I dry heaved earlier, the acid roiling in my belly and needing to come up, they came in to check on me and took it upon themselves to teach me a lesson for soiling the ground. The last thing I want is for them to teach Sienna a lesson.

"Yeah, something smells rancid," she says.

"Like death," I tell her. The guards told me this is where they take care of people who are a problem. This is probably where our mom died, and unless a miracle occurs, this is where we'll die.

"Hey, El, did anyone—"

Before she can finish her question, she's throwing up again and again. I don't know what's wrong with her, but it can't be good. And when I ask her what's wrong, she shocks the hell out of me when she says, "I'm pregnant." She closes her eyes and lays her head against the rough wall. "I only just found out."

It takes a second for the words to wrap around my brain, but once they do, I start to freak out. "What?" I gasp, wishing it weren't true. "No...No. No. No." I shake my head, fresh tears gliding down my cheeks. "I did this. This is all my fault. I went to go see him and now—"

Now my sister, who's pregnant with my niece or nephew is going to die. She'll never be able to give birth, raise her baby. I've taken away her happiness because of my stubbornness. I should've listened to her.

"Hey, stop it," she says. "You couldn't have known. Don't worry, we'll get out. Micah will find us."

"No, you don't get it. She's going to kill us. She—"

"Well, aren't you observant?" Arielle says, walking into the room. "You are nothing but a stupid *bastarda* born from a whore." She steps toward me and fists my hair. I should probably fight her, but I just don't have it in me. I've fought and fought and every time I've lost. "You don't deserve anything," she spits. "And I'm going to ensure you never get a dime."

Before she can do anything else to me, Sienna jumps in. "Don't you dare speak to my sister like that." When she gets in Arielle's face, it forces her to let go of me.

"Back up," the guard barks. I glance at him, and shivers wrack my body, remembering what he did to me earlier. "Or I'll have to teach you some manners, the same way I taught your—"

His words are what spur me on. The thought of him doing to Sienna what he did to me. Hurting her and her baby...

"Leave her alone!" I hiss, refusing to let him get near her. She's spent so many years protecting me. I need to protect her. "Don't you touch her!"

"Looks like you haven't learned your lesson," the guard says.

"I've had enough!" Arielle hisses. "Sit down and shut up!" She shoves Sienna backward and she loses her footing, falling to the floor.

It all happens so quickly. Arielle steps toward her, and Sienna curls into a ball, trying to protect her unborn baby.

I snap, grab the gun out of the guard's waistband, unlock the safety, and shoot, refusing to let that woman hurt my sister. My life is already over, but I'll be damned if she hurts the only person in the world who's always had my back, has always protected me.

As Arielle hits the hard ground with a thud, red spreading across the concrete around her, the guard snatches the gun from me and barks out, "What the fuck did you do?"

"Enough!" a loud voice rings out, making us all look at the man who's walked in with his own gun in hand. My biological father. "Give me that gun." The guard nods and hands it over.

The men speak in Spanish for several seconds, and then Eleazar glares at me.

"First, your whore of a mother killed my father. Now, my daughter, my own flesh and blood, kills my wife. I should shoot you dead..." I don't bother to argue because at this moment, I would welcome death, but then, instead of pointing the gun at me, he points it at Sienna. "But I need you, so instead..."

No, he's going to kill my sister!

"Wait, please," I yell. "It's not her fault. I did this. I killed Arielle. She kidnapped me and..." I ramble on, trying to explain what happened, begging him to not take it out on my sister. I'm in the middle of asking to make a deal, saying I'll do whatever he wants if he keeps her alive, when a gunshot rings out, and Eleazar's body hits the ground, landing on his wife's.

A few seconds later, Lincoln enters the room and shoots the guard in the head, taking him down. And then Micah is running straight for Sienna, while Lincoln scoops me up and carries me out of the warehouse. He holds me in his arms the entire drive back to the hotel and continues to hold me once we're back home.

I nuzzle my face into his neck, breathing in his scent, using it to block out everything that's happened. He rubs my arms up and down soothingly, murmuring, 'Everything's going to be okay," and I try with everything in me to replace the guards' touch and words with his.

I know later, the nightmares will come, but for a little while, in Lincoln's arms, I pretend like everything is going to be okay.

Four

ELLIE
PRESENT DAY

"So, why didn't you have sex with him?" Raelyn asks. "You clearly trust him."

"Because I left before I turned eighteen." I found out Eleazar left me everything, making me a multimillionaire. Micah helped me sell off the illegal shit and keep the clean money. For the next three years, I was barely a shell of myself. "I couldn't tell Sienna what happened because she told me not to go to Eleazar. I put her and her baby at risk." Thank God they were both okay, and several months later, she gave birth to the most beautiful baby girl, London. "She would've blamed herself, then tried to fix me," I choke out. "And well, I'm broken, Rae, and no amount of tape or glue can change that."

She wraps her arms around me, and I sigh into her hold. "You're not broken, Ellie. You're just a little banged up."

"Regardless, she doesn't know. Only you do. I left at the end of my senior year and have only gone home a handful of times."

"You should tell her," she says, pulling back and meeting my gaze. "I can see it in your eyes. You hate the rift in your relationship."

"It's better this way. We might not be close, but she's happy, finally living the life she deserves. She has a wonderful husband and two beautiful little girls." I sniffle back a sob that's trying to break free. "Telling her will only make her feel guilty, trust me. She'll shoulder the blame and won't stop trying to fix it. She'll hate herself for not protecting me, even though it wasn't her fault. It was mine."

"Okay, so instead, continue to have a strained relationship with your family." She rolls her eyes. "But that doesn't explain why you never hooked up with Lincoln. He's clearly the answer to your intimacy issue."

"He doesn't see me like that."

"Umm, have you seen yourself? Maybe not when you were fifteen, he didn't. But now, you're twenty-one and hot as fuck. Hell, I don't swing that way, and even I'd fuck you."

I'm laughing at her ridiculousness when my phone goes off. "I better get that."

We get off the floor and I grab my phone to check it. It's Sienna...

SIENNA

Please tell me you're coming home for the holidays.

I text back that I'm not sure if I'll be able to make it, hoping she'll let it go. But of course, she doesn't.

SIENNA

Please, El. The girls made you a special present and want to give it to you in person. They're also in the Christmas pageant at the dance studio. You have to come home and see it. Please. We miss you.

As much as I want to say no, I know if I don't at least make some sort of appearance, she'll never let it go. And I do miss my family.

"Maybe when you go home, you can talk to your sister," Raelyn says, nosily glancing over my shoulder.

"And ruin Christmas? Not happening."

"Well, I'm sure Lincoln will be there, right? You could always ring in the new year with him inside of you." She waggles her brows and I shake my head, typing out a message to Sienna.

ELLIE

I can probably come home for Christmas, but only for a few days. I'm busy since it's my senior year and I'm graduating soon.

The truth is, I have nothing going on right now. Classes are over, and my new ones don't start until January, but thankfully she doesn't call me out on it, instead texting back:

SIENNA

Thank you! We'll take whatever time with you we can get. See you soon. Love you.

"You're not broken," Raelyn says again. "But you do need to figure your shit out. Get help, talk to someone, talk to your sister. Get laid. You're living in denial instead of facing the reality. You and Sienna both survived, but she's the only one truly living." She places her hand on my shoulder. "It's time for you to live."

"AUNTIE ELLIE!" MY ADORABLE FIVE-YEAR-OLD NIECE SHOUTS, running toward me. "I missed you so much. Are you home forever?"

"Home forever?" Brooklyn, my other—just as adorable—three-year-old niece parrots.

"Aww, girls, I missed you." I pull them into a hug and inhale their sweet scent. "I'm not home forever. I'm still in school. But I brought you presents," I say, hoping it'll distract them.

I pull the two packages I brought out and hand one to each of them, and they squeal in delight, plopping onto the ground and tearing the paper open.

"What are you going to distract me with?" Sienna asks, raising a single brow.

"How about a hug?" I offer, opening my arms. She sighs and steps into my embrace.

"I've missed you. Thank you for coming home."

"Of course," I murmur like it's not a big deal. "It's Christmas."

"Look who it is," Micah booms, walking over and pulling me into a hug. "Missed you, kiddo. How's the West Coast?"

"Warm," I half-joke.

"Aww, you saying you don't miss the frigid winters here?"

"I'm saying, the second I stepped off the plane, I almost stepped back on it."

He chuckles then sobers. "In all seriousness, thank you for coming home. Your sister was worried you wouldn't show."

I nod in understanding, but the lump in my throat doesn't let me speak. Not that I'd know what to say even if I could. I had thought about using this time with Sienna to tell her everything, but now that I'm here, I realize that's not a good idea. It's Christmas Eve. The girls are dressed in pajamas with candy canes on them. There's a huge tree in the living room. And the smell of ham and cookies is floating in the air.

Now is not the time.

After the girls finish opening their gifts—princess dresses, heels, and tiaras, since Sienna said they're on a Disney kick and will be going to Disney over spring break—they take off to go change into their outfits before dinner. I head up to the guestroom that used to be my room.

When I first left for college, Sienna refused to change a single thing about it, saying it would always be my room. But when I came home to visit for the first time after being gone for almost a year, seeing my stuff everywhere brought back memories of *that night* and all the nightmares that followed. I packed up and threw everything away and then insisted she turn it into a guestroom. The hurt look on her face isn't one I'll ever forget, but it was for the best because Tesoro isn't my home anymore—it's more like hell.

The thought has me getting emotional and needing to get some air. Since we still have a bit before dinner, I sneak up to the rooftop garden. It's freezing outside, so I grab a jacket, knowing that probably won't help, but once I'm up there, I realize it's almost not needed, because surrounding the couches are heating lamps.

"Your sister said you were coming home," a masculine voice says from behind me. "Figured you'd come up here at some point."

"So, you bought me heating lamps," I choke out, trying and failing to rein in my emotions. No matter how long I've been gone, my feelings for Lincoln Alexander never seem to waver.

"Didn't want you to freeze your ass off," he says nonchalantly.

I turn around and take him in: strong jaw, eyes, the color of melted caramel, black button-down shirt with the sleeves rolled to his elbows. Jeans that mold to his muscular thighs. It's been a while since I've seen him, but he still looks as gorgeous as ever. I do the math...He must be in his mid, maybe late thirties now. I always assumed the older you get, the more your looks deteriorate. Yet somehow Lincoln's managed to get even better-looking with time. *Figures...*

"Everything okay, El?" he asks, stepping toward me.

"Yep," I say robotically, but the way his lips turn down tell me he's not buying it.

"Let's try this again. Everything okay?" He steps closer, and I swallow thickly, wondering how my body will react.

Of course, instead of doing what it usually does—vibrating with nervous energy and dread—butterflies swarm my belly, and my heart picks up speed.

"I'm okay," I say because it's the half-truth. I am okay. I'm alive and safe. I have money in the bank, and I'm only a semester away from graduating. So, yeah, I'm okay. Aside from dreading any man touching me intimately and lacking a relationship with my sister, I'm okay.

He eyes me for several beats then nods. "Your sister misses the hell out of you. Any chance of you moving home in May?"

I swallow hard, not wanting to lie to him. "I'm not sure," I admit truthfully. "Just taking it one day at a time."

Another nod. "You know I'm here if you need anything, right?"

This isn't the first time he's said this. He's told me that several times over the years, especially following the events that went down that day in the warehouse when he carried me out with me clinging to him like he was my lifeline. As I sat, curled up in his arms, he whispered *everything will be okay* repeatedly, and ever since then, every time I see him, he asks me the very same question.

"I know. Thank you."

I settle myself on the couch, and Lincoln turns the heating lamps on, warmth immediately emanating off them. I wonder if he's going to sit with me, but my thoughts are answered when he reaches over, squeezes the top of my shoulder, and then disappears back inside, leaving me alone.

I sit like this for several minutes, getting lost in my own head, breathing in the fresh air that goes untouched by the pollution because we're so far up. Up here, it's easy to miss home. The quiet, easy feel of being close to my family. It's when I'm forced to look at my sister and know that I'm not being completely honest with her that it gets hard. When I think about the way she looks at me, knowing something is wrong but not knowing how to fix it. When I walk down the streets of Tesoro, I'm reminded of the evil that lurks in the shadows. Eleazar might be dead, but his spirit still haunts me. Sometimes, it even feels as though he's watching me. I know that's impossible, that it's my mind playing tricks on me, but it doesn't stop my brain from believing it to be true.

Which is part of the reason why I never wanted to tell Sienna the truth. I thought if I was the only one suffering, then it was for the best. But maybe I was wrong. Maybe if I lay it all out for her, leaving no secrets between us, we can finally start to work past it all. Sure, she'll be hurt, but will it be any worse than the way she looks at me now? And maybe I can shine a light on the demons hiding in my closet and rid myself of them once and for all.

"There you are," Sienna says. "I forgot about this place." She glances around, clearly confused as to how the heating lamps got here, but I don't bother explaining.

"Dinner ready?" I ask, standing.

"Yeah, but umm..." She looks at me with longing in her eyes, and my stomach tightens, hating that it's all my fault. Everything is my fault. "I just wanted to see how you're doing. How school is going. You're always so busy."

"It's going good," I say, skipping over her first question.

"So, are you still planning to move home in May? Because I've been thinking a lot about the studio and you taking over. Micah and I found out we're expecting again and—"

"You're pregnant?"

"Yeah." A warm smile spreads across her face. "We've decided this baby will be the last one." Her hand protectively goes to her still flat belly and flashbacks to the day in the warehouse surface. Her throwing up, Arielle shoving her, Eleazar pointing a gun at her. Afterward, her bleeding and going to the hospital...I can't do it. I can't tell her the truth. It will only upset her, and that's the last thing she needs while she's pregnant. She's happy and deserves to stay that way.

"I don't know if I'm moving back home," I blurt out before I can stop myself. Sienna flinches, and I hate myself even more. "I was offered a job in California," I say, the lie sliding right off my tongue and leaving a nasty taste in its wake.

"Oh."

"If you need to sell the studio, please don't feel like you need to keep it. I bought it for you to do whatever you want with." When I found out I was left Eleazar's estate, the first thing I bought was the studio Sienna and I danced at. It was always our dream to open our own dance studio. The plan was for me to go to college and once I graduated, we would teach together. But then that day happened and everything changed. She had given me so much over the years, and I just wanted to give her something back.

"What? No." She shakes her head, her eyes turning glassy with emotion. "The studio will be here, always. Whenever you're ready to come home, it'll be here. We'll be here." She bridges the gap between us and takes my hand in hers. "I miss you so much. I don't know what's going on, why you continue to push me away, but I'm always going to be here. *Always*. You're my ride or die, and that will never change. Please consider moving home. Even if it's not here with us. Just being close to you again would be amazing."

"I'll think about it," I say, choking up with emotion, wanting to tell her everything, and hating that no matter how much I push, she keeps pulling. But then I remember that she's pregnant, and I can't do it. Stress isn't good for her or the baby.

So instead, I vow to get my shit together. She'll never know what happened—and that's for the best—but if I can just get past my own demons, I can push what happened aside and fix my relationship with her. I can do the one thing she wants and move home. Because she deserves that. Hell, she deserves more than that, but at least this is something I can give her.

Now I just need to focus on fixing my shit. I have five months before I graduate and move back home.

First step: Figure out how the hell to be touched by a man.

"It's not happening." Sienna shakes her head and takes a

sip of her water.

"Well, your name is on the list, just in case," Lincoln says with a shrug.

"List for what?" I ask, clearly walking into the middle of a conversation. After dinner, I spent time with Brooklyn and London, trying to make up for lost time. After we set out the cookies and milk for Santa, I read them a Christmas story before bed. I thought maybe Sienna would be hurt that they insisted it be me and not her, but all she did was smile and say she's glad I'm home.

"Elite is having a masquerade party on Valentine's Day," Sienna says with an eye roll. "And my dear brother-in-law thinks Micah and I should go."

"It's going to be the event of the year," Lincoln says with a smirk. "We recently added a few backrooms."

"Backrooms?" Sienna questions.

"Some places call it a darkroom or a black room," Lincoln explains. "The rooms are pitch black. You can't see anything."

"How would you know who you're having sex with?" Sienna asks.

"If you're there with someone, you'll know, but you won't see them. Instead, you have to rely solely on your other senses: taste, touch, scent...Or you can book it anonymously." Lincoln Grins wickedly. "Nothing hotter than anonymous, no-strings sex."

"I don't need anonymous sex," Micah says, pulling my sister into his side. "I like knowing I'm making love to my wife."

Lincoln groans. "You're missing the point. It's Valentine's Day, and you guys never go out. You're always home, and now with another baby on the way, it's only going to get harder. Have our parents watch the little rugrats while you enjoy an adult night. Pretend you're strangers...Flirt, hookup. Live a little."

"Maybe," Sienna says noncommittally. "We'll have to see how my morning sickness is. With Brooklyn, it was more like night sickness."

"I give up." Lincoln sighs, making Micah and Sienna laugh. "I'm going back to my place. Let me know when Santa comes, so I can come over."

"You watch the girls open gifts?" I ask.

"Of course," Lincoln says, standing and walking over to the door. "I wish they didn't get up at the ass-crack of dawn, but the look on their faces as they open their presents is worth it."

His words make me realize how much I've missed by staying away. I came to visit last year, but it was only for a few days after Christmas, leaving before New Year's.

Once he's gone, I excuse myself to my room to give Sienna and Micah some alone time. While I'm getting changed for bed, my phone goes off with a text from Raelyn asking how it's going. Instead of texting back, I hit call, and she answers on the first ring.

"You fuck him yet?" she asks without so much as a hello.

"Yeah, right under the Christmas tree," I say, sarcasm dripping in my words.

Raelyn laughs. "Damn, talk about unwrapping presents."

"Ha ha," I deadpan.

"In all seriousness, how's it going?"

I sigh and plop onto my bed. "I've decided not to tell her anything."

"El," she groans.

"She's pregnant again and happy, Rae. So fucking happy. Telling her will only open old wounds that she's had a hard enough time closing. I'm not doing that to her."

"So, what are you going to do? Avoid her forever?"

"No, I'm going to figure my shit out once and for all. Then I'm going to move home in May and be the best damn sister and aunt I can be."

"And how are you going to do that?"

"The masquerade party."

Five

ELLIE
SIX WEEKS LATER

"This is a mistake."

"No, it's not," Raelyn argues. "We'll go in, you'll *finally* get laid, hopefully overcome your aversion to being intimate with the opposite sex, and then we'll get out. *And* while I'm waiting for you, I'll hopefully get laid too." She waggles her brows suggestively, and I groan, praying this plan doesn't come back to bite me in the ass. In my head, it sounded like the perfect plan: show up, have anonymous sex with a guy I trust, and then leave. But now, as we walk toward Elite, a million thoughts are plaguing my mind.

"What if I can't do it?" I stop and look at Raelyn, my heart pounding behind my ribcage. "What if I freak out? It's anonymous sex because it's in a dark room. What if all I see are those men who—"

"Stop," Raelyn says gently. "We've talked about this. You'll focus on his voice, his scent. And you'll take charge, insisting on being on top so it's all in your control."

"Okay, right, yeah." I nod nervously.

"It'll be okay, and if it's not, you'll get out of there, and I'll be right outside the door waiting for you."

"And what about you getting laid?" I lift a brow.

"You know I was only joking," she says with a pointed look. "We're here for *you* and I have your back."

"Thank you." I glance behind me and take a deep breath. "All right, let's do this." We both put on our masks and walk around the corner toward the entrance of the underground sex club. "And don't forget you're me," I remind her. "And I'm Sienna." If we're questioned, I know enough about my sister to bullshit my way out of it, and Raelyn knows enough about me. But my hope is that once I flash Sienna's ID, they won't ask for mine, so it'll be as if I was never here.

I hand the bouncer Sienna's license that I swiped out of her wallet on our way out, when I told her we were going to watch a late Broadway show in the city. Despite her being surprised to see me visiting so soon after my last visit, she was so excited to see me again, she didn't question it.

"She's with me," I tell the bouncer when he glances from me to Raelyn. "My husband should be here soon." I'm lying through my teeth—the kids are with their grandparents, so Sienna and Micah can enjoy a romantic Valentine's Day at home—but I just need the lie to stick long enough to do what I came here to do. If all goes as planned, I'll get in and out without anyone ever knowing I was here—or questioning if Sienna was ever here.

"Sounds good," the bouncer says. "Have a nice evening, Mrs. Alexander."

As we walk through the club toward the bar, I keep an eye out for Lincoln. Because there's no way to recognize someone with their mask on, I snuck into his place earlier today and snapped a picture of his mask, so I'll be able to recognize it. Thankfully, it was on his desk, in his home office. Otherwise, I'd be going at this blind, and that would not be good.

We do a couple laps around the club, and a few guys eye us, but we don't give them a chance to approach. The club is filled with various shades of black and grey with a hint of red throughout, giving it a mysterious yet sensual vibe. There are lounge chairs and couches in various locations, making the area feel spacious yet intimate. Everyone is wearing masks, but a lot of them are only covering the minimum, so you can sort of see what their face looks like. Raelyn and I both went simple in little black dresses, unsure what the vibe would be, and I'm glad we did, because while a few went for a dramatic vibe, most are dressed in various sexy dresses—the men sporting suits.

I check the main area, then walk down a few hallways that are open and lead to different rooms and a couple of small bars. I'm about to suggest we get a drink at the main bar and wait, when I spot Lincoln strolling through, wearing the silver mask I saw— his tie matching.

"That's him," I murmur to Raelyn, nodding toward Lincoln. Even if I hadn't seen what his mask looked like earlier, I'd still be able to recognize him. I spent years watching him, crushing on him. And even with me away, Sienna posts pictures of him all the time when they're at family functions that I miss. "He's heading toward the bar."

"Good luck," she whispers over the music. "And remember, I'll be close by. If anything changes and you can't do it, I've got your back."

I wait for Lincoln to have a seat at the bar and order a drink before I sidle up next to him, having a seat and playing it off like I don't notice him.

When the bartender asks what I'd like, I debate whether I should order something alcoholic, but figure one drink won't hurt and will hopefully lessen my nerves a bit.

"A mojito," I tell her, going with a drink I normally wouldn't choose just in case. Lincoln and I have never hung out where there's alcohol involved, but I'm not chancing ordering my usual—whiskey sour—since Sienna is the one who put me on to it.

While I wait for my drink, I focus on calming my heart rate. With Lincoln next to me, I'm suddenly having a *"what the fuck am I doing?"* moment.

There's a part of me that feels guilty for concealing my identity from Lincoln and seeking him out for anonymous sex, but the other part of me justifies it because, if by some miracle I pull this off, it will be completely consensual. Still, it feels deceitful.

It'll just be one time and then we'll go our separate ways, I tell myself.

"A duck?" a masculine voice asks, forcing me out of my thoughts.

I glance at Lincoln, who's looking at me. "Huh?" I say dumbly, mesmerized by his hazel eyes that are shining bright against the silver mask that covers the top half of his face, exposing his full lips and clean-shaven jawline.

"A duck," he repeats, nodding toward where I was absentmindedly creating an origami duck out of my napkin, a nervous habit I picked up when I was younger.

"Quack, quack," I say, pretending the duck is real because apparently, I've lost my damn mind.

Lincoln eyes me for a moment and I worry I've already fucked up—I'm attempting to talk lower to disguise my voice without sounding like an idiot, but I have no clue how intuitive he is—when a smile spreads across his face, his eyes light up with mirth, and he throws his head back in laughter.

"I don't think I've ever seen you here before," he says once he's stopped laughing.

"How would you know?" I shrug. "I'm wearing a mask." It's a black and gold gorgeous Venetian cat mask. It hides most of my face, leaving only my eyes and lips on display. I've given myself smoky eyes to blend with the mask, creating a dark, mysterious feel, and my lips are painted a dark red matte, outlined to look plumper than what they are. On top of that, when I went in for a haircut yesterday, I added caramel highlights to my hair, something I've never done before. As long as Lincoln's known me, my hair has always been one color—brown—and I almost never wear makeup, especially lipstick as bold as what I'm wearing tonight.

"Very true," he says, "but as the owner of this establishment, I make it a point to get to know my guests, and I would've remembered that duck...and those green eyes."

My eyes. Oh, shit. I should've worn colored contacts. What the fuck was I thinking? Luckily, based on the way he's running his gaze over my body—his eyes that were just filled with laughter, now full of desire—he must not recognize me. Because if he knew these green eyes belonged to his much younger sister-in-law, he wouldn't be checking me out the way he is.

"I've only been here a handful of times," I tell him, trying to be as honest as possible.

The bartender sets my drink in front of me, and I take a sip, relishing in the way the alcohol slides down my throat and warms my insides.

"Are you here with anyone?" Lincoln asks, his eyes trained on my face—well, my mask.

"Nope," I reply. "I'm new to all this. It makes me...nervous," I say, my words true. "But with the anonymity tonight's event brings, I'm hoping to meet someone."

"What do you think about Elite so far?"

"I think—" I lock eyes with him, trying to up my seduction game since my time is limited "—it has potential."

A small smile quirks in the corner of his lips, and I wonder how this man has managed to avoid being tied down. Somehow, he's managed to only get better looking with time.

"We'll have to see about turning that potential into life changing."

That's what I'm hoping for, I think but don't say. "And how would *we* do that?" I ask, taking a sip of my drink as I turn toward him, so my bare knee rubs against the side of his leg.

He does the same, and because we're so close, when his knee slides past mine, he's able to capture my leg in between his own. My insides warm at the way we're connected, and when he reaches over and snags a lock of my hair, twirling it around his finger, that warmth morphs into a fire.

"First, you can start by telling me your name," he says.

I thought about this ahead of time, knowing this question would be a possibility. "Liz," I tell him, using a piece of my name.

"Liz," he repeats. "I'm Lincoln. It's very nice to meet you."

I smile softly, wishing that I were here under different circumstances. Wishing I was older and had a chance with Lincoln. When I was younger, I would fantasize about what it would be like to have his attention like this. And now that I have it, instead of enjoying it, I'm freaking out, praying that I can simply get through what I came here to do. Knowing that if tonight somehow happens, it'll be the only time I'll ever be with Lincoln like this.

Lincoln glances over my shoulder, and my heart drops, assuming he's found someone he'd rather speak to, until he stands and extends his hand. "Dance with me?"

Butterflies swarm my belly as I take another large sip of my drink before I stand and put my hand in his. "I'd love to."

He guides us over to a corner of the club and, as if everyone knows exactly who he is, they part, giving us plenty of room. The music playing is a sexy remix with a good beat. Lincoln reaches out for me, his fingers landing on the curves of my hips, and pulls me close, so our bodies are almost touching.

I wrap my arms around his neck, and we sway to the music, our eyes locked on each other. The song playing transitions into another, and then another. I couldn't tell you how many songs we dance to, or which songs are even playing. Time seems to stand still, everyone else disappearing, leaving only Lincoln and me and our bodies moving and grinding in perfect rhythm with one another.

Lincoln pulls me close, so our bodies are flush, and runs his nose along the curve of my neck, only the tip grazing my flesh. "Vanilla," he murmurs, getting my signature scent correct. "You smell delicious."

We dance like this for several songs, neither of us speaking, instead, allowing our bodies to do the talking. But then a gentleman taps Lincoln on his shoulder and whispers something into his ear, and I'm reminded of where we are.

Lincoln nods once and the gentleman walks away, and then his eyes are on me. He opens his mouth, and I hold my breath, hoping whatever he was told won't affect the chemistry that's sizzling between us, but then his eyes glitter with regret, and I know he's about to walk away.

He gently shakes his head, and I want to beg him to tell me what he was about to say. But before I can get a word out, he bridges the tiny gap between us that he created when he was tapped on the shoulder and leans in, his masculine scent wrapping around me like a warm blanket on a cold night.

I stay still, waiting to see what he's about to do, knowing deep down, this is the end. He's about to tell me goodbye and walk away. I can feel it.

His warm lips press against the sensitive spot just below my ear, and my entire body reacts in the best way possible. With other guys, being touched filled me with dread, but right now, *his* touch is causing my belly to tighten and the area between my legs to clench. My nipples are hardening, and my heart is beating rapidly behind my ribcage.

"I'm sorry," he says softly into my ear, forcing my eyes to flutter shut in disappointment. "I have to go, but I *really* enjoyed this dance." And then he's gone.

A few seconds later, I open my eyes and glance around, and it's as if he was never here. I stand frozen in my spot, until Raelyn joins me.

"Holy shit, you guys were so hot together," she says. "I thought flames were going to explode from your bodies."

"Not hot enough, apparently," I say, my body still buzzing with electricity.

"Wait, he left?"

"Said he was sorry and that he had to go but he enjoyed dancing with me." I release a harsh breath. "Let's get out of here."

Raelyn's brows shoot up to her forehead. "Seriously? You're leaving, just like that? Maybe he had to take care of something and will be back. What if—"

"I can't do this," I blurt out. "It's for the best that he walked away."

"Why? Did he make you feel uncomfortable? If you're not ready—"

"No, no." I shake my head. "He made me feel the opposite. I've never felt this turned on in my life." After what I went through, I thought the idea of sex would always turn me off...Until now.

"Okay, then why the hell aren't you going after him?"

"Because this was a stupid idea. I spent years crushing on him and then several more years making it a point to get over him. I accepted that there would never be anything between us—that our relationship would always remain platonic. But tonight proved otherwise. The way he looked at me, with heat and desire in his eyes." I sigh, wishing I could've snapped a picture and captured that look forever. "If I sleep with him, if I actually go through with it without freaking out, where will that leave me?"

"One step closer to taking your life back," Raelyn says.

"I can't do it. I can't be with him and then walk away. I can't sleep with him and then pretend like it never happened. Let's go."

"How about we go to the bar and have a drink first?" she suggests. "Once we leave, you might not be able to get back in, so let's think about this rationally."

"Fine, but having a drink isn't going to change anything."

We sidle up to the bar and each order a drink. I expect Raelyn to drone on about why I should be chasing after Lincoln, but instead we sip our drinks quietly. When our glasses are both empty, and we've paid our tab with cash, she turns to me and says, "Now that you've calmed a bit, are you sure you want to leave?"

Do I want to leave? No. But is it for the best? "Yes, I'm sure."

Without giving Raelyn a chance to argue, I drop a couple bills onto the bar top to leave a tip and then get off my barstool, pushing through the throng of people who are dancing, flirting, and kissing—some are doing a lot more than that—determined to get out of here. I'm halfway down the hallway, near the entrance, when I run straight into a hard chest that nearly knocks me over. But before I fall on my ass, strong hands grab my hips, keeping me upright.

I'm about to push him off me, but I notice the hazel eyes, strong, clean-shaven jawline, silver mask—Lincoln.

"You're still here," he says.

Maybe I'm projecting, but his words almost sound relieved.

"I'm here."

A couple tries to walk past us, but we're standing in the middle of the walkway, so Lincoln pulls me to the side to get out of everyone's way. I'm not sure where Raelyn is, but I'm assuming she's made herself scarce.

"Everything okay?" I ask.

"What?" His brows crease in confusion, but then he must remember because he says, "Yeah, just a work thing. All part of owning a business."

I nod, and then we stand here, Lincoln's body pressed against mine, our faces only inches apart. I can practically feel the sexual tension rolling off us in waves, but I don't know what to do, what to say. A moment ago, I was telling Raelyn I couldn't do this and was ready to leave. But now, at the feel of Lincoln's body melding into mine, our gazes locked and filled with desire, all my previous thoughts have evaporated.

I want Lincoln. I want to be with him, even if it's just once. I want to know what it feels like to be with a man by choice, a man I'm sexually attracted to. He's the only man—aside from Micah, who's like an older brother to me—that I trust, and I want him to be the first person I freely give myself to. I might not be a virgin because of what those men did to me, but I'll never consider them my firsts.

They took what wasn't offered.

I want to give myself willingly to Lincoln.

And I know if I don't do it now, in this club, where I have anonymity on my side, it's never going to happen.

"Do you want—?"

"Would you—?"

We both speak at the same time and then laugh at the awkwardness.

"You go first," he murmurs, his lips so close to mine I can smell the smoky scent of the whiskey he was drinking earlier.

"I was going to ask if..." I swallow nervously. I can do this. The worst thing he can say is no.

"If..." he prompts.

"I was wondering if you'd like to join me in a backroom."

His eyes light up. "How do you know about the backrooms?"

Oh, shit. Fuck. Why is he asking me this? Wouldn't every member know about the amenities offered at the club they're a part of?

"I heard someone mention it," I lie, praying he doesn't hear the shakiness in my voice.

He nods slowly. "Must've been a VIP. The backrooms aren't available to everyone yet," he explains. "You know what they're for, right?"

"Yes," I breathe, lifting my leg slightly and rubbing my knee against his groin to let him know how serious I am about this. Even though we're wearing masks, and he obviously doesn't recognize me, being in a dark room will help to ensure that he never does.

Lincoln groans softly, and his eyes burn bright with want. "You sure you're ready for that?"

No. "Yes." I reach out and tug slightly on the top of his dress shirt. "I want you."

"There's something you need to know first. I'm not looking for anything more than one night. What we do in that room is all I can offer you, so if you're looking for more, I'm not the man for you."

I already know this about him. I've heard his conversations with his brother and my sister countless times about not wanting to settle down. He's told them if he meets the right woman, he's not opposed to it, but he's not willing to simply *settle*. So, instead of wasting the woman's time, he makes it clear that he's not looking for anything more than sex. That way she won't be hurt when he walks away—and he always walks away.

"Good," I tell him. "Because that's all I want with you."

He stares at me for several beats, his eyes searching for something...what? I don't know. But when it seems he's found whatever it is he's looking for, he nods once and then takes my hand in his, pulling me down the hall.

And as I follow behind, with my heart beating fiercely in my chest, I say a prayer to whatever sex god is up there that I can get through this. Because if I can't...Fuck, I don't even want to think about how that will go down.

Six

ELLIE

THE ROOM IS DARK. AS I EXPECTED IT TO BE. TO GET INTO THE backroom, we had to walk to the end of the hall and go through a pair of large, black, wooden doors that took us into a darkened area where the music disappeared and was replaced with a low, seductive tune meant solely to fill the silence. We passed several doors and then stopped at door number one. If I wasn't so nervous, I would've made a joke about selecting the prize behind this first door.

Lincoln pulled a keycard out of his pocket and pressed it to the access box. The light turned green, and he opened the door. For a moment, I could see inside the room because of the bit of light coming from the hall, but all I could make out was a bed before we stepped inside, where the room was shrouded in darkness.

My eyes are still adjusting, so I can't see Lincoln, but with his fingers still threaded in mine, I can feel him. He squeezes my hand

and then I'm tugged toward him, my body not stopping until it's pressed up against his own.

"Can I take your mask off?" he asks, running his finger along my jawline.

"No," I say, wishing I could tell him otherwise. "I want this to be completely anonymous."

"All right," he concedes. "What are your hard limits?"

For a second, I'm dumbstruck, wondering why he's asking me that. But then I remember where we are—at a sex club—and since this wasn't planned, and we don't know each other, we don't know what each other is willing and not willing to do.

Shit. I clearly didn't think this through. He owns a damn sex club—of course, he's into kinky shit...and he's going to expect it. Only there's no way I can give him what he wants. I don't even know if I'll be able to go through with sex, let alone allow him to do other things to me.

When I don't respond, he backs up slightly. "If you don't want this..."

"I do," I choke out, "but...I'm new to all of this. My prior experience wasn't—" I swallow nervously, unsure how the hell I can explain to him what's going through my head.

"Wasn't what?" he prompts.

"It wasn't good," I tell him truthfully. "That's why I'm here. I want to be with someone who knows what he's doing. Who will show me what good sex feels like, and then, like you, I want to walk away." I release a sigh of relief at having told him the truth. He may not know it's me, but at least I was honest with him as much as I could be.

When he doesn't say anything right away, I worry he's going to walk away—and I wouldn't blame him. This isn't what he was expecting at all.

But then he gently pushes me backward until my back hits the wall, and his breath feathers across my face. "If there's anything you don't like, you need to speak up. Tell me. Being in the dark means I can't read your features, and sometimes our bodies and minds don't react the same."

"Okay," I breathe, realizing this is happening. I'm about to have sex *willingly* for the first time, and it's with Lincoln fucking Alexander.

With his fingers still linked with mine, he raises our hands above my head, forcing my face to tilt to the other side. With my neck exposed, he places an open-mouthed kiss to the sensitive spot just below my ear and then trails more kisses along my heated flesh, across my jaw, and then places one more to the corner of my mouth. My entire body shivers in response, and he chuckles darkly at my unbridled reaction.

"Tell me what was bad last time," he whispers against my lips, "so I can make sure it's better this time."

"Everything," I croak out, not wanting to relive what happened to me years ago, wanting to stay in the moment with Lincoln. "Please," I beg, "just make it feel good...make *me* feel good."

At my words, his mouth connects with mine. The kiss is firm yet gentle. Hard but still somehow soft. Our lips curl around each other, moving in tandem. Lincoln's tongue seeks entrance and I welcome him, sighing into the kiss as we taste one another. I wasn't sure how it would work with us both wearing masks, but they do nothing to deter the way we want each other.

All we're doing is kissing, but it feels like so much more. My body is on fire, the apex of my legs is clenching with want, butterflies are swarming my belly, and my heart is racing in the best way possible. I've never felt like this before, and it gives me hope that I'll be able to get through this without freaking out. That the trust in him is enough to make me feel safe with my emotions.

I'm so lost in my thoughts that I don't realize the kiss has ended until I hear Lincoln whisper into my ear, "You taste so good. Can I find out if you taste as good everywhere?"

Oh, fuck. "Yes." I nod frantically, even though he can't see me.

He unlinks our hands, and his touch disappears, reappearing seconds later with his fingers skating down my arm and stopping at my breast. He pulls down that portion of my dress, along with my bra cup, and exposes my nipple. The cool air causes the peak to harden, and when his wet tongue circles the tip and then sucks, I let out a heady moan, my eyes closing as I relish in the pleasure.

Big mistake.

The second my lids close, and Lincoln bites down on my nipple, images of *that night* surface.

The force.

The begging.

The agony.

The pleading.

I try to push the flashbacks away, but they're too strong, feel too real. Every ounce of pleasure is replaced with the memory of pain. My moans are on the verge of morphing into a cry for help.

I'm about to tell him to stop, that I can't do this. But before I can get the words out, a husky yet gentle voice is at my ear. "I've got you, Kitten. Focus on me, on the pleasure I'm giving you. You're in control here." And then his tongue is back on my nipple, licking and sucking.

I release a calming breath, doing as he said, focusing on him, on the pleasure, reminding myself that I'm in control and if I want him to stop, he will.

With those thoughts, my body relaxes. I'm back in this room, with Lincoln, in the moment. It's the first time I've made it through a flashback, and I want to cry in happiness. But instead, I drag my fingers through his hair and tug on his head gently. I can't see him, but I can feel his eyes on me.

"Thank you," I whisper.

I don't know how he knew what was going through my head—and maybe he didn't. Maybe he could *feel* the change in my body—but in this moment, I know I did the right thing by coming here tonight. Trusting him with my body and mind.

Lincoln responds by pulling the other side of my dress and bra down and giving my other breast attention. I run my fingers through his hair as he removes my clothes and works his way down until he's pressing a soft kiss to my lace-covered mound.

"Fuck, you smell like vanilla here too," he murmurs. "Can I taste you now?"

"Yes," I breathe, wanting nothing more than for him to put his mouth on my body some more.

Once he's removed my panties, he lifts my leg onto his shoulder and starts to lick my center. He focuses on my clit, gently massaging circles on the swollen nub, and I let out a loud groan, loving the way his tongue feels on me. I've used a clit stimulator many times to get myself off, but it's never felt like this. Soft yet firm. A slow climb higher and higher. The more he licks, the wetter I get. I can feel my orgasm cresting, but my body is fighting it, fighting the pleasure, as my mind wars with itself.

Pain. Pleasure.

Screams. Moans.

Fear. Trust.

"C'mon, Kitten," Lincoln says, pulling me back into the present. "Come for me. Let go, and come all over my face."

His words are my undoing. My body relaxes, allowing the pleasure to dominate, as the most intense orgasm takes over my body, waves of pleasure washing through me.

I've barely come down from my climax when I'm lifted and carried over to the bed. My back hits the soft mattress, and Lincoln's mouth presses against mine. I revel in the taste of him, of the taste of *me* on him. I'm not sure when his clothes came off, but when he spreads my legs and begins to guide himself inside me, my hands wrap around his neck, the feel of his naked flesh under my fingertips.

He continues to kiss me, devour me, consume me, as he slowly enters me inch by delicious inch. I haven't had anything inside me since *that day*, so it hurts, stings. To drown out the pain, I try to focus on Lincoln, on his scent, his taste, the way he's kissing me, but I fear that my haunted past will continue to prevail by overshadowing the present.

I keep my eyes open, even though I can't see anything, and pretend I can see his face. His strong jaw and Roman nose. His hazel eyes and his boyish, playful smile. It's one of the things that drew me to him. His smile. He's always happy, never lets anything bring him down. He doesn't stress, let's everything roll off his back.

Lincoln must feel the tension I'm emanating because he slows down, allowing me time to adjust to him as my body fights against itself.

"Breathe," he murmurs against my lips. I do as he says, sucking in a harsh breath and then releasing it slowly. "That's it," he coaxes. "Fuck, you're so tight. You feel so good."

I wish I could say the same—that he feels good—but right now, all I feel is pain.

I continue to breathe through it, though, trusting in him to make this good. A couple months ago, I couldn't even make out with a guy without freaking out, but tonight, I've already experienced my first orgasm that wasn't self-induced. So, I'll take that as a win.

When he's all the way in, he starts to move. Little by little the pain begins to morph into pleasure as something deep inside me starts to build. My legs wrap around Lincoln's waist, and he cradles me protectively in his arms. I pull his face back down to mine, needing to taste him, smell him. I need him surrounding me—in me, on me, all over me.

My release hits me hard, my entire body trembling as I scream out in pure ecstasy. Without meaning to, my eyes close, but instead of flashbacks hitting me, all I see is Lincoln.

Kissing me.

Touching me.

Consuming me.

I'm not sure if the force of my orgasm causes me to black out, but when I come down from my high and open my eyes, Lincoln is no longer on top of me.

I lie here for several seconds in the quiet darkness, wondering if I dreamt the entire thing, but then I hear shuffling. A moment later, there's a dip in the bed, and strong hands are spreading my thighs. I jump at his touch, and he chuckles softly as warmth touches between my legs.

A washcloth. He's cleaning me up. Taking care of me.

As he gently wipes me down, I choke up with emotion. I'm not sure why, after everything that's taken place tonight, but the idea of him caring for me like this feels more intimate than anything else he's done to me.

I swallow down my emotions and blink back my tears, refusing to lose it now. Later, when I'm alone, I'll allow myself to let go. To remember. Lincoln has no idea what he's done for me tonight, but I'll forever be grateful to him for giving me my intimacy back. Without realizing it, he's replaced the most horrid memories with pleasurable, treasured ones.

When he's finished cleaning me, I assume we're going to get dressed and leave, so I'm shocked when he climbs onto the bed and lies next me. His strong arms pull me into his side, and he whispers into my ear, "Tell me I can have you again because once wasn't enough."

And because what he did to me felt so good, because I know this is the only time that I'll be able to have this with him, I can't help but say, "Okay," so we can do what we just did all over again.

"If you could wish for one thing, knowing it would come true, what would it be?"

"Peace," I answer without hesitation. Because all I want is to be at peace with myself, much like how I feel right now, lying in this bed with Lincoln. I don't want this feeling to end, and I know it will once we walk out the door. "What about you?" I ask in return.

After the first time we had sex, we laid in bed and talked about life and love and everything in between. I worried he'd recognize my voice, despite me disguising it, but I think because he was too caught up in the moment, the thought that it could be me never crossed his mind.

Once we were both rejuvenated and ready for round two, Lincoln brought me to orgasm once again before he flipped me onto all fours. A flashback hit me hard, but he immediately felt me tense up and instead rolled to his back, pulling me on top of him and giving me a sense of control. With his help, I brought us both to another orgasm, and after he cleaned me up again, we lied back in bed and proceeded to play a form of twenty questions.

At some point, we're going to have to call it a night, but if he's not ready to do that yet, I'm okay with prolonging the inevitable. With each new joining of our bodies, a piece of me is put back together. I might still be a bit battered and bruised on the inside, but I can honestly say that I'm not the same broken girl that walked through the doors of this club tonight.

"For you to let me inside you again," Lincoln says in response to my question.

"Well, then," I tell him, rolling over so our eyes lock. "Your wish is my command."

Seven

LINCOLN

AT TWELVE YEARS OLD, I KISSED A GIRL FOR THE FIRST TIME. We were at the movies, and I leaned in and pressed my mouth to hers. I was young, but even back then I could appreciate how soft her lips were. The way our lips curled around one another. The way she moaned into my mouth, urging me for more. We spent the rest of the time making out, and when the credits began to scroll up, I couldn't tell you what the movie was about.

At fourteen, I got my cock sucked for the first time. It was in the locker room at school before football practice, and even though I didn't last long—shooting my load straight down her throat about a minute after she started—the feel of her warm mouth on me as I chased my orgasm was one of the best highs I'd ever felt.

At fifteen, I fucked a girl for the first time. I had snuck into her room while her parents were asleep. She was a little older and more experienced, and I never told her I was a virgin. The kissing lasted longer than the sex itself, but during those few short minutes when I was inside her, I can remember being amazed by the way our bodies connected on such an intimate level.

At sixteen, I got my first taste of pussy. When she suggested that I go down on her, I had no idea what I was doing, and it took forever—as well as her guidance—before she orgasmed. But when she did, when her entire body shook and she came all over my sheets on my bed and my mouth, I felt like I had been given a superpower. Pizza had always been my favorite food, but after that day, pussy became my new favorite thing to eat.

With every new experience, I fell deeper in love with the opposite sex. The female body is beautiful. Thin, thick, curvy, toned...blonde, brunette, redheaded. Large breasts or small. I don't have a preference. I've been with damn near every type of woman, and I appreciate them all in their own way.

It's why I opened Wanderlust and Elite. Because I love women. Their soft lips, feminine curves, their sweet scent, the sounds they make when they come. Some people are addicted to cigarettes, drugs, food, alcohol. My addiction is women, and I have no problem owning it.

Whether it's dancing with them, talking to them, watching as they come all over my cock or my fingers or mouth, I can't get enough of them.

It's also why I never understood how my brother could get married to Sienna, chaining himself to one woman for the rest of his life. Don't get me wrong. She's a cool woman, and I love her like a sister. My nieces are adorable, and I love being an uncle. But why would I ever want to be stuck eating the same food for the rest of my life when I could have a variety?

At least that's what my mindset was...Until now.

As I sit on the edge of the bed, watching the silhouette of the woman I just spent hours with get dressed, for the first time ever, I don't want to say goodbye.

We've had sex three times. I've tasted her sweet cunt just as many. But it's not enough. I want more. I want her to take her mask off and let me turn on the lights. I want to see every inch of this woman that I've spent the past few hours touching, kissing, caressing, worshipping.

Normally, when the night comes to an end, I have no problem walking away. But there's something about this woman that's calling to me. And I have no idea what to do about it.

I can't blame it on not knowing what she looks like because I've had plenty of anonymous sex and had no issues walking away afterward.

Maybe it's the mystery behind her reason for coming tonight: wanting to replace a horrible experience with a good one. Though, I know damn well I rose to the challenge, and she's leaving here completely satisfied.

I don't know. I can't put my finger on it, and it's driving me nuts. My brother once said he knew Sienna was *the one* the first time that he laid eyes on her, and I thought he was fucking insane, but right now, I'm thinking maybe he wasn't so crazy after all because something deep inside of me is telling me not to let this woman walk out that door.

"Thank you for tonight," Liz says softly, her husky voice breaking through the fog of my thoughts. "I had a really good time."

Her silhouette moves toward the door, and I get up and meet her there, my hand landing on hers as she reaches for the doorknob, preventing her from turning it. I've already asked her to take her mask off, but she said no. I asked if we could turn the lights on, but she refused. I can't adequately describe the sensation settling over me, but there's a weird feeling of desperation that's vibrating through my body, making me jittery, like an addict who needs his fix—despite having had this woman several times tonight.

"Stay with me," I murmur, my front pressing against her back.

"I can't," she says apologetically, almost as if she wishes she could say yes.

"Can I have your number?" Fuck, I've seriously lost my shit, but I don't even care. The thought of never seeing her again is driving me senseless.

"You're the one who said you're not looking for anything more than one night," she points out, throwing my earlier words back in my face.

She's right. She's so damn right, but..."I've changed my mind."

"I'm sorry," she mutters, "but I have to go."

And with those words, I back up and watch as the first woman I've ever wanted something more from walks out the door and out of my life.

"I've stopped by the club every damn day but nothing. If she's returned, it's not when I've been there." It's been over a month since Valentine's Day—six weeks to be exact—and I can't get the woman off my mind. I even checked the cameras to zoom in on her, but with the mask she was wearing, the only thing I have to go off of is her brown hair with blonde highlights, green eyes, and full, kissable lips. I did notice she has a tattoo on the inside of her wrist, but I couldn't make out what it was.

Pretty much, I have zilch, so I doubt I'll ever see her again.

"Never thought I'd see the day," Micah says. "My baby brother is in love."

I roll my eyes and take a swig of my beer, focusing on the basketball game that's on the screen. It's Sunday, and I'm hanging out at my brother's place watching the game while Sienna cooks dinner.

"Did I just hear Lincoln's in love?" Sienna asks, setting a bowl of chips on the table along with some dip. She's got the phone pressed to her ear, obviously talking to someone, but she's looking at me, waiting for an answer.

"He's in full-on stalker mode," Micah says with a smirk.

"I'm not stalking," I correct with a glare. "I'm searching for her."

"You hear that?" Sienna says to whoever is on the phone. "Stalking must run in the family."

"That better not be my mom you're talking to," I hiss. The last thing I need is for her to get it in her head that I'm looking to settle down. The minute I turned thirty she started giving me shit and hasn't stopped. It's not that I'm unwilling...I'm not a commitment-phobe like she thinks. I've just always been content with my life and haven't seen any reason to settle down. If someone wants to get married, good for them. If they want to settle down and start a family, that's great. I've just never had the desire...Until now.

Fuck, this is so stupid. I don't even know what the woman looks like. Under that mask could be a fucking alien for all I know.

But she smells sweet like vanilla and tastes even better. Her lips are soft, and her skin is creamy. And when I'd make her come, she'd release the sexiest moan.

Nope, definitely not an alien.

"I'm not talking to your mom." Sienna giggles. "Though, they are on their way with the girls, so if you don't want her to know, make sure you don't talk about this mystery woman when they're here."

"So, if you're not in love," Micah says, "why are you searching for her?"

"The woman from Valentine's Day," Sienna says to whoever is on the phone.

"Sienna, stop telling people my business," I bark, which only makes her roll her eyes.

"It's just my sister," she says. "Now answer Micah's question. Why are you searching for this woman? What was her name again?"

"Liz." Or Kitten, as I called her due to the Venetian cat mask she was wearing. "And I'm searching for her because..." I scrub my hand over my face, fully aware that what I'm about to say is going to sound insane. "Because I think she might be the one."

"What?" Sienna gasps. "What do you mean *the one*? Like the woman you want to spend your life with? How could you possibly know that after one night?"

"Micah knew you were the one after only seeing you once," I point out.

"He's not wrong." Micah shrugs.

"Yeah, but you don't even know what she looks like," Sienna argues.

"Doesn't matter," I tell her. "I know what I felt. When we kissed, when I was inside her…What we experienced runs deeper than looks." When we were lying in bed between rounds to give our bodies time to recoup, we talked, connected on a deeper level.

"Sometimes it feels like my life isn't my own," she whispered in the dark. *"But tonight, you gave me back a part of myself."*

I wanted to ask her what happened, but I didn't want to ruin the moment. So, instead, I pulled her into a kiss, which turned into another round of sex and orgasms.

"Holy shit," Sienna breathes, snapping me from my thoughts. "You really do have feelings for this woman."

"I do," I tell her. "And when I find her, I'm going to make her mine."

Eight

ELLIE

"I'm going to tell him."

"What?" Raelyn asks, confusion marring her features. "Tell who what?"

I've just gotten off the phone with my sister, and I'm in shock. "Lincoln. He's looking for me...well, the woman from Valentine's Day. Remember how I told you he asked for my number, wanting to see me again?" She nods. "He's been looking for her—me. I'm going to tell him I'm her."

I haven't been able to stop thinking about that night since I walked out the door, which was the hardest thing I've ever had to do. But I did it. Because despite Lincoln saying he wanted more, I was scared that once he knew it was me, it would ruin everything. And since that night was without a doubt the best night of my life, I couldn't risk it.

But now, knowing he's been searching for me at the club for

weeks, it's worth the risk if it means I can be with him again.

"Okay, so let me get this straight," Raelyn says. "You snuck into a sex club, pretending to be your sister. Convinced Lincoln to have anonymous sex with you. The same guy who you said would never give you the time of day because he's older and your sister's brother-in-law. And you're planning to waltz in there and tell him you're the one he fucked seven ways to Sunday and is obsessing over and you think he's just going to be like, 'Cool, marry me?' Sure, Ellie, let me know how that goes."

"Well, when you put it like *that*, it sounds bad." I glare at her, ignoring the fact that she might be right. *Okay, is probably right.* "But you weren't there," I argue. "In the room where he made love to me over and over again, worshipping me. Making sure my needs were met and I was satisfied. And you didn't hear him over the phone. He thinks I'm the one."

"He doesn't think *you're* the one," Raelyn says. "He thinks the woman he spent the night with is the one."

"Which is me," I counter. "I didn't lie about anything. We talked and danced and then went into that room and had sex multiple times, and in between the sex, we talked some more. I might've been vague, but I never lied. I need to tell him. It's like fate."

Raelyn shakes her head. "I think you're making a big mistake, but you know I'll support you regardless."

I pull her into a hug. "Thank you. I'm going to book a flight. My sister and her husband are taking the kids to Disney for spring break before she gets too pregnant. It'll be the perfect time to go there and talk to Lincoln without them around."

"Do it after practice," she says. "We need to go, or we'll be late."

I glance at the clock and see that she's right. Even though it's Sunday, we're meeting with our group to go over our routine for the end-of-the-year showcase. With all of us being busy with our final year of classes, we practice several evenings during the week and on Sundays. This showcase is a big deal for many students looking to begin their careers post-college. Since my plan has always been to teach dance with my sister, the showcase is simply my final grade in order to graduate.

"Alright, from the top."

The music starts, and we all move into position. We've been at this for hours, and I'm sweaty, thirsty, and have a splitting headache, but since nobody else is complaining, I keep my mouth shut.

We go through it once more before Miguel suggests we break into smaller groups to go over the transitions. Because the last part of the routine had me on the floor, I stand, but when a bout of nausea hits me, I find myself sitting back down.

"Ellie, are you okay?" Raelyn asks, handing me my jug of water as everyone stops and watches to make sure I'm good.

"Yeah, I think I'm just thirsty." I take a large sip of water and then go to stand again, but when I do, blackness shrouds my vision and I wobble on my feet.

Something's wrong. I don't know what, but I can feel it.

My body is weak, my bones and muscles feel like Jell-O.

I try to open my eyes, but everything is swirling around me, as if the room is spinning. And then everything goes black.

"You have an iron deficiency," the doctor says, "which has led to pregnancy anemia."

I eye him in confusion, wondering what the hell he's talking about. "I'm sorry, can you repeat that?" Because I'm pretty sure he has the wrong patient being that in order to have pregnancy anemia, the person would actually have to be *pregnant*.

His brows furrow. "According to the blood work, you have a severe iron deficiency which has caused pregnancy anemia. Luckily, we've caught it quickly. But I noticed you didn't put down who your obstetrician is, so we'll need to..."

He glances up at me and must see the shock in my features, because his eyes go wide. "You didn't know you were pregnant, did you?"

I shake my head slowly, trying to wrap my head around what he's saying.

I'm pregnant.

I'm pregnant.

Holy, motherfucking shit. I'm pregnant.

"I'm sorry," he says, wincing. "It's been a busy day, and I wasn't thinking." He scrubs his forehead. "Let me start over." He sits in the chair Raelyn just vacated, who left to go find us some food. "According to the bloodwork, you're pregnant."

"Is it..." I clear my throat. "Is it possible you have the wrong patient?" I glance over at his chart. "I'm Eliza Bardot."

He looks down at his chart and back up. "Yes, I have the right patient, and based on your hCG levels, I'm guessing you're probably around six weeks pregnant."

"Okay." I nod emphatically, trying like hell not to freak the fuck out. "Is it possible the tests got mixed up? Like, maybe my bloodwork got mixed up with someone else's and now some poor woman who was hoping to be pregnant has no idea that she actually is?"

The corner of the doctor's mouth twitches, but he has the good manners to keep it in check. "It's possible," he says, "but not likely. However, since you weren't aware of your pregnancy, we can do a transvaginal ultrasound to confirm. How does that sound?"

I nod again as I try to take in what he's saying.

Pregnancy.

Ultrasound.

Anemia.

What the hell is going on? "I thought I was just thirsty," I whisper.

"That's because of the anemia," he says. "You were a bit dehydrated, so we're giving you fluids." He points to the bag of dripping liquid that's flowing into my IV.

"I'll put the order in," he continues, "and then once we've confirmed your pregnancy, we'll discuss the anemia."

Another nod. Still in shock and confused and *what the fuck?*

The doctor leans over and squeezes my hand, smiling softly at me. Then he stands and steps out, leaving me to my thoughts.

I pull my phone out and click on the calendar app, counting back six weeks. Valentine's Day. My period comes the first of the month like clockwork. I had it in February. I remember because when I went to the store to buy tampons, I also bought Raelyn and me some Valentine's Day candy.

Holy shit, Valentine's Day.

Elite sex club.

Lincoln and me.

Three amazing rounds of sex.

Fuck.

I scan my calendar, trying to jog my memory. Did I get my period in March? I don't think I did. I look at the date and see it's now April. I should've gotten it three days ago, but I didn't. I'm staring at my calendar, trying to have this all make sense, when Raelyn walks in.

"They didn't have any muffins, but I got you a—"

"Are you on your period?" I blurt out.

"Umm, yeah," she says, drawing out each word. "Why?"

"I haven't gotten mine."

"Okay..." She looks at me like I'm crazy. "I'm sure it will come—"

"No," I cut her off. "Not this month. Last month. I got it in the beginning of February, but it never came in March, and now it's April, and I always get it the day after you. Always." Our cycles synced halfway through our freshman year of college and ever since they have always been the same.

Her eyes widen, catching on. "You don't think...You used protection, right?"

"No, we didn't. Oh my God, Rae. I'm so stupid. I didn't even think about it. I'm not on birth control because I wasn't sexually active, and deep down, I knew regardless of how many guys I attempted to have sex with, I couldn't follow through with it."

"But you had sex with Lincoln..."

"Three times with no protection."

"Why the hell wouldn't he use protection?" she shrieks.

"I don't know. I don't know how it all works..." Which, in hindsight, was irresponsible of me. "But I do know that every member has to submit a clean bill of health, and women have to show proof that they're on birth control."

I know a little of how Elite is run because I grew up around it. I might not have been in the actual sex club, but I would overhear the adults talking when I would go to Wanderlust, where my sister once worked as a stripper.

"I wasn't thinking," I say out loud. "I was so focused on simply trying to get past my shit, I didn't think about it. And now..." I glance at Raelyn.

"You might be pregnant," she finishes for me.

"According to the doctor, I *am* pregnant, and the reason why I felt nauseous and dizzy and blacked out is because I have pregnancy anemia, caused by an iron deficiency *in pregnant women*."

Her eyes widen in shock. "Oh, shit."

Oh, shit, is right. If the doctor is correct, I'm pregnant...with Lincoln's baby.

⟡

*W*HOOSH, *WHOOSH, WHOOSH.*

Spoiler alert: The doctor was right—I'm pregnant!

I stare at the screen as the ultrasound tech explains that based on my measurements, I'm seven weeks along, and my estimated due date is November twenty-first. Raelyn is holding my hand, and neither of us have said a single word. I think we're both in utter shock. It's one thing to talk about me being pregnant, but it's a whole other to see the fluttering heartbeat on the screen.

But for me, it's more than just shock. I've never known what it feels like to fall in love. For your heart to be completely owned by someone else. As I stare at the little blob on the screen, I've finally fallen...Because my heart has left my chest and now belongs to the baby in my belly.

"What are you going to do?" Raelyn asks once Dr. Gerard has finished discharging me—leaving me with a prescription for prenatal vitamins, an iron supplement, and a recommendation for an OB/GYN.

"I don't know," I tell her honestly.

"If you don't want to have the baby..."

At her words, my hand flies to my stomach protectively. Growing up, my mother never once protected me. Every day I was around her, I was put in horrible situations, and even in her death, she put me in harm's way. If it weren't for Sienna taking care of and protecting me, I can't imagine what my life would've looked like. Even when I didn't listen to her and put myself in danger, she literally risked everything in order to save me.

"This baby might not have been planned, but he will be loved and protected by me," I tell her. "He will grow up knowing what it feels like to have a mother who cares and would do anything for him. I might not be perfect, but I have the money and means to take care of him, and I will love him with everything in me."

Him...I'm having a son. The gender was revealed in the bloodwork, and I wanted to know. The more prepared I am, the better.

"I keep hearing you talk about *you*, but not once have you

mentioned the father," Raelyn points out. "Does that mean you're no longer going home to tell him that you're the woman he's been searching for?"

I shake my head, my heart sinking at the thought. "I can't do it," I tell her. "I'm going to eventually tell him. I would never keep him from his son, but I messed up badly and can't go home like this. He thought he was having sex with a member of the club who was on birth control. He trusted the woman he was with, and she broke that trust. *I* broke that trust."

"So, what are you going to do?"

"I'm going to graduate and spend the summer here. I have until the end of November to figure out how to handle this situation. But I'm not going to force Lincoln to be in this baby's life. He didn't ask for this, and he shouldn't be punished for my choices."

"I wish I could stay," she says softly, "but—"

"Stop, you have an amazing job waiting for you when we graduate." She was hired by a prestigious dance company in Chicago where her family lives. It's literally her dream job. "You have to go. I get it. Luckily, since I own the condo that we live in, I can stay for however long I want."

When my bio dad—Eleazar—died, I inherited his entire fortune. After selling off everything, and donating all the blood money, I was left with a little over two hundred million dollars. Those who know me don't understand why I even bothered going to college. Originally it was because I wanted to major in dance therapy, but when I got here, I wasn't in the right mindset to take classes that would force me to analyze human behaviors— especially since I can barely handle my own on a good day—so I changed my major to dance and spent the past four years dancing my way through school while hiding from my past and home.

"But you're going to tell him, right?" Raelyn presses. "You're going to give him the choice."

"Of course," I tell her. "I just need some time to figure out how to blow his world apart."

Nine

LINCOLN

"I can't find her." I've spent months searching for this woman, but it's as if she doesn't exist. I've gone through every member of the club, starting with the ones named Liz and Elizabeth who attended the masquerade party on Valentine's Day. All the members' cards get scanned when they enter and leave, so it's all timestamped. Normally, her card would've been scanned for the backroom as well, but I fucked up and didn't ask for her card since I have access to everything. Had I asked for it, I wouldn't be where I am: at a fucking loss. Because even after combing through every damn member, I still can't find her, which makes no sense, unless she lied about her name.

"Maybe it's not her you're after," Micah says from the visitor seat in my office. Since we have access to everything electronically, we do the majority of our business at Alexander Enterprises, which is located in downtown Tesoro. "Maybe being with her made you realize you're ready to settle down, but it's not actually her you want." When I hit him with a hard glare, he sighs. "Go on a few dates and see how it goes."

"How is taking some woman to dinner going to compare to being inside my mystery woman?"

"Okay, then fuck someone else and see if it's just as good."

"Not happening," I tell him. I know I sound crazy, but I'm not ready to give up yet. Maybe it's because she's the last person I had sex with, but I can still remember how smooth her creamy flesh felt, still smell her vanilla scent. When I close my eyes, I can feel the way her body fit perfectly with mine. The way she tasted. I always use a condom—always—but that night I was so enraptured by her, I went in raw every single time. It wasn't smart to go without a rubber, but I can't say I regret it because fuck, I can still remember the way her warm, tight cunt wrapped around my cock every time she came. Yeah, it was worth it. Thankfully, when I went and got tested afterward, I was given a clean bill of health.

"What are you two gossiping about?" Sienna asks, strolling in.

"Men don't gossip, they discuss," Micah corrects, making her roll her eyes as she leans down and kisses him on his lips. She attempts to back away, but he pulls her into his lap, making her squeal, and I can't help but smile at how happy they are. Before I spent the evening with my mystery woman, Liz a.k.a. Kitten, I was in no rush to have what they have. I was content with my physical relationships, but now, I want more. I want the closeness, the conversation, the family, and I want it with *her.*

"My bad," Sienna jokes. "What were you two *men* discussing?"

"Your husband was just telling me to get laid and see if her pussy is as good as my mystery woman's," I say, knowing I'm throwing my big bro under the bus.

His eyes widen at the same time Sienna gasps. "Micah!"

"What?" he says with a shrug, playing it off. "He's obsessed over this woman and whining like a little girl. Something needs to give. His mood is killing my vibe."

I chuckle when Sienna playfully slaps his chest. "Could you replace my pussy?" she asks with a laugh as her phone begins to ring and she reaches into her pocket to grab it.

"Fuck no," Micah says immediately, not falling for that trap.

"Exactly," I agree. "I want *her*. Not some cheap knockoff."

"Except you don't know who she is," Micah points out. "So, unless you want to remain celibate for the rest of your life, you're going to have to get back out there. And I've had enough of your crankiness. You need to get laid."

Ten

ELLIE

I'm going to do it. I'm going to tell my sister. She's texted me asking if I'll be home for my birthday or if we should celebrate early, when they come for my graduation. It's been over a month since I found out I was pregnant, and since then, my body has already started to change. My breasts are fuller and slightly sensitive, I have a bit of morning sickness, but thankfully the iron supplement and prenatal vitamins are keeping the dizzy spells away, and my belly is starting to form a little bit of a bump. It's not huge, but since I'm tiny, it's making the changes in my body more prominent.

Because of exams and the showcase, I couldn't fly there like I wanted to, so it has to be over the phone. The longer I wait, the harder it will be. They're flying here next week for my graduation, and the last thing I need is Sienna finding out I'm pregnant before I've told her.

Before I can talk myself out of it, I hit call and a couple rings later, Sienna answers the phone, laughing over the line.

"Hey, sis, how's it going?"

"Okay," I say vaguely. "How are you?"

"Oh, I'm good," she says, cackling. "But Lincoln just showed up and apparently has a broken dick."

"What? Why?" I gasp, wondering what the hell happened, when I know for a fact, it was working just fine a few months ago.

"He's obsessed with finding the mystery woman," she says. "So, Micah told him to go out with other women."

"He told me to *screw* other women!" Lincolns yells over the phone, and I'm momentarily distracted by the sound of his voice. No matter what's going on, he's always smiling and laughing. His voice, while masculine and deep, is constantly filled with happiness. Just listening to him speak soothes me…Until I think about the words he spoke.

He's having sex with other women…Moving on. That's good. This is for the best. If he finds someone else, he'll be too distracted to be pissed when he finds out what I did.

Yes, Lincoln moving on is definitely a good thing…

"Whatever," Sienna says flippantly. "*Screw* other women. He was cranky, so Micah told him to find someone else so he would go back to being his usual happy self. But based on the way he's pouting, I don't think it went well."

"It didn't go at all," Lincoln says. "I'm broken. She broke my dick."

Oh God. This isn't good. When he finds out it was me who broke him, he's going to be pissed. My sister is going to be pissed. Micah is going to be pissed.

"Hey, Sienna," I choke out. "I gotta go."

"What? You just called," she says.

"I know, but…I have to go. I'll call you later."

Before she can argue, I click end on the call and then turn off my phone. My head is resting in my hands as I freak out, when

Raelyn walks in and plops down on the bed.

"What's going on?" she asks.

I raise my head and sigh. Then I explain to her what happened when I called Sienna. When I finish, she says, "Maybe this is a sign."

"A sign? For what? Me to leave the country?"

"No." She snorts out a laugh. "A sign that he'll forgive you. He obviously wants this mystery woman something fierce."

"Yeah, the mystery woman. Not me."

"Maybe he'll be so happy to finally know who the mystery woman is, he'll overlook how it all went down and that she's you."

"No way." I drop my head back onto my pillow and stare up at the ceiling. "Once he knows she's me, he's going to lose his shit. I never should've done what I did..."

But even as I say the words, flashes from our night together hit me, the way he worked my body, making me feel only pleasure. The hours of talking in between. I've never connected with someone on such a deep level.

My thoughts flit to hearing my baby's heartbeat in the hospital, seeing his tiny body on the screen...and I know I don't mean the words I just said. That night changed my life in so many ways, including giving me the baby I'm carrying. He's only been a part of me for a short time, but I already love him something fierce.

"You didn't do anything wrong," Raelyn says.

"I snuck into his sex club, one I'm not a member of, and had sex with Lincoln without being on birth control. Something that's required to be a member. Then, I got knocked up. What part of that isn't wrong?" I feel like we've had this same conversation more times than I can count, and I'm sure she's sick of having it with me, but I appreciate how she continues to support me every time I freak out and debate whether or not I should tell Lincoln and my sister. Raelyn is the definition of a true best friend, and I don't know what I would do without her in my life.

"Okay, well, first of all, even if you had been on birth control, it's not one hundred percent effective, so you still could've been in this position." She shrugs. "And you didn't set out to hurt anyone. You just wanted to feel whole again, and Lincoln is someone you trusted to help fix what was broken. And look on the bright side." Her eyes go wide. "It worked!"

"It worked? It worked?" I splutter, sitting back up. "That's what you're focusing on, Rae? I'm pregnant with Lincoln's baby." I lift my shirt and show her the tiny bump as evidence. "And when my family finds out, they're going to hate me."

"Stop," she chides. "Your sister could never hate you. She loves you. And you need to tell them soon because we graduate next week, and you're supposed to be moving back to Tesoro for good."

"Or maybe I don't move back," I say. "I can tell them something came up and I can't make it to graduation, and I won't be moving back home. I can tell them I took an unexpected job."

"So now you're lying to them?" Raelyn raises a brow. "You can't not tell him, and lying is only going to make it worse. Besides, you already admitted to being completely yourself that night, which means the woman Lincoln fell for is you. That has to mean something, right?"

"It means he's going to be pissed when he learns it was me." I sigh in frustration. "Damnit, I need more time to figure this out. Maybe it's for the best if I stay here. It'll give him time to get over his mystery woman so then he won't feel pressured into being a part of this baby's life once he does learn the truth."

Raelyn nods. "You know I've got your back no matter what you decide."

I spend the night tossing and turning, trying to figure out what to do. Grades close the next morning, and with the credits I've earned, I'm officially a college graduate.

In the afternoon, I go to my three-month checkup where I hear the heartbeat again, which only has me falling even more in love with my baby boy. As I listen to the whooshing sound, I wonder if my mom felt an ounce of the love I feel when she was pregnant with me. And when I think about the answer, I come to a conclusion regarding the matter at hand.

"I'm staying here," I tell Raelyn when I walk through the door. "Lincoln didn't ask for this, and the last thing I want is to force him into fatherhood."

"I understand what you're saying," she says, "but I think you need to leave that up to him."

I place a protective hand over my little bump, remembering how my mom used to treat me. "I was a mistake, Rae, and my mom made sure I never forgot that. I won't put my baby in the same position, risk him being looked at the way my mom looked at me—with regret."

I pull out my phone and send a text to Sienna. I know it'll hurt her but it's for the best.

ELLIE

> Hey sis! Sorry to do this, but I got an amazing job opportunity and had to take it. Unfortunately, that means I won't be able to attend graduation, and because it's for the entire summer, I won't be coming home. I'll call you soon. xo

Within seconds, she responds:

SIENNA

> Was looking forward to seeing you graduate and spending your birthday with you, but I get it. I just want you to be happy. If anything changes, let us know and we'll be on the next flight out. I look forward to hearing about your job, and just know, this will always be your home if you ever change your mind. Love you.

"What'd she say?" Raelyn asks.

"She understands," I mutter. I should be grateful that she's not arguing or asking questions, but somehow her understanding only makes me feel that much worse.

❦

ONE WEEK LATER

"I wish you were here," Raelyn says over Facetime. Today is graduation, but since I told Sienna I couldn't make it, there's no point in going. Walking across the stage won't be the same without having her in the audience.

"Are you at least going to come to the after party?" She pouts, and I roll my eyes.

"I'm pregnant, Rae. I'm tired, hormonal, and I can't fit into half my clothes. The only place I'm going to is the mall to buy some jeans that don't make me feel like I've eaten an entire chocolate cake in one sitting." Mmm...chocolate cake. Maybe I should stop by the bakery on the way and get a slice.

"Fine," Raelyn relents. "But tomorrow is our day. I need to pack Saturday because I leave Sunday to go home."

"You got it," I tell her. "Have a good time. Love you."

"Love you more." She blows me a kiss and then ends the video call.

I drop my phone into my purse, hook it over my shoulder, and then swing the front door open, ready to get out of here and get some clothes that fit and a slice of chocolate cake.

Only when I go to step out, I'm blocked...by my brother-in-law. As I stare at him in shock, trying to make sense as to why he's here, I don't think about the fact that I'm dressed in tiny cotton shorts and an even tinier tank. Not only is it hot as hell here, but I wasn't kidding when I said my clothes don't fit. I'm only a little over three months along, but my belly already has a noticeable bump that makes it hard to wear my clothes that had fit me like a glove before I got pregnant. The second his eyes stop on my belly, I know shit's about to get real.

Never one to beat around the bush, he asks what we both know he's thinking. "Are you pregnant?"

I swallow nervously as my hand instinctually goes to my protruding belly. I should deny it, tell him he's crazy and then slam the door in his face, but there's no point in delaying the inevitable.

"Does your sister know?" he asks when I don't verbally confirm. "Who am I kidding? Of course, she doesn't know," he adds, answering his own question. "If she knew, she'd be all over you...Which is why you haven't told her. Why you canceled our visit for your graduation and said you were taking a job here this summer. Holy shit," he breathes. "You weren't planning to tell her, were you? You were going to keep this from her." He shakes his head, and my stomach sinks at his evident disappointment.

"Who's the dad?" he asks.

His question causes me to panic. I wasn't planning for an interrogation. And I sure as hell can't tell him who knocked me up.

"Ellie!" Micah barks, obviously fed up with my silence. "Who the hell got you pregnant?" If I was considering telling him the truth, the crazy in his eyes would stop me dead in my tracks.

"I-He's not exactly in the picture," I tell him, speaking around the truth.

He stares at me for several seconds and then nods. "You're coming home."

Oh, shit. Fuck. "What?" I say, as my heart picks up speed. "No...I can't. I—"

"Stop," he says, cutting me off. "I don't know what the fuck is going on, but I'm not going to listen to your half-truths anymore. You're done with school and there's no summer job. You're coming home with me now, where your family is, and we'll deal with this together."

"No." I shake my head, my blood pumping so fast I'm slightly dizzy. "I can't. Sienna is going to get upset." I back up slightly. "I messed up, but she's pregnant and shouldn't be stressed." I plead with him with my eyes, begging him not to do this, even though it's futile. "Please, Micah. Pretend like you didn't see me. Please.

I can't go home. Everyone is going to hate me."

"Impossible. You're family. We deal with shit together. The stress of you trying to handle this on your own, hiding it from your sister, isn't good for you or that baby. You've been gone long enough. It's time to come home." He extends his hand, silently telling me to take it.

"Wait," I tell him. "My stuff...I need to—"

"We'll pay someone to pack it up. We're leaving now. Let's go."

The drive to the airport is awkwardly quiet, and the long flight in the private plane is as well. I spend the time I'm not sleeping trying to figure out how to get out of this mess. I text Raelyn to let her know what's happened, apologizing that I won't see her before she leaves. Of course, her only concern is for me and texts that if I need anything to let her know.

The moment we're through the door, Sienna throws her arms around me, ecstatic to see me. "What are you doing here?" she asks, backing up and looking at me with tears in her eyes. Since she's several months pregnant, she's sporting the most adorable bump under her pretty floral sundress.

I'm about to respond, when her eyes, just like her husband's, go to my bump. "Oh shit," she breathes. "Are you...are you pregnant?"

The emotion in her eyes is my undoing, and before I can think about what I'm doing, I blurt out, "Yes, I'm pregnant...with Lincoln's baby." Sienna and Micah gasp, but I don't stop talking, needing to get it all out before they freak out on me. "I'm so sorry. I know I fucked up, but I swear I didn't mean for this to happen, and I'm not expecting anything from him. That's why I wasn't going to come home. I didn't want him to feel responsible. It's not his fault that—"

"Like fuck he's not responsible," Micah barks.

It takes me a second to catch up, and I realize he's pissed because he's assuming Lincoln knew he was sleeping with me. Jesus, I need to explain. This is all such a mess.

But before I can, Micah is storming out of the penthouse, the door slamming open so hard that it damn near falls off the hinges. "Where is he go—?" And then it hits me. Lincoln! Fuck.

Eleven

LINCOLN

"With Rosa having to leave unexpectedly, I'm going to have to look into—"

Bang. Bang. Bang. "Lincoln, open the fucking door!"

"Let me call you back," I say, hanging up without waiting for Lisa to respond—my only concern, my brother.

"Everything okay?" I ask, swinging the door open. I barely get my question out before my brother cocks his fist back and then clocks me straight in the jaw, forcing me to stumble backward.

"What the hell!" I bark, torn between confusion and anger. Micah's been my best friend my entire life, and while we have disagreements, neither of us has ever put our hands on the other.

"You fucked her? What were you thinking?" He stalks toward me and grabs me by my collar, slamming me up against the wall. This time, when he goes to punch me, I'm ready and duck just before his fist connects with my face.

"Stop!" I yell, having no idea what he's going on about. "What are you talking about? Fucked who?"

"Micah, stop!" a feminine voice yells. "Please, don't do this." I glance around my brother and find Ellie standing there with a pained expression etched into her features. "Please, let me explain."

"Explain what?" I ask, confused as hell by what's going on. I didn't even know she was back in town. The last I heard she was staying in California for at least the summer.

"You fucked her," Micah spits, "and now she's pregnant."

"Who?" I ask again.

"Her!" he barks, pointing his finger at Ellie.

I bark out a humorless laugh, because this must be some kind of joke, only the look on Micah's face tells me he's being dead serious.

"Bro," I say slowly, shaking my head. "I don't know what's going on, but I've never touched Ellie." I glance at her briefly. "Tell him. Tell him I've never touched you."

I've known her since she was fourteen and, yeah, we've always had a good relationship, and I care about her, but it's never been like that. Hell, she's fourteen years younger than me.

"Lincoln," she sighs, tears filling her green eyes. "I..."

The regret in her features confuses me. "Ellie, what's going on?"

"Lincoln, stop playing stupid," Micah says. "She might not want to hold you accountable, but you were raised better than that. She's pregnant, and you're the father, and whether you like it or not, you're going to man the fuck up."

"What?" I look at Ellie again. "I don't understand." I step over to Ellie, who's got her arms wrapped around herself and is sobbing softly.

"I'm so sorry," she cries. "This wasn't supposed to happen."

"What?" I ask carefully. "Come and sit down." I take her hand in mine and bring her over to the couch. If what Micah is saying is true and she's pregnant—not by me—it can't be good for her to be this stressed out.

"I'm so sorry," she says again, covering her face with her hands.

"For what?" I ask gently. "Ellie..." I tip her chin up so she's forced to look at me. "What happened? You know whatever it is, I've got your back." When she was younger, I was someone she confided in—school, her sister, asshole guys who didn't deserve her time, her mom—I was even the one who got her out of a shitty situation with her bio dad. But after that day—when she was held captive and almost killed—she started to shut everyone out. I tried to be there for her, but when she moved, and we no longer lived on the same floor in the same hotel, we didn't really keep in touch.

"I'm pregnant," she murmurs, liquid emotion filling her lids, "and the baby's yours."

I freeze, unsure why the hell she's saying this. It makes no sense. I've never been with this woman before, yet she's sticking to this claim.

"Ellie, why are you saying this?" I ask, trying to keep the anger out of my voice. Clearly, something is wrong for her to go out of her way to lie about me being the father of her baby, but she must know by saying this she's causing a shitstorm of issues for me with our family. "Did something happen with the guy you slept with? Did he hurt you?" If he did, Micah and I will no doubt be on the next flight out to kill him.

She shakes her head, and her hand goes to her belly. "The baby is yours. We had sex...on Valentine's Day."

The baby is mine.

We had sex.

On Valentine's Day.

I repeat the words several times in my head, trying to wrap my mind around what she's saying. But it doesn't make any sense because on Valentine's Day I was with...

Green eyes.

Brown hair with caramel highlights.

No. No. No. This can't be happening.

Her name was Liz, not...Eliza.

My hands clench and sweat dampens my palms.

There's no way. She wouldn't...She couldn't.

I try to think...There's no way my mystery woman could be her.

And then I remember the tattoo I saw on the camera. I grab Ellie's left wrist, and on the inside, in script, it reads 'Survivor.'

A tattoo on her wrist, just like my mystery woman.

Fuck. No. This has to be a coincidence. A sick, twisted joke.

But when I look at her face riddled with guilt and regret, and Micah, who's standing nearby, glaring daggers my way, it's clear that neither of them think this is funny.

I stand and back up, needing space. Needing to think. This can't be right. There's no way...I would've known if I was sleeping with Ellie. Right?

But as I stare at her, assessing her features—features of the woman I've been fantasizing about for the past three months—I have no choice but to admit the truth. "I didn't know," I say out loud. "I didn't know it was her."

Micah's eyes alight with fury. "How the—?"

"Stop!" Ellie begs. "He's telling the truth. He didn't know. That's why I didn't want to come home. I messed up, and it's not his fault."

I didn't know, but she did, which means..."How the fuck did you get into my club?"

Ellie flinches. "I pretended to be Sienna."

Jesus, I scrub my hands over my face. This is so messed up. But it also makes sense as to why I couldn't find my mystery woman in the system. And since Sienna is family, not a member, the bouncer would've let her in without scanning her card.

"You're telling me you snuck into my sex club by pretending to be your sister, sought me out, and had sex with me, knowing who I was?"

She nods. "I'm sorry."

"You're sorry?" I bark out a humorless laugh. "You're sorry? Did you think this was funny? Some kind of joke?" I get in her face, my body vibrating in anger. "Did you fuck me with the hope of getting pregnant? Huh? Did you do this on purpose?" The tears that had filled her lids, spill over, but she doesn't answer me, and I need answers because this is bad, really fucking bad. "Answer me! Did you—?"

"Stop it!" Sienna suddenly appears and pushes me back. "Stop yelling at my sister. Can't you see she's upset?"

I bark out another laugh, wondering if I'm dreaming...No, screw that, having a nightmare. Because there's no way any of this can be real.

"You're worried about me upsetting her?" I say, glaring at Sienna. "She pretended to be you to get into my club and then seduced me, so I'd have sex with her without knowing who she was."

Sienna gasps and glances at Ellie. "Is that true?"

"No," Ellie sobs. "I mean, it is, but it wasn't like that." Her cries get harder, and I want to feel bad, but fuck that, she did this. And now her decisions have consequences. "I just wanted to have sex," she blurts out. "I mean..." Sobs now rack Ellie's body as she tries to get words out, but she's crying too hard. Sienna sits next to her sister and wraps her arm around her, comforting her.

"El, talk to us, please," Sienna pleads. "Did you try to get pregnant with Lincoln's baby?"

"No," Ellie chokes out. "I just wanted to know what it would feel like to be with someone by choice. Someone who makes me feel safe. Someone I trust." She glances up at me. "I'm sorry. I tried so many times to have sex with other guys, but I couldn't do it, and Raelyn said it's because I didn't trust them. I didn't believe her, but I was desperate to feel good. To take away the images and pain..."

As she explains herself, my thoughts go back to our night together. What she said to me...She wanted to replace the bad experience with a good one. She wanted me to make her feel good. At the time, I thought she meant she had shitty sex, but now...

"I was raped," she says, just as the same thought hits me. "When Arielle took me, she allowed the guards to rape me." Her body trembles, and my fists clench at my sides, wishing all those fuckers were still alive, so I could slowly torture and kill them one by one.

"It was horrible, and it hurt so much," Ellie murmurs. "And every time a guy touches me, the memories resurface." She locks eyes with me. "Until you."

Fuck.

"Oh my God," Sienna breathes, holding her sister. "Why didn't you tell me? You've been keeping this to yourself all these years?"

"I couldn't tell you," Ellie mutters. "You told me not to go, and I didn't listen. It was my fault, and you were pregnant with London and almost lost her. You were bleeding and were nearly killed because of me. You would've felt responsible, and I couldn't let you shoulder that blame."

It all makes sense now. The way Ellie clung to me the day I saved her from the warehouse. We thought we got there just in time, but the fact is, we were too late. The damage had been done. Sure, they were alive, and we blew up the warehouse, killing everyone involved, but we had no idea that Ellie, only fifteen years old, had been raped. She hadn't told a soul.

"Oh, El." Sienna starts to cry. "Is that why you moved away?"

Ellie nods into her sister's chest. "I couldn't be here, with all the memories of that day...And I couldn't tell you. So, I ran to California."

Sienna always questioned why Ellie never dated after that day, why she was so quiet, and when she announced that she was moving to the West Coast, Sienna hadn't understood why. But now, all the pieces of the puzzle fit together.

"But none of what happened excuses what I did." Ellie pulls away from Sienna and focuses her attention on me. "I messed up. I wanted to be intimate with someone I could trust, someone I knew wouldn't hurt me, would be gentle and treat me right, so I could move forward. I honestly didn't even think it would happen, and when it did, I figured we would go our separate ways and you'd be none the wiser."

"Only you weren't on birth control," I add, "and we didn't use protection."

My thoughts go back to that night. The talking, the touching, the kissing. How perfect it felt being inside of her without a condom. I came inside her several times without thought.

She nods. "And I got pregnant."

"Were you going to tell me?" I ask, remembering that Micah said I should take responsibility, as if he assumed I knew and wasn't going to own up to what Ellie and I created. Holy shit, we created a baby. I can't believe this is happening. One minute, I was desperate to find my mystery woman, and the next, I discover she's Ellie, who is pregnant with my baby.

"Of course," she says. "I just needed some time to figure it all out. I was raised by a mom who didn't want me, and Sienna's dad didn't want her. The last thing I want is for this baby to ever feel unwanted." She stands, and when her fingers splay across her abdomen, I notice a tiny but noticeable bump. "I know this is my fault," she says, sniffling back her tears. "You went into that room thinking I was a member of the club who was on birth control. This baby is not your fault, and I won't force you to be in his life."

"His?" I ask.

She nods. "There was an issue, and I had to go to the hospital..."

"What?" Sienna gasps. "What issue? Are you okay?"

"Yeah," Ellie says softly. "I have pregnancy anemia. I didn't even know I was pregnant. I got dizzy during practice for the showcase..."

"You said it was canceled." Sienna pouts.

"I didn't want you to come," Ellie admits. "I knew if you came to see me, you'd take one look at me and know I was pregnant, so I lied to keep you away. About the showcase, the job, not being able to attend graduation. I've told so many lies, and I'm so sorry. It feels like everything has spun out of control, and I don't know how to fix any of it."

Sienna sighs. "Are you okay now? Is the baby okay?"

"Yeah," Ellie tells her with a small smile. "I'm taking prenatal vitamins and iron supplements. Because of how far along I was, they were able to tell me the gender. I'm having a little boy."

Sienna smiles and gives her sister a hug. "Congratulations! How far along are you?"

"A little over three months. I'm due November 21st."

"Eek!" Sienna squeals. "Our babies will only be three months apart! Obviously, we don't know if we're having a boy or girl yet, since we like to be surprised, but it won't matter. Our babies will grow up together and be best friends. How cool is that?" She turns to Micah, whose face is devoid of all emotion, and she drops her smile, suddenly remembering the elephant in the room.

"Oh, shit," Sienna murmurs. "You're pregnant...with Lincoln's baby."

"Yeah, she is," I agree, wondering where we go from here.

Ellie's emerald eyes meet mine—eyes I've been fantasizing about—and I suddenly can't breathe. Because she might be several years younger than me and off limits, but that doesn't change the fact that I fucked her...several goddamn times. I ate her sweet cunt and feasted on her perfect tits. I held her and talked with her and...Fuck! She was my mystery woman. No, not *was*...she *is*. She's the woman I've been searching for, hell-bent on finding. She broke my goddamn cock.

"Lincoln," Ellie says gently, carefully, not wanting to poke the beast. "What are you thinking?"

"I'm thinking about how I was determined to find the woman whom I thought was 'the one.' My mystery woman. I didn't think

I'd ever find her." I wave my hand toward her. "I guess the joke was on me." I snort out a harsh laugh. "Because even though she's standing right in front of me, the truth is, she never existed."

Ellie opens her mouth to say something—what, I don't know—but I can't take another moment of being in the same room as her, so I raise my hand to stop her and then stalk out, slamming the door behind me.

Instead of taking the elevator, I take the steps, needing to burn off the raw emotions coursing through my veins. When I get to my car, I go straight to Elite without thinking, with only one purpose in mind: needing to fuck that woman right out of my head.

Only it's easier said than done. Because when I get there and find a willing participant, I realize far too quickly that my cock doesn't want this woman.

He wants the woman with the green eyes.

Who smells like vanilla.

With the chocolate and caramel hair.

And perfect, luscious tits.

As I sit in my office and stare at the grainy image of the mystery woman, who I now know is Eliza Bardot, I realize I'm screwed. Because despite the fact that she's too young, too off-limits, and that she fucked up big time, I still want to feel her under me, on top of me. I want to inhale her sweet scent, taste her delicious cunt. Sink into her body and get lost in her.

And now, instead of running the fuck away from her, in a few months, I'm going to have a baby with her.

"Figured I'd find you here," Micah says, walking into my office and sitting across from me. "You okay?"

"No," I tell him honestly.

"What can I do?"

I drop the picture onto the desk and look at him. "You can tell me that I'm an idiot."

"You didn't know."

"No, not because of that."

"Then why?"

"Because despite knowing who the mystery woman is, I still want her."

Micah's eyes widen in understanding. "Fuck."

"Yeah," I agree. "Fuck."

"You know you can't have her, though, right?" he states matter-of-factly, giving me a look that says it's non-negotiable, that being with Ellie is off the table. A look that has me wanting to argue but knowing I can't because she's Sienna's little sister, Micah's sister-in-law. And he's my brother. But more than that, he's my best friend, and I'd never do anything to mess up our relationship. Which means, Ellie is completely off-limits.

"Yeah, I know," I say, scrubbing my hands over my face. "She's off-limits." And doesn't that just fucking suck. Knowing the woman I want is right there, within my reach, knowing the way she tastes, smells, feels, and also knowing I can never have her again.

Twelve

ELLIE

"You know I'm here to talk any time," Sienna says, taking a seat next to me on the couch. "Even if you just need someone to listen. I'm not going to judge, and no matter what you say, I won't get upset."

It's been two days since my truth bombs exploded all over everyone. Lincoln left, Micah went after him, and Sienna gave me my space when I excused myself to cry.

She's been bringing me my meals since I've refused to get out of bed, but today is Mother's Day, and Sienna deserves to be spoiled. So instead of hiding myself away, I woke up early with my nieces, Brooklyn and London, and we made Sienna breakfast in bed. The girls surprised her with the most adorable cards and homemade gifts, and Micah bought her jewelry.

Normally, they would go to Micah's parents' place for brunch, but since Donna and Michael are vacationing in Europe, we spent the morning and early afternoon hanging by the pool. Now, the girls are napping, and Micah excused himself to handle some business, leaving Sienna and me alone.

"I know," I say with a forced smile. "And I appreciate that, but I don't want to put you in the middle of this mess."

"I already am," she says, reaching over and squeezing my hand gently. "We're family, and we'll get through this together. What happened to you..." Tears fill her eyes, but she quickly swipes them away. "I'm sorry. I told myself I'd keep it together, but I just can't even imagine...Have you talked to someone? A professional?"

"Yeah, though, probably not as consistently as I should. It just feels like by talking about it, I'm forcing myself to relive the trauma, and all I want is to move on."

"I get that, but maybe in order to move on, you need to face what happened to you in the past. Like how you faced having sex."

My thoughts go back to the night with Lincoln and how, despite him not knowing what I was going through, he helped me face my fears head on. That night was better than I could've ever imagined my first time would be. The way he touched and caressed and—

"What's going through your head?" Sienna asks, pulling me from my thoughts.

"I think you're right. Facing my issue with sex head on worked, so maybe I should give speaking to someone another try." I've told myself so many times I would do it, but now, I need to actually put forth the effort. In a few months, I'm going to become a mother, and it's important that I'm the best version of myself.

"Speaking of which..." Sienna smirks and edges a bit closer. "How was it?" she whispers.

"How was what?"

"You know." Her cheeks tint a light shade of pink and she waggles her brows. It takes me a second, but once I catch on to what she's asking, I bark out a laugh.

"Are you asking me how Lincoln was in bed?"

"Well, yeah." She shrugs. "I mean, you don't have to get into the details, but we missed out on this. The girl talk." Tears fill her lids, and she smiles a watery smile, and I pull her into a tight hug, needing to be close to her. Sienna is right. We missed out on a lot because of what happened and because I ran. But I'm back home now, so I'm going to do everything in my power to make it up to her.

"It was good," I murmur as we break apart. "Really freaking good. So good, I have no idea how I'm going to be with someone else in the future and not compare them to Lincoln."

Sienna chuckles. "It's the Alexander genes. They're good at everything. It really isn't fair."

"What are we good at?" Micah asks, as he strolls into the living room.

"Sex." Sienna giggles.

Micah's jaw tenses, his eyes going dark. "Ellie," he says, his tone serious. "You know nothing will ever come of you and Lincoln again, right? He's too old for you. What you did..." He sighs, and his expression slightly softens. "I get it. I don't agree with how you handled it, but you're young and you've been through so much—"

"Wait a second," Sienna cuts in. "Are you saying that Lincoln and Ellie can't be together?"

"That's exactly what I'm saying," Micah says.

"You are aware that she's an adult, right?" Sienna glares. "If she and Lincoln want—"

"He doesn't," Micah says, cutting her off. "He agrees with me completely."

"Agrees with what?" she asks.

"That Ellie's off-limits," he says in a tone that conveys this conversation is over.

"You can't—"

"Stop," I say, not wanting them to fight. This is precisely why I didn't want to come home. I knew once everyone found out, lines would be drawn, and it's not fair to put them in the middle of this.

Sienna deserves to be happy, and I'm not going to be the reason she and Micah argue.

"I agree," I say to them. "Like I told Lincoln, if he doesn't want to be a part of this baby's life, he doesn't have to be. And I'm definitely not expecting him to get down on one knee and propose." I laugh awkwardly to cover up my hurt. I didn't really think the idea of us was a possibility, but that didn't stop me from wishing...

"If you're worried about Lincoln not being there for the baby, don't be," Micah says. "He's upset right now, shocked at the turn of events, but he'll come around and do the right thing."

*The right thing...*Because this baby wasn't conceived out of love. It was a one-night stand gone wrong. The same way I was conceived.

My stomach knots as the realization hits—that despite never wanting to be anything like my mom, I ended up in the same position she was in—knocked up by a man who doesn't want me or our baby.

"If you'll excuse me"—I stand and force a smile to cover up how sick I suddenly feel—"I'm feeling kind of tired."

❦

LINCOLN

SHE'S OFF-LIMITS.

I know this, hell, I agree with this, but it's hard to accept. Because every time I close my eyes, I can't get her out of my head. The way our bodies fit together so perfectly. The way her warm, tight cunt gripped my cock.

But it was so much more than that. It was the conversation. The feelings that ran deeper than I've ever felt. I don't believe in love at first sight, but the chemistry between us was undeniable.

And had she been anyone else, I would've taken it as a sign. I've been thinking about her for months, fantasizing about the day I'd find her. And just when I thought all hope was lost, she appeared at my doorstep.

Only the joke was on me because my mystery woman wasn't just any woman—she's Sienna's much younger sister.

She's without a doubt the youngest woman I've ever slept with. It's not that I'm opposed to younger women, but older women tend to know what they want, and they are a helluva lot more mature. They don't cling. They don't play games. They know the score.

But with Ellie, it was different. I had no idea she was so young because she didn't play games. She knew what she wanted, and she went after it. And in that short amount of time, we connected on a deeper level.

Or maybe my memory of that night is distorted, and it wasn't as earth shattering as I remember. Maybe I'm reaching, like Micah said.

It doesn't matter, though, because Ellie is definitely out-of-bounds, and the only part I should focus on is that she's pregnant with my baby.

The truth is, since the day I found out she was pregnant, I haven't thought about much else.

I've known Ellie since she was a teenager, and during that time, I was always in awe of her strength and courage. She took each shitty situation her mom thrust upon her and handled it like a little badass. Left to fend for herself, she had little choice but to grow up fast.

Ellie went to work with Sienna and did her homework in the dressing room of a strip club every damn night. Her sister busted her ass to pay the bills, and since their mom didn't help at all, there was no money left over to pay for shit. So Ellie worked hard to make good grades in school to get a scholarship, and when she wanted to go to dance camp, she went behind my back and tried to work at Wanderlust—my gentleman's club—to make enough money to go. Of course, Micah found out and put a stop to it, paying for it himself, but the point is, Ellie was willing to work for what she wanted.

But her mom continued to wreak havoc when she poisoned Eduardo—the dirtiest underground criminal on the East Coast—then told his son, Eleazer, that he was Ellie's sperm donor to try to save her ass, which ultimately backfired when he killed her and left her for dead. Ellie went after him on her own to try to stop him from taking her away from Sienna. Not just for her own sake, but for Sienna's, who would've been forced to go on the run and leave Micah behind.

Then, when Eleazar's wife, Arielle, tried to harm Sienna and her baby, Ellie shot her fucking dead.

And the one that nobody had any idea about until recently...

Ellie was raped by several men while she was held captive by Arielle. She hid it from everyone to spare her sister any undue guilt because she knew that Sienna took her responsibility for Ellie seriously. Soon after, she went off to college and got a degree. And then she took control of her sexuality by seeking out a man she trusted enough to be intimate with. And succeeded.

I want to be pissed at her. I want to yell and scream and tell her that she fucked up. Not only did she pull one over on me, but in the process, she managed to get pregnant. So, yeah, I want to be pissed, but what she did is just so typical of Ellie. She took matters into her own hands, like she always does, and made it—well, I guess in this case, *me*—her bitch.

And fuck if I didn't submit...No, nope, not going there. It's one thing to give credit where credit is due, but it's another to go *there*. Back to the club, in the backroom, where I had the best damn sex of my life. Nope, not going there. Ellie might be a badass, she might've left her mark on me, but she's still off-limits.

My phone rings with an incoming call from my mom, and I cringe. Micah promised not to say anything, so I could tell her and our dad myself, but me knocking up Sienna's twenty-one-year-old sister isn't a conversation to be had over the phone.

Since it's Mother's Day and I can't *not* speak to her, I hit accept. "Hey, Mom. Happy Mother's Day."

"Thank you. How are you?"

"Good. Busy as usual."

"If you keep working the way you do, you'll never meet anyone," she chides, and since I don't want to touch that subject with a ten-foot pole, I quickly change the subject by asking about their trip.

After she tells me about the places they've visited since the last time we spoke, she lets me know they'll be home in the next few weeks, making me promise to come over for dinner once they're back. And when we hang up, I wonder how the hell I'm going to tell her that I'm finally giving her the grandbaby she's been begging for, only it's out of wedlock and with a woman she views as family.

Thirteen

ELLIE

"Happy Birthday, Auntie Ellie!" London and Brooklyn shout as they run into my room—well, my old room that's now the guest room, which is supposed to be converted into the new baby's room. Which reminds me: I need to find somewhere to live. I love my sister, but after being gone for four years, I feel like an outsider. Lincoln used to come around, but he's been MIA since I came home, Micah's been quiet since he told me on Mother's Day that Lincoln doesn't want me and never will, and Sienna is overcompensating for both of them by being overly nice and attentive.

I've also walked in on them having sex in the middle of the night...Twice—once on the kitchen counter and another time on the table. Yeah, I definitely need to get my own place.

"Wow," I say, sitting up and taking the gifts they're holding from them. I read the card that Sienna must've helped them write, then glance up at her standing in the doorway, smiling softly, watching as I open the gift. It's a whitewash picture frame with adorable little blue footprints all over it, and on the bottom, it reads *Love at first sight*. Inside is the sonogram of my little blob from when I was in the hospital.

My finger runs over the image as tears prick my eyes. I haven't heard from Lincoln since the day everything was revealed and he walked out. I've considered texting him and telling him that I can draw up papers for him to sign away his rights, but I keep hoping that maybe he'll come around, since Micah said he was certain he'd do the right thing.

"Auntie Ellie, are you okay?" London asks, shaking me from my thoughts.

I glance up at her and wipe my eyes. "Yes, thank you for this gift. It's the best gift ever."

"London said our new baby is hers because she's older," Brooklyn says. "Can your baby be mine?"

Sienna chuckles, and I can't help but crack a smile. "Only if you'll share him with me," I tell Brooklyn with a wink.

"Of course!" she says. "Mommy says sharing is caring."

"C'mon, girls," Sienna says. "You need to get ready for school."

"But my belly hurts," London complains.

"Mine too!" Brooklyn agrees.

"Probably because you're both hungry," Sienna says.

After the girls wish me a Happy Birthday one last time and run out of the room, Sienna steps farther inside. "How are you feeling?"

"Okay."

"You have your checkup today, right?"

"Yeah." Since I moved back here, I needed to change doctors, so I decided to go with Sienna's OB, whom she loves. I'm going to meet her today and have a checkup at the same time.

"If you want me to go..."

"I appreciate it, but I'm okay going alone." It won't be the first or the last time I go by myself. It's something I need to get used to. Even if Lincoln comes around and wants to be in the baby's life, at most, we'd be co-parenting.

"I know you're okay going alone," she says, stepping into the room and sitting on the edge of the bed, "but that doesn't mean you have to. It's okay to let people in."

"Like who? Lincoln? Since he found out about the baby, he's been avoiding me like the plague."

"I think he just needs a little time to sort through what he's feeling. But I'm here."

"I know you are." She's told me as much on several occasions, but since our conversation on Mother's Day, where she and Micah almost got into an argument because of me, I've made it a point to keep to myself, not wanting to put them in the middle.

"But you have a family. You have the girls and Micah, and soon you'll have this little one." I pat her belly gently. "Plus, you have the dance studio. I don't want you to worry about me. I'm actually planning to go house hunting after my appointment."

"El." She sighs. "There was a time when we were each other's only family. And yeah, along the way, I've added a few more people to the picture, but you're still my family. And you're welcome to stay here as long as you want or need to."

My heart swells at her words, thankful to have such an amazing sister. But even though she has good intentions, things have changed, and she needs to put Micah and her kids first.

"If this is about what Micah said..." She adds, but I don't let her finish her thought.

"It's not. I appreciate you letting me stay here, but with both of us having babies, we're going to need our own space." She opens her mouth to argue, but I quickly change the subject. "Are you going to the dance studio this morning? I haven't danced in weeks, and I'm dying to get into the studio to get my blood pumping."

"Yeah, I try to go every day. But with Nora and Paula taking over my classes until after I give birth, and Samantha now running the front, I feel like I'm no longer needed," she says with a laugh.

"If you want, we can go by the studio for a bit and then head to my appointment together. Maybe you can check out some places with me afterward."

A smile spreads across Sienna's face, and I know I've said the right thing. "That would be great. And we can do lunch for your birthday. Let me get the girls off to school. Then I'll meet you at the studio." She pulls me into a hug. "Happy Birthday, El. I'm so glad you're finally home."

After taking a quick shower to rinse the sleep off of me, I throw on a maternity tank and sweats, pack a change of clothes for my doctor's appointment, and then head out.

I'm pressing the button for the elevator when the sound of footsteps hits my ears, making me tense. Micah, Sienna, and the girls already left for the day, which means...I glance back and see Lincoln walking toward the elevator, his head down, staring at his phone. He looks up and our eyes lock. The look on his face says he wants to go back to his place to hide until I'm gone, but it's too late now.

"Hey," I say, as the elevator doors open, and we step inside. It's a private elevator, so we're the only two on it.

"Hey," he parrots.

We stand in awkward silence for several moments before I decide to rip the Band-Aid off. "We should probably talk about the baby."

His eyes descend to my swollen belly, and he nods. "Yeah, sorry, I've been busy." He sighs. "This is all just so..."

"I know," I tell him, not needing him to finish his sentence. "I really am sorry."

He shakes his head. "What's done is done." The doors open and we step out. "We just need to focus on the situation at hand. Figure out how to deal with it."

The way he says 'deal with it' rubs me the wrong way, reminding me of what Micah said about him 'doing the right thing,' and before I can stop myself, I open my mouth. "Our baby isn't something to be dealt with. It's a *he*...And he deserves to feel loved and adored. He's not a business acquisition gone wrong, nor is he a *situation*. I know this isn't what you wanted, and I already told you that I won't force you to be in his life, so you don't need to worry about *doing the right thing*. I'd rather you walk away than treat him like he was a mistake you have to deal with. So, let me know if that's what you want, and I can have an attorney draw up papers to terminate your parental rights once the baby is born."

Without waiting for him to respond, I take off out of the hotel lobby and onto the street, my heart racing and my blood boiling. I get that I messed up, that I caused all of this, but he's not discussing a business transaction—he's talking about my baby—*our* baby.

Since the studio isn't too far, I decide to hoof it there instead of waiting for an Uber, so I don't risk seeing him again.

On my way, I pull my phone out and read my weekly 'what to expect' post in the app I downloaded. When I turn the corner, I'm not watching where I'm going, and I run smack dab into someone.

"Sorry," I breathe. "I wasn't watching where—"

The gentleman doesn't even acknowledge me, though. Instead, he continues to stalk in the opposite direction. Rude.

I'm about to turn around when he looks back, his gaze crashing with my own. His glare doesn't hold for long, but the coldness in his eyes during those few short seconds is enough to send a chill up my spine, despite it being over ninety degrees outside. The look in his eyes sparks a flashback, and I force myself out of my head, refusing to let my return to this town get to me. Then I resolve to find someone to talk to—ASAP.

Once I arrive, I get lost in dancing. It's always been my way to escape, and for the next few hours, I do just that—everything else fading away.

Fourteen

LINCOLN

"My baby isn't something to be dealt with...he deserves to feel loved and adored. He's not a business acquisition gone wrong...I can have an attorney draw up papers to terminate your parental rights once the baby is born."

Ellie's words run on repeat all morning while I try to get some work done. *Try* being the operative word because I've been staring at my screen for who the hell knows how long, and I haven't gotten shit done.

"Hey Lincoln, Micah just arrived, and he doesn't look happy," our secretary, Rita, says from the doorway. Her words snap me out of my thoughts, and I slam my laptop closed. Until I figure out how I'm going to handle the situation I've found myself in, I have a feeling I won't be getting much done.

When I step into Micah's office without bothering to knock, I find him barking orders over the phone. While I handle the entertainment aspect of Alexander Enterprises—hotels, clubs, restaurants, etc.—Micah handles the business side of it all, including the not-so-legal shit. Part of owning the majority of Tesoro means sometimes having to get our hands dirty.

"Big bro," I say, dropping into the visitor seat once he slams the phone down. "How's it going?"

"Two of Ricky's men were found dead down at the marina..." Ricky is a huge player in the underground world. When Eleazar died, leaving everything to Ellie, we took over the territory temporarily so shit wouldn't hit the fan. A lot of men wanted what Eleazer left behind, but we ended up making a deal with Ricky De La Cruz. Unlike the Gutierrezes, he doesn't kidnap and traffic women. His main focus is on drugs and weapons. With the assurance he would clean up the streets of Booker Park—the south side of Tesoro that had gone to shit thanks to Eduardo—we created a partnership of sorts.

"Bruno was also killed," Micah adds, referring to one of the men who's been working for us for years.

"Bruno?" Fuck, he knows how to handle himself. For him to have been taken out must mean..."Ambush?"

Micah nods. "The shipment was stolen, and they left the bodies there."

Everyone in Tesoro knows not to fuck with Ricky or us, so for someone to not only steal from Ricky at our marina, but then leave the bodies to be found, tells us one thing. "Someone's trying to send a message."

"Yeah, and until we find out who, we need to be cautious." He opens his mouth to say something else, but his phone rings. "Hellcat, everything okay?" he asks when he answers, using the nickname he's dubbed his wife with.

Whatever she says must not be good because he immediately switches to speakerphone. "What's wrong?" he asks, and the tone of his voice puts me on high alert. With the news of the ambush, my thoughts jump to the worst possible conclusions.

"The girls are sick," Sienna says. Micah glances at me and shakes his head, obviously having had the same thoughts as me.

"What's wrong with them?" he asks, keeping the phone on speaker.

"I thought they were fine this morning. They wished Ellie a Happy Birthday and gave her a special gift. Though, now that I'm thinking about it, they did mention their tummies hurt, but I thought they were just hungry. On my way to the studio, I got a call from the school clinic. They're both running fevers, and London threw up. I'm on my way to get them now."

"You have Ricardo with you, right?" Micah asks, referring to Sienna's personal bodyguard. Even though things have been calm the past several years, Micah doesn't take chances with his family. Ricardo has been with us for a long time and would do anything to protect Sienna and their girls.

"Of course," Sienna says flippantly.

"You make a doctor's appointment?"

"No, it's probably a stomach bug of some sort. But I feel bad because it's Ellie's birthday, and I was supposed to meet her at the studio and go to her OB appointment with her. She's meeting with her new doctor and seeing the baby today."

Mention of the baby has me shifting in my seat. It doesn't help that Micah's eyes land on mine. "Do you need me to come home so you can go with her?" he asks.

"I want to say yes, but with the girls so sick, I don't want to leave them, and it's probably not a good idea to be around Ellie in case I get sick as well. She might have already been exposed, but in case she hasn't, we should probably book her a room for a couple of days. There's nothing worse than being pregnant and sick."

We live on the top floor of Hotel Blu—an upscale hotel Alexander Enterprises owns. When we were constructing it several years ago, we designed it so the entire top floor would be occupied by us. We have a private elevator that only goes to our floor, access to the roof, private pools on our terraces, in-home gyms, underground private parking, and round the clock security. It doesn't get much safer or convenient than that.

Micah shakes his head. "You're pregnant."

"I know, but I'm a mom. It's different." One of the things I love about my sister-in-law is how much of a devoted mother she is. She reminds me so much of my mom, the way she loves her family so fiercely.

"I'm leaving now and will meet you at home," Micah says.

"You don't have to—"

"Hellcat, I'm on my way. I love you."

After she returns the sentiment, he hangs up and looks at me. "Fucking woman is so stubborn."

"It's one of the many things you love about her."

"True," he agrees. "You should go to that appointment."

"What—?" I start to play stupid, but when he hits me with a hard glare, I close my mouth.

"She's the mother of your baby. You need to work shit out, unless you're planning to have nothing to do with your child." Micah quirks a knowing brow, and I sigh.

"Oh, and can you maybe take her to lunch afterward for her birthday?" he says, standing. "It'd make Sienna feel better knowing her sister isn't spending the day alone. Plus, trust me when I say, you'll regret missing out on these moments."

I HAVE NO CLUE HOW I GOT HERE—AT LIVE, LOVE, DANCE— the dance studio Ellie bought for Sienna years ago when she found out she was rich, thanks to her dead sperm donor. But here I am, watching Ellie dance her heart out. She's strong yet graceful as she moves to the beat, having no clue that she's no longer alone.

When I arrived, Samantha was confused to see me, which makes sense, since the only time I come here is when my nieces ask me to come watch them, and neither one is here today. She was even more confused when I asked where Ellie was—which tells me Ellie hasn't told anyone I'm her baby daddy yet.

Fuck, I'm someone's baby daddy.

She pointed me in the direction of studio B, where I found Ellie immersed in the beat of the music.

When her eyes lock with mine in the mirror, she stills, then turns around and cocks her hip, her telltale sign she's about to give me shit.

"What are you doing here?" she asks, her full lips forming a sexy pout. Fuck, no, not sexy. She's not fucking sexy. *But she really is.*

As she sashays over to me, I can't help but rake my gaze down her body. Her eyes are bright green and expressive today. Her slim neck is exposed, thanks to her hair being pulled up in a messy bun. Droplets of sweat are trailing down into the small sports bra she's wearing, and my thoughts immediately go back to the night we spent together. I couldn't see her well in the dark, but I remember after the third time we fucked, tasting her salty flesh. She had passed out from exhaustion, and instead of waking her up, I spent several minutes memorizing every inch of her body, knowing we'd part ways once she woke up, and I'd likely never see her again.

"I asked you a question," she repeats. My eyes are currently on her toned legs, and when my gaze begins to ascend back to her face, I stop at her tiny bump. The bump that's there because she's carrying my baby. A baby we created during a night filled with passion.

And then I spent months searching for her...

"The girls are sick," I blurt out, shaking myself from my thoughts. It doesn't matter how attracted I was to her—*okay, still am*—this is Ellie, and I have to remind myself that she'll always be off-limits, despite being pregnant with my baby.

"Oh no," she says, moving past me and grabbing her phone. "I had my phone on silent, so I missed Sienna's calls and messages.

She just sent me one a few minutes ago, saying the girls are throwing up and running fevers. Poor things." She types back a response and then says, "Shoot, it's a good thing you interrupted me. I need to get ready to go to my appointment. I didn't realize I had been dancing for so long."

She grabs her stuff and is about to head out of the room when she realizes I'm still standing here. "Umm, thanks for letting me know about the girls."

"I was actually thinking I could go with you to your appointment," I mention. I wasn't sure until I got here what I was going to do. Yeah, the baby is mine, but until he's born, I figured it wasn't really necessary to be actively involved. It's not like *I'm* carrying the baby.

But as I stand here, taking her in, I realize that despite how fucked up this all is, I want to be involved.

"That's not necessary," Ellie says. "I've gone to all my previous appointments alone. It's all good. I promise."

"I know. You're strong and independent, and you don't need anyone." I don't mean for it to come across mockingly, but I can see how she'd take it that way.

With her brows furrowed, she cocks that hip out again. "That's right, I am. When you've lived the life I have, all you have is yourself."

"Actually," I say, stepping closer, without realizing what I'm doing before it's too late and we're only a few inches apart. This close to her, I can smell the vanilla, a scent I've been fantasizing about since the moment I smelled it on her that night at Elite. "You have other people. You just choose to push them away, starting with your sister."

"I'm pretty sure she's at home with her daughters," she argues. "As she should be."

"That's not what I meant, and you know it. You've been gone for four damn years, Ellie. You chose to go away to school. You chose to keep her at arm's length. And now you're doing it with me."

"What?" she scoffs. "How do you figure?"

"Before you even gave me time to process the bomb you dropped on me, you were throwing shit at me about terminating my parental rights. After you're the one who fucked up...*Liz*." Yeah, the moment I realized she gave me a part of her real name, I wanted to slam my fist into a wall. Looking back, so many signs were there flashing at me, but I didn't see them because Ellie wasn't on my radar. "Well, guess what, *Kitten*? I'm here, and I'm not going anywhere. You can try to push me away all you want, but I won't budge. That baby you're carrying is half mine, and I plan to be in his life, starting with this appointment."

Her eyes widen, and then for a brief moment, they seem to soften, before they turn hard again, hiding whatever emotion she almost let slip. "I need to rinse off," she mutters, stalking past me.

The drive to her doctor's office is filled with awkward silence. When we arrive, the receptionist at the front desk gets her checked in, wishing her a happy birthday as she does so, reminding me of what day it is and that Ellie just turned twenty-two. At her age, I was usually partying with my friends and only working when Micah and my father insisted on it. Ellie, on the other hand, just graduated from college and is expecting a baby. I talk shit about how young she is, yet she's more mature than I ever was at that age.

We're brought back to a darkened room, where a woman by the name of Nayloni introduces herself and says she'll be conducting the ultrasound today.

Ellie lies back, and Nayloni asks her a few questions, inputting her answers into the computer. When she rattles off her date of birth, Nayloni says, "Happy Birthday."

"Thanks," Ellie says softly. "I can't think of a better gift than getting to see my little blob today."

Nayloni chuckles. "Blob, huh? That's a new one."

She lifts Ellie's shirt and squirts blue shit onto her stomach. A few seconds later, the screen fills with a black and white image of a tiny baby.

"Yep," Ellie says, "best present ever."

When I glance at her, the tips of her lips are curved into a huge grin, her gaze trained on the screen, and so much love in her eyes, it makes my heart squeeze in my chest.

"Heartbeat is 148," Nayloni says, taking my attention away from Ellie and back to the screen.

"Is that good?" I ask, having no clue about any of this.

"Yep. It should be between 120 and 160, so he's got a good, strong heartbeat."

He...Because we're having a little boy.

Ellie reaches out and touches the screen, her fingers sliding across his body. "He looks like a gummy bear," she says, her smile lighting up the dark room.

"Oh, so he's been upgraded from a blob to a gummy bear? Nice," Nayloni says with a playful wink. Ellie laughs, and the melodic sound goes straight to my heart. I heard her laugh a few times the night we were together, and then I tried to remember it once she was gone. But my memory didn't do it justice.

And now, as I listen to it, I know why I didn't recognize it— Ellie barely ever laughs. When she was younger, she laughed, but after that day, after she was taken and raped, the laughter stopped. Ellie grew up, her body and voice and personality changing. And her laugh changed too, but I never heard it because life was cruel and didn't leave her with much to laugh about.

And I don't know why, but in this moment, I vow to make her laugh more often. To make her smile. Ellie's strong and resilient and a goddamn survivor, but she deserves more than to merely survive...she deserves to be happy.

Fifteen

ELLIE

I GLANCE OVER AT LINCOLN AND FIND HIM STARING AT ME WITH a look that I can't decipher. For as long as I've known him, he's always been the chill brother, nothing seeming to rattle him—unless you do stupid shit like me and have sex with him and get knocked up, then he shows a bit of emotion. But right now, as he looks at me, his features are filled with raw emotion, and I'm not sure why.

"You okay?" I ask as Nayloni goes about getting the baby's measurements.

"Yeah," Lincoln says with a tight smile. "It's just all so surreal. To think in a few months, we'll be parents of a tiny, helpless baby, who'll depend on us for everything."

I nod in understanding, getting a bit choked up at his words. Despite being pissed at me for what I did, I should've known he would do the right thing, which is a huge relief. Still, I feel like utter crap for what I'd done. My stupidity put him in this position, leaving him no choice but to either step up or be a shit father.

Nayloni lets us know the baby's measurements are perfect, and after printing updated pictures for us, she gives me a moment to wipe off the gel and then escorts us to the examination room, where she says the doctor will be in shortly.

"I'm sorry," I tell Lincoln the second the door closes. "What I did was wrong, and I'm so sorry I put you in this position. I had a one-track mind, and I didn't consider the consequences. Just like I didn't when I went to talk to Eleazar after Sienna told me not to. Had I—"

"Stop," Lincoln says gently, pressing his palm to my cheek in a comforting manner. "I agreed to have sex with you. It was completely mutual, and the fact is, even though condoms are up to the guest, I always use them. But I didn't with you, and even if you had been on birth control, nothing is one hundred percent effective. We both made our own decisions, and there's no sense in pointing fingers or living with regrets."

"You don't regret spending the night with me?" I choke out, shocked by his admission.

"I wish I could say I did," Lincoln admits with a shake of his head. "But that night, I connected with someone on a deeper level, and through that connection we created this." He holds up the sonogram picture. "How could I possibly regret what happened, when, as a result, we created such a beautiful miracle?"

Holy shit. I never thought I would hear him say something like this. Since the moment I found out, I prayed for him to come around, to be a part of our baby's life. When I was little, all I ever wanted was a family, but I accepted at a young age it would never happen, and when I found out I was pregnant, I was devastated because I knew Lincoln would be so mad, there'd be no hope of giving this baby a real family—one I never had. But now...is it possible?

"I want this baby," he continues, his eyes locking with mine.

"And I forgive you. It might not have happened how either of us planned, but we're going to have a baby together, and I want to raise him with you. There's no reason why we can't do that as friends."

Friends. Right. Of course. What was I thinking? That he'd declare his undying love for me after what I did? Sure, he's a damn good person—which is why I knew I could trust him—and is willing to forgive me, but that doesn't change the fact that he doesn't see me as anything more than Ellie Bardot, his much younger sister-in-law, who he's now stuck raising a baby with.

Fuck, I really did mess up.

"Knock, knock," the doctor says, stepping into the room. "I'm Dr. Peterson." She shakes my hand and then Lincoln's.

"I'm Ellie, and this is the baby's father, Lincoln."

"It's wonderful to meet you both. I spoke to Sienna at her checkup the other day, and she mentioned you've moved home and would be coming in." Her smile is friendly, and I know right away why Sienna loves her.

"Why don't you have a seat on the examination table" she continues. "I'd like to take your blood pressure."

"Oh, it was done when I first got here," I remark, sitting on the table.

"Yes, I saw. I'd like to double check it." She puts the cuff on me and pumps it up until it's beyond tight before slowly releasing the air. After she removes the cuff, she types something into her iPad and then has a seat in front of me.

"I'm concerned," she says. "Your blood pressure is a bit high, which is common for women who have pregnancy anemia. You're taking your supplements and iron, right?"

"Of course," I say, starting to get worried.

She nods. "I'd like for you to pick up a blood pressure monitor. Take and record your blood pressure three times a day in a journal. I'm also going to suggest modified bed rest."

Wait, what? "Bed rest? Like, I can't get out of bed? I don't understand. I feel fine. I'm young and active and eat healthy for the most part, aside from a few cravings. What am I doing wrong?"

Dr. Peterson rests her hand on mine, noticing that I'm starting to freak out. "Pregnancy anemia paired with high blood pressure can lead to preeclampsia as well as other more severe complications. Right now, I'm not ordering you to go on bed rest, but I want you to try to relax, take it easy. We'll reevaluate at your next appointment. If it worsens, we'll have to consider medication as well as bed rest."

When my face falls and my hand goes to my belly, the doctor pats my hand. "The baby is perfect. Sometimes things happen that are out of our control, but unlike years ago, we now have modern medicine on our side. Keep taking your supplements and vitamins, monitor your BP, and don't stress." She glances at Lincoln for backup. "Make sure she doesn't stress."

"You got it," Lincoln says, stepping closer to me and putting his hand on my shoulder. He squeezes gently, and when I glance up at him, he smiles softly. "No stress."

I nod in response, but my mood has officially sunk. Sure, my baby is doing okay right now, but low iron and high blood pressure can't be good.

When we get into Lincoln's car, I pull up Google and type in the terms the doctor mentioned, but before I can click search, my phone is snatched out of my hand.

"Hey!"

"Nope." Lincoln pockets my phone. "Doctor Google never goes over well for anyone."

I huff in annoyance and glare his way, but it only makes him chuckle.

When I notice we're not headed in the direction of home, I ask, "Where are we going?"

"It's your birthday, and I imagine you're hungry since you haven't eaten recently. I'm taking you to lunch, and then we'll go by the store and get you a BP monitor and journal, and then you're going to do as the doctor said and relax."

I want to argue with him, but since he's not wrong, I simply nod. A little while later, I recognize where we are: Elite. My heart clenches in my chest, and I glance at him, silently asking why we're here. There's no way he wants to—

"Figured we could have lunch at Impulse," he says, cutting off my ridiculous thoughts. "I know how much you used to love the food here."

I did. It was my favorite place to eat, and it also helped that eating there meant spending time with Lincoln. The last time we ate at Impulse was for my graduation dinner before I left for California.

Lunch is good, and Lincoln and I spend the meal talking about school, the baby, and how I like being back at home. It's not awkward at all, and we keep it light, staying away from anything too deep. It reminds me of before everything changed—when things were a bit simpler.

After we're done eating, Lincoln surprises me with a birthday cake that's beyond delicious. Since it's only the two of us, the waitress boxes up the rest for later. After stopping by the drug store, we head home.

"I don't think you should go back to your sister's place," Lincoln says as he drives toward Blu.

"What?" I jerk my head toward him, wondering what the hell he's talking about.

"The girls are sick, and you're already dealing with enough." He nods toward the bag containing my new monitor and journal. "The last thing you need is to get sick on top of everything else."

"Sienna's pregnant and—"

"...she's their mother," he finishes. "And Micah texted saying he's handling it, so she's exposed as little as possible, but there's no reason for you to be exposed as well."

"Yeah, that makes sense," I agree. "As much as I love staying with them, I was planning to find my own place anyway," I admit.

"The room I'm staying in was set to become the baby's nursery. Sienna said it was fine, but I know she'd love to be able to decorate it once the baby is born and they know the gender. Plus"—I mock shiver—"I've caught them having sex twice."

Lincoln barks out a laugh. "I've walked in on them a few times."

"Yeah, well, twice is two times too many for me. It's time to go."

When we arrive at Blu, instead of going to the elevator, I head over to the front desk to see about renting a place.

"What are you doing?" Lincoln asks, pulling me to the side.

"I need to find my own place, but until then, I was thinking I'd rent a room here."

"Or you can stay with me," he says, shocking the hell out of me. Before I can argue, though, he adds, "The doctor said you need to rest. I'd feel better knowing you're under my roof where I can make sure you guys are okay." He says, 'you guys,' but for some reason—maybe it's the hormones—all I hear is 'our baby.'

"You don't think I can take care of him?"

"What? No." He shakes his head. "I mean, of course, you can take care of our baby. You can take care of the entire world if you wanted to..."

"Then what's the problem?"

"Sometimes, it's okay to let someone take care of you too."

His words make me pause. "You want to take care of me?"

"Ellie," he says. "You're pregnant with our baby. We're in this together. Of course, I want to take care of you. You just have to let me."

"I'M SO SORRY," SIENNA SAYS WITH A POUT OVER FACETIME. "I hate that you spent your birthday alone. If I wasn't afraid of passing this stomach bug on to you—"

"Hey, stop," I say, shifting on the lounger to get comfortable. "Lincoln went with me to my appointment and took me to lunch afterward for my birthday. He even had a cake brought out. I promise, I had a good birthday, even though it wasn't spent with you and my favorite nieces."

"Okay, good," Sienna says, then squints. "Hey, where are you? That looks a lot like Lincoln's terrace."

"It is," I tell her. "I'm staying with him. Didn't Micah tell you?"

"No, but I did just wake up from a nap, so he probably hasn't had the chance. So, you're like moving in with him?" she asks cautiously.

"No, I'm going to find my own place. I'm just staying with him temporarily since the girls are sick and the doctor wants me to rest."

"Why? Is everything okay?"

I tell her about my appointment, and when I'm done, she says, "I'm glad you won't be alone and that Lincoln is stepping up. Do you need anything of yours from here?"

"Lincoln already handled it. He must've come by when you were sleeping."

After Lincoln gave me a tour of his place and showed me to my room, he went by their place to get a bunch of my stuff before going to the office. He said he'd pick up dinner on his way home, and since I have the place to myself and it's such a nice day out, I figured why not throw on my bikini and spend some time on Lincoln's terrace. The doctor did say to relax, and there's nothing more relaxing than lounging by the pool.

"Okay, cool. Enjoy the rest of your birthday, and once the girls are better, we're having a redo. Dinner, cake, the birthday works."

"You got it, sis."

After we hang up, I remove my cover up and connect my phone to the Bluetooth speaker. With the sun shining down, I lie out on the lounger and close my eyes, taking a moment to relax, just like the doctor ordered.

Sixteen

LINCOLN

"Did Rita misunderstand? Are you working from home indefinitely?" Micah asks over my Bluetooth as I drive away from the office, files stacked on my passenger seat.

"She didn't misunderstand. I'll be working from home for at least the next few weeks."

"Because Ellie's staying with you?"

Because I googled pregnancy and high blood pressure. I told Ellie not to do it, but then, after I arrived at the office, I did it anyway. And what I found scared the shit out of me. Which led to my decision to work from home. The doctor doesn't feel she's at risk at the moment, but the only way to ensure she stays that way is for her to relax, and the only way to make that happen is for me to be there with her.

"Because the doctor put her on bed rest." Okay, not really, but she suggested it, and I'll be damned if something happens because we didn't take her suggestion seriously. For the next few weeks, I'm making it my mission to make sure Ellie stays calm and comfortable and stress free.

"Oh, shit. Is she okay?"

I explain what happened at the appointment, and once I'm done, Micah agrees it's a good idea for me to stay home.

"So, when are you going to tell our parents they're about to be grandparents again?" Micah asks, and even though I can't see him, I can imagine the smirk he's sporting.

"I think that's something that should be told in person, so I'm going to wait until they return from their trip. They mentioned being home in time for your baby shower."

Micah barks out a laugh. "You're such a pussy."

He's not wrong. "Can you blame me? When Mom finds out that I knocked up Ellie, her sweet pseudo daughter, she's going to kill me."

"She's not going to kill you," Micah argues. "She'll probably be a little disappointed because she was hoping for you to settle down, which probably looked a little different than knocking up your one-night-stand, but she'll be so excited to have another grandkid to spoil, she'll get over the unconventional way it's happening."

"Fuck," I mutter. "I can't get over this. Seeing him on the screen today was so damn surreal."

"But beautiful, though," Micah adds.

"Really beautiful," I agree. "I just...I'm at a loss," I admit.

"Because Ellie's the mom?"

"Because Ellie's my mystery woman."

"Who's off-limits," he says, his tone brokering no room for argument.

This is where I'm supposed to agree, the way I did last time, but after spending the morning with Ellie—the woman who rocked my world on Valentine's Day and is now swollen with my child—it's hard to see her as the same person Micah sees as taboo. At twenty-two years old, she's all grown up and well over the legal age. Not to mention, wise beyond her years. The woman has been through more shit than most people her age. Truthfully, there's no reason why she and I can't be together if that's what both of us really wanted.

When I don't say anything, Micah says my name to get my attention. "She's off-limits, right?"

And because the last thing I want to do is to start issues within our family, I reluctantly agree. "Yeah, of course she is."

But when I stroll into the penthouse with Mexican food—one of Ellie's favorites—and find her lying on the lounger, in a tiny as hell bikini, her eyes closed and her belly sporting the sexiest bump, I know it's going to be easier said than done. Because as I stare at this all-too-grown-up version of Ellie, my head, heart, and cock have all ganged up on me and are demanding I make her mine in every damn way.

"Hey," Ellie says, scrubbing her eyes and sitting up. "I must've fallen asleep. What time is it?"

"Almost five. I left work early and picked up Mexican for dinner. It's in the kitchen."

She stretches her arms above her head, and her breasts, which are damn near spilling out of the small triangles, thrust outward. I try to avert my gaze, but it only fucks me harder when my eyes land on the equally small triangle that's being held together by two strings and barely covering her cunt. That same cunt I spent hours feasting on, tasting, licking, sucking, devouring.

Fuck! What the hell was I thinking suggesting she stay here? And I'm supposed to be working at home for the next several weeks? I should've gotten her a hotel room and paid someone to take care of her.

"Hey, are you okay?" Ellie asks, her brows furrowing in concern.

"Yeah," I choke out, grabbing the towel and tossing it to her. "Maybe, uh, you should check out maternity suits if you're going to be spending time by the pool."

She quirks her head to the side. "Yeah, probably. But this one still fits, and nobody's here but us." She wraps the towel around herself, covering her body, and I'm finally able to release a harsh breath.

As she saunters inside, completely unaware of the effect she has on me, I follow behind, wondering how the hell I'm going to get through the next several weeks. And then it hits me. It's not just a few weeks I have to get through. It's months, no, scratch that, *years*. Ellie being pregnant means we'll be connected through this baby in some shape or form for the rest of our lives. I'll have to see her every day, knowing I can never have her again.

"This smells delicious," she says, as she pries open the bag and dramatically inhales the scent of the food. When she reaches in and grabs the top container, she pulls the lid off and dips a finger into the *queso* and then pops that finger into her mouth. As she sucks the liquid cheese off her digit, her eyes roll backward, and the most erotic moan escapes her, reminding me of the sounds she uttered as I made her come over and over again.

Fuck, I can't do this. This is goddamned torture. "I need to shower," I choke out as I stalk out of the room to my en suite bathroom, where I proceed to rub one out.

Only when I fist my cock, images of Ellie come to mind—writhing underneath me, begging me for more. It doesn't matter that I couldn't see her...I could feel her, taste her, smell her...

Refusing to get off to the image of her while I'm in the shower, I let go of my shaft and press my head against the cool wall, wondering not for the first time what the fuck I'm doing.

When I walk back out to the kitchen—my body tense due to the lack of release—Ellie's sitting at the island bar, eating her food. She looks up, her green eyes locking with mine, and a small, unsure smile quirks at the corner of her lips. "I made you a plate."

"Thanks." I sit next to her and notice she's reading on her phone. When she was younger, she always had a book in her hand. Her sister is the same way.

"Reading anything good?" I ask, attempting to make conversation as I take a bite of my quesadilla.

"Apparently when I give birth there's a chance that I'll shit myself."

I'm in the middle of chewing when she says this, so I not only choke, but my food goes flying out of my mouth and all over the counter.

"What?" I ask, sure I heard her wrong.

"That's what it says," Ellie replies, looking at me with wide eyes.

"What the hell are you reading?"

"*What to Expect When You're Expecting*. I figured the more I know, the better I'll be prepared." Her words come out nonchalant, but I can hear the undertone in them—she's scared. She never had a mom growing up, aside from her older sister, Sienna, who took on the mother role, which isn't the same. Sienna grew up having to care for Ellie, so becoming a mom was natural to her, but Ellie doesn't have any experience with taking care of anyone but herself, and she's worried she won't be good at it.

I lean over and palm her face, turning her head so she's forced to look at me. "We've got this, Kitten. This baby will be loved and cared for and want for nothing. Hell, he's already loved and he's not even here yet."

Tears prick her eyes, and I move my thumb to wipe one that escapes. "Thank you," she says softly. "I know I messed up, but—"

"Enough of that," I tell her, dropping my hand from her face. She might've made a bad choice, but she didn't do it maliciously. She was desperate to feel again, to be intimate with someone, and she trusted me enough to know I would never hurt her. "I'm glad it was me you went to. Some other guy might not have understood your cues."

I could tell from the moment we met at the club, she was skittish and needed to be handled with care. I tried to walk away, telling myself I didn't want to deal with it, so when one of my employees told me someone was asking to speak to me, I took that as my sign. But then fate intervened, and I ran into her when she was heading out. And I knew I needed to have her. I could tell she wasn't experienced, and she confirmed that the little experience she had wasn't good, but I didn't know how deep the demons went that haunted her.

"That's what happened before," she admits. "I tried being with other guys. Once in high school and then a few times in college, but every time, I'd freak out. They would be too rough, too selfish. I didn't know how to explain what I needed because I wasn't sure myself. And then Rae said I needed someone I trusted, and you were the only one I thought of."

"And how was it?" I ask, genuinely wanting to know—but also curious, since I'm the only person she's been with—yeah, I'm refusing to count those fucking assholes who raped her.

Ellie's cheeks tint a light shade of pink, and I immediately wonder if they were that color the night we were together. "Well, I don't have much to compare our night to..." She smiles sheepishly. "But it was good...Really good, actually. Like, you totally put my vibrator to shame. Whoever comes next will have a lot to live up to," she says with a laugh.

But I don't join in because the thought of her being with someone else isn't funny—at fucking all. The idea of some other guy seeing her naked—when I didn't even get to do that—or kissing her and feeling her soft, creamy skin and then sliding inside her warmth as she moans in pleasure, causes my blood to boil and my fists to clench.

Fuck that, Ellie is mine.

And before I can think about what I'm doing, I'm wrapping my fingers around her nape and pulling her face toward me, fusing our mouths together. My tongue demands entrance, and she opens, granting me access.

My hand ascends, fisting the back of her hair, and I deepen the kiss, our tongues tangling as we greedily taste one another. She tastes spicy with a hint of something that's all her. And when I suck on her tongue, and she moans into my mouth, I'm instantly hard, desperate for more than just her kiss.

I need every goddamn part of her. The parts I've already savored that left me hungering for another taste. The parts I never got to experience.

Every. Fucking. Part.

I lift her onto the island and spread her legs, so I can stand between them, and then yank the towel off her body. I step back for a moment, wanting to take her in now that we're in the light, needing to rememorize every goddamn curve on her.

Micah's cautionary words creep into the back of my mind, but the second our eyes connect, and she looks at me like I'm everything she could ever want or need, I shove his words out the door, slam that bitch shut, and lock it.

Breaking our gaze, I notice her cheeks are flushed, and her lips are swollen from being kissed. Her hair is messy from my fingers running through it. Her chest is heaving rapidly, and her nipples are poking through the thin material of her bikini top. I want to continue to drink her in, but I'm dying of thirst and need an actual taste.

"Take your top off," I demand. Without argument, Ellie reaches back and unties the knots, the material falling into her lap and exposing her luscious tits.

I waste no time, taking one in my hand and kneading it, while my lips wrap around the other. Her moans of pleasure spur me on, as I lick and suck on her nipple, while my thumb continues to stroke and caress her other peak. I don't stop until she's writhing against me, her legs tightening around my waist, and then she's coming...fucking coming from my touch alone. I remember Micah mentioning how sensitive Sienna is when she's pregnant, but holy shit, this is insane.

"Oh my God," Ellie moans, clearly as shocked by her quick

orgasm as I am.

"Did that feel good?" I ask, trailing fiery kisses over her breasts, not wanting to stop touching her. Knowing the moment I do, I'll have to deal with the reality of my actions.

"Yes," she breathes.

"Good, because you're about to come again."

I push her chest back slightly, so she's forced to lean back on her elbows, and when she does this, her belly pushes out, showing off her bump. I never found pregnancy attractive, always associated it with crying babies and losing your freedom, but as I kiss her swollen belly, I can't help but reconsider my stance. This woman is carrying my baby, protecting and nurturing him, until he's ready to enter this crazy world. And if that isn't sexy, I don't know what is.

I press a kiss to the top of her naval and remember something from Sienna being pregnant. "Can you feel him?" I ask, glancing up at Ellie.

"Not yet. I read around twenty weeks."

I make a mental note of that and continue my explorations, kissing each side of her hips. When I press an open-mouthed kiss to the material covering her cunt, my lips go wet from her arousal. She's so turned on, she's soaked her bikini bottoms.

Instead of having her remove them, I pull the strings myself and watch as the front triangle flops downward, exposing her neatly trimmed pussy.

"Put your feet on the counter."

She does as I say, and her lips spread slightly, her arousal glistening in the light.

"Fuck, Kitten. You're dripping."

My words must embarrass her because she attempts to close her legs, but I'm not having it. "Keep 'em open," I order. "I'm about to eat this pussy, and when I'm done, you'll be sitting in a fucking puddle."

"Oh, Jesus," she groans as she spreads those toned, tanned legs wider, giving me the perfect opening to put my face between them and eat the hell out of her.

I could easily focus on her clit and bring her to a climax quickly, but instead, I make a show of feasting on her, sucking her juices, licking everywhere but the spot that will set her off. She moans and begs, but it's not until her fingers delve into my hair and demands I make her come that I finally give her what she craves. I glide the flat of my tongue up her center until I settle on her clit, massaging it in slow circles until she's coming all over my tongue, her juices sliding down and covering the counter just as I predicted.

Without waiting for her to come down from her high—because I need to be inside her right fucking now—I pull my sweats down, then pull her toward me, so her ass is hovering off the counter. Her eyes widen, and her body tenses, and I stop in my place, remembering her past.

"Hey," I say, making her expressive green eyes look at me, "you're here with me. In my penthouse, on my kitchen counter, about to be fucked until you come for a third time all over my cock."

She nods in agreement, her body instantly relaxing, and I take that as my cue to slowly guide my hard shaft into her hole. With our eyes staying locked on each other, I lean over and kiss her softly, then murmur against her lips, "Wrap your arms and legs around me." The night we were together, she never said it, but I could tell she preferred to be on top and in control. And now that I know what she went through, it makes sense.

Once our bodies are flush, I lift and carry her over to the couch, sitting on it with my cock still inside her. The position forces me to go deeper, and Ellie moans in pleasure.

"That feel good?" I ask, reinforcing that it's me inside her and not one of those fuckers from years ago.

"Yes," she breathes, "so good." She's now completely relaxed, confirming my suspicions. When those fuckers raped her, she had no control, but when she's on top like this, it makes her feel like she has all the power—and I'm completely okay with that.

"When you're ready, I want you to move," I tell her, squeezing the curves of her hips gently. "Find what feels good."

She visibly swallows, and then a few seconds later, she starts to move. While I let her do her thing, I focus my attention on her rosy nipples, leaning forward and licking them. When my lips wrap around the hardened peak and I bite down, her walls tighten, telling me she's close—which is good, since I haven't had sex since I was with her, meaning I won't be able to last much longer.

"I...I can't," she whines, her hips rolling and grinding. She's new to this, and she knows what feels good, but it's not always easy to get there, especially like this.

"I've got you," I murmur, taking over from the bottom and searching for her sweet spot. I know I've found it when she moans and begs me not to stop. I keep going, hitting the spot until she's screaming out my name, her walls choking my cock like a vice and sending me over the edge right along with her.

It's when we've both caught our breaths and she attempts to climb off me—the mixture of our cum sliding out of her and down my dick and balls—that it hits me what we just did, and what's worse, it only took mere hours of her staying with me for it to happen.

"I'm gonna go clean up," she says, sounding off.

Before I can say anything, though, she's padding across the marble floor and disappearing down the hall to her room, the sound of the door slamming closed echoing behind her.

I should go after her to make sure she's okay, but I'm frozen in place, wondering not for the first time what the fuck I'm doing.

I ate her.

Fucked her.

Gave her three goddamned orgasms.

It was good. No, fuck that...It was amazing. Just as I

remembered it being with her. Better this time because I could see her.

It wasn't enough. I already want her again. I'm addicted.

And that sucks because it can't happen again.

Because she's off-limits.

Fuck.

Seventeen

ELLIE

ONE MINUTE, I WAS DEVOURING THE MEXICAN FOOD LINCOLN brought home, and the next, I was being devoured by him. I don't even know how it happened, but I guess the how doesn't really matter. It happened, and it was even more amazing than the night we spent together at Elite. Not only could I feel him, taste him, and smell him, but I could watch as he kissed and consumed and devoured me like he was starved, and I was the only thing that could satiate his hunger.

This entire day has gone completely off course in the best way possible. When I woke up, I thought I'd spend the morning dancing, then go to my appointment where I'd get to see my baby, and then have dinner with Sienna and her family.

But instead, Lincoln not only showed up and made it clear he wants to be part of our baby's life, but he went with me to my doctor's appointment and then took me to lunch for my birthday, complete with a birthday cake. After spending the afternoon lounging by the pool and relaxing, I ended my birthday with a taste of Lincoln—and yummy quesadillas.

But, of course, you can't have the good without the bad, right? It has to balance itself out, which is why I'm sitting in the living room alone, staring at the television. After Lincoln and I came down from our orgasms, we cleaned up and ate at the island. He at least didn't make it too awkward, instead talking about the appointment, when the next one is, if I've checked my blood pressure...But he ate quickly and then used the excuse that he has work to do before hightailing it out of there and closing himself off in his office for the rest of the evening.

I should probably call it a night, but I'm afraid if I go to sleep, I'll wake up and it'll be like nothing ever happened. So, instead, I'm sitting on the couch, watching mindless television and hoping Lincoln will come out and give me some kind of sign as to what the hell this means. At least then I'll know where to go from here.

The night we hooked up at Elite, I assumed after we had sex, Lincoln would be done, but instead, he took me in his arms and held me. We connected. And I guess I was hoping that would happen again. But with him closing himself off, it's left me questioning everything: Was it a mistake? Does he regret what happened? Is this normal after sex, for people to go their separate ways? Am I overthinking this?

I want to ask Sienna, but a huge red flag would be raised, and the last thing I want is to make our family dynamics even more awkward.

One show bleeds into another...Raelyn calls and wishes me a happy birthday, and I avoid telling her what happened. Another show, and Sienna calls to see how the rest of my day was. Again, I keep it simple, and she updates me on the girls and their stomach bug. Micah is working from home, and they're all quarantining in the penthouse. London's birthday party is postponed until they're all healthy.

I fall asleep sometime during the third show and wake up to the smoky scent of whiskey and something that's all Lincoln as he carries me to my room and lays me on my bed. I'm already in my pajamas, so he unfolds the blanket and then covers me with it.

"Goodnight, Kitten," he murmurs, thinking I'm asleep, as he leans over and kisses my forehead.

"Wait," I say, latching onto his wrist before he can leave. "I…" I want to ask what today meant, but when I open my eyes and find his features a mixture of confusion and pain, almost as if he's at war with himself, I lose the courage to ask, afraid of what his answer might be. Afraid that if I try to slap a label on what this means, I won't like the label he gives me.

So, instead, I go with the whole *ignorance is bliss* mindset, and when he raises his brow, silently prompting me to continue with whatever I need to say, I change my direction. "I want you," I tell him brazenly, sitting up on my knees so we're almost eye level. He swallows apprehensively and flinches slightly, and then he stares at me for several seconds, like he's trying to figure out what to do or say. When he stays motionless for what feels like an eternity, I assume he's going to tell me no, and then I'll have my answer to the question I was afraid to ask anyway.

But instead, he shocks the hell out of me when he cups the side of my face and his mouth descends on mine. Unlike the frenzied kiss earlier, this one is soft and sensual. He kisses my top lip first and then moves to my bottom, sucking it into his mouth before he deepens the kiss. As his lips glide against my own, he gently pushes me onto my back and spreads my legs, so he's hovering above me, his arms caging me in like a protective cocoon.

"We shouldn't be doing this," he murmurs, his voice pained, "but I can't stop wanting you." His defeated tone has me closing my eyes, wondering if I should put a stop to this. I am the one who started it after all.

But before I can decide one way or another, Lincoln makes the decision for us by pressing his lips to mine once again. He tastes like whiskey and a hint of Lincoln, and I wish I could bottle it up and save it for when he stops thinking with his dick and puts a stop to all of this and I'm left with only the memory of the times we spent together.

I'll be sad, and I'll miss this—the chemistry and connection I feel when we're intimate in this way—but I'll also always be grateful to him for helping give me a piece of myself back. He could've held a grudge, but he didn't. And I never expected him to give me anything more than what he gave me that night at Elite, so every time he gives me a little more, I relish the extra gift I've been given.

As his lips linger on mine, warmth spreads through my body. And then he breaks the kiss and trails his lips across the curve of my jaw to my ear. "Vanilla is my new favorite scent," he whispers, causing the warmth to morph into an inferno. "I dreamed about this scent for months after that night...Fantasized about it. But fuck, Kitten, they didn't do it justice."

He runs the tip of his nose along my neck, inhaling my scent, and I briefly wonder if I should put the flames out now, before the fire inside me gets out of control and sets my heart ablaze. But I've learned that life is short and unpredictable, and all we can do is live in the right now because there might not be a tomorrow. So, that's what I'm going to do—live in the moment with Lincoln.

Tomorrow, he might not want me. He might wake up and regret everything we've done. He might insist we take a step back and focus on the baby we've created since we have years of co-parenting ahead of us. But today, Lincoln wants me. And for someone who went years craving yet fearing being wanted, being intimate with Lincoln, having him want me and me not push him away, feels pretty damn good.

"Take this off," he commands, sitting up on his haunches and helping me lift the tiny tank top I was wearing to bed. Because I'm braless, my breasts are immediately on display, and Lincoln wastes no time taking one in his hand and wrapping his lips around my nipple. He licks and sucks on the hardened peak, and I moan in pleasure. I never knew how good being intimate with someone could be. The men who raped me hurt me, and the boys I tried to be with afterward obviously didn't know their way around a woman's body, nor did they understand how to pleasure one. Until Lincoln, I felt broken, but little by little, he's piecing me back together.

Lincoln's tongue trailing down my torso takes me out of my thoughts as I focus on the way he's kissing and licking his way down my body. When he removes my cotton shorts and panties, he spreads my thighs slightly and lifts them to my chest. I'm not sure what he's doing, but since I trust him, I don't question it until his tongue lands on my puckered hole and flashbacks from that day crash into me like the strongest, unexpected wave, knocking me back and causing me to choke on salt water.

Force.
Pain.
Tearing.
Blood.
Screaming.
Begging.
Crying.

"Stop, please!" I choke out, the memories hitting me so deep, they've taken my breath away. Blackness prickles at my vision. White noise clogs my hearing. And then like a light switch, everything turns off. And I feel like I can finally breathe again.

Eighteen

ELLIE

"There she is," Lincoln says when I open my eyes and take in my surroundings, trying to remember what the hell happened. He's sitting against the headboard of my bed, and I'm cradled across his lap. I glance down and see that I'm dressed, and then it all comes back to me. Embarrassed by what transpired, I try to scramble off Lincoln, but he's not having it.

"Stop," he says gently, holding me tighter against him and palming the side of my face. "Talk to me. What happened?"

I hesitate to answer him, in fear of the flashbacks hitting me again, but when he pinches my chin and tips my face up to look at him, my body instantly relaxes. This is Lincoln. I can trust him. It was stupid to expect that because I haven't freaked out on him yet that it would never happen.

I keep my eyes on Lincoln as I speak, needing to remind myself that I'm here with him and safe. "When I was raped, they did it...

in every hole. But the worst was when they did it from behind, in *that* hole."

Lincoln's eyes darken in understanding. "Not now, but at some point, I need you to tell me what happened."

"No." I shake my head. "I can't do that. Please..."

"It's the only way I can assure what happened today doesn't happen again," he explains, and while what he says makes sense, the thought of verbalizing what they did makes me feel sick to my stomach. It doesn't matter that it's been years since it happened. Every time I think about it, it's as if it just happened.

"Everything we've done has been amazing," I whisper. "I just wasn't expecting that. But I'll be okay next time."

"Kitten..." Lincoln lays me on the bed and wraps himself around me like the most comforting blanket, trapping my legs in his. He slides one arm under my head and the other glides across my waist, resting on my hip. "You said you wanted to be with me because you trust me, right?"

I nod. "I trust you more than anyone else."

"Then I need you to trust me with what happened. It's the reason members of the club are required to fill out a form with their limits. Something you should've done. Luckily, nothing I did that night triggered you, but it could've. I never should've touched you without scanning you into the system, so I'd know your limits."

"If you would've done that, we never would've been together," I mutter.

"Probably," he admits, "but being the owner of Elite means I'm held to a higher standard, and what I did that night was irresponsible, and something could've gone seriously wrong."

"Why didn't you scan me in?" I ask curiously.

"I was too wrapped up in you. It's no secret I've been with my fair share of women..." When I pout at his admission, Lincoln chuckles. "Not as many as you're thinking."

"How many?"

"I don't keep track, and whatever number I give you won't make a difference. But the point I was trying to make is that even though I've been with other women, something about you felt different. From the moment I saw you at the bar, the chemistry between us was off the charts, and I was so shocked by my reaction to you, all my common sense got shoved out the door."

I can't help the smile that spreads across my face at the fact Lincoln just admitted that the connection he felt was between *us* and not some mystery woman. That night meant so much to me, and it warms my heart that it meant something to him as well.

"I'm glad it did," I tell him honestly. "I know that might be wrong of me to say, but you have no idea how many times I tried to be intimate with guys. I was afraid it would never happen."

"Which is why, as your partner, I need to know what happened. Not just for you but also for me, so I'm not caught up in my head worrying about what might trigger you."

"I don't want you to see me as that person," I say, closing my eyes. "I like the way you look at me. And I'm afraid if you know what they did...*What they made me do*, the way you look at me will change."

"Let me make something very clear," Lincoln says, palming the side of my face. I open my eyes and our gazes lock. "There's nothing those pieces of shits could've done to you that would make me want you any less. When I look at you, all I see is the beautiful, sexy woman who did what no other woman has ever done—made me want more." He presses his lips to mine and then breaks our connection far too quickly. "One day, you're going to tell me all that happened, and nothing you say will change a damn thing about how I see you, but for now, just tell me this: what is it you want?"

"You," I say without hesitation.

A small smile quirks in the corners of his lips. "And what do you want from me?"

"Everything," I tell him just before I wrap my arms around his neck and pull his face toward mine, kissing him with everything in me.

Our lips caress each other for several seconds before I pull back slightly. "I don't want them to win," I murmur against his mouth. "I don't want what they did to define me. I want to be with you in every way possible, for each memory we create to replace the one they burned into me."

Lincoln nods in understanding, and then his mouth is back on mine, kissing me with the type of passion that sends electrical currents through my body and to the apex of my legs. I break our connection to pull his shirt over his head, and he does the same to me, removing my shorts and panties as well.

Once I'm naked, he gently rolls on top of me, and our eyes meet. "I'm going to do what I did before," he says. "I want you to keep your eyes open and on me, and if you can't handle it, you have to tell me. Okay?"

"Okay," I breathe, a mixture of nervousness and excitement making my heart kick into overdrive. I've heard anal play can feel good, but since my experience was beyond painful, I never planned to find out. Now, with Lincoln, I want to see how good it can be. Everything we've done thus far has only brought me the best type of pleasure, and I have no doubt, he'll make this good too. I just have to hope I can stay in the moment with him.

"Focus on me," he says, noticing that I'm already lost in my own head. He kisses his way down my body, his eyes never leaving mine, and then spreads my thighs wide. Instead of going to my butt like he did last time, he focuses on my pussy, giving it attention until I'm dripping wet and begging for release. Then, he adds two fingers while massaging my clit, and I fly high onto the most amazing cloud of bliss.

Before I can come down from my high, my legs are pushed back, just like last time—only my eyes are on Lincoln's as he does it, so I know it's coming, allowing me to stay in the moment, in this room, in this bed, with him.

With his gaze never leaving mine, he dips his chin and makes a show of licking the juices that dripped down, his tongue gliding from the bottom of my ass and stopping once he's reached my pussy. Instinctually, I tighten my anus, the feeling foreign, but I don't freak out.

Lincoln continues to lick me from bottom to top, his tongue caressing and massaging my hole and then working its way to my clit. Every time his tongue ascends, he shifts my lower body downward, and when his tongue descends, it's shifted upward, creating a rhythm.

Up. Swipe. Lick. Suck. Down. Massage. Repeat.

Little by little, the past is replaced with the present.

Pain. Pleasure.

Screams. Moans.

Fear. Trust.

"That's it," he murmurs. "I can feel your orgasm. Come for me, Kitten."

Another swipe. Another Lick. One more suck. And my body detonates. The orgasm is so strong, my hips lift off the bed, and my legs tremble. Lincoln keeps me grounded, and when I've finally caught my breath and sit up, I feel like I've won yet another battle against my past.

When I scoot back, needing to clean up, a huge wet circle on the sheet catches my attention. Oh, God. Did I...?

"It's not urine," Lincoln says, as if he can hear my thoughts. "That's from you coming twice." He smirks, clearly happy with himself for making me do that, and I refuse to be embarrassed.

"I need to shower," I tell him, sliding off the bed while avoiding the spot—I'll deal with that after I'm clean.

When Lincoln makes no move to join me, I take his hand in mine and try to pull him off the bed, but he shakes his head, not budging. "I already showered before I came to find you in the living room."

"Fine, then." I grab his crotch that's sporting a hard-on. "I'll just have to dirty you up, so you'll be more inclined to get clean with me."

His hazel eyes widen, taken off guard since I've yet to give him head. The truth is, I've never given anyone head. Never wanted to.

"Ellie," Lincoln says softly, pulling me toward him. Because he's sitting and I'm standing, I have to glance down at him. "You don't have to do that. If you want me to shower with you, I'd be more than happy to do so."

"I've never done it before," I admit. "But I want to, so you'll have to help me since I'm sure you know exactly how you like it."

He searches my eyes for the truth in them, and when he sees that despite me being nervous, I truly mean it, he releases a sigh and nods. "Okay, but if at any point—"

"I'll stop and tell you," I finish.

Lincoln leans back and spreads his legs slightly. "I'm all yours," he says with a twinkle of mischief in his eyes. "Just don't bite and we'll be good."

When I flinch, his eyes cut into thin slits. "Talk to me."

"When I was raped, I never stopped kicking and screaming. I refused to accept what they were doing to me. One guy practically shoved it down my throat and began fucking my mouth, but I refused to accept what he was doing to me, so I bit down and drew blood. He slapped me so hard that I was flung across the room, but at least nobody else tried after that."

Lincoln's jaw tightens, and despite him saying he wants to hear everything that happened to me, I worry that I shouldn't have said anything.

"Good," he says, his tone dark. "If those assholes were still alive, I'd torture them until they begged for death."

"Knowing they were dead is how I got through many nights." I step toward him and reach out, pressing my palm to his heart. His body is like a work of art—chiseled and toned and perfectly tan. "I don't want to think about them. I want to forget. I want to move forward and live my best life with you"—I press my other hand to the curve of my belly since I'm still naked—"and our baby. I spent years fighting for my broken pieces to heal, and thanks to you, they're finally doing just that."

I glide my hand down the hard ridges of his abs and stop where his happy trail meets the waistband of his pants. "I want to taste you, just like you tasted me." I pull his pants down, and he lifts slightly, helping me push them down his muscular thighs. "I want to make you feel as good as you make me feel." I kneel between his legs. "I want to replace another horrible memory with a good one."

I wrap my fingers around his shaft, getting a feel for the velvety smooth skin, and then I lean over slightly and give the head a hesitant, open-mouthed kiss.

When a low growl vibrates through Lincoln, hitting my lips, I do it again, this time, sliding my tongue across the tip so I can taste him, the salty liquid hitting my taste buds.

"Jesus, Kitten," Lincoln groans, "you trying to kill me slowly?"

His words spur me on. Parting my lips, I glide my mouth down his entire length, stopping just before the head hits the back of my throat and then come back up, stopping at his crown. When my eyes meet his and see that they're filled with molten desire, my confidence rises, and I take him into my mouth again, this time suctioning my lips around his shaft.

"Fuck yes," he moans as I bob my head, creating friction with my saliva. When I glance back up, wanting to see the pleasure on his features, Lincoln locks eyes with mine. "You're doing so good...Fucking perfect."

At his praises, I take him deeper, suck him harder, and I don't stop until he's cautioning me that he's going to come. But I ignore his warning, wanting to swallow every last drop of him.

Once I've licked him clean, he pulls me up, so I'm tucked into his side, my head resting against his chest. We lie like this for several minutes in silence, and I start to wonder if he's fallen asleep, but then he reaches up and tips my chin, forcing me to look at him.

"Ellie, I..." he begins, and I hold my breath, having no clue what he's going to say. He doesn't finish his thought for several seconds, but the turmoil in his eyes causes my stomach to roil, and I pray he doesn't tell me this can't happen again.

"Yeah?" I prompt, the suspense damn near giving me heartburn.

"We should shower." He forces a fake smile and then slides out of bed and pads toward the bathroom. When I don't follow, wondering what he really wanted to say but too scared to ask, he glances back. "C'mon, dirty girl. I need to clean you up." He shoots a playful wink my way, and I tell myself it's for the best because my heart might not be able to handle what he was about to say.

Ignorance is bliss, right?

Nineteen

LINCOLN

Delicious curves.

Vanilla scent.

Plump lips that are parted slightly.

Soft snoring.

I can't stop watching her sleep. Yesterday never should've happened. Eliza Bardot is not available for the taking—at least not by me. I knew that, but that didn't stop me from taking her in my living room on the goddamned couch and then in my guest room and again in the shower.

I've thought about my mystery woman for the past several months, and if I were honest, I considered that maybe I'd just imagined the connection. That once I found her and was with her again, I'd realize that I had worked it up into something more than just your typical one-night-stand—something I've done many times and never thought twice about.

I was wrong, though. My memory of that night didn't do the chemistry between us justice. It's deeper, stronger, and I'm completely fucked because regardless of how many times I've already crossed that line with Ellie, I had promised Micah that his sister-in-law would always remain off-limits to me.

Ellie inhales a sharp breath and then releases a sigh, turning slightly onto her back. I slide my gaze down her perky breasts that are hidden by the tiny tank she's wearing, her nipples poking through the material, and land on her swollen belly.

She's pregnant with my baby. We heard his heartbeat yesterday, which was surreal. I've listened to Micah talk about Sienna's pregnancies, but experiencing the ultrasound for myself, was unlike anything I've ever experienced.

My hand goes to her belly, gently laying my palm flat against the baby bump, just as Ellie's eyes shoot open. She blinks several times before her gaze descends to where my hand is resting.

"Sorry," I mutter, pulling back. "I didn't mean to wake you."

"I'm a light sleeper," she murmurs groggily.

We stare at each other for several seconds, and there's so much I want to say, but I'm confused by my feelings and wouldn't even know where to start. In the world I live in, when you want something, you go for it. Our dad raised Micah and me to work hard, and while I'm a bit more carefree than Micah, I still bust my ass every day to create the life I want.

Yet, here I am, lying in bed with a woman whom I'm attracted to, who's carrying my baby, who's within touching distance, and no matter how badly I want to have her, I know I can't. Last night, despite how amazing it was, never should've happened, and once we leave this bed, I need to ensure that it doesn't happen again. And that is something I need Ellie to fully understand. But first, I need to apologize for giving in to my baser instincts. Beg her to forgive me for not being the responsible one when I unequivocally know better. She's young and pregnant and vulnerable, and I took advantage of that.

"What are you thinking about?" Ellie asks, edging closer and palming the side of my face. Her touch causes me to flinch, and the corner of her lips turn down into a frown in response.

"I have a lot of work I need to do," I answer lamely.

She nods in understanding and backs up. "I should probably go to the studio..." Her words trail off and she sighs, shaking her head. "Well, shit, I'm supposed to be taking it easy, huh?" She laughs humorlessly. "Guess no studio...And Sienna's quarantined, so I can't see her or my nieces." She pouts, clearly getting more annoyed by the second. "Guess I'll shower and start looking online for a place to live." She shrugs and slides off the bed, leaving me lying here wondering how the hell we went from fucking all night and me holding her while we slept, to her looking for a place to live.

Oh, right. I know how we got here: Me...Because I'm a bastard who fell for a woman I'm not supposed to have.

"Happy Father-To-Be Day." Ellie hands me a square box that's been giftwrapped in silver paper. I look at the box for several seconds, wondering what the hell she's talking about, until it hits me—it's Father's Day. And I'm an expectant father. And then I feel like shit because when it was Mother's Day, I didn't acknowledge that Ellie was an expectant mother. In my defense, however, I had only just found out she was pregnant and wasn't in the mindset to think about things like that. I had wished my mom and Sienna a Happy Mother's Day—after Micah reminded me—and avoided everyone else, lost in my own head.

I take the gift from her and unwrap it. Inside is a black book. When I open it, I find a couple of sonogram pictures with the dates written underneath it. The rest of the pages are empty.

"It's a baby book," Ellie says. "Women tend to have cuter ones, but I figured black was more your style. You can add to it as the baby grows and then more after our son is born. I got one for Micah when they were expecting London, and he keeps it on his desk at work. I figured you might like one as well."

Our son.

Ellie and I are having a son.

"This is awesome," I tell her, leaning in and kissing her cheek, while struggling to fight back my feelings toward Ellie that are threatening to break free. "Thank you."

It's been a rough several days since I woke up in bed with Ellie and reminded myself that I need to maintain a safe distance. Avoiding a woman who lives in your home that you are attracted to on a deeper level has a way of testing a man's restraint like no other. I can't even count the number of times I've jacked off in the shower. She probably thinks I have some sort of OCD about being clean.

"You're welcome," she says with a small smile before heading into the kitchen to make her morning tea. Every day she starts with tea and breakfast, then she moves on to yoga and a shower. From there, she spends her day television surfing, lounging by the pool, and reading—avoiding Ellie doesn't mean I've stopped paying attention.

"How's it going?" Micah asks.

I glance at the plans I'm looking over and sigh into the phone. "It's going…" If going means reading the damn thing five times because I can't get a certain brown-hair, green-eyed woman off my mind. Living with her is turning out to be quite the distraction, especially since I spend most of my time fantasizing about what I wish I could have but can't.

"The kids and Sienna are finally one-hundred-percent again, so we're planning to have London's party on Sunday."

"Sounds good."

"How's Ellie? Sienna said she's been kind of quiet. She's tried to video chat with her since she couldn't see her in person, but she's not very talkative."

That's probably because I fucked her seven ways to Sunday, spent the night in her bed, and then pushed her away. And aside from the necessary questions like "I'm ordering food. Want anything?" or "How's your blood pressure doing?" I've been avoiding her like the plague. And she's caught on, glaring at me every time I run into her.

"She's been taking it easy," I tell him honestly. "I'm sure once Sienna sees her in person that will help with them reconnecting."

"Yeah, I hope so. Well, at least now Ellie can move back in here and get out of your space."

"Yeah," I agree noncommittally, my stomach tightening at the thought of Ellie no longer sleeping under my roof. It's been a test to my restraint living with a woman I want every single second of every day, but I'm handling it, and once the baby comes, I'd like for us to co-parent together. She mentioned getting her own place, but I was hoping she'd consider living with me instead.

My stomach growls, reminding me that I haven't eaten since early this morning. "Hey, listen, I need to grab something to eat and send the plan revisions for the hotel and casino to the architect. Text me a calendar invite for London's birthday, so I don't forget."

We hang up and I head out of my office, starved and hoping there's something good to eat in the fridge. I ordered Italian last night, and I'm pretty sure there was some chicken fettucine leftover…Only when I step out of my office and see Ellie, dressed in tight leggings and a tiny sports bra that has her breasts practically spilling out of the top, the only thing I'm suddenly hungry for is her.

She's on her mat, on all fours. Her face is pointed toward the ceiling, and her eyes are closed. Her back is arched, and her round ass is sticking up in the air. With the music playing in the surround sound, she isn't aware she has an audience, and my only thought as I watch her inhale and exhale while she stretches is how easy it would be to get on my knees behind her, tear those pants down her legs, and eat her pussy and ass from behind.

My cock, clearly on the same page, starts to swell in excitement, and I know if I don't get the hell out of here, I'm going to do something I'll regret again.

But before I can make my feet move—no clue if I'm going back to my office to hide some more or making a run for it out the front door—Ellie's face lowers as she turns to the side, her eyes opening and connecting with mine. And one day when I look back, I'll remember this as the moment that I knew I was utterly screwed because my need to be with this woman outweighs my ability to do the right thing by staying away from her.

"Nice of you to come out of hiding," she says, finishing her stretch and then standing. The perspiration glistening on her neck and chest descends into the swells of her breasts, and it takes everything in me not to close the distance between us and lick the salty liquid off her flesh. I'd bet my entire bank account she smells like the perfect mixture of sweat and vanilla.

"I'm hungry."

She stares at me for several seconds, her expression looking as if she wants to say something, but instead, she simply nods and walks away, her pert ass swaying as she goes. I watch, mesmerized, until she disappears down the hallway, and her door shuts behind her.

And then I continue to stare because I can't stop wishing the circumstances were different so I could make her mine.

After forcing myself to go to the kitchen to make myself something to eat, I'm in the middle of heating up some leftovers when a loud scream comes from Ellie's room. I drop what I'm doing, and without knocking, plow through her door. My only thought is that I need to get to Ellie. Something could be wrong with her or the baby. What if she slipped?

But when I get inside her room, she's rushing out of the bathroom at the same time, and we collide—her very wet, naked body running straight into my arms, soaking my entire front.

"Are you okay?" I choke out, trying like hell to focus on her and not the way her dripping wet flesh is pressed up against me.

"There's a huge ass spider in there, like the size of my freaking head. And I'm pretty sure it has babies."

"What?"

"A spider! Lincoln, go kill it!" She breaks our contact and shoves me toward the bathroom door. "Go, please!"

Stifling my laugh, I do as she says and head into the bathroom with her following behind. I immediately spot the spider in the corner of the shower and, with balled up toilet paper, smash it and drop it into the toilet, flushing it straight to hell.

The second it's gone, Ellie breathes a sigh of relief. Then, as if suddenly realizing that in her moment of panic she ran out naked, she glances down at herself and then up at me, her cheeks flush and eyes wide.

She attempts to cover her breasts and pussy the best she can, but it's too late. I've already seen her. And fuck if I don't want her. She's still dripping wet, and all I can think about is drying her off inch by inch with my tongue.

My brain tells me to run, but every other part of me begs me to stay. I'm unsure which way to go, until Ellie sucks her bottom lip into her mouth as her hooded emerald eyes rake over my wet shirt that's clinging to my upper torso. Decision made.

Without giving myself time to change my mind, I bridge the gap between us, but I don't need to go far because Ellie does the same, meeting me halfway. Our bodies and mouths collide, and I lift her onto the counter, stepping between her parted thighs, ready to devour her in this bathroom.

And then the doorbell rings throughout the penthouse. *Fuck.*

"I better go get that," I murmur, stepping back and refusing to make eye contact with the woman who's supposed to be prohibited but who I still almost fucked again.

Without waiting for her to respond, I hightail it out of the bathroom and head straight to the door, pulling it open without considering how I might look.

Well, in hindsight, I should've considered it because when the door flies open, standing on the other side are none other than Michael and Donna Alexander, my parents.

"Why are you soaked?" Dad asks, stepping around me.

"You look flushed, honey," Mom says, pressing her palm to my cheek. "Are you coming down with that bug the girls had?"

"What? No, I'm fine," I tell them, closing the door behind me. I glance down the hall, praying Ellie stays in her room until I can tell them about her. Because one look at her swollen belly and they're going to know I knocked up the woman they view as family.

"What are you guys doing here?" I blurt out, making Mom frown. "I thought you weren't coming home for a couple more weeks."

"We decided to fly home in time for London's party," Mom says, having a seat on the couch. "Got in this morning."

"And you came straight here?"

"You've been acting strange," Dad says. "Your mother is concerned."

"I'm—"

There's a bang and then a "Shit! Ow, ow, ow!" And without thought, I run straight to Ellie's room, concerned she—or the baby—is hurt.

"What's wrong?" I ask, when I find her sitting on the bed, her face etched in pain—and thankfully dressed. Her hand is holding her side, and there are tears in her eyes.

"I tripped and hit my side on the corner of the dresser." I kneel in front of her and lift her top, exposing the area already bruising on her side.

"Should we go to the hospital?" I ask.

"No, it just hurt really freaking bad."

"Oh, Ellie, what are you doing here?" my mom asks.

Out of shock, we both stand at the same time, and because I had lifted her shirt up, her round belly is still showing.

"Oh my God!" Mom gasps. "Are you pregnant?"

Dad steps into the room, next to mom, his gaze flicking from Ellie to me. "Son, don't tell me..."

"Is this why you've been acting so weird?" Mom says. "Ellie's staying with you?"

Oh shit.

The look on Dad's face tells me he's put the pieces together. Mom...Not so much.

"Lincoln," he barks. "Did you do this?"

"What?" Mom looks from us to my dad in confusion. "What are you asking, Michael?"

"He's asking if I'm the father of Ellie's baby, and the answer is yes."

Mom's eyes go wide. "Oh," she breathes, her gaze darting between me and Ellie, who's standing frozen in her spot, watching this train wreck of a conversation come to a head. "So, are you two together?"

"No," I blurt out. "It was an accident."

Mom's eyes bug out of her head, Dad's turn into thin slits, and Ellie drops her head, hiding the frown I saw before she could hide it.

"I don't understand," Mom says. "You slept with Ellie casually? Of all the women you could've been with..." She shakes her head in disappointment. "I thought we raised you better than this."

"It's complicated," I tell my parents, knowing that's not enough of an explanation but not wanting to throw Ellie under the bus, and really...I'm not lying. It is complicated.

"Donna," Ellie cuts in. "This wasn't Lincoln's fault."

"Ellie," I warn, shaking my head.

"No, I'm not going to let them look at you like that," she says. "This is my fault." She places a protective hand on her belly. "I went to Elite and sought Lincoln out on Valentine's Day. He didn't know it was me because I was wearing a mask for the masquerade party. We spent the night together, but I failed to think about birth control beforehand. I didn't plan to get pregnant, but my irresponsibility is the reason why I am. Not Lincoln."

She sniffles back her tears. "I wouldn't blame Lincoln if he didn't want anything to do with this baby. He didn't ask for this. But you raised him right, so he's agreed to be a part of the baby's life. I'm so sorry," she says, swiping away her tears. "Your family has been so good to me and my sister, and I messed up big time. But please don't blame Lincoln. It's all on me."

"It's on both of us," I say, refusing to let her take all the blame. "I might not have known who Ellie was, but I was completely on board with having sex with her at the club. And not using protection was on me as well."

"So, what now?" Dad asks.

"Now we take it one day at a time, starting with getting ready for our son to arrive in November."

"Your son?" Mom asks, perking up. "You're having a little boy?"

Ellie nods, a small smile gracing her face. "We got to see him at the ultrasound. He looks like the cutest little gummy bear." Then, as if she forgot she shouldn't be happy because of my parents being upset, she schools her features. "I really am sorry," she says to my parents. "I know what a mess I've created."

"Oh, honey." Mom pulls Ellie into her arms. "It's all going to be okay. I'm a firm believer that everything happens for a reason." Mom's eyes meet mine, and she smiles softly, silently telling me that she's no longer upset. My shoulders slump in relief. I don't know what the future holds, but what I do know is that we're going to need our family by our side.

Twenty

ELLIE

"Oh my God. He's so precious." Sienna coos over the sonogram picture in a way that only a mother can do while staring at a black and white grainy photo.

"He looks like a gummy bear, right?"

She stares at the image closely then barks out a laugh. "He totally does." She sets the picture down on the island and looks at me. "How are you doing?"

It's Friday, and I've spent the week at Lincoln's since he insisted that I stay with him so he can keep an eye on me because of my high blood pressure—which has been doing better. While he's made sure the fridge is stocked and we've eaten a few times together, he's also avoiding me.

"I'm okay." I shrug. "I need to find somewhere to live." I sigh, and Sienna quirks her head to the side, picking up on the uneasiness I'm feeling.

"Obviously you can afford a place, so what's wrong?"

"Being here dredges up old memories I wish to leave in the past," I admit. "I know one event shouldn't change the entire course of my life, especially since the people involved are all dead, but I can't help feeling like this town is tainted. At least in California, I could live in denial. Here, not so much."

Sienna nods in understanding. "For a few years, I refused to drive on the side of town where the warehouse was. It's been turned into a shopping plaza, but when I go by it, all I see is that day."

"I never should've gone to see Eleazar."

"You were trying to protect us," she says, placing her hand over mine. "We were going to run, and I was going to have to leave Micah behind, and all you wanted was to stop that from happening. We've always had each other's backs, El. You believed in Micah and me before I did, and you couldn't have possibly known what that crazy psycho woman was going to do. None of us blames you. Hell, I wouldn't have the family I have, if it weren't for you."

I blame me...And I always will. But it's pointless to argue. Sienna only ever sees the good in me.

"Is everything set for London's party?" It's taking place at the indoor water park on Sunday, and despite having to be in the same vicinity as Lincoln, I'm looking forward to spending the day with my nieces in the water, even if I can't go down the good waterslides.

"Yep. She's excited."

A beep sounds through the room, and a second later, the front door opens, and Micah and Lincoln are sauntering inside while they talk business.

"There's my beautiful wife," Micah says when he sees Sienna and I are sitting in the kitchen. He palms her cheek and gives her a kiss that borders on inappropriate, and I can't help but wish, not for the first time, that I was loved and adored the way my sister is.

I look away to give them their privacy, and my eyes land on Lincoln, standing in the corner, staring at me with a mixture of heat and lust in his gaze.

Ever since I returned home and he found out I'm pregnant with his baby, he's been hot and cold. First, ignoring me for weeks. Then, on my birthday he went from sweet—going to the doctor with me and then taking me for lunch—to taking me on the counter and couch and again in the shower. The next morning, he was cold again, obviously having regretted what went down between us the night before.

Honestly, I was shocked he let it happen at all. But then again, from what Sienna told me, he was very much attracted to his mystery woman, *Liz*, when he didn't know she was me. Between Valentine's Day, my birthday night, and the other day in the bathroom when he almost took me on the counter, it's clear Lincoln wants me, but he doesn't *want* to want me because I'm so much younger than him, and he believes that's a definitive line he shouldn't cross.

And since I'm the one who created this awkward as hell situation by getting knocked up, I feel like I don't have a leg to stand on. But at the same time, I'm not about to become his doormat.

Which is why I need to find my own place, so the temptation will be gone, and we can focus on co-parenting because that's what's most important—the little gummy bear in my belly who I'm determined to make sure has two loving parents and a better life than I ever had.

"Micah, stop," Sienna says through a giggle. "I'm having coffee with Ellie. Go run your empire."

Micah chuckles. "I'd rather run you straight to bed."

"Ugh, so cheesy." Sienna shakes her head. "Go away so we can have our girl time."

"Actually," I say, standing and clearing my throat. "I need to get going anyway." I force a smile on my face. "I'm beginning my house hunting today." I don't actually have any appointments scheduled, or a realtor hired, but how hard can it be to find someone to show me some places that are for sale?

Sienna pouts but doesn't argue. "You want me to go with you? I can."

"Nope, I'm good. But if I find something I like, I promise to get your approval first."

I give her a kiss on the cheek and then smile awkwardly at Micah, hating that it will probably never be the same between us since I had sex with his brother and ended up pregnant.

Without giving Lincoln a second glance, I head out. Only instead of him staying with Micah, he follows me out and down the hall back to his place.

"You know you can stay here, right?" he says once we're inside. "We're having a baby together..."

"And we can co-parent from different homes," I finish. "I appreciate you letting me stay here while the girls were sick and you arranging to work from home to watch over me, but my blood pressure is improving. It's going to take some time to find a place, so hopefully the doctor will give me the all-clear by then so I can move into my new place and get settled before the baby comes."

Lincoln nods, but his pinched brows and pursed lips tell me he doesn't agree with what I'm saying, so I break it down for him in a way he'll understand.

"Linc, living together long term would never work. One day you're going to want to date, or I will, and then what? We bring them here? Put a scrunchie on the doorknob to alert the other person that we're having sex? I spent years living in fear of being sexually intimate with a man, and now that I've experienced how good it can feel, I want that."

"While you're pregnant?" Lincoln clips, making me roll my eyes.

"Obviously not while I'm pregnant. But after I give birth, I don't see any reason why I can't be a mom and still continue to date. I have no intention of bringing any man around my son until

I know he's good enough to be in his life, but I'm young and…" I swallow anxiously. "I want what Micah and Sienna have. I want to fall in love. I want to meet a man who will sweep me off my feet and love me the way I deserve to be loved. And I don't see that happening if I stay here."

Lincoln sighs. "You've always been a romantic."

"When you grow up in a world like mine, all you have is the hope of something better. It's why I clung to you when I was younger. You were the good in a world filled with so much bad. But I took advantage of your good, and for that I'll always be sorry."

"I already told you—"

"I know, I know." I laugh lightly. "You forgive me. But it's more than that. I never wanted to be anything like my mom, but here I am, pregnant from a one-night stand."

I rub my belly, hoping my baby will feel the love I already feel for him. "I have the money she didn't have, and thanks to you being so good about this, we'll give him two loving parents. But one day, I'd like to meet someone. I want the house filled with love and happiness. I want the shit you see in movies, like the perfect Christmases and family dinners. Sienna never imagined having it, but there she is, living her best life, and I want that too. But I can't have it with you. So, I'd rather move out now and start working on creating the life I want for myself and my baby."

"Our baby," he interjects.

"Our baby," I agree. "A baby we'll be raising together for at least the next eighteen years."

Lincoln nods in agreement.

"So, I was thinking…" I swallow thickly, hating the thought that's crossed my mind while I was pouring my soul out to him, but if we have any chance of getting through this parenting thing together, it's something that should probably happen. "I think we should agree to be friends."

"We've always been friends," Lincoln says, confusion etched

across his features.

"Eh." I tilt my head to the side and shrug my shoulder. "I think it was more of an 'I worshipped the ground you walked on, and you dealt with my teenage one-sided infatuation' sort of relationship, but I wouldn't call it a friendship."

Lincoln chuckles and shakes his head. "Trust me when I tell you that the infatuation was *very much* returned in recent events."

"But only because you didn't know it was me," I say, trying to keep the disappointment out of my voice. "So, friends?"

Lincoln doesn't look sold on the idea, and a part of me wants to ask if it's because the infatuation is still there and he craves more, or if being my friend is something he isn't interested in. But really the answer won't matter because regardless, Lincoln doesn't see a future with me, and we both deserve to find the person we want to spend our lives with."

"Friends," he finally says.

"Good." I plaster on a smile I hope one day will become real. "Now, I need to start house hunting. Wish me luck, *friend*." And with a playful wink, I disappear into my room to find a realtor.

"Have you had any luck finding a place yet?" Sienna asks, as we wade in the pool at the water park. Because it's indoors, they keep it at a perfect eighty degrees. We're both floating on our backs, relaxing with a virgin daiquiri in our hands.

"I have an appointment this week to see a few places." I take a sip of my drink and glance at Lincoln, who's chatting with his brother and dad. Unlike his usual businessman attire, today he's sporting board shorts that are hanging low on his hips, sans shirt.

"Lincoln mentioned that he told you he wants you to live with him."

"Yeah, but he's not thinking clearly. We can barely be in the same room as each other without fuck—" I cover my mouth, realizing my error too late, as Sienna scrambles to stand up, her drink falling into the water.

"You what?" she hisses, her gaze flitting between me and Lincoln.

"Nothing," I choke out, standing as well. "Nothing." I repeat.

"El, I heard you," she whisper-yells. "Please don't lie to me."

"I—" She arches a brow, daring me to lie, so I switch gears. "It's not that I want to lie to you," I say, glancing at the guys to make sure they're out of earshot. "But Micah's your husband, and you don't keep secrets."

"You're my sister," she says. "Whatever you say, stays between us."

"I don't want to put you in that position."

"You're not. I don't tell Micah everything. And I wouldn't tell him whatever you tell me unless you were in danger or something. You're not only my sister, but you're my best friend, and I've missed you these past several years. I want you to be able to talk to me. To trust that you can tell me anything. Please, no more secrets." The hurt on her face has me sighing in defeat.

"Okay, fine. While you guys were quarantined, Lincoln and I..." I clear my throat. "We had sex."

Her eyes go wide. "So, what? You're together?"

"No, that's the thing. He has it in his head that I'm off-limits, so afterward, he regretted it and then began avoiding me."

"That's because of Micah," she says with a frown. "He told Lincoln that you were too young and that he can't be with you. You were there."

"Yeah, I know, but that doesn't mean Micah's word has to be law."

"No, but you are several years younger than him."

I roll my eyes, hating that people take one's age so seriously. "Age is only just a number," I point out. "But it doesn't matter because Lincoln obviously agrees with Micah. And after his constant hot and cold crap, I finally had enough and told him we need to be friends if we want to co-parent. Hence, me needing to find a place to live."

I glance over at Lincoln and find him staring at me, his gaze burning with desire as he drags his eyes down my bikini clad body. Unlike some women who hide their pregnancy, I love my bump and have no problem sporting it.

"Holy shit," Sienna murmurs. "He's practically undressing you with his eyes."

Because she's right, and it's Lincoln's fault for not hiding his blatant lust for me better, I don't bother to deny it. "Which is why I need to move out. He may consider me off-limits, but his dick doesn't agree."

Twenty-One

ELLIE

"I'm starved. Any chance we can stop by the Mexican place on the way home? Oh! Or the sushi place. Mmm…Or Thai."

Lincoln chuckles from the driver's side. Since the water park was a bit of a drive, we carpooled because I haven't gotten a chance to buy my own vehicle yet. I'm putting it off, knowing I'm going to have to buy some sort of mom mobile like Sienna. Well, maybe not as mom-ish, since I'll only have one baby and she's about to have her third. "Which one?"

"Huh?"

"Which place," Lincoln asks. "Mexican, sushi, or Thai?"

"Oh, right. All three?"

I bat my lashes playfully, and he shakes his head.

"Okay, fine. Mexican…No, Thai…No, sushi. Actually! You know what we should totally do?"

I wait for him to play along, and he doesn't disappoint. "What should we do?"

"Pickup ice cream for dinner!"

Lincoln barks out a laugh. "We just had cake and ice cream at the party."

When I give him a *so what* look, he chuckles. "Ice cream, it is."

Ice cream turns into banana splits, and once we have everything we need to make the best ones ever, we head home.

While I'm setting up shop, Lincoln sits at the island and we talk, something we haven't done much of since everything went down. Sure, we've fucked a couple of times, but we haven't actually had a real conversation.

"Have you thought about what you want to do after the baby is born?" he asks.

"Like, if I want to work or stay home?" I cut the bananas and place them into the bowls.

"Yeah."

"I'd like to stay home with him for a while." Weighing my options is something I've given a lot of thought to. But ultimately, my decision came down to one thing. "I spent most of my life home alone," I tell him while I open the containers of ice cream and scoop it out. "I don't want that for my baby. If I didn't have the money I have, if it was necessary for me to work, that would be one thing, but since I can afford to be at home, I want to be there for him. And if I do choose to go to the studio, I can always bring him with me."

I glance up and find Lincoln smiling softly. "If you didn't have the money, I'd make sure you could stay home."

"Because your mom was a stay-at-home mom?" I guess, in a way she still is. Err, or is it a stay-at-home wife? She's never worked a day in her life and seems to be content with that. She loves her life as a mom and a wife.

"No, if you wanted to work, I would support that decision too. But you're telling me that what you really want is to stay home with our child, and I don't care what it takes, I'll always make sure you and our son have everything you guys want and need."

His words cause me to choke up, and I look away, using the ice cream as an excuse to avoid eye contact. When I sniffle too loudly, Lincoln asks what's wrong.

"I'm just glad I'm having this baby with you. I grew up around a lot of bad men and thought that's how they all were, until I met you and Micah." I sniffle back my tears. "You guys are a rare breed."

Lincoln nods in understanding but thankfully lets it go by changing the subject. "So, you're planning to stay home. What about the studio?"

"Oh, that doesn't count as work," I say, pouring the chocolate syrup on top. "Our son will grow up there with his cousins and aunt." I look up at him. "And if you even think about giving me shit for planning to teach him how to dance..."

Lincoln raises his hands in surrender. "Never crossed my mind. I don't care if our son wants to play football or dance or join the chess club. As long as he's healthy and happy, I don't give a shit what he does."

"Good, then we're on the same page." I squirt the whipped cream on top and then hand him his bowl, sitting next to him.

We both take a bite, moaning in unison, which makes us both laugh.

"Now for the tough discussion," he says, glancing over at me. "Baby names."

"Ugh." I take another bite of my food. "I'm going to need some more sugar in me before we go there."

Lincoln laughs. We both take another bite. And that's how we spend our evening. Talking and eating ice cream. It's the most normal thing we've done, and it reminds me of when I was younger, when things between us were simple. Despite the age difference, I'd like to think we were friends. And more than anything, I miss that. Lincoln was always someone I could talk to, and my hope is that someday we can get back to that.

"Morning, sleepyhead."

I drag my feet into the kitchen and plop onto the bar stool. "I think I have a hangover."

Lincoln laughs. "I wouldn't doubt it. I told you that third bowl was too much, but you didn't listen."

"Yeah, yeah. I need—" Before I can finish my sentence, Lincoln places a plate of eggs, toast, bacon, and fruit in front of me, along with a cup of coffee.

"Half decaf," he explains, knowing I need and love my morning coffee, but since I'm pregnant, I now take it with only half the caffeine.

"Oh my God," I groan at the sight and smell of the food and drink in front of me. "You are the best baby daddy ever."

Lincoln barks out a laugh. "Remember that when I tell you what name I want for our son."

"Nope," I say, covering my ears. I read the biggest argument couples have is over the name of their baby, and since what you name your child is so important, I don't want to mess this up. Take my name for example—Eliza, named after my psycho bio dad. Or London and Brooklyn, named after where their parents fell in love and renewed their vows. And so because naming our child is a really huge deal, I'm not ready to discuss it yet, even though Lincoln thinks he has the perfect name. I'm a mood reader, a mood dancer, a mood decision maker. If I'm not in the right mood, this name thing can go either way.

"Fine," he says dryly. "Eat your food. By the way"—he smirks—"see that mango?" He nods toward the pre-cut fruit on my plate. "When it's put together, that's the size of our baby."

I glance at it, then snort out a laugh. "I don't even want to know where you learned that."

"I looked it up. Apparently, there are pregnancy growth charts that compare baby sizes to either fruits or vegetables. According to the fruit chart, next week he'll be the size of a banana."

I stare at him, oddly touched that he's looking up stuff about our baby, and a bit disturbed that people compare them to foods.

"Huh. Thanks for that tidbit of info. Let me know when he's the size of a watermelon. It's my favorite fruit."

"Won't be for a while," he says with a shrug. "Watermelon is the endgame. When he's that size, he'll be ready to come out." Suddenly his eyes go comically wide, as if he's suddenly thought of something.

"What's wrong?" I ask, taking a bite of my delicious bacon.

"Nothing...It's just..." He clears his throat. "How the hell do you think a baby the size of a watermelon slides out of a woman's hole? I mean, I know some women are loose...But take you for example. You can't be more than the size of a lemon. I just don't see how the hell a watermelon is fitting inside of a lemon without causing major damage to both of you."

I'm in the middle of drinking my coffee when he says this, so my drink flies out of my mouth and all over the place.

"Oh my God, Lincoln! Thank you for the visual," I splutter, grabbing a napkin to wipe my mouth. "The hole widens to accommodate the baby. Sometimes there's tearing and it has to be stitched up, but for the most part, the woman's body stretches open for the baby."

Lincoln looks at me, part amazed and part traumatized, and I note not to let him anywhere near my lower half when I give birth.

"Any plans for today?" he asks after a few quiet moments.

I roll my eyes. "You know I'm supposed to be relaxing."

"True," he agrees. "Which is why I got you this."

He pushes a paper across the island, and I pick it up and read it. "A pregnancy spa day?" I ask. "What's the occasion?"

"For you to relax." He smiles sheepishly. "Consider it a belated Mother-To-Be Day gift."

"You know how much I love the spa here." Technically, since Lincoln and Micah own the hotel, they also own the spa, but I learned a long time ago that just because you own it, doesn't mean you don't have to pay just like everyone else. But cost aside, this was very thoughtful of Lincoln.

"I do," he agrees. "And I booked it for both you and your sister so you can have a girl's day, considering it's been a while since the two of you have had one. Sienna already knows and is excited. My mom's taking care of Brooklyn and London today since they're out of school for the summer."

"Thank you!" I get up and kiss his cheek, then sit back down so I can continue to eat because I'm starved. Maybe this whole friendship thing isn't so bad after all.

"I can't remember the last time I spent so many hours being pampered," Sienna says as we float out of the spa several hours later, both of us on cloud nine from the treatment we were given. Not only did we get manis, pedis, facials, and pregnancy massages, but we also received fresh haircuts and color. I feel like a new woman.

"Same. I didn't realize how badly I needed that. Although, is it weird that despite feeling calm, I could totally do with a nap?"

Sienna laughs. "It's the baby. They suck everything out of you: beauty, energy, sex drive. I could go to sleep and wake up when the baby comes."

I nod in agreement, not bothering to tell her that beauty and energy I feel on a deep level, but the sex drive... Well, that's a whole other story. Maybe it's because I've only just recently become sexually active, but I crave it all the damn time. Since I'm almost five months pregnant, and Lincoln isn't an option, I'm having to resort to the battery-operated toy I recently purchased.

When we get up to our floor, Sienna gives me a hug, telling me that she had a wonderful day, and then we part ways. I might not be too keen on being back in Tesoro, but I'm loving being close with my sister again, and it feels damn good for everything to be out in the open.

The second I walk through the door, I smell the Mexican food, and my stomach grumbles in anticipation.

"Perfect timing," Lincoln says, handing me a plate filled with all my favorites. "Figured you'd be hungry."

"You figured right." I have a seat on the barstool and start chowing down. "My God, this is so good. Thank you, thank you."

"Good enough to thank me twice?" he says with a laugh as he sits down next to me.

"I'm thanking you for me and the baby. Trust me, he's just as happy as I am."

Lincoln chuckles and reaches over, his hand rubbing my bump. "Is that true, little guy? Do you love Mexican as much as your mama does?"

Him talking to the baby, calling me mama, and touching my belly shouldn't affect me the way it does, but I can't help the way my heart pounds against my rib cage, how my tummy tightens, and the area between my legs throb. I'm blaming it on the pregnancy hormones because there's no way it's normal to get choked up with emotion and turned on at the same time.

Yep, I need to move out stat, because I can't see how I'm going to survive living with Lincoln much longer.

"Stainless steel appliances, marble floors..." When Franco, the realtor who has been showing me places all afternoon, notices I'm no longer paying attention—instead, focused on the view of downtown Tesoro—he stops rambling and steps next to me. "Not what you're looking for either?"

I shake my head and wrap my arms around my belly protectively. Franco has shown me several beautiful, expensive, luxurious places, but none of them feel like home. Then again, I'm not sure what home is supposed to feel like. I've only had one *true* home my entire life, and it was when I lived with Sienna and Micah. I felt safe and comfortable there. I knew that no matter what went wrong in the outside world, once I was under their roof, between their four walls, I would be okay. And that's how I want my baby to feel. But none of the homes I've seen today give me that same feeling. And if I don't feel it, how will my baby?

"It's not you," I begin, and Franco barks out a laugh.

"Sorry," he says. "You sound like my ex-girlfriend when she was preparing to dump me."

I think about what I said, and once it clicks, I laugh as well. "That's not what I meant. I just have a certain *type* of place in mind...No, it's more like I'm seeking a certain *feeling*, and none of these houses have felt like my home yet."

Franco glances at me and smiles softly. "We can find that place. If it's available in Tesoro, we can find it. Why don't we head back to my office and regroup? We can go over what you liked and didn't like in the places we saw and go from there?"

"Or," I say, when my belly grumbles in protest, "we can do it over dinner because I'm freaking starved. And my baby agrees."

Franco chuckles. "We can do that."

Twenty-Two

LINCOLN

"Hey, Rita. I'm meeting with Brody Fields to discuss the hotel and casino investment proposal, and I left—" My words come to a halt as my eyes land on Ellie sitting in a booth closest to the entrance of Catch 52, one of the many restaurants that Alexander Enterprises owns. Her head is thrown back in laughter, and her hand is covering her belly—something she does often without realizing it, like she's worried something will happen to him and she instinctually needs to protect him. She looks breathtaking, and it kills me to know that I can't have her. That I have to look at her every goddamned day but can't touch.

I step toward her table, figuring I'll say hello before my meeting—that's the friendly thing to do, right?—when I take notice of someone sitting across from her. The person who's making her laugh. A man.

"Mr. Alexander," Rita says, confused as to why I stopped

speaking mid-sentence.

"I'll call you back." I click end on the call and then watch as Ellie and this guy talk and laugh, oblivious to everyone around them, seemingly lost in their own little world. I can't see the guy's face because his back is to me, but Ellie's eyes are shining bright with happiness, something I rarely see on her, and it makes me want to punch something—preferably him. Because he shouldn't be the one making her happy. That should be me. Only, it can't, since Ellie remains off-limits. *Fuck, I'm so goddamn sick of those words.*

And then it hits me: she's on a date.

I'd like to say she's only doing this to make me jealous, playing games to get my attention. But she had no idea that I'd be here. This meeting was rescheduled last minute, the location being changed not even thirty minutes ago.

She barks out a melodic laugh that has several patrons glancing in her direction, and it takes everything in me not to yank her from that table and take her away from here.

And then, as if the electric current between us is so strong, her gaze moves to me, her eyes locking with mine. She says something to the guy she's with, offering him a small smile, and then slides out of the booth to come speak to me.

As she saunters my way, I fully take her in. The floral mini dress she's wearing dips low on top, and her already nice-sized breasts—that have grown exponentially thanks to her pregnancy— are spilling out. All I can imagine is placing my lips to the swells of her breasts and kissing and licking her creamy flesh.

She's donning heels that somehow make her tanned, toned legs even sexier. I picture her wrapping those legs around me, her heels digging into my back as I fuck her against the wall.

"Linc," Ellie says, once she's in front of me. "What are you doing here?"

My eyes home in on her plump lips that are covered in pink gloss, and when my brain envisions her wrapping those lips around my cock, I lose my ever-loving shit. That's my only explanation for what I do next.

Without answering her question, I snatch up her hand—even though I'd like to throw her over my shoulder, but she's pregnant, so that can't happen—and drag her toward the back where I know there's a private office.

The manager is sitting behind the desk when we enter, and he stands in alarm at having the owner show up unannounced. "Mr. Alexander—"

"Out! Now," I bark.

He jumps into action, hauling ass out of the office.

The door is barely closed before I'm pushing Ellie against the wall. "You said you weren't going to date while you're pregnant."

Her lips purse and her brows furrow, but I don't wait for an answer, growling "mine," and then start attacking her mouth like a goddamned animal possessed by the woman in front of me. She tastes sweet like pink lemonade and something that's simply her, a taste I can't seem to get enough of as I fuck her mouth.

It takes her a second, but then she's kissing me back as fiercely as I'm kissing her. Her clothes are ripped off, mine next. And then I'm carrying her over to the desk, setting her down and spreading her thighs open. "You better wrap those sexy heels around my waist, Kitten," I murmur against her mouth. "Because I'm about to show you who you belong to."

She does as I say, and I waste no time, thrusting into her warm cunt that I swear to God was made just for me. She moans in pleasure once I'm all the way in, and I swallow it down, wanting to take and keep everything she gives me.

I'm worked up and know damn well I won't last long, so I reach between us and circle her swollen nub, determined to get her off. Her climax builds quickly, and once she's close, dangling over the precipice, I release her mouth and pull her nipple between my lips, sucking on the hardened peak until she falls over the edge, taking me right along with her.

As we take a moment to catch our breaths, neither of us move—her legs are wrapped around my waist, her heels digging into my back, and I'm still inside her. And then she shocks the hell out of me when she shoves me away.

"What the hell?" I ask, when I stumble back, my wet cock leaking all over the place.

"I should be asking you that!" Ellie sits up and jumps off the desk, collecting her clothes and throwing them on, piece by piece. "One second, I'm in a meeting with my realtor, and the next, you're fucking me on a desk." She puts her dress back on and glares my way.

"Your realtor?" Shit, I totally misread that situation. "I thought you were on a date."

Ellie barks out a laugh, then schools her features. "Wow." She shakes her head. "So this"—she waggles her finger back and forth between us—"was nothing more than a jealousy fuck."

I step toward her, but she retreats, and because I'm still naked, when she hauls ass out the door, I can't follow. I quickly get dressed, but by the time I make it out to the lobby, Ellie is nowhere to be found and Brody Fields has arrived for our meeting.

"Hey, I've been trying to get ahold of you," he says.

"Sorry, I had a bit of an emergency."

"Everything okay?"

"Eh, not really." I shrug. Brody's a family man, so I give it to him straight. "I'm having some woman troubles."

Brody chuckles. "I know all about that. If you need to reschedule..."

"You sure? This isn't usually how I do business."

"It's all good. But when we reschedule, you're coming down to my neck of the woods." He extends his hand, and I take it.

"Thank you. She's pregnant and..."

"Say no more. Good luck, man."

"Thanks." I start to head out when Brody calls my name.

"Buy her sweets. Pregnant women love sweets."

I take his advice and stop at the bakery on my way home. When I arrive, Ellie is nowhere to be found, but since Oscar was outside on security duty, he told me she arrived a little while ago and was visibly upset.

Her door is closed, so I knock, but of course, she ignores me. "Ellie, please, let me in."

Silence.

I try the knob, but it's locked.

"C'mon, please. I want to apologize."

Crickets.

I glance down at the bag in my hand. "I have double chocolate cake."

Nothing...And then the door swings open, Ellie snatches the bag from me, and then slams the door shut. "Hey!" I yell. "C'mon." I turn the knob, and it opens. "Can I come in?"

"What were you doing at that restaurant?" She glares. "Were you spying on me?"

"What? Why the hell would I do that? I had an investor meeting scheduled, and we agreed to meet there for dinner."

"Quick dinner."

"I rescheduled, so I could chase after you."

"Whatever," she mutters, pulling the box of cake out of the bag.

I walk inside and sit on the edge of the bed. "I'm sorry."

"For what?" She raises a challenging brow.

"For thinking you were on a date and then acting like a jealous asshole when I have no right to behave that way."

"And..."

"I'm not going to apologize for taking you on that desk." I smirk playfully, and she rolls her eyes.

"We're supposed to be *friends*, Linc."

"What if I want to be more?"

Her brows kiss her forehead. "What...What are you saying?"

"I'm saying..." I snatch the box out of her hands, setting it on the nightstand, and then push her back, crawling carefully over her and settling on her legs. "I want you, Kitten. Ever since we spent the night together at Elite, you've owned every one of my damn thoughts and fantasies." I press my lips to hers, nipping her bottom lip playfully. "Tell me I can have you."

"Linc," she sighs, sounding as if she's going to tell me no, but when I trail kisses along her jawline, she tilts her head so I can run my nose along the curve of her neck, inhaling her sweet vanilla scent.

"You smell so good." I press my lips on her heated flesh and suck on it, eliciting a moan from her. "Tell me, baby. Tell me I can have you."

When she sighs in defeat, I can feel it...She's about to give in. And then she lifts her shirt over her head, exposing her luscious tits, and I know I have her. I was just in her less than an hour ago, but my cock is already hard.

"Fuck, yes. These tits are mine," I murmur, taking her nipple into my mouth and sucking on it so hard that it draws a loud moan out of her, which makes my cock that much harder.

I suck on her other nipple, then move down to her belly, giving it a kiss. "This baby you're carrying is mine." I glance up and find her staring at me, her emerald eyes filled with heat.

"And this pussy..." I rip her panties clean off her and spread her thighs, then run my tongue straight up her center. "This pussy is all mine." I suck on her clit, then glance back up at her. "Tell me, Kitten. Tell me you're mine."

She stares at me for several seconds, and I worry she's going to deny it, but instead, she nods. "I'm yours."

Those two words stir something deep inside of me. I have no idea what I'm doing or where this is going. All I know is that I want to make this woman mine. Maybe I'm selfish and irresponsible to take what I know I shouldn't have, but I'll deal with the fallout later. Because right now, all I want is her.

A RISK WORTH TAKING

MY PHONE GOING OFF JARS ME AWAKE, AND WHEN I OPEN MY
eyes, I find Ellie curled into a gorgeous ball against my side,
snoring softly. I grab my phone, careful not to jostle and wake
her up, and see it's still early. My thoughts go back to the way she
screamed my name repeatedly last night and into this morning.

Ellie sighs and snuggles closer to me, reminding me that we fell
asleep naked when she slides her leg over mine and the heat from
her bare cunt warms my flesh.

I'm debating whether to pull her on top of me so we can have
morning sex, when my phone goes off again—the entire reason
why I woke up in the first place. Fuck, it's so easy to get lost in
this woman.

Before I can click on the message, my phone rings. Not wanting
to wake Ellie up, I gently slide out from under her and answer the
call once I'm in the hall and her door is shut.

"Jesus, fucking finally," Micah barks. "I was about to come
bang on your damn door."

"Sorry, I was—"

"Doesn't matter. Ricky called. Two of your women were left
for dead last night. One died, but one survived."

"My women?" I ask, confused as hell, since the only woman
on my mind is sleeping in the bed under my roof.

"Issa and Olga."

Fuck, he's referring to two of my dancers who also work at the
sex club. "What the fuck happened and why wasn't I called?" I
bark. "Where are they now?" I rush to get dressed. The women
who work at my club know they're safe. This never should've
happened.

"He called me because I'm his point of contact."

"They're my girls! What the hell did he do to them?"

"It wasn't Ricky. I'm leaving to speak to him now."

"I'll meet you in the garage."

"Issa didn't make it," Micah says once I get into his SUV. "Olga did, but she's in rough shape. Ricky has her at his place with a private doctor."

"What the fuck happened?"

"That's what we're about to find out."

When we get to Ricky's, we're patted down, and Micah's asked to leave his gun with security. He glares but obeys, and then we're brought back to Ricky's office.

"Stay calm," Micah says before we enter. "If Ricky did this, he wouldn't have contacted me."

"Gentleman," Ricky says, standing to shake our hands.

"What the fuck is going on?" I ask, getting straight to the point, because screw staying calm.

"From what I've gathered, the women were hired for a private party. Two of my men were invited...Friends of friends." He shrugs. "When they got there, the women were being fucked in every hole. Nothing unusual for that type of party. But then they noticed the women were tied up and crying, begging to be let go. Both high as kites."

"They don't do drugs." I have the girls tested on a regular basis. "Who did this?" I growl, my entire body vibrating with anger.

"According to Olga...You."

"What?" I bark, standing so abruptly, my chair flies backward.

"I'm not saying you did this," Ricky states calmly. "But whoever did, wanted the women to think you were hosting a party and invited them to attend. They showed up and quickly realized you weren't there, but it was too late. They were tortured and fucked and then beaten and left for dead at the marina."

"Who found them?" Micah asks.

"My men followed them."

"And the guys who dropped them off?" I ask.

"We're looking for them now. They took off after dumping the bodies while my guys were focused on saving the women."

I nod in appreciation. "Did they hear anything at the party?

Who might be responsible for this?"

"Only your name was mentioned, but I'm looking into it. I don't find it to be a coincidence that my men were invited to a party they thought you were hosting only weeks after my shipment was ambushed and our men were killed."

"Fuck," Micah hisses. "Someone is trying to fuck with us. Possibly pit us against each other."

"Anyone come to mind who might hate you?" Ricky asks. "Normally, I'd say it's business-related, but leaving two women for dead on your doorstep? That screams personal."

"No damn clue," Micah tells him, "but we're going to find out."

"And when we do, whoever is fucking with us is dead," I add, because Ricky is right, this shit just got personal. It's one thing to fuck with us and our business, but to go after two innocent women. Fuck that.

After discussing this a bit more, Ricky takes us to see Olga, who's barely awake, but who will thankfully—according to the doctor—make a full recovery.

"It goes without saying that I'll cover all of this," I tell Ricky, referring to the cost of the doctor and making sure Olga is taken care of. I'll also be contacting Issa's family to cover the cost of her funeral expenses.

"I need to hold a meeting at the club," I tell Micah once we're back in the vehicle. "Those women never should've agreed to a private party outside of Elite or Wanderlust."

"I'm putting extra security on Sienna and the girls," Micah says.

Speaking of which...Micah's phone, which is hooked up to Bluetooth, goes off, and he clicks answer. "Hellcat, everything okay?" I can hear the worry in his voice. This has shaken him up. Before he became a family man, shit like this would've gotten his adrenaline rushing, but since Sienna and his daughters, he works hard to make sure this type of stuff doesn't happen so his family isn't placed at risk.

"Yeah, you left without waking me up." I can practically hear the pout in her voice.

"I'm sorry," he tells her. "Some shit hit the fan at work, and Lincoln and I had to go deal with it."

"Oh, Lincoln's with you? Perfect! Your parents want to meet for brunch. I'll text you the location. We're on our way, and Ellie's meeting us there too."

"Okay, baby. See you soon."

I chuckle over the fact that she doesn't even ask, just demands, and Micah doesn't argue. Simply agrees. I used to think it was because he was pussy-whipped, but now, I'm starting to get it. He loves Sienna and wants to see her happy. He's not pussy-whipped—his wife owns his heart. All these years, I didn't understand it. Couldn't imagine a woman ruling my every move. But now, when I do something that makes Ellie happy, and she hits me with that beautiful smile, I absolutely get it. Because that's all I want—for Ellie to be happy.

Fuck, Ellie! I left without letting her know. I consider calling her, but then I glance over at Micah and change my mind. We're going to need to have a conversation about Ellie and me, but now isn't the time.

Twenty-Three

ELLIE

I WAKE UP TO AN EMPTY BED AND A SORE BODY—THANKS TO being thoroughly fucked—and sigh, wondering when I became such a pushover. I blame Lincoln. I've been in love with him for so long that I allow my feelings for him to cloud my judgement. Any other guy playing this hot and cold game would've been thrown to the curb, but when Lincoln goes all caveman and demands I'm his, I turn into a puddle of Jell-O. I should be stronger than that, demand that he stop playing games, but the expert way he works my body is enough to drive me to stupidity. I'm calling it dick brain. Lincoln fills me with his dick, and I turn into a dumbass.

My phone pings with a text, and when I open it, I find a message from Sienna asking to meet everyone for brunch. I don't know who everyone is, but I'm assuming she's referring to her and my nieces, so when I show up at the restaurant she messaged, I'm confused to find Donna and Michael there as well.

"Hey, sis!" Sienna says, getting up to give me a hug—well, as much of one that she can give with both of us being pregnant. "The guys are on their way." Hmm, nice of Lincoln to let me know.

She pulls back and looks down at my belly and grins. "You seriously have the cutest bump. Why can't mine be this adorable?"

"Oh my God." I roll my eyes. "Yours is adorable. You're just almost eight months along, while I'm barely half-baked."

"How are you feeling?" Donna asks. It's been a little awkward with Michael since they found out I was expecting Lincoln's baby, but Donna has been sweet, texting me to make sure I'm okay.

"I'm good," I tell her, walking over and giving her a kiss on her cheek before I sit down. Sienna sits on one side, with Brooklyn and London on each side of her. So, I leave the chair open for Micah to sit with his family and sit on the other side between Donna and the empty seat.

We're just ordering drinks when the guys stroll in, intense expressions on their faces.

They stop at their dad first to give him a hug and then their mom, both of them kissing her on her cheek. I hold my breath as Lincoln scans the table for an empty seat, hoping that the things he said last night weren't just his jealousy and dick talking, but when he strolls past me without so much as a hello, while Micah gives Sienna a kiss that rivals those in the romance books I read, my heart cracks.

He orders a drink, then turns his attention on me. "How are you feeling?"

"Cold," I mutter, sounding as bitter as I feel.

"Do you need a jacket?" he asks, already moving to remove his like the perfect gentleman he is.

"No," I bite out, then take a sip of my coffee.

"Hey, Lincoln," Micah says from across the table. "How did the meeting go with Brody yesterday?"

"I had to reschedule," Lincoln tells him.

"What? You've had that meeting scheduled for months. You told me you'd handle it. He's a major player—"

"Something came up," Lincoln says, cutting him off. "He understood."

"What the hell came up that had you blowing off Fields?"

Lincoln opens his mouth, then closes it, and it hits me that the meeting he blew off to chase after me yesterday is the one they're talking about.

"There was an issue at the club," he lies.

It's not that I expected him to go into full detail about what happened between us in front of everyone, but the way he flat out lies makes me feel like I'm his dirty secret. Like he gets off on fucking me behind closed doors, but I'm not good enough to be anything more than that.

My thoughts take me back to high school when I went on a study date with Jameson, a kid from my school. I thought maybe he was interested in me, but he was only interested in fucking me. Told me that I was the type of girl guys fucked, not dated. It didn't matter that I was living in Micah's expensive hotel and attending an elite art school, I was still the poor girl from Booker Park. Lincoln sat with me and told me that guy was wrong, yet here we are, years later, and he's fucking me in secret, embarrassed to tell his family about me.

Maybe Jameson was right...

Needing to escape before I start crying, I quickly mutter an excuse about needing to use the bathroom and take off toward the restroom.

I've barely made it there, when arms gently wrap around me from behind.

"Let me go!" I yell, already knowing from the scent that it's Lincoln.

"Stop, please," he says, spinning me around and pushing me against the wall. "I'm sorry."

"You seem to be saying that a lot lately," I say dryly, sniffling back my tears. "I don't even know why you followed me."

"Because I could tell you were upset."

"Yeah, well, now your family might think you actually care about me, and we know you don't want that." I glance to my left and nod toward the women's restroom. "Hey, look...If we're quick, you can fuck me in there and make it back out before we need to order, and nobody will ever know."

"Kitten, please stop," he murmurs, pressing his forehead against mine. "I didn't want to lie, but—"

"Auntie Ellie!"

"What the hell is going on here?"

"Ohhh, Daddy, you said a bad word!"

We both jump and glance over, finding Micah and Brooklyn standing in the hall.

"Brooklyn, go use the bathroom," Micah bites out.

Once Brooklyn has disappeared into the bathroom, he asks, "What's going on?"

I wait for Lincoln to answer, refusing to lie and hoping he won't either, but when he says, "It's complicated," my heart shatters.

"Actually, it's not," I tell Lincoln, fed up with his shit. "You and me, we're done. Done fucking, done living together, and done being *friends*. There, now it's *un*complicated."

Pushing him away, I take off out the back door, needing to get some fresh air. It's a beautiful day out, so I chose to walk here since the restaurant was close. After rounding the corner of the building, I step onto the sidewalk to head back to the hotel.

I'm pulling my phone out of my back pocket to let Sienna know I left when someone bumps into me. I'm not expecting it, so I stumble to the side, trying to catch my balance. But before I can, I'm shoved again, this time harder.

"Ow," I hiss, unsure what is happening. In a flash, someone grips my bicep tightly, shoving me toward the street. Just then, my name is called, and when I try to turn to see who it is, I'm catapulted forward, losing my footing in the process. In an attempt to protect my belly, I twist my body, praying I land on my side. My butt hits the cement first, and for a split second, I think I'm going to be okay. But the force is too strong, and I bounce off the ground, my head smacking against the concrete. Then, everything suddenly goes black.

As I lose consciousness, my last thought is that I hope my baby is okay.

Twenty-Four

LINCOLN

THE SECOND THE WORDS *IT'S COMPLICATED* COME FLYING OUT OF my mouth, I want to take them back, but it's too late, and now I need to do damage control. But before I can try to explain to Micah what's going on, Ellie snaps on me, telling me we're done, and then takes off out the back door.

"Fuck!" I bark, knowing I messed up. I wasn't expecting to have a goddamn family gathering the morning after telling Ellie I want more with her. I thought we'd discuss shit further once I got back, and then shortly afterward, I'd sit down and have a conversation with my brother and parents.

"What the hell is going on?" Micah asks. "Are you fucking with Ellie?"

The door slams closed, and I run after Ellie. I can deal with Micah later. Right now, she needs to be my priority.

When I get outside, the brightness of the morning momentarily blinds me, but my vision adjusts just in time to see Ellie turn the corner. The hotel is only a couple blocks away, so she must've walked here. I pick up my pace so I can catch up with her, and when I turn the corner, I spot her on the sidewalk, only she isn't alone.

My first thought is that she ordered a ride, since the black town car's door is open, but when I get closer, I see the hooded figure isn't helping her into the car but dragging her toward it. And he's got company. Another hooded figure is standing by the door, and someone else is in the driver seat.

She screams out in pain, confirming my thoughts: they're trying to kidnap her. I yell out her name, hoping to get her attention. Only instead, it gets the attention of her would-be captors. The guy holding onto Ellie shoves her in the opposite direction, and since I'm not close enough to catch her, I can only watch helplessly as she stumbles backward, her body hitting the ground while her head bounces against the cement like she's on a trampoline and not the hard, unforgiving sidewalk.

As I watch the guys who did this pile into their car and peel away, my gut tells me to chase them down so I can torture the fuck out of them until they tell me why they were going after Ellie. Then, slowly and mercilessly, I would end their lives. But with Ellie lying on the ground unconscious, both her and our baby at risk, I have no choice but to focus on getting help.

"Ellie, baby, can you hear me?" I ask once I've reached her. "Ellie, please," I beg, needing her beautiful eyes to open and look at me, for her to tell me she's okay.

When she doesn't respond, I pull my phone out and dial emergency. As I explain to the dispatcher our location and the situation, I run my hand along Ellie's face and body, trying to check her out without moving her. Thankfully, when she fell, she landed on her back, but that also means she hit the back of her head.

Once I hang up with the dispatcher, who assures me that an

ambulance is en route, I dial Micah's number.

"Are you coming back—?"

"Ellie's hurt!" I bark out. "Meet us at the hospital."

There are a few different hospitals in Tesoro, but in this part of town, there's only one they would take her to.

There's a crowd forming around Ellie, who's yet to wake up, but I ignore them, focusing on trying to comfort her until the ambulance arrives. I've never felt so damn helpless in my life.

When the paramedics finally show and check her out, her lids flutter, and I pray to whatever God is up there that Ellie and our baby will be okay. After placing a neck brace on her, they work together to lift her onto a gurney, while one of them asks me questions. I only know so much, but their main focus is on her pregnancy.

Since there isn't enough room in the back of the ambulance, they offer to let me ride in the front, but I opt to drive myself instead, so I'm not at the hospital without a vehicle. I arrive right behind them, but I'm stopped from entering the emergency entrance, so I walk around to the front where Sienna and Micah—and Sienna's bodyguard, Ricardo—are already waiting.

"What the fuck did you do to my sister?" Sienna shouts, tears streaming down her cheeks as she throws herself at me, punching my chest repeatedly until Micah pulls her away.

"Someone tried to take her," I tell her honestly, not having the time or inclination to filter what I say to keep from scaring her. Between what transpired earlier this morning and having just witnessed Ellie's near abduction, Sienna needs to know what we're up against.

"If I hadn't shown up..." I swallow hard, not wanting to think about what would've happened had I not gotten there in time. "When I called her name, they got spooked. The guy dragging her to the car, pushed her, and she lost her balance and fell."

"Did you recognize them?" Micah asks, his face devoid of any emotion. He's in boss-mode.

"No. There were three guys, all in black hoodies that hid their faces, driving a black town car. I was too focused on Ellie to chase them."

Micah immediately pulls his phone out and starts barking orders, demanding the cameras to be accessed and to find the guys who did this. As he does, he holds Sienna, comforting her so she'll calm down. With her only a couple of months away from giving birth, the last thing she should be is stressed.

Micah hangs up and dials again. "I need a team to go to my parents' and stand guard. My kids go nowhere. I don't know who is fucking with us, so we trust no one."

"I don't understand what is happening," Sienna says once he's hung up.

"I don't know yet," Micah says, lifting her chin and kissing her softly. "But we'll figure it out."

Sienna nods and then turns her attention on me. "She wouldn't have left if you hadn't upset her. What did you say to her?"

"Hellcat," Micah begins, but I shake my head because she's not wrong.

"No, she's right. I fucked up, and if something's happened to her or the baby…" I choke out, the reality of the situation hitting me like a tidal wave.

I did this.

I was so focused on right and wrong, on what my family would think, I kept her at arm's length instead of embracing my feelings for her. I knew the moment I found out she was the woman from the club, I wanted her, but I was stuck on the fact that she was also the same *teenage girl* who once had a crush on me.

"What happened?" Sienna asks.

"I'm falling in love with her," I admit out loud for the first time.

"You're what?" Micah barks. "I told you that Ellie is off-limits."

"No, she's not," I argue, done with those fucking words. "*Teenage* Ellie was off-limits, but twenty-two-year-old Ellie is a consenting adult."

"We agreed," Micah seethes.

"We didn't agree to shit," I counter.

"She's still a fucking kid!" he shouts.

"She'll always feel that way to you," Sienna says, "because you see her as a little sister. The girl who grew up under your roof. You helped raise and protect her. But she's not a kid. She hasn't been for a long time."

"She's fourteen years younger than him!" Micah barks.

"So what?" Sienna argues. "I'm eight years younger than you. Who cares as long as my sister is happy? He didn't go after her when she was fourteen. You were there, and you know damn well Lincoln never crossed any boundaries. Don't turn this into something sleazy when it's not. Ellie was twenty-one and a consenting adult when Lincoln saw her as anything more. She's the one who made the choice to seek him out. And can you blame her? Your brother is one of the best men I know, besides you."

Her words cause a lump of emotion to settle in my throat, and I have to force it down in order to speak. "I tried to stay away from her," I tell Micah. "After I found out she was my mystery woman, despite knowing how attracted I was to her, I tried to stay away. But then I spent time with her...And fuck, bro, chemistry aside, how could anyone not fall in love with her? I love her being in my home, occupying my space. I've never been inclined to converse with a woman, but when I'm with her, I don't want the conversation to end."

My thoughts go to her calling me out on my shit when I fucked her on the desk after thinking she was on a date. Doing yoga in the living room. Lying out by the pool. The way she reads about her pregnancy and focuses on our baby all the time. She wants so badly to be a good mom...To be nothing like her own. She's constantly rubbing her belly and talking to him, so completely in love with our son already. What she doesn't get is that she's already a better mom than the woman who gave birth to her.

Visions of our future flash in front of me: Late nights in bed, talking, making love. Family trips. Sharing a home, creating memories. Ellie in a white dress, walking down the aisle toward me. Pregnant with more of my babies...

Fuck, they have to be okay.

"You really are falling for her," Sienna says with a watery smile.

"And you're really okay with that?" Micah asks.

"I am," she says, "because my fully-capable sister deserves to fall in love, to be cared for and cherished. Falling in love with you was the best thing to ever happen to me"—fresh tears fill her lids—"and if Lincoln can love her the way you love me, why would I not support them? If he's capable of being the hands-on dad you are to our girls, of creating the kind of life with Ellie that we share...Why wouldn't I want that for my sister? Who cares if he's older, if he's your brother? My sister deserves to be fucking happy." Tears skate down her cheeks, and Micah swipes them away.

"If you hurt her..." Sienna says to me.

"If she gives me another chance after today, I'll do everything in my power to make sure she's never fucking hurt again. Everything you said...I want that with her." I glance at Micah. "I don't need your permission or approval, but as my brother, as my best friend, I'd really like your blessing."

It takes him a minute of staring me down before he nods once. "Then you have it. Just don't fuck it up, because you might be my brother, but I'll kill any motherfucker who hurts Ellie."

"Good, then we're on the same page," I tell him. "Because I plan to do the same...Starting with whoever is responsible for putting her in this fucking hospital."

Concussion.

Medically induced coma.

Monitoring for bleeding.

I'm trying to listen as the doctor discusses Ellie's diagnosis and what they've done to ensure she'll be okay, but it's hard to focus when all I want is to see Ellie with my own eyes, to pull her into my arms and hold her, to check that she's okay for myself.

"And the baby?" Sienna asks nervously.

"As of right now, the baby is stable. We're going to monitor them both for the next few days as we slowly wake her," he says, and I sigh in relief. They're both okay. She'll need more time to recover, to heal, but they're okay. "If you have any questions, I'll be back around once they move her to a private room."

"Raze is already here, ready to guard the room," Micah says once the doctor has left. "They'll do shifts. Nobody is getting near her."

I nod, thankful my brother can handle shit under pressure because right now I can't think about anything other than getting to Ellie and our baby.

The next couple of days are spent watching Ellie sleep. They're monitoring her and the baby closely, so we can hear the baby's heartbeat, which is definitely reassuring, but what I really want is for Ellie to wake up so I can start making shit right. After running tests, the doctor tells us that Ellie is out of the woods, so he lowers her meds, which means she can wake up any time.

And then, in the middle of the night, her emerald eyes open, and it feels like I'm finally able to take my first real breath. She coughs lightly, and I hand her a cup of water. She takes it from me, and while she sips on it, I buzz the nurse, who says she'll get the doctor.

While we wait, I tell her the baby is okay, and she nods, giving away no emotion. I have no idea where her head is at, until the doctor comes in and asks her a bunch of questions: What's her name? Her date of birth? What's the month and year? And then...

"Do you know why you're in the hospital?"

"Yes," she says, her voice still devoid of all emotion. "I hit my head."

I assume that's all she remembers, and I'm prepared to explain it further, but when the doctor leaves—after letting her know that she and the baby are doing well and will be discharged in a couple of days as long as nothing changes—before I can even speak, Ellie glances over at me and says, "I want you to leave, too."

Twenty-Five

ELLIE

"Hey, can I come in?" Sienna asks from the doorway, obviously being careful since I just kicked Lincoln out, refusing to let him explain anything to me.

"Of course." I force a smile on my face, and she nods, walking in and letting the door shut behind her.

"How are you feeling?" she asks, sitting in the chair next to me.

"Like I hit my head on the concrete."

She waits for me to indicate I'm joking, and when I don't, she sighs. "Ellie..."

"I don't want to talk about it." I close my eyes, refusing to let the stupid traitorous tears fall.

"We need to discuss it. Someone obviously tried to abduct you."

At her words, my lids pop open, my mind confused. I assumed

she wanted to discuss Lincoln and me…"What are you talking about?"

"When you fell…Do you remember what happened?"

"Lincoln upset me, and after telling him off, I left. While I was walking down the street, I ran into someone." I try to remember exactly what happened, but it is all a blur. One minute, I was heading toward the hotel and the next…

"The man you ran into was planning to kidnap you," Sienna says. "It wasn't a coincidence that you bumped into him. He followed you to the restaurant and was waiting for you. What he wasn't expecting was for you to leave early or for Lincoln to follow you out. He seized the opportunity and grabbed you, trying to shove you into the car, but Lincoln called your name, so the guy pushed you in order to get away. You lost your balance and fell, hitting your head."

"How do you know all this?"

"Micah had the surveillance cameras pulled. They're trying to figure out who was trying to abduct you and why."

I take a moment to absorb what my sister is telling me. For years, after Eleazar died, I constantly looked over my shoulder, afraid someone would come after me. Worried those same people might go after my sister and nieces. It felt too easy to simply tear down Eleazar's illegal businesses, liquidate his assets, and keep the clean money—donating the dirty.

It wasn't until I moved across the country that I felt like the chains shackled to me loosened slightly. I started moving forward with my life. Trying to find my way in this world. And now, not only am I finally living, but thanks to Lincoln, I've been able to move past my intimacy issues.

I can't let my past catch up to me, hold me down, and restrain me once again. I refuse to go back to being the woman I was. I'm finally free, and I won't have that freedom taken away.

I glance down at my baby bump and stroke it gently. Now, not only do I have myself to protect, but also my baby, and I'll be damned if I let anything happen to him.

"El?" Sienna saying my name snaps me out of my thoughts. "Micah and Lincoln are going to find whoever is responsible and make sure they never touch you again."

On the outside, I nod and force a smile, but underneath, my heart is pounding in my chest. Unfortunately, with the monitors hooked up to me, as my blood pressure rises, the beeping increases.

Sienna notices. "Ellie, calm down, please. I promise everything will be okay."

"I know," I lie. "But you can't blame me for being worried. I have a baby to protect. And what if whoever this is goes after you and the girls?"

I need to get out of here. Get as far away from this town as possible. Away from my family and disappear. I have enough money to make it happen.

"Don't worry about us," Sienna says. "Micah is handling it. He would never let anything happen to us. What can I do for you? You shouldn't be stressed."

"Can you find my purse?" I choke out, a plan forming in my head. It will suck doing what I need to do, but it's the only way I can ensure everyone I love is safe.

"Umm, sure." She walks over to the cabinet and pulls it out. "I grabbed it when we left the restaurant."

"Thank you. It has my phone in it, and I'm sure Raelyn will be worried since she hasn't heard from me." Despite us being long distance, we still chat every day.

I take my purse from Sienna and quickly discover my phone is dead. Thankfully, there's a charger plugged into the wall, so I set my phone up to charge.

"I'm actually really tired," I tell Sienna. "I think I'm going to take a nap."

"Oh, okay." She forces a smile. "I'll come back later to check on you."

"Sounds good." I fake a yawn.

"I love you, El. And I'm so glad you're home. We'll get through this together."

Emotion clogs my airway, so I simply nod in response, then choke out, "I love you too."

Sienna stares at me for several seconds, then sighs. With a kiss to my forehead and another *I love you*, she leaves.

Once she's gone, I grab my phone and start working on my escape plan.

Twenty-Six

LINCOLN

"How's she doing?"

"Okay. Quiet as usual," Sienna says with a shrug. "She's being discharged in the morning and asked me to bring her some clean clothes."

"Did she say where she's going?"

"No. I haven't asked. I'm assuming to my place since she hasn't settled on a home yet."

I scrub my hands over my face in frustration, unsure what the hell to do. It's been two days since Ellie woke up and demanded I leave. I only know she and the baby are okay because Sienna gives me updates. But they're not enough. I need to see her, speak to her. I need a fucking chance to make this right.

"I know this sucks, but right now, the focus has to be on her remaining stress-free and safe."

"I know. Everything just feels like it's so fucked right now."

The men who went after Ellie have disappeared, and despite having access to the cameras, they were smart and covered their tracks. Our guys are still searching for answers, but as of now, we've got nothing. All I want is to wrap Ellie up in my arms and keep her safe. I want to tell her how I really feel and beg her for a chance to see where things go with us. But until she agrees to see me, there's nothing I can do or say to make anything right.

"The doctor said she and the baby are both doing great, and the guards will keep her safe," Sienna says. "Just give her time." She reaches out and squeezes my arm. "I'm going home to make dinner. Why don't you come home with me and eat with us?"

I open my mouth to say no, but before I can get a word out, she adds, "And before you say no, I wasn't really asking. Let's go." She hooks her arm in mine. "You need a home-cooked meal and a shower. Tomorrow, Ellie will be discharged, and we'll figure this all out."

"Boss, we have a problem," Oscar says through the phone, and my blood goes cold. He's on guard duty tonight, which means whatever he's about to say is regarding Ellie. "She took off."

"What do you mean she took off?" I ask slowly, trying hard not to freak the fuck out.

"The doctor came by to check on her, and when he left, I heard him tell the nurse he's discharging her early. I assumed someone knew and would soon be by to pick her up and take her home. But she was alone when the nurse came back a little while later with a wheelchair and escorted her to the door. By the time I realized what was going on, she was getting into a town car and taking off. Deandre is tracking the vehicle now."

Fuck. This makes no sense. Where the hell is she going? "Once he has a location, send it to me, and stay on her. I'm leaving now."

Snatching my keys off the counter, I fly out the door, cursing myself for not putting a location tracker on Ellie's phone.

I'm just getting into my car when Deandre sends me the location. I don't know where she's headed, but I input it into my navigation so I can follow it. About thirty minutes into the drive, I catch up to the car and know exactly where he's taking her. Sure enough, fifteen minutes later, my thoughts are confirmed when Ellie gets out of the vehicle and walks across the tarmac and up the steps of a private plane.

Without giving it a chance to take off without me, I jump out of my car and run after her. The flight attendant looks like she wants to stop me, but the glare I hit her with has her eyes widening as she backs up.

The second I step onto the luxurious plane, my gaze collides with Ellie, and she looks a mixture of scared and pissed.

"Get off!" she yells, going with pissed.

"Not without you." I step toward her.

"Did you seriously have me followed?"

"Did you think we'd leave you at the hospital alone? There's been a guard protecting you 'round the clock since you were brought in. He saw you take off and followed you here."

As soon as I'm standing in front of Ellie, I kneel so we're at the same level. "Where are you going, Kitten?" I ask gently.

Tears fill her lids. "Don't call me that," she mutters, "and away from here."

"Without saying goodbye to your sister and nieces? You know Sienna is going to worry."

"I..." She swallows thickly and sniffles back a sob. "I have to protect them."

"By leaving?"

A tear slides down her cheek, and I reach out, gently wiping it away. The sight of her crying has my stomach roiling. Ellie is one of the strongest people I know, an expert at hiding any signs of weakness, so to see her showing emotion is rare.

"By disappearing," she whispers, and then it hits me. She's

hoping whoever came after her will leave Sienna alone if she's gone. And by disappearing, she's protecting herself and our baby.

"Oh, Ellie." I sit next to her and pull her toward me, cupping her cheek. "Don't do this, please. Let me protect you. I promise I'll keep you and our son safe."

"It's pointless now anyway," she mutters. "You found me."

"Yeah, I did, and I always will," I vow. "But I don't control you, and I would never lock you up. If you want to run, you have the money to do so. So, I'm asking you not to. We can figure this out together. Trust me."

"You hurt me," she says softly, her accusation cracking my damn heart. "And now I don't know if I can."

"Baby, no," I plead, locking eyes with her. "I know I fucked up, but I need you to give me a chance to make this right."

"It's too late," she says stubbornly. "My only concern now is my baby." Her hand goes to her belly protectively, and I know I need to take a step back. Ellie's hurt and scared, and I can't force myself on her right now. I need to take it one step at a time.

"Okay, but this baby"—I place my hand over hers—"is *ours*, and even though you're upset with me and can't trust me with your heart, you know you can trust me to protect him. Please, at least come home with me so I can protect you both. Running away isn't going to fix this. Whoever is after you also wants to fuck with Micah and me."

"What do you mean?"

"We think the same people who tried to abduct you are also responsible for the shipment that was ambushed and stolen."

"The one that killed Bruno?"

"Yeah. And the morning I left you in bed..." Her lips turn down into a frown, and it takes everything in me not to kiss away her sadness. "I left in a rush because two of my dancers were attacked at a private party that they thought I was hosting. One of them was killed."

Ellie gasps, having had no clue because Sienna kept it quiet, not wanting to stress her out. And while I agree with her logic, I also think she needs to know how serious this is and that whoever is responsible isn't only going after her—they're coming for us all.

Thankfully, Ellie lets me take her back to my place, but once we're there, she shuts herself in her room, claiming to be tired, when really, she's just trying to avoid me. But I accept it for now, content with knowing she's under my roof and safe.

After I call Micah and Sienna to let them know everything that transpired—and promise Sienna she can visit tomorrow—I knock on Ellie's door to check on her. She might not want anything to do with me, but she hit her head less than a week ago, so she isn't going to stop me from making sure she's okay.

When she doesn't answer, I try the doorknob. It turns, so I peek in, finding her curled into a ball asleep. The last time I saw her in this bed was the night we spent together before brunch. The side I fell asleep on is empty, and I probably shouldn't do it, but I kick my shoes off and climb into the bed, maintaining a little space between us.

Only she must sense my presence because she cracks a single eye open. "I told you to go away," she murmurs groggily.

"I know." I brush a few wayward strands of hair out of her face. "But I had to make sure this is real."

"What?" she asks, opening both eyes and furrowing her brow.

"That you're here, under my roof. Alive and safe." I swallow, and the ball of emotion gets caught in my throat. "When I saw you fall..." I release a harsh breath, unable to hold back my emotions. "You were so still, lifeless. I thought you were dead." I palm her face, needing to feel her warm flesh. "I don't want to live in a world where you're not in it, Ellie. I'm falling in love with you."

I didn't plan to say those words, but the second they're out, I realize I don't regret them in the slightest. I knew I was falling for her, but the truth is, I've already fallen hard.

"Lincoln," she breathes, "you can't say stuff like that. It's not fair."

"Why? It's the truth."

"You're only saying that because you thought I was dead."

"No, I'm saying it because I do." I bridge the gap between us and run my hand down her curves to her ass, then pull her toward me. "I love you, kitten, and I know it's hard for you to believe me since I managed to fuck everything up. I allowed societal views and my brother's disapproval to get inside my head and dictate my actions. But I don't give a shit about our age difference. I felt the pull between us on Valentine's Day, and it's only grown stronger since then."

"That's just chemistry," she argues, refusing to make shit easy on me. But I'm okay with that because she deserves to have someone fight for her.

"Part of it, yeah. But I also love the friendship we've been developing. I love the way you fiercely protect the one's you care about. The way you already love our baby."

I cup the side of her face, and when she leans into it and sighs, my hope is renewed that she's going to forgive me. "You've been through some major shit in your life, but instead of letting it keep you down, you've risen. You're the strongest person I know."

"My sister used to say that men are good with pretty words, but it's their actions that show who they really are. If you want something between us, you're going to need to show me."

"Okay." I nod in understanding. "I will. But since it's late, and we're both exhausted, I was hoping I could just hold you and our baby tonight. I almost lost you both."

She stares at me for several moments before she turns her back on me. I assume that's her way of telling me it's not happening, but then she reaches back and grabs my hand, pulling my arm around her and placing it on her protruding belly. She snuggles against me, and I lay my head on the pillow, sliding my other arm under her, nuzzling my face into her neck, and inhaling her vanilla scent.

Within minutes, she's asleep, her soft snores the only sound in the otherwise quiet room. I remain awake, holding her tight, thanking God for protecting her and our unborn baby. Then, I think of all the ways I plan to show Ellie that I love her.

"STUPID THING. DOES THERE REALLY NEED TO BE THIS MANY buttons on a damn remote? Why can't you just have the ones that are necessary?"

I chuckle, watching Ellie bitch at the remote for a few seconds before I take pity on her and pluck it out of her hand.

"Hey! I was using that."

"You were yelling at it." I drop onto the couch and then reach out and bring Ellie down with me. She falls into my side, and when she tries to move away, I wrap my arm around her waist, holding her firmly so she can't get away.

When I woke up this morning, her side of the bed was empty. I jumped up and went in search of her, worried she took off, but calmed down once I found her in the kitchen making herself a cup of coffee. She's spent the morning avoiding me. I've caught her cleaning the bathroom, doing yoga, reading a book on the terrace, and speaking to her realtor about new places that have become available. I shut down her cleaning, watched her sexy ass do the downward dog, ordered her some new books that will arrive soon, and glared at her on the phone, which had her telling that asshole she'd call him back later.

It's now early afternoon, and she must've run out of shit to do because she's trying to watch a movie out here since my guest room doesn't have a TV.

"So, what are we watching?" I ask, looking down at her.

"We?" she squeaks out. "Don't you like, have work to do? I'm sure you have better things to do with your time than watch a movie with me."

"Watching a movie with you sounds like the perfect way to

spend my afternoon. Should we grab some snacks, though? I haven't seen you eat."

Just as I finish my sentence, her stomach growls, and she flushes a light shade of pink. "Food would be good. I think the gummy bear is—Oh my God!" She jumps up, her hand going to her belly.

"What? What's wrong?" I'm on my feet, ready to scoop her up and take her to the hospital.

"I think I felt him," she breathes, looking over at me with glassy eyes.

"What?" I glance down at her belly. "Can I feel him?" I place my hand on her stomach but don't feel anything.

"Oh! I felt it again. I think it's a flutter."

"A what?" I remove my hand.

"A flutter. The doctor said I'll feel him stirring inside me before I feel him kicking. He's getting big enough that I can feel him moving around." Her smile is so big and bright, if it were the sun, it would blind the fuck out of me. "I can't believe I can feel him," she murmurs. "He's real and alive in my belly."

"He is," I choke out, my emotions getting the better of me. But I can't help it. It was only a few days ago I thought I was going to lose them both. But here she is, alive and smiling and talking about our baby moving around inside of her.

"When you were in the hospital, I was looking up names on my phone to pass the time. I came across one name that I think would be perfect for him...I mean, only if you like it."

"What happened to the name you originally wanted?" she asks.

"I think this name would better suit him."

"Okay, what is it?"

"Donovan. It means 'strong fighter.' I saw it and it made me think of you. You're a fighter, El, and I have no doubt our son will have the same strength as his mother."

Tears fill her lids, and she grants me the most beautiful, watery smile before she says, "I love it."

"Yeah?"

"Yeah." Her eyes descend to her belly. "Hello there, Donovan. What do you think? Do you like that name?" She giggles and glances back up at me. "He fluttered again. So, I'll take that as a yes. What about the middle name? Any traditions you guys have?"

"Our middle names were derived from our grandfathers. Micah's is Eugene, named after our paternal grandfather, and mine is Thomas, named after our maternal grandfather.

"We could continue on with the tradition," she says. "Donovan Michael Alexander has a nice ring to it. Unless Micah already called dibs on it."

"Micah's going to end up with another girl," I tell her with a laugh. My brother already has two girls, and they've decided this baby will be their final one. I think part of him is hoping for a boy to even out the gender playing field, but if they have another girl, he'll be completely okay with it. Both of his daughters are total daddy's girls.

Ellie laughs. "Probably. But maybe you should ask just to make sure before we settle on it, since Sienna is giving birth before me."

"I'll ask, but I'm sure it will be okay. Now, what are you and Donovan hungry for?"

"Mmmm...Pizza...with ham and pineapple." Her eyes light up. "Yes, with extra pineapple."

"Alright, so one Hawaiian pizza for you plus a normal one for me. Got it."

"Hey!" She playfully smacks my arm. "Hawaiian is normal."

"Sorry, Kitten, but nothing about fruit on pizza is normal."

I order the food and then make her some popcorn, since she wants it to snack on while we wait for the pizza. And then I find the movie she wants to watch. Since it's not on any of the streaming services, I buy it from Amazon.

"Save the Last Dance? It's not one of those cheesy dance movies, is it?" I've seen my nieces watching those, and if I'm going to have to sit through two hours of that, I at least want to mentally prepare myself.

"It's not cheesy," Ellie says. "It's my favorite. And in the movie, Derek takes Sara to see the Joffrey Ballet in Chicago. I've always wanted to go."

As she tells me more about the movie—and the Joffrey Ballet—the dreamy look in her eyes reminds me of the old Ellie. The one who was in love with dance and ballet and dreamed of performing professionally one day. Before the dark parts of life snuffed out her light—and dreams.

When she finishes telling me the premise of the movie, I click play, and that's how we spend our evening—watching two teens from different worlds fall in love while they fight for their futures. Occasionally, I glance at Ellie as she watches the movie. She laughs and cries, and when the couple manages to work through their shit, she clutches her chest, making me realize just how much of a romantic Ellie really is. Which means, I need to tap into that romantic side of her if I have any hope of ever winning over her heart.

Twenty-Seven

ELLIE

"How does it feel to be halfway there?"

I glance over at Dr. Peterson, reluctantly prying my eyes away from the monitor displaying my son. Normally, ultrasounds aren't done at every appointment, but when you fall and put yourself and your child at risk, you get to see your baby more often. I'd prefer for my son not to be at risk, but I do love to see him swimming around in my belly.

"I feel like the pregnancy is both flying by and moving along at a snail's pace."

The doctor laughs, and Lincoln chuckles.

"I've started to feel him fluttering around." Ever since I felt him that day on the couch when Lincoln and I were getting ready to watch a movie and discussing baby names, I've felt it more often.

"Soon you'll be able to feel him from the outside," the doctor says with a soft smile.

She spends the next several minutes going over everything with us, as well as running tests that are required at this stage in my pregnancy. Thankfully, the baby is perfect and shows no signs of distress from the fall I took. All the measurements are on par with how far along I am, and, according to Lincoln, the baby is now the size of a papaya.

When the doctor's done, she gives us a printout and then moves on to my blood pressure. "Based on your charting, your BP seems to have improved slightly. I would like for it to be a little lower, but the fact that it hasn't gone up is a good sign."

"Does that mean I can resume normal activities?"

"It does...However, due to your fall, I would still like for you to take it easy."

"Oh, that's a given," Lincoln murmurs from next to me, prompting me to look at him. When I raise a questioning brow, he shrugs. "Between the anemia, high blood pressure, and the fall, I'm considering wrapping your pregnant behind up in bubble wrap."

I bark out a laugh, but Lincoln doesn't join in. "I'm serious, El. You need to relax. I caught you on your hands and knees cleaning the bathroom, for God's sake."

"Well, in my defense, your cleaning lady isn't good." And I was also avoiding Lincoln, something I'd been doing since I woke up the morning after he told me he loved me. That is, until he cornered me with the promise of my favorite movie and yummy pizza, causing me to cave way too easily.

One part of me wants to believe him, throw caution to the wind and tell him I love him back. But the other part of me is afraid that if I give in too quickly, I'll appear weak. Like my mother. She let her emotions steer her actions—and look where that got her...Six feet under, after spending her life drugged up with her legs spread for a man who showed her how much he loved her by pimping her out.

Okay, obviously, her life was a bit darker than mine, but she did go from being a talented dancer to a prostitute. Decisions were made, and I'll be damned if I make any decision that can lead me down the same road my mom took. Which means I need to make sure Lincoln means what he says when he tells me he loves me and wants a future with me.

"She's been let go, and a new one has been hired," he says, snapping me out of my thoughts. "The new person is at the house cleaning as we speak."

Dr. Peterson chuckles. "Any plans for the Fourth of July?"

"What?" I ask, doing the math in my head. Holy shit, I didn't realize we were already into July. I'm about to tell her that I have no plans, but before I can get the words out, Lincoln speaks first.

"We're going away."

I whip my head around to look at him, and he shoots me a wink that has my legs clenching. I might be reluctant to believe he wants a future with me, but my body still craves his touch.

After wishing us a good holiday and saying she'll see us next month, the doctor walks us to the check-out desk where I schedule my next appointment. We then head for home, with my assigned bodyguard, Oscar, trailing closely behind.

When I asked Lincoln why I needed Oscar when he and I are out together, he said, "I won't risk getting distracted by you and not paying attention to our surroundings."

"How would you get distracted?" I asked.

"Have you seen yourself, Kitten? You're breathtakingly beautiful, fucking mesmerizing. It's all too easy to get lost in you and forget everything and everyone around me. I do it several times a day, and I won't take the chance of something happening to you."

His words had my heart swelling, but I didn't show any emotion on the outside, not wanting him to know how much what he said meant to me. Maybe I'm being overly cautious keeping my heart protected by several layers, but if Lincoln wants to break through them, he's going to have to do more than spout a few pretty words.

"So, where are we going?" I ask once we're back in Lincoln's car.

"It's a surprise, but don't worry, we'll be back before Sienna's baby shower this weekend."

The surprise is a trip to New York City, but I have no idea why. We get checked into a beautiful hotel, where there's a large black box with a red ribbon waiting for me on the bed.

"For me?" I ask dumbly.

"For you," Lincoln says, leaning over and kissing the top of my head. "Be ready to leave at five o'clock."

I open the box and find the most gorgeous one shoulder, sparkly emerald maternity evening gown that matches my eyes, complete with matching black, sparkly ballet flats, and a sexy yet comfy-looking maternity bra and panties—also black.

I don't know how Lincoln did all of this without me knowing, but when I put it all on and it not only fits but makes me look like a pregnant fairy-tale princess, I send him a text thanking him, then go about doing my hair and makeup. I keep my look simple, my hair down in beach waves, and my makeup on the natural side, using a bit of mascara and eyeliner to make my eyes pop. I might be five months pregnant, but even I can admit I look sexy.

After shooting a selfie I take using the floor-to-ceiling mirror and sending it to Sienna—who responds that I look beautiful and to have a good time, confirming that she knows precisely where we're going—I reply that I love her and then head out to the main room of the suite to find Lincoln standing next to the wet bar, looking handsome in his suit. When he lowers his hand that's holding a drink, I notice he's sporting an emerald tie, and my heart soars. He planned this. I don't know what *this is* exactly, but he took the time to plan the little details, and that gives him extra points in my book.

"Kitten," he purrs, his eyes igniting with heated lust. "You're sexy as hell in your yoga attire, but fuck, you look exquisite like this."

I can't help but laugh at his yoga remark since I do tend to live in my yoga pants, sports bra, and tank.

"This is for you," he says, setting his crystal tumbler down and pulling an oblong black velvet box out of his jacket pocket. I take the delicate box from him and pop it open, not expecting what I find nestled inside.

"It's a Venetian cat mask," he explains, as I take in the beautiful silver and black mask that's attached to a delicate chain. "It's as close as I could find to the one you wore that night."

He takes the necklace out of the box, and I turn around, lifting my hair up so he can clasp it around my neck. Once it's fastened, it drops against my chest, and I look down to admire the lovely gift.

"Why?" I ask, turning around to face him, confused as to why he bought this for me. Sure, that was one of the best nights of my life, but that night changed the course of his life entirely.

When he raises a questioning brow, I explain. "That night changed everything for you. I not only turned your entire world on its axis by getting pregnant, but you've had to deal with the fallout with your family. You went from the carefree bachelor to living with a hormonal pregnant woman." I chuckle, self-deprecatingly. "It's beautiful, Linc. And I love it because for me that night changed my life for the better. If it weren't for you, I would still be hiding from my past and from my sister. And I'd still be afraid to be intimate with a man. But...Well, I guess I don't understand what meaning it holds for you."

He shakes his head and gently cups the side of my face. "You're right, that night changed my life, but Kitten, it changed my life for the better too. That night was the first time I connected with a woman on a deeper level. Before you, sex was just sex. It was fun and a good release. I enjoyed exploring, but I never felt anything like what I felt with you. I didn't understand it when my brother said he knew Sienna was the one for him the first time he saw her dancing on stage—not until that night I spent with you.

"From the conversation we shared, to the dancing, to our time in the backroom, I felt everything. And after you left, I couldn't stop thinking about you. All I wanted to do was find you."

"Because you didn't know it was me," I mutter, my gaze descending.

"No," he says, tilting my chin up to look at him. "I didn't know my mystery woman was you, but that doesn't change the connection we shared. And since learning it was you who I shared that connection with...Spending the past couple of months with you...That connection has only deepened for me.

"Yeah, I was scared to admit my feelings because the fact is, I am a lot older than you, and to a lot of people that looks bad. But I'm done giving a fuck about what shit looks like. I love you, El, and I love that you're carrying my baby."

He moves his fingers from my chin, back to the side of my face, and with his other hand, squeezes the curve of my hip, pulling me closer. "I'm not saying I want to keep knocking you up like my brother and your sister keep doing..." The corner of his lips quirk into a sexy smirk. "But watching you grow my baby inside of you is one of the most beautiful things I've experienced. Just knowing that we created him during that night we spent together is such a turn on...So I definitely wouldn't object if you wanted to make a couple more babies with me."

I choke out a watery laugh as butterflies attack my chest. "We'll see if you say that after the baby is born and we're sleep deprived from him waking up all night."

"You're really not going to make this easy on me," he says with a groan. "My point is that yes, my life changed that night we were together but only for the better, El. Before that night, I had refused to settle down, not wanting to ever *settle*, wanting to make sure the woman I ended up with was the person I could see myself creating a life with. And when I look at you, I see all of that. I see our future...Babies, a home filled with love. Holidays, birthdays, family vacations...Lazy mornings in bed, late nights spent with me inside you. I want it all, and I want it with you."

"Lincoln," I breathe, getting choked up with emotion from his words. He doesn't get its significance because he's always had it—the loving family, holidays, vacations, birthdays—but all those things he says he wants with me are all the things I've always wanted but feared I'd never have.

"I want that," I whisper, afraid if I say the words too loudly, the universe will rescind the offer.

"Give us a real chance, Kitten, and I promise I'll spend every day showing you how much I love you and how much I want this life with you. I'm not saying every day will be perfect, but we can have the life we both want, together."

I should probably make him work harder for it. It's only been a short time since I pushed him away and told him he'd have to prove his love for me, but as I look into his hazel eyes, I realize I don't want to play games. I've learned the hard way how cruel life can be, how quickly it can change at the drop of a dime. All we have is right now, and I want to spend it being loved by Lincoln.

"Okay," I breathe. "I'll give us a real chance."

His features morph into pure happiness, and the way my heart swells tells me I made the right decision. I love Lincoln, and I want this life with him. I want to love him and be loved by him. Hell, I've loved him in my own way since I was fourteen years old. Not because he was hot and older—though, he definitely was— but because even back then I felt the strength of his love. It was the kind of love that wrapped me up like a warm blanket on the coldest winter night and made me feel safe. Only now that love has blossomed into something more...Something deeper. Something I want to spend the rest of my life nurturing, so it will continue to grow.

"I love you," he says, pulling me into his arms. "And I promise, you won't regret it."

His mouth descends on mine, and I sigh into the kiss, getting lost in him. It's only been a short time since I've felt Lincoln's mouth on mine, but the moment our lips touch, I instantly crave more of him, more of his touch, his scent, his taste.

When I encircle my arms around his neck, wanting to deepen the kiss, he chuckles into my mouth and breaks the kiss. "Baby, we have plans tonight."

"Screw the plans," I mutter, trying to pull him back to me. It's impossible for me to compare my turbo-charged sex drive to that of someone who's not pregnant, and it could be because I've only just recently found how pleasurable sex and orgasms can be, but I find myself wanting Lincoln often.

"Not happening," he says, untangling us and taking my hand in his. "You look too beautiful not to take out, and the plans we have, I think you're going to regret missing...Even if the sex is that good." He shoots me a flirty wink, and I laugh at how adorably sexy he is.

"Fine," I say, caving since it really would be a shame not to put this dress to use. "But when we get back here..."

"Oh, Kitten, when we get back here, it's on."

The ride in the elevator is spent with Lincoln holding me and kissing me. He draws me in just enough to turn me on and work me up but leaves me hanging and craving more.

I quickly learn that our dinner reservations are for a restaurant in the hotel. We're sat in a private room where we enjoy a delicious meal. We keep things light with small talk, and it's nice, being able to talk and laugh without having to focus on the heavy shit that'll be waiting for us when we return. After dinner, we have dessert, and then Lincoln guides us outside to where a limo is waiting for us.

As Lincoln opens the door, and I slide inside the spacious area that could easily seat several people, I consider what it would be like to lift my dress, push my panties aside, and ride him into oblivion.

He must sense my thoughts because he shakes his head and laughs. "I haven't been inside you in over a week. When I'm finally balls deep in your perfect cunt, I'm not planning to leave for a while."

My lady parts clench at his dirty talk, wondering if wherever we're going is worth prolonging him from doing just that.

But then we stop in front of the infamous Lincoln Center, and I gasp, knowing there's only one reason we would be here.

"Are we here to see...?" I choke out, unable to finish my words.

"The American Ballet?" he finishes. "Yeah, I wanted to fly us to Chicago to see the Joffrey Ballet, but—"

"They don't have summer productions." I know everything there is to know about damn near every dance company. When I was a little girl, all I wanted was to one day tour the world dancing. As I got older, my dream changed to dance therapy, wanting to help others the way dance helped me. But then I was raped, and everything changed. So, I bought Sienna a dance studio and took off to the other side of the country for college.

"We're here to see Romeo and Juliet," Lincoln says, snapping me out of my thoughts.

"This is amazing," I tell him once we've stepped out of the limo. "It's always been a dream of mine to come here, but at first I was too broke and then I moved..."

"Well, I'm honored to experience this with you for the first time," he says, hooking his arm in mine and guiding me toward the Metropolitan Opera House.

It's not until about halfway through the show that it hits me just how much I've missed dancing. Even simply watching it is soothing.

"What's going through that beautiful head of yours?" Lincoln asks, picking up on my mood change like he always does.

"I miss dancing," I admit. "The calmness it brings. I want to talk to Sienna about working at the dance studio once Donovan is born. And I think I want to go back to school to get my master's in dance therapy like I originally planned. I know that's a lot, especially with a new baby, but—"

"But nothing," Lincoln says. "You're not in this alone anymore.

If you want to teach dance, you will. And if you want to further your education, I'll support you." He leans in and presses a soft kiss to my lips. "Your dreams are mine," he murmurs against my mouth. "Your future is mine."

Twenty-Eight

LINCOLN

THE EVENING SO FAR HAS GONE BETTER THAN I PLANNED. FOR one, I didn't expect to have such a deep conversation with Ellie before we left our room. I bought her the necklace to symbolize the night we spent together. To show her that despite how we started, I wouldn't change a damn thing. I never imagined a future with Ellie, I never saw her that way, but now, I can't imagine a life without her, and I need her to know that.

What I wasn't expecting was for that necklace to open a line of conversation that would lead to Ellie agreeing to give us a real chance. From then on, the night only got better. She opened up to me, sharing her wants and dreams for the future. With me being older and working from an early age for my family's business, there isn't much I want or need. I've always been content. But listening to her tell me about wanting to get her master's and work at the dance studio reminded me of just how young she is. She has her entire future ahead of her, and I'm going to ensure that every one of her dreams and goals eventually come to fruition. But to do that, we need to find out who the fuck is after us—especially Ellie.

As we ride back to the hotel, with Ellie's body pressed up against mine, her head resting on my shoulder, I type out a text to Micah, asking if our guys have found anything yet.

MICAH

No. Not a damn thing. Either none of the big players know shit, or they're keeping secrets.

MICAH

How's it going in the city?

LINCOLN

Ellie loved the ballet, and she's agreed to give us a real chance. We need to find whoever is fucking with us soon. When we get back, I want in.

MICAH

I'm working on it. You need to focus on Alexander Enterprises, so I know it's being handled. Sienna is due in a month, and the last thing I want is her giving birth with a threat looming over our heads. She and the girls are getting antsy at home, but traveling this far along isn't advised in case she goes into labor early.

LINCOLN

I want in.

MICAH

We'll talk when you get home.

"Everything okay?" Ellie asks when I sigh loudly.

I consider saying yes, not wanting to ruin the evening, but I don't want to lie to her. "We still don't have any leads as to who is coming after us."

She snuggles closer to me, and I wrap my arm around her, needing to hold her tight.

"I wish we could stay here forever," she murmurs after a few minutes. "I like this, being with you away from Tesoro. I feel content and safe."

"I'm going to make sure you feel that way *in* Tesoro," I tell her, kissing the top of her head. "Micah and I won't stop until you do."

When we arrive at the hotel, Oscar escorts us to our suite, doing a search of the place before we enter. I've barely closed the door behind us, when Ellie is on me, her arms wrapped around my neck, and her mouth attacking my own.

My first instinct is to lift her like I'm a fucking caveman and take her against the wall, that's how badly I want to be inside her, but with her being pregnant, I remind myself that I need to be gentle.

So instead, I break the kiss and then lift her onto the dining table, taking a step back to admire the beautiful woman in front of me. Her lips are slightly bee-stung from our kiss, her face and neck flushed a gorgeous shade of pink. Her chest is rising and falling in quick succession, and when her eyes meet mine, they're hooded over with lust.

When I pull my phone out, needing to capture her like this, she tilts her head to the side. "What are you doing?" she asks, her voice breathy.

"Taking a picture of you."

"We took pictures of us earlier, at the ballet."

"Not like this." I snap the picture and then put my phone away.

"Like what?" she questions.

"Like you're mine." I capture her lips, and she moans into my mouth. We kiss for several seconds, until I can't take it any longer, needing to feel more of her.

"How do I get this dress off of you?" I ask. I might've picked it out, but the only thing I know is that it matches her beautiful eyes.

"Like this." She pulls the string on the side, and the dress falls open, exposing the black lace bra and panties I also bought.

With a groan, I step back and kneel in front of her, then remove her ballet flats, dropping them to the side. I glance up and find her peering down at me, her emerald eyes filled with desire.

I take her foot in my hands and press a soft kiss to the instep. Everything about Ellie is feminine, even her feet. I kiss the inside of her ankle, and then I work my way up her smooth calf and thigh. Once I get to the top, I start all over again with her other leg, memorizing every inch of her. When I arrive back at the top, I spread her thighs and suck on her flesh, leaving a tiny hickey that only she and I can see, needing in some way to mark my claim on her.

As if she can hear my thoughts, she giggles, making me look up at her. "I think the baby I'm carrying by you proves that I'm yours."

"The only thing that will prove you're mine is when you're wearing my ring on your finger and your last name is Alexander."

Her eyes go wide, and I chuckle at having shocked her. "No, I'm not proposing," I say. "I want to, but I'm afraid you'll think it's only because of the baby. So, for now, I'll mark you with my mouth, watch our son grow in your belly, and convince you to live with me. Then, after the baby is born, I'll beg you to become my wife."

I spread her legs wider and press my nose to the lacy material covering her cunt and inhale her scent.

"Lincoln!" she squeaks.

"Stop." I playfully bat her hand away. "I've missed your smell." I inhale again, and she groans but doesn't stop me.

After I've gotten my fill of her for the moment, I press a kiss to the top of her mound and then work my way up to her protruding belly. It's crazy how much it's grown since I found out she was pregnant. I kiss just under her naval then above it, and I'm shocked as hell when I feel it bump against my lips.

"Holy shit," I breathe. "Did you feel that?"

"I did," she says, her eyes wide. "Oh my God. He kicked. Like, actually kicked."

"Amazing," I murmur, peppering several kisses to her belly. And then it hits me. "You don't think he'll know...?"

Ellie barks out a laugh. "No. And if you even think about stopping right now, I'll be forced to finish myself."

The idea of Ellie fingering herself almost has me wanting to stop just so I can watch that happen, but my need to be inside her is too strong.

"Another time," I tell her, standing so I can give the rest of her body attention. Her breasts are covered in lace, just like her panties, so I take a second to appreciate them before I pull both of her cups down and watch as they spill out, her hard nipples beckoning me.

"Your tits are perfect," I say, pulling a nipple between my lips and sucking on the rose-dusted peak.

She moans in pleasure and then says, "You better enjoy them now. Soon, my body will be destroyed. My boobs will be saggy, and my stomach will be full of stretch marks. I won't be perfect."

I stop what I'm doing to give her my attention. "Are you serious right now?" I ask, annoyed that she thinks I could be that shallow. "I've never seen a woman after she's given birth, but if you think your body changing due to you carrying and protecting and growing our baby inside of you for nine damn months is going to make you any less perfect to me, you need to think again."

Without giving her a chance to argue, I devour her mouth. One hand cups her breast, plucking and tweaking her sensitive nipple, while the other pushes her panties to the side and plunges two fingers into her. She's warm and wet, and so goddamned *perfect*.

"Oh, shit," she moans into my mouth. "Harder, Linc, please."

I love that she's slowly getting comfortable enough to ask for shit like that. That she's taking control of her sexual needs and refusing to let the fuckers who raped her win.

I do as she requested, going deeper without being too rough. I work her up, fucking the hell out of her cunt until she's coming around my fingers and screaming my name.

"I was thinking," she murmurs against my mouth once her breathing has calmed slightly. "Maybe we could..." She clears her throat, and I back up so I can look at her, not liking the nervousness in her tone.

"What is it, Kitten?" I ask, when I notice her skin is a dark shade of pink.

"I want to replace the bad with the good."

"Was what we just did bad?" I ask, confused. She was just screaming like—

"No!" She shakes her head. "It was amazing. The way you make me come blows my mind. I meant that I want to replace the bad memories of before with the good ones now."

"Okay...I thought that's what we're doing every time we're together like this."

"It is, but I was thinking we could do anal," she says softly. "When you did it before with your finger, it felt good. I think I'm ready for more." Jesus, this woman. Her strength and courage know no bounds.

"Hold on to my neck," I tell her as I scoop her up into my arms bridal style and carry her to the bedroom. Once I've laid her on the mattress, I grab the lube from my toiletry bag in the bathroom and then head back to the bedroom.

Ellie is quiet, probably lost in her own thoughts, so I throw the lube to the side and climb onto the bed to kiss her. She sighs into the kiss, the tension slowly melting away.

"You're in charge," I remind her. "Everything we do is your choice. You want me to go harder, I go harder. You want me to stop, I stop. Got it?"

She nods in understanding.

"I need to hear the words, Kitten."

"I got it. I'm in charge."

"Damn right you are. Now tell me what you want."

I expect her to hesitate, so I'm pleasantly surprised when she says with determination in her voice, "I want you to fuck my ass."

And since I would give this woman anything she wants—and let's be real, what man doesn't enjoy anal?—I do exactly that.

After making sure she's ready—and working her up to the point that she's about to explode—I wrap my arms around Ellie and slide into her from behind. While I slowly fuck her ass, I stroke her clit and pepper kisses along her shoulder and neck, reminding her that I'm here, that it's me who's inside of her. And when she comes, it's my name she screams out in pleasure.

"Thank you," she murmurs with tears in her eyes.

Once I've pulled out, I hold her for a moment before we take a shower. "You never have to thank me, baby. We're in this together." I kiss her soft lips, tasting the saltiness of her tears. "Nobody is ever going to hurt you again."

Twenty-Nine

ELLIE

"I can't believe he took you to the American Ballet." Sienna smiles softly. "And look at this necklace." She fingers the charm on my neck and then glances at Micah. "Remember when you took me to London and got me this necklace?" She touches the ballet slipper charm that's resting on her neck. "Not only are we dating brothers, but they think of the same ways to spoil us."

"Great," Lincoln groans. "Just what a man likes to hear...How unoriginal he is." He glares at Micah. "When I ran my idea past you, why didn't you mention you did the same shit for Sienna?"

"Hey," I say, palming Lincoln's face. "My sister and I both love dance. It wouldn't be hard to come up with the same idea to take us to see a show. And this necklace was so thoughtful. Who cares if he did it first? It wasn't the same. The memories aren't the same. And it's something I'll remember for the rest of my life."

"Fine," Lincoln grumbles. "But I'm going to come up with an

original surprise that Micah's never done."

"Don't worry," Sienna says. "Micah doesn't surprise me anymore. We're an old, married couple now."

"Excuse me?" Micah growls. "I'll show you an old, married couple!" He grabs Sienna by the neck and kisses her hard. And for a moment, I wonder if maybe Lincoln and I should give them some privacy. But then London and Brooklyn come running out and they break apart with a groan.

"You know," I say. "I was going to go in the pool. Would you girls like to join me?"

"Yes!" Both of them cheer.

"Go grab your suits. You can change at my place."

"Your place, huh?" Lincoln says when the girls run off. "I like the sound of that." He pulls me into him and kisses me. "Say you'll live with me. Make my place *our* place. I don't want you to move out, El."

"I'll live with you," I agree.

After the girls go home from spending the day swimming—while Micah proves he and Sienna aren't an old, married couple (*gag*)—Lincoln insists we move my stuff into his room. So, we order in Chinese and spend the evening intertwining our things.

"I've never shared a room with anyone," I admit once all our stuff is sorted and put away.

"Me either," Lincoln says. "I always preferred to have my own space." He pulls me into him, so our legs are entangled. "But I think I'm going to enjoy sharing a space with you." He nuzzles his face into my neck and nips playfully at my flesh.

"I think I'm going to enjoy it too," I agree.

SIX WEEKS LATER

"I can't believe Sienna seriously blew me off." I glance at

my phone again, still no message from my sister. With her being due in two weeks, and my due date just a few months after, I suggested we have a sister day since we'll both be busy once the babies are born. She told me that sounded great, and then at the last second, she canceled.

"I'm sure she had a good reason," Lincoln says as we step off the elevator and head to our door. When I told him she canceled, he offered to take me to breakfast.

"I guess." I pout, feeling super emotional lately. The books all say it's normal during pregnancy, but it feels like something more. Like I'm constantly waiting for something bad to happen, and it's stressing me out.

After we returned from our trip to the city, another major incident occurred at the dance studio. I was there after hours, dancing, when the place suddenly caught fire. Thankfully, Oscar was with me and ushered me to safety, and the damage was minimal. But upon inspection, we learned someone had hacked into the server to ensure whoever was responsible wouldn't be caught by taking the cameras down.

And then a couple of weeks ago, Lincoln's club, Wanderlust, nearly flooded. This time, his security team was able to keep whoever was responsible from hacking the server, but when they found the culprit, he was being pulled out of the water in the marina—his heart no longer beating. They know his name and that he lived in Booker Park, found out he was into drugs. But nobody knows why he did what he did or who he was working for. He wasn't connected to the club in any way. And the phone on him couldn't be recovered. Nothing is adding up...Or maybe we're missing something.

Lincoln keeps telling me not to stress, that it's not good for me and the baby, but it's hard not to worry when bad things keep happening around me.

"While you're adorable when you pout, I prefer to see you smile," Lincoln says as he hits the code and swings the door open, holding it for me so I can walk through first.

"Then tell my sister—"

The lights flip on, and several people shout, "Surprise!" at the same time, nearly giving me a heart attack.

"Tell me what?" Sienna says with a knowing smirk as she waddles over to me. "Happy baby shower!" she says, enveloping me in a hug.

I can't help it. The dam of emotion breaks open, and right in front of everyone, I start bawling. Overwhelmed, I'm hit hard by a myriad of feelings, ranging from worry to happiness and everything in between.

"Oh, El, don't cry," Sienna murmurs.

"Sorry." I sniffle back my sobs. "Thank you." I glance around at the room decorated in blues and greens. Balloons everywhere. There's a huge cake, tons of desserts, and food laid out on tables. And standing behind Sienna are the people who mean the most to me.

Lincoln's parents, Donna and Michael, are both here, smiling softly. It started out rough, but I quickly learned that Donna was more upset with Lincoln thinking he manipulated me. When they learned it was all me, they opened their arms, offering love and support.

My nieces are jumping up and down, holding gifts in their hands. Micah is standing next to them, looking a mixture of happy and pissed off—so, pretty much how he always looks. A few girls from the dance studio are here that I've become close to. And then, standing in the corner of the room, is my best friend.

"Raelyn!" I shriek, running over and attacking her. We text and talk and video chat almost every day, but I haven't seen her in person since I left California after we graduated, and I miss the hell out of her.

"I can't believe you're here!"

"And miss my bestie's baby shower? Not a chance." She pulls back and places her hand on my belly. "I can't believe how big you've gotten." Her gaze flits behind me, and then she says softly, "And holy shit, girl. It seems when we talk, you leave stuff out. Like the fact that your baby daddy is in love with you."

I glance back at Lincoln, who's smiling at me, and feel my cheeks flush. "I was afraid it wasn't real or that he'd change his mind," I admit to her. "I didn't want to look stupid."

"Oh, Ellie, when will you realize how lovable you are?" She hugs me again and kisses my cheek. "We'll catch up later. Right now, you have a baby shower to enjoy."

"Later?" I ask hopeful.

"Lincoln booked me a room here for the week."

"Yay!" I cheer, so excited to have my best friend for the entire week.

The baby shower is beautiful. Sienna planned everything to a T, including the delicious lunch and desserts. They make me open gifts, and Lincoln surprises me by showing me that the nursery has been painted without me knowing.

I couldn't ask for a better day, and I can't believe Sienna did all of this, less than a month before she's ready to pop.

"You made mine just as special," she says when I thank her after everyone but Raelyn and Lincoln have left. "I'm so proud of the woman you've become, El, and I have no doubt you're going to be an amazing mom."

"You're gonna make me cry," I half-joke.

"I'm serious," she says, giving me a watery smile. "Thank you for coming home. I know Micah forced your hand, but you could've left. I'm so excited to raise our babies together. I love you."

"I love you more."

Once she's gone, Lincoln insists Raelyn and I go relax by the pool while everything gets cleaned up and says he'll order something in for dinner later.

"Thank you," I tell him, giving him a quick kiss. "Today was perfect."

Raelyn and I change into our bathing suits and are lying out by the pool, talking about everything that's been going on with her in Colorado, when my phone rings with a call from Sienna. "It's time!" she squeals. "Apparently, the excitement from the baby shower was too much, and my water broke!"

"Oh my God!" I sit up. "Do you need me to watch the girls?"

"Could you, please? Donna is on her way to stay with them, but she just got home, so it will be a little while."

"I'm on my way!"

After letting Lincoln know I'm heading over to Sienna's place, Raelyn and I take off over there. I give Sienna and Micah both a hug, wishing them luck, and they depart for the hospital. Donna arrives about an hour later, but we stay and hang out, keeping the girls entertained while we wait to hear from Sienna and Micah.

About three hours later, after the girls have fallen asleep, Micah video calls to let us know the baby has arrived and that both mom and baby are doing fine.

"Well, don't keep us in suspense," Lincoln says, having joined us about an hour ago. "Is it a girl or a boy?"

"It's a boy," Micah chokes out. "A beautiful, strong, healthy little boy."

He moves the phone, bringing Sienna and the baby into view. She looks exhausted, but in the best possible way, as she holds her little bundle of joy and waves to us.

"And what's his name?" Donna asks.

"Colton Lincoln Alexander. Colton because we like it, and Lincoln in honor of my brother, since he's the reason we met." Micah's eyes move to where Sienna is sitting. "If he wouldn't have hired her, I'd be a lonely old man."

Everyone chuckles at his dramatics.

"That's a beautiful name," I tell them. "Congratulations. Let us know when you're up for company and we'll come by."

"You can come now," Sienna says. "Donna is going to bring the girls in the morning."

"We're on our way!" I jump up, excited to meet my nephew in person.

After changing, since I was still in my bathing suit and cover-up, we drop Raelyn off at her room with plans to have brunch in the morning, and then we head to the hospital.

Baby Colton is absolutely precious, and if I could, I would hold him forever. But since it's late, we only hang out for a little while, taking some pictures and making sure Sienna and Micah don't need anything.

"This will be you in a few months," Sienna says with a smile when I place Colton back in her arms so she can feed him.

"I'm scared shitless," I admit with a laugh. "You make it look so easy."

"It's not always easy, El," she says. "Parenting has its good moments and bad. Happy and sad. Some days, you'll question what the hell you're doing." She looks at me with a soft expression. "But then your baby will smile at you, tugging on your heartstrings, and it will all be worth it."

"I wish I would've been worth it," I blurt out, immediately regretting bringing up our past.

"You are," Sienna says. "Maybe not to *her*, but you've always been worth it to me."

"And to me," Lincoln adds, squeezing my shoulder. "And it's because of what you've been through that you'll be the most incredible, loving mom to our babies."

"Babies, huh?" Sienna laughs, lightening the mood. "Already planning the next? Guess it runs in the family." She smirks at Micah, who shrugs, and we all laugh.

After saying goodbye to them, Lincoln and I head out of the hospital. Since we drove ourselves—with Chris, another one of Lincoln's guys, following as protection—we walk back to the parking garage. Lincoln opens my door for me, and as I get in, a weird feeling comes over me. I glance around from the passenger seat, and my eyes lock on a gentleman standing in the darkened corner, a chill racing up my spine.

I take my eyes off of him for a second to see where Lincoln is, but when I glance back, the man is gone, leaving me wondering if my mind is playing tricks on me.

"What's wrong?" Lincoln asks when he gets in, attuned to my emotions.

"I thought I saw someone."

"What?" He looks around and pulls out his phone, already dialing somebody. "Who?"

"I don't know. He was standing in the corner, and then he was gone."

"Did you recognize him?"

I think hard on it. Something about that man felt oddly familiar, but I can't place him now…"I don't think so."

Lincoln relays the information to whoever's on the other end of the line, then hangs up and says it's being investigated.

When we get home, we take a shower together, something that's become a part of our routine, and then after we're both dressed, we cuddle in bed. I'm exhausted from today's events, and it doesn't take long before my eyes close and I fall asleep…

Emerald eyes.

Cold.

Calculating.

"You're supposed to be my dad! Please, if you love me, you'll let me stay with Sienna."

"Love you?" He scoffs. "Love doesn't belong in this world. It makes you weak. My family didn't get to where they are with love. We got here with power, brains. We made smart choices."

"Okay, but what does that have to do with me?"

"You will be a smart choice."

"I don't understand."

"You're my blood, Eliza. And from what I've been told, a virgin. In my world, that's worth a lot. There are many men who would pay a considerable amount in both money and favors to marry you."

"What?" I shriek. "You're going to sell me? Are you crazy? I'm your daughter!"

"Enough! Everyone has a part to play. You will play your part, or your sister will pay the price."

"Ellie...Ellie, wake up."

I snap my eyes open and find warm, hazel eyes staring at me instead of cold, emerald ones.

"You were having a nightmare."

"Yeah," I choke out. It was actually a memory, but nightmare works as well. "But it's over now." I wrap my arms around his neck and pull him over to me. "Thank you for being my safe place."

"Want to talk about it?"

I think about that for a second, unsure how to tell him what I'm feeling when I don't even really know myself. "I feel like we're missing something. I don't know what, but last night when we were in the parking garage...The guy I saw. I don't know. He looked familiar, but I can't place from where."

Lincoln nods in understanding. "I'm going to keep you and the baby safe. I promise. Please don't stress over this." He places a kiss to my nose, each of my cheeks, and then finally my lips. "Nothing will happen to either of you."

Thirty

LINCOLN

"Holy shit, El. You feel so good." I thrust into Ellie from the bottom, massaging her breasts while she rides me. Her hands are resting on my shoulders, using them as support, and I never want this to end. She's thirty-two weeks pregnant, and with her bump growing more and more every day, she prefers to be on top, and I'm not complaining. The sight of her tits bouncing as she rides my dick like a stick shift in a sport's car is a fucking turn-on.

"I'm so close," she mewls, trying to find the spot that will set her off. Since I've spent months learning her body, and I know it better than she does, I grip her hips and find the spot for her. It only takes seconds in this position before she's flying over the edge and taking me with her. She doesn't stop until she's milked me dry, and then with a quick kiss, she climbs off, so we can take a shower and start our day.

"You're having breakfast with Sienna?"

"Yep," she says, soaping up her body. "I can't get enough of Colton. He's so sweet."

"Soon, we'll have one of our own." I grab the shampoo and turn her around so I can wash her hair, knowing she loves when I do it. Just as I suspected, the minute my fingers delve into her hair, her body relaxes, and she groans in pleasure.

"I have some business to handle. A meeting for the casino we're building."

"Can you still go to my doctor's appointment?"

"Of course." I turn her back around and kiss her wet lips. "If I lose track of time, just come and get me when we need to go."

ELLIE

"You're the cutest little baby, aren't you?" I say in a baby voice to Colton. He's seriously the cutest freaking baby ever—after London and Brooklyn of course. But when London was born, I was young and didn't enjoy her like that. And I had moved to California shortly after Brooklyn was born.

"He's the devil," Sienna groans with a laugh. "London and Brooklyn were both sleeping for several hours a night by six weeks old, but not him. He's going to give me a run for my money, I just know it."

"Just like his daddy," I coo, making Colton smile.

"I'm going to make myself a sandwich. You hungry?" Sienna asks, standing.

"Oh, I—" I check my phone and see the time. "Shoot, no. I need to get going. I have my thirty-two-week checkup today."

"Getting close."

"Yep, it's crazy to think that by Thanksgiving, Lincoln and I will be joining the parent club." I set Colton in his swing and give him a kiss on the forehead. Then hug my sister. "I'm really glad we'll have you and Micah next door to help us. I'm excited, but I'm not going to lie. I'm also a bit nervous. Being responsible for someone's life is a lot. And watching how badly mom failed..."

"You're not Mom," she reminds me. "And I'll be there with you every step of the way. And you'll have Lincoln. He's a wonderful uncle, and I have no doubt he's going to make a great dad." She kisses my cheek. "Let me know how it goes."

"Will do."

When I get inside, I call out Lincoln's name, but he's nowhere to be found. I check his office, our room, the gym, but he's not here. I shoot him a text, but he doesn't respond, so I pop my head out of the door. "Hey, Oscar, have you seen Lincoln?"

"Not since he left about an hour ago. Everything okay?"

"Yeah, we need to leave for my doctor's appointment, or we'll be late." I could've sworn he told me to come and get him when it was time to go, but maybe he said he'd meet me there? With my pregnancy brain, anything is possible. "Can you take me? I'm assuming Lincoln is going to meet us at the doctor's office."

"Of course, ma'am. You ready to go?"

"Yep." I grab my purse, and then we take off down the elevator. I check my phone again to see if Lincoln's responded, but the elevator has no service. The second we step out the back door, my phone pings with a text from Lincoln telling me he's sorry and will meet me at my appointment.

I'm typing back a response when Oscar yells, "Watch out!" I look up to see what's going on, just in time to hear a gunshot ring out and then see him fall to the ground.

"Oscar!" I yell, running toward him.

"Ellie, run!" he chokes out.

It takes a second for his words to resonate in me, but once they do, it's too late. I'm being yanked up by two men wearing all black. My hands are pulled back and restrained, and my phone falls out of my hand, crashing to the ground.

I scream and cry, hoping to get someone's attention, but before anyone can come to my rescue, I'm shoved into the back of the car, and some kind of material is placed over my mouth, immediately silencing me.

"Don't forget the jewelry," the guy who gets into the driver seat says. The guy who got in next to me snatches my necklace and tosses it out of the car, then yanks my watch off, chucking it as well.

"Done."

Knowing there's no way out, I calm myself so I don't raise my blood pressure and put stress on my baby. Since they didn't bother to blindfold me, I watch the outside so I can try to see where we're going. If I can somehow escape or find a way to get ahold of Lincoln, I'll need to know where we are.

The ride isn't long, and what scares me is that these guys don't even try to hide where we're going, and everyone knows the only reason bad guys don't care how much you see is if they don't plan to keep you alive.

When we pull up to a small, rundown house on the outskirts of Tesoro, my first thought is that maybe they took me for my money. But if that's the case, why did they do everything else they did? Was it to scare us, so when they took me, I'd be more inclined to pay them?

My line of thoughts and questions come to a halt when I'm taken out of the vehicle and brought inside to find the man from the hospital parking garage standing in the living room, staring at me. It was months ago, but the look on his face is engrained into my brain.

And then he steps forward, the light from outside shining in, making his green eyes sparkle. And I gasp, only knowing one other person who has those eyes besides me...

But it doesn't make any sense because that man died in the fire.

And the man in front of me doesn't look like him.

"Welcome, *daughter*," he spits.

My eyes go wide at the confirmation. He's alive. But how is that possible? And why the hell does he look so different?

"I know I look a bit different," he says, as if he could hear my unspoken question. "But, yes, it's me. While you were dismantling everything my father and I worked to create, I was fighting for my life. While you were spending my money, I was having skin graphs and surgeries. It took years to recover from what you did."

"What do you want?" I choke out. "The money? You can have it all! Just let me go, please."

Eleazar chuckles, and the sound sends chills up my spine. He might look different, but between the green eyes and that laugh, I know it's him.

"Oh, you're going to pay me back, *mi hija*. But the money is only the beginning. I lost seven years of my life because of you, you little bitch. And then, when I return, I find you've destroyed everything. Every business, my home. You ruined it all. So, yes, you are going to pay me back...Starting with giving me the heir you owe me."

"What?" I gasp. "I don't understand. Just take my money. I have millions. You can have every penny—"

"It's not just the money!" Eleazar barks, grabbing my face and squeezing it painfully. "You ruined everything my family worked for. I am nothing now because of you, but once I have the money you took *and* my heir, I'll be able to start over, build again."

"You can't sell me off!" I hiss, pulling my face out of his grip. "In case you didn't notice, I'm not a fifteen-year-old virgin anymore."

"Oh, I know," he says, his face filled with disgust. "You're damaged goods. But you do have something that is of value to me." He glances down at my belly, and I take a step back.

"You can't be serious," I choke out.

"Oh, I am deadly serious," he says. "That baby you're carrying will be mine."

"And what about me?" I whisper.

"Once you've served your purpose, you won't be needed any longer. And I'll do what you intended to do to me...End your life."

LINCOLN

"Sir, if you need to reschedule..."

"Can you give me a couple of minutes?" I ask the front desk receptionist, who smiles and nods politely.

Ellie should've been here by now, and with her not answering my calls or texts, I'm worried she's pissed at me for leaving this morning without telling her. In my defense, when Dad called and said that one of our guys had captured an intruder, I took off wanting to be there to interrogate whoever it was, hoping to learn who's targeting us.

Of course, after hours of our men torturing the guy, we only learned that he was hired to break in and cause a scene. He doesn't know who hired him or why, only that he would be paid 10k cash if he was able to get away. Whoever it was, either hadn't counted on us having a guard watching our parents' house until shit gets sorted, or wanted him to get caught. But the question is why? Why would anyone pay to have someone break into our parents' house without wanting him to hurt anyone or take anything? Something isn't adding up.

I click on the tracker app I installed on Ellie's phone, and it shows she's still at the hotel. It's not like her to miss a doctor's appointment. She loves going to them and hearing the baby's heartbeat. It doesn't make any sense.

I dial Oscar's number, and it rings until it goes to voicemail, so I start to worry something's happened. I'm about to dial Sienna's number, since I left Micah back at our parents' house when I left for the doctor's appointment, but my brother's name pops up on the screen.

"Hey, I'm trying to get—"

"Ellie's been taken."

Three words. That's all it takes to bring me to my knees, right there in the doctor's office. My eyes close, and I pray to God that I heard my brother wrong. After a moment of silence, though, he continues...

"Oscar was shot in the parking garage. He hit the panic button on his watch, but he bled out before the ambulance could get there. Max tried to call us, but we were underground."

Underground...We were underground interrogating some asshole who broke into our parents' place while Oscar was shot and Ellie was taken.

"The police were called," he continues while I remain on the floor, unable to move. "They found her phone, necklace, and watch, but Ellie is still missing. Max confirmed her abduction. He's checking all the cameras now, trying to see if he can track where they took her."

I pry my eyes open, knowing I need to stand and walk out of this waiting room, out of this office. I need to find Ellie and bring her home. But my body doesn't want to move.

I failed her.

I failed our baby.

I promised I would keep them safe, and I failed them both.

While she was being taken, I was— "It was a setup."

"What?" Micah asks.

"The guy who broke into our parents' house. It was a setup. Whoever did this, knew we'd go running to our parents' place. They must've known Ellie had a doctor's appointment. I left, and in doing so, made her vulnerable."

Fuck! I never should've left her. Or I should've put more guys on her. If I would've—

"Stop," Micah says, snapping me from my thoughts. "Thinking about the 'what ifs' isn't going to change shit, so don't do it. We'll get her back, bro."

"Yeah, we will," I agree. "And when we find who took her, heads will fucking roll."

Thirty-One

LINCOLN

"How many times are you going to watch those videos?"

When I ignore my brother, my eyes staying trained on the computer screen, watching as Ellie kicks and screams and gets shoved into the vehicle, he reaches over and presses pause.

"You've been watching these same videos for the past four weeks. You've got to stop before you drive yourself crazy. We already know that aside from them heading to a backroad where the cameras cut off, they don't contain anything worth a shit that will lead us to her."

I swallow heavily, my eyes closing slightly from the lack of sleep. If I'm not out searching for answers, threatening and bribing people for information, I'm watching the videos. Over and over again. Because it's all I can do.

Ellie's been gone for thirty-five days. Thirty-five fucking days without sleeping with her cuddled into my side. Without seeing her doing yoga in the living room. Without smelling her sweet vanilla scent. Thirty-five days without watching her read her romance books while she lays out by the pool. Without seeing her smile, hearing her laughter.

Our baby has grown another four weeks, is now the size of a honeydew. I haven't felt him kick my hand, heard her talk to him. She hasn't rearranged the nursery or bought anymore baby outfits. I have no idea if her blood pressure is up, if she's able to take her anemia medication.

It's been thirty-five days, and we're no closer to finding her. It's as if the car she got into drove off the face of the Earth. Nobody's reached out wanting a ransom, her accounts haven't been touched. We've hired the best of the best, and nobody has any answers.

I press play, and the frame picks up where it left off with Ellie disappearing into the car. A second later, the window goes down, and her necklace and watch are thrown out. Her phone is on the ground already, having fallen from her hand when she was grabbed. Before the window goes up, my screen is slammed shut.

I spin around and stand, cock my fist back, then hit Micah square in the jaw. He stumbles back, but once he's gathered his wits, he comes for me, tackling me to the ground. I expect him to punch me—hell, I'd welcome the pain—but instead, once he's got me pinned, he grips my wrists and holds me down.

"Fucking stop!" he barks. "I get it. You're—"

"No!" I shout back, my heart racing behind my ribcage. "You don't fucking get it. Sienna was missing for a few hours. Ellie's been gone for weeks! Motherfucking weeks! Back then, we knew who took Sienna. But right now, I have no fucking clue where Ellie is!" I lift my legs, causing Micah to fall forward and off balance. I shove him to the side as I climb to my feet. "Watching these videos, searching for her, asking everyone questions are the only things keeping me from falling apart!" I pound my fist against my chest.

"She's somewhere out there, God knows where, probably

fucking scared. For all we know, she's been trafficked. She could be anywhere at this point. In someone's basement, in a shipping crate on the way to another country to be sold," I say, imagining all the horrific possibilities and scenarios. "She's due in a few weeks, and I don't know how to get to her." I choke out the last words, emotion clogging my throat as tears fill my lids. I close my eyes, wishing the world around me would disappear. If something's happened to Ellie...Fuck, I don't want to be in a world where she doesn't exist.

"Lincoln," Micah says, palming my face. Prying my lids open, I look into my brother's eyes which are filled with emotion. "We'll find her."

"You don't know that." I shake my head and move past him, unable to look at him any longer. All I want is to be alone.

"I promise, we won't stop until we do."

"Yeah," I agree, more so to get him to go away.

"Come to dinner tonight, please," he says, following me to the front door. "Colton has a checkup we need to take him to, but when we get home, come over and eat with us."

"I'm not good company."

"Nobody expects you to be. But right now, whether you want to admit it or not, you need to be around family."

"What I need is to find Ellie." Snatching my keys, I head out, having no idea where I'm going but needing to do everything I can to try to find her...To find someone who has information regarding Ellie's captor and where he's taken her. Somebody has to know something.

❦

ELLIE

"Is she ready?"

"I'm only thirty-six weeks!"

"I didn't ask you," Eleazar barks, shooting me a glare. "Dr. Pasquale, if she were to give birth right now, would the baby survive?"

"M-Mr. Gutierrez," the doctor stammers, terrified of Eleazar—which makes sense, since he's coercing the poor doctor into doing as he demands by threatening his family. "Technically, yes, but—"

"No buts." Eleazar raises his hand. "I'm tired of waiting. The Alexanders are circling. They're asking too many questions, and I can't hide for much longer. When I take back my life, I need to make a grand entrance. And the only way I can do that is with my heir in my arms."

I close my eyes and try to tune out his grand plan. Since he has no intention of letting me survive past giving birth, he's had no problem speaking in front of me—dead people can't talk after all.

At first, I was confused as to why he hasn't killed Micah and Lincoln yet, but when he shared his plan, I realized Eleazar Gutierrez has lost his damn mind. In time, he does intend to kill them, but not until he's shown Lincoln that he will be raising his son and has reestablished his rightful place in Tesoro. Since he holds them both responsible for trying to kill him and then dismantling his empire, Eleazar doesn't just want to take his life back—he wants retribution for the time he's lost.

"I'll need to run a few tests to make sure, but—"

"Then do it!" Eleazar barks.

"I'll need a nurse to assist and equipment."

"Fine." Eleazar steps toward him and gets in his face. "Just remember that if anyone finds out, I'll not only have your wife and daughter raped while you watch, but they'll be tortured and murdered as well. And I'll leave you alive, so you'll be forced to remember every day the consequences of having betrayed me."

"I-I understand, sir."

"Good! I'm tired of waiting for what's owed to me. Today is the day I finally take back my life." He glares my way. "And everyone else loses theirs."

Eleazar stalks out, leaving the doctor and me alone, but I don't bother begging him to help me. I learned the first time I did that, the room where I'm being held captive is monitored. When I tried to bribe the doctor for his help, Eleazar punished me by covering my mouth for what felt like days, which prevented me from eating and drinking. As much as I want to fight back, I can't risk my baby being hurt in the process. My only hope is that Lincoln somehow manages to find and rescue us. It's the only thought that keeps me going every day.

When the doctor leans in close, I flinch, unsure what he's doing, why he's suddenly so close to me, until his lips brush my ear and he murmurs, "I'm going to find a way to save you."

Just as quickly as he leaned in, he stands upright, and when he leaves the room, I'm left wondering if I just imagined what he said.

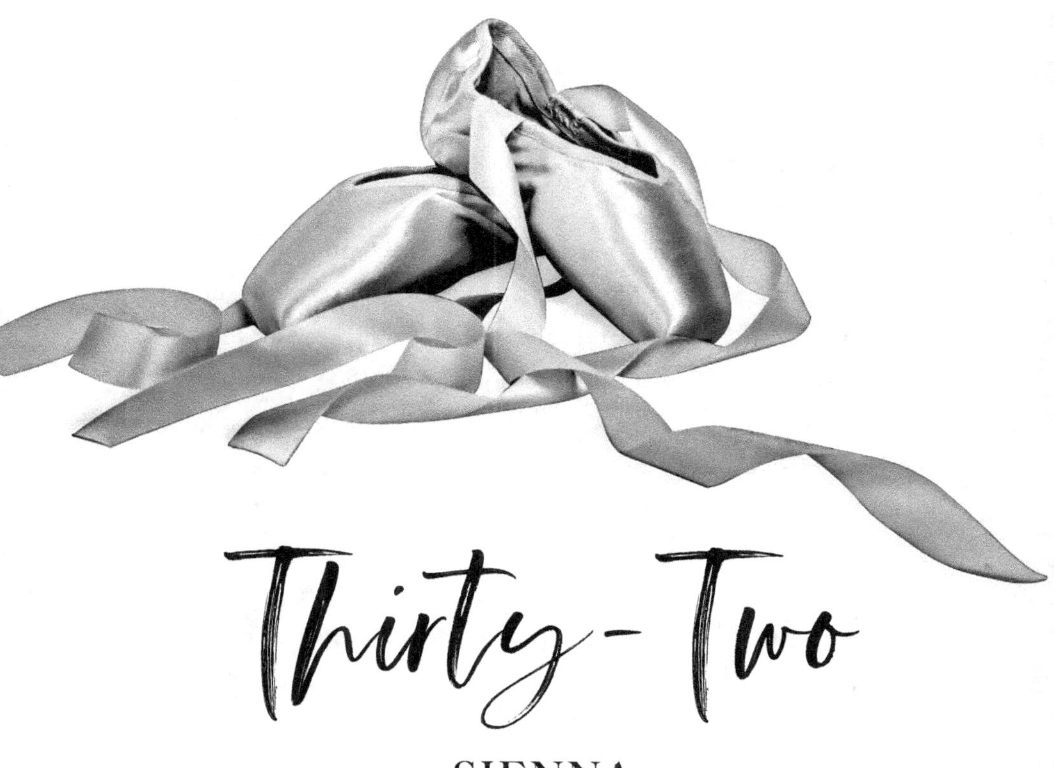

Thirty-Two

SIENNA

"Thank God his lungs are clear." I place Colton back in the car seat and buckle him in, giving him a soft kiss to his forehead. About a week ago, Colton caught a cold from the girls. We had the pediatrician come check them out. Luckily, London and Brooklyn's immune systems are strong, and aside from a cough, they're okay. But Colton is younger, so he's struggling a bit more than them. The pediatrician recommended having his chest x-rayed to be on the safe side, and thankfully, everything is okay.

"And did you see he weighs twelve pounds?" I add. "He's getting so big so fast. It feels like he was just born, yet he's already two months old."

"Time doesn't stop," Micah mutters, a sardonic smile spreading across his face. It's been a month since Ellie was taken, and even though he's right, time doesn't stop, it also feels like someone pressed pause on our lives the moment she disappeared.

"How's your eye feeling?" I reach up to palm the side of his face, hating how badly it looks. When Lincoln punched him, he got him good. It's only been a couple of hours, but there's already an intense bruise forming.

"It's fine." He tilts his head to the side, avoiding my touch. I try not to take it personally, knowing he's not upset with me but worried about his brother and the search for Ellie—just as I am— but it still hurts. "We should head home."

Ever since Ellie went missing, Micah insisted on homeschooling the girls, not wanting to risk anyone else's safety by any of us leaving the hotel. The only reason we're out right now is because Colton needed to have his lungs checked for fluid, which needed to be done at the hospital.

When we walk past the cafeteria, the scent of caffeine permeates the air, and I make a last second decision to grab a cup of coffee from here. I know from our Lamaze classes that they sell coffee from Coffee Grind, a local coffee shop that I love.

"Hellcat," Micah grumbles.

"I'll just be a second. I'm running on fumes."

While I get in line, Micah stands off to the side with Colton, holding the stroller. And two guards, who are there to protect us, monitor the area.

As the line moves forward, I step up to the counter, ready to place my order, when a woman walking past bumps into me, nearly knocking me over.

"Oh, I'm sorry," she says. "Please excuse me."

I'm about to tell her it's okay, when she shoves something into my hand, stunning me silent. I watch as she continues on her way and then open the paper in my hand.

Follow me to Eliza. She's in danger. Please bring help.

I read the words once, twice, a third time before they sink in, and I rush after her. I have no idea where she's going or if this is a trap, but I'll be damned if I don't do as she says.

"Sienna," Micah hisses, catching up to me. "What are you doing?"

"I'm—" It hits me just before I start explaining that there must be a reason why the woman gave me a note instead of telling me. Someone might be listening.

"I need to use the restroom," I say instead. I hand Micah the paper and take over pushing the stroller so he can read the note.

The second his eyes land on the words, his steps falter slightly, his gaze flying around the area until they land on the woman I'm following. And then he pulls out his phone and starts typing.

She leads us outside, and just as I begin to worry about keeping up with her—since we have the baby with us and our vehicle is parked on the other side—two cars pull up.

"Get in with the baby," Micah says.

"What? No. I need to go to my sister."

"You need to go home with our son where it's safe. When we get Ellie, she's going to need you."

I want to argue, but he's right, and I don't want to waste time when I know he'll never let me put myself in harm's way. So instead, I pull him into a quick hug, telling him that I love him and to please bring Ellie home.

He nods into my hair. "I love you, and I will."

And then Colton and I get into the car with one of the guards, and I pray my husband comes back alive with Ellie in tow.

Thirty-Three

ELLIE

"Please! No!" I scream, trying with everything in me to shake my body enough that the doctor won't be able to cut me open. "Please," I beg. "Don't do this! It's not time!"

The doctor gives me a look of sympathy, and tears fill my eyes, knowing he has no choice. Either I was imagining that he said he would get help, or he was unsuccessful. Either way, he's numbed me from the waist down, has prepped me for a caesarean delivery, and is about to cut me open and tear my baby out of me, and there's nothing I can do to stop him.

"I'm waiting on the other nurse to arrive," he says to Eleazar. "She's the pediatric nurse. We need her to—"

"I'm done waiting!" Eleazar barks. "Cut her open now!"

"Please! You can't—"

"Shut up!" Eleazar slaps me across the face so hard, I nearly black out. "Shut her up!"

"I don't—" the doctor begins, but Eleazar cuts him off.

"Shut her up, or I'll kill your entire family."

The doctor nods and grabs something from the table. When I glance over, I see it's a needle.

"Please don't," I whimper.

"I'm sorry," he mutters almost incoherently. "This will put you to sleep," he says a bit louder, "so you won't feel any pain."

I swallow nervously, staring at him as he sticks me with the needle. A few moments later, everything begins to turn hazy. I try to keep my eyes open, but they're too heavy.

There's a loud bang followed by several more bangs, and I want so badly to see what's going on, but my eyes give up, closing of their own accord as everything around me fades to black, and I pray that my baby's okay.

LINCOLN

From the moment I got the text from Micah telling me they have a lead as to where Ellie might be, followed by his location, everything kicked into overdrive.

I wasn't sure what the hell was going on, but I knew my brother wouldn't fuck with me, so I followed the location until it led me to a back road with fresh tracks.

But instead of taking that road, I kept following where Micah was leading me. When I saw his vehicle, I pulled up and got out.

"Where are we? Where is she?"

"I think she's down the road we passed."

"How the hell do you know?"

"A nurse tipped Sienna off. She drove down that road, but I kept going. She wrote that Ellie is in danger."

"So, what the fuck are we waiting for?" I start heading back to my car, but Micah gets out and catches up to me.

"Stop. We don't know what we're walking into. This could be a trap. Whoever has her is most likely armed, probably with an army of men who've been told to shoot without question. We need to be smart about this. I sent Max the location, and he's gathering information."

Fuck, I know he's right. But the idea of us being so close to Ellie and unable to get to her has me shaking.

"Yeah?" Micah says, putting his phone to his ear as two more vehicles arrive with our men inside. "Okay, thanks."

He hangs up. "He was able to hack into a satellite nearby. There's an abandoned house about a mile back. Two guys are guarding the front door, two in the back. He can't see inside, but..."

"But the chances of this being a coincidence is slim. Ellie's got to be in there." For the first time in a damn month, I have hope that we're going to find her.

"Yeah," Micah agrees as we're handed Kevlar vests and weapons.

We go over the game plan, with the goal to get in and get out with Ellie—as well as the nurse who Micah believes put her life on the line to deliver the message to Sienna—and then we pile into two vehicles, leaving the others here. Since driving up would tip the guards off and risk Ellie's captor doing something crazy, we pull over halfway up the road and park, getting out and walking the rest of the way.

Because they're not expecting anyone to be approaching by foot, we're able to surround the area. We take out the guards quickly, and Micah and I run in, knowing our men have our backs.

We listen for voices, and once we have a location, we approach the room slowly, careful not to tip off whoever's here. But when we arrive, and I take in the sight before me, I fear we are in fact too late.

Ellie's on a medical table, her eyes closed. A doctor is standing over her with a nurse next to him. Another nurse is standing to the side. And then there's a man in a suit. I don't know who he is, but what I do know is that he doesn't belong, and my suspicions are confirmed when he barks out, "Hurry the fuck up!"

I spot the gun in his hand, aimed at the doctor's head, and I aim my own gun and shoot, taking the man in the suit out. He flies back, blood and brain matter hitting the wall, and the doctor sucks in a harsh breath.

"Stop!" I demand, but he shakes his head. "Stop, or I'll shoot you just like I shot him."

"I-I can't," he says. "It's too late."

I step further into the room, my gun now aimed at the doctor's head, and faintly hear someone saying, "All clear," but my only focus is on the huge gaping hole in Ellie's stomach.

"What the fuck did you do?" I hiss, ready to blow this fucker to bits.

"Mr. Gutierrez made him," the nurse rushes out. "The doctor tried to stall, but he forced him to cut her open."

"Mr...?" I glance at Micah, whose eyes are as wide as mine probably are.

"Eleazar Gutierrez," the doctor clarifies. "He's been threatening my family to get me to cooperate. He wanted the baby. I'm so sorry," he says, his eyes and words pleading with me. "It's too late. I have to deliver the baby. She's already been exposed."

"Fuck," Micah hisses. "I'm calling an ambulance."

"Is Ellie okay?" I choke out, brushing several sweaty strands of Ellie's hair out of her face.

"She's sedated," the doctor says. "She'll wake up soon, but right now, I need to deliver this baby."

"It's too early. She's still got a month to go."

The doctor nods as he goes back to what he's doing. "His lungs are developed. It will be okay."

Micah and I watch as the doctor and nurses work in unison to deliver Ellie's and my son. I'm not sure what they're doing, but the moment I see a head full of hair, it feels like my heart leaps out of my chest. A moment later, Donovan's shoulder and upper body appear, and then the rest of him is pulled out. He's covered in blood, and I hold my breath, praying he's okay.

And then the most beautiful sound fills the room when our son lets out a cry for the very first time. The doctor hands him off to the nurse before returning his attention back to Ellie. I'm torn between watching him work on Ellie and making sure our child is okay.

As if Micah can sense my turmoil, he says, "Go make sure your son is taken care of, I'll watch the doctor."

"Thank you."

I go to the nurse, who cleans Donovan off and suctions shit out of his nose. "I don't have all the equipment to check him here," she murmurs, "but he looks healthy." She wraps him in a blanket before extending her arms out to me. "Would you like to hold your son?"

I nod, choked up with emotion. After putting the safety back on my gun and stowing it away, the nurse places my son into my arms. His eyes are closed and he's whimpering, still with a bit of blood and shit on him, but he's the most perfect thing I've ever seen in my life.

"Welcome to the world, Donovan Michael Alexander." His eyes flutter open, as if he already knows his name, and his lips purse together. He lets out a soft cry, and my heart swells inside my chest. I walk him over to Ellie and hold him next to her. "This is your mom. She's asleep right now, but trust me when I tell you, you're already her entire world."

ELLIE

THE FIRST THING I HEAR WHEN I COME TO IS HIS VOICE. "...SHE has the most expressive, beautiful green eyes and the sweetest smile. And when she looks at you, it's as if you're the only person that matters. She's strong and resilient, and even though life dealt her a shit hand, she never let it get her down."

I'm not sure who he's talking to or where I am, but his voice is soothing, and I'm tired. I want to open my eyes, but it feels like I just need a little more sleep...

The sound of what I assume is a door creaking open hits my ears, and then I hear my sister speak. "She's still asleep?"

"Yeah, but I'm sure she'll wake up soon. How could she not when she's got this perfect little miracle waiting to meet her?"

Huh? Who's waiting to meet me?

Before I can give it much thought, my sister says, "Did all the tests come back okay?"

At first, I think she's talking about me, until Lincoln responds. "He's perfect, despite that asshole having him ripped out of Ellie's womb early."

My eyes shoot open at his words, my hand going to my belly, as everything comes rushing back to me: Oscar being shot, me being taken and held captive by Eleazar, and then Eleazar forcing the doctor to deliver Donovan early.

Where my bump was, it's now flat, and I gasp out loud, realizing I'm no longer pregnant. "My baby," I choke out, my gaze landing on Lincoln.

"Hey, hey, it's okay," he says, standing. And it's then that I see the bundle of blankets nestled in his arms. "Ellie, I'd like for you to meet your son." He leans on the edge of the bed and places my baby boy in my arms, and I immediately start to cry, my emotions overtaking me.

"Is he...Is he okay?" I choke out, my eyes glued to the sweet little baby who's now cradled in my arms. His eyes are closed, and his lips are pursed, making a sucking motion. He's got a bit of dark hair on the top of his head and the cutest button nose.

"He's perfect, El," Sienna says. "He's six pounds and twenty and a half inches. His lungs are fully developed, and he passed all the testing they ran on him once he arrived."

I sigh in relief, thankful that the doctor was telling the truth when he told Eleazar that the baby was okay to be delivered. Speaking of which…"What happened? Is Eleazar…?"

Lincoln's jaw clenches. "He's dead. And this time, he's not coming back. I blew his head off his goddamn shoulders."

"Micah and Lincoln said it barely looked like him," Sienna adds. "But a rush DNA test confirmed that you guys are related."

"Yeah, it's him. Someone saved him from the fire and nursed him back to health. He was in a coma for a while and had to have skin graphs and surgeries, which is why he didn't look the same. Once he'd finally recovered and returned, he was pissed to discover that everything he built had been destroyed. But he didn't just want everyone involved dead, he wanted revenge.

"His plan was to kidnap and sell me like he originally wanted, but then I slept with Lincoln and got pregnant. So, he changed his plan…"

"To take our son," Lincoln guesses.

"Yeah. He was going to take him and then kill all of us. Was it the doctor who saved me? He told me he would, but I wasn't sure…"

"Yeah," Sienna says with a small smile. "A nurse approached me at the hospital and had us follow her. The doctor asked her to get help, but she couldn't find us at first because we were at an appointment for Colton. Luckily, she stumbled upon the appointment information when she logged into the hospital's database searching for any particulars that might help her locate us. That's how she was finally able to track us down.

"By the time we found the location where you were being held and were able to go in and get to you, it was already too late," Lincoln says.

"Looks like you showed up right on time," I say, leaning

over and inhaling Donovan's baby scent. I glance up at Lincoln. "Thank you. This is the second time you've saved me."

Lincoln shakes his head. "I never should've had to—"

"Stop." I reach out and place my hand in his. "Everything is okay, and beating yourself up over what happened isn't going to help anything. Our baby is here, and he's perfect. Eleazar is gone, and we're all okay."

"Everyone except Oscar," Sienna murmurs. "He didn't make it."

Tears fill my lids. I had a feeling that the shot might've killed him, but I was hoping that wasn't the case. "He was a good guard," I say through my tears. "A good man. I know he wasn't married and didn't have kids, but I'd like to pay for his funeral and make sure his mom is taken care of."

"We did all that," Lincoln tells me. "It was a few weeks ago. We made sure he had a good service, and we took care of his mom."

"Oh, right...Because I was gone for over a month."

"There she is." A doctor I don't recognize walks in. "Glad to see you're awake and holding your baby. How are you feeling?"

"I'm still a bit out of it," I admit.

"That's to be expected."

The doctor explains everything my body went through, what I can expect healing wise, and then asks if I'm planning to breastfeed. Since I am, he offers to call in a lactation specialist and says he'll be back later to check on me. Sienna tells us she's going to let Micah know that I'm awake, giving us a few minutes alone.

"It's so crazy," I say once Sienna and the doctor are gone. "I went to sleep pregnant and woke up a mom."

Lincoln chuckles. "It's probably for the best. Seeing your insides is something I'll never forget." He leans over and palms my face, pressing his lips to mine. "I'm so thankful we were able to find you, Kitten. Don't be surprised if I don't let you or this little guy leave my sight for a while. I never knew what I was missing until you came back into my life. Now that I know, I couldn't handle losing either of you."

"Well, then it's a good thing you'll never have to find out." I move over so he can join me on the bed, and he climbs on, pulling me and the baby into his arms. "When I snuck into your club hoping to seduce you, I never thought it would end up like this," I half joke, making him laugh. "But I have to say, the risk was definitely worth the reward."

Epilogue

ELLIE
FOUR MONTHS LATER

"So, you haven't seen him all day?"

"Nope. He said with the Valentine's event happening at Elite, he would be home late," I tell my sister as I walk into the penthouse with a sleeping Donovan wrapped in my baby carrier. When I find Lincoln's parents sitting in the living room, I screech in shock.

"Everything okay?" Sienna asks.

"Yeah, sorry. Donna and Michael are here. Let me call you back."

I hang up and drop my bags onto the counter. "Did we have plans?" I ask, trying to remember if I made plans and completely forgot. It wouldn't surprise me. Baby brain is a real thing.

"No." Donna laughs. "We're actually here to watch our precious grandbaby."

"What?" I shoot her a confused look, since in the four months Donovan's been alive, I've yet to have anyone watch him. If he isn't with me, he's with Lincoln. It's not that I don't trust our family, but after what I went through, I can't seem to let my son out of my sight. I know it's unhealthy, which is why I've started to attend therapy on a regular basis. Lincoln even attends with me sometimes, and it feels like it's really helping.

"You have a note waiting for you in your bedroom," Donna says with a grin.

After I unwrap Donovan and lay him in his crib, I go to my bedroom to see what Donna's talking about, and sure enough, there's a large red box with a black bow on the bed. I open it and find a note on top.

Happy Valentine's Day,

It was one year ago today that our lives were forever changed. I've enclosed something for you to wear, and once you're ready, there will be a limo waiting to take you to me.

Love,

Lincoln

P.S. I know you're freaking out about leaving Donovan with my parents, but it's only for a few hours, and Sienna and Micah are right down the hall.

He's right, I am freaking out. But my excitement over whatever Lincoln's planned is helping a bit. Setting the note down, I open the tissue paper and find the most exquisite little black dress and heels. Underneath is a lacy set of lingerie and nestled at the bottom is the same Venetian cat mask I wore to the masquerade party one year ago.

Butterflies erupt in my belly in remembrance of that first night I spent with Lincoln. The gentle way he taught me what it means to make love while rocking my world. I thought that night could never be topped, but I was wrong because Lincoln has spent the past year showing me repeatedly just how amazing sex can be with the person you love.

After I've gotten ready, fed Donovan, and have gone over everything with Donna and Michael, I head out with my new guard, Westley. Just as Lincoln wrote, there's a limo waiting for us. Westley opens the door for me and helps me in and then sits in the front with the chauffeur.

The drive to Elite is short, and once we're there, I expect to be taken around back, but instead, we go through the front just like I did last time. The bouncer nods in greeting as I make my way in, a confirmation that there's no need for pretense like last year. As I enter, I quickly realize that Westley's no longer trailing behind. And when I step inside the club with my mask on, I'm taken back to last Valentine's Day. Only this time, instead of the fear and uncertainty running through my veins, I'm buzzing with electricity at the thought of spending time with Lincoln.

Unsure where to go, I head straight for the bar, since that's where I encountered Lincoln on Valentine's night one year ago today. I situate myself on the barstool, and the bartender brings me over a mojito without me having to ask. It's only then that I realize Lincoln is recreating that very momentous night. Although we've never discussed the particulars of that night, Lincoln clearly remembers everything about it. I love that he remembers even the smallest details, such as what I wore and what I drank.

I take a sip of my drink, and even though I'm not nervous, I create an origami bird while I wait for Lincoln to appear.

A few minutes later, a gentleman dressed to the nines in a sexy tux takes a seat next to me. He orders himself a drink before casually glancing over. "Not a duck."

I giggle at his perception. "A bird." I place it in front of him and slowly look up. With his mask on, just like last time, the only features I can completely make out are his beautiful hazel eyes.

When his gaze meets mine, he shakes his head and chuckles. "How did I not know it was you?" He palms the side of my face. "I would recognize those gorgeous emerald eyes anywhere."

"I'm glad you didn't," I admit. "We wouldn't be where we are if you had."

"I'd like to argue, but you're right. I wasn't ready for you yet. But I am now." He leans in and presses his lips to mine. "Dance with me?"

His question is simple, yet the meaning is so deep my belly knots. "I would love to."

With our fingers entwined, Lincoln guides us onto the dance floor and pulls me into his arms. With my head on his chest, we sway to the music in comfortable silence for several minutes before Lincoln speaks.

"I became obsessed with vanilla after that night. Had I been around you afterward and breathed in your intoxicating scent, I would've known it was you." He inhales deeply, dragging his nose along the curve of my neck, and the area between my legs tightens in anticipation, knowing that soon we'll make our way to the backroom.

When Lincoln doesn't make any move to leave the dance floor, I whisper, "I want you," and he chuckles, the deep yet melodic sound doing crazy things to my insides.

Without saying a word, he drags me down the hall to the same room as last time. He presses the card to the door's sensor, and we step inside, the bit of light from the hall disappearing the second the door closes behind us.

Lincoln pushes me against the door, and memories from that night come rushing back. Only now, the fear and uncertainty have been replaced with hunger and confidence.

Our mouths connect in a passionate kiss filled with love and desire. I don't have to see him to know that he loves me and craves me. I can feel it in the way his mouth moves against mine. In the way his hands roam along my body.

"Jesus, baby. I can't get enough of you," he murmurs, nipping my bottom lip before he trails open-mouthed kisses along my neck and collarbone. We work in unison shedding our clothes, and once we're both naked, he turns me around so my ass is jutted outward, and my hands are against the wall.

"Spread those thighs, Kitten."

I do as he says, and a second later, he parts my cheeks, and his tongue glides across the tight rosebud. "Oh, fuck," I moan, knowing he needs to get me ready first, but wanting him deep in my ass right now. Lincoln works me up, taking me to the edge, but before I can jump, he pulls back and twirls me around and into his arms. He carries me to the bed and lays me down.

He kisses me hard, then demands, "Get on your knees."

He doesn't have to tell me twice. Once I'm positioned, he slides inside me. He's hard and thick, and as he grips my hips and fucks me with abandon, I'm reminded of how perfectly we fit. I scream out my orgasm, and before I've come down, he's thrusting into my ass.

I never imagined that one day, I'd not only be comfortable enough with a man to have sex, but I would enjoy anal. But I know it's only because I'm with Lincoln. I feel safe with him, knowing I can trust him with every part of me.

I climax again, this time taking Lincoln with me. And when we've both come down from our orgasms, he lifts me once again and carries me to the bathroom. Unlike last time—when I refused to let him see me in the light, in fear of him finding out who I was—we remove our masks and shower together, making love under the water before we get out.

I expect for us to get dressed, so I'm shocked when he guides us back into the dark room and over to the bed.

"Haven't gotten your fill yet?" I joke, when he hovers over me and nuzzles his face into my neck.

"Not possible," he murmurs, pressing a soft kiss to the sensitive spot just under my ear. "The more I have you, the more I want you."

"Never know," I say with a laugh. "One day you might get sick of me."

"Not happening. But how about we put it to a test?" He nibbles my flesh, and I moan in agreement.

"Okay, sure." I tilt my head to give him better access. "But how do you suppose we test this theory?"

"By you marrying me," he says, shocking me still. "And spending the rest of our lives together." Because we're in the dark, I can't see him, but I can feel when he takes my left hand in his and slides something onto my third finger.

"Lincoln," I breathe, my heart pounding against my ribcage.

"I love you, Ellie," he says, his lips pressing against mine. I close my eyes, and when I open them, the light is on, and Lincoln's looking down on me, his eyes filled with warmth. "Until you, I could never imagine settling down. I was content with keeping shit light and casual. But now, I can't imagine going back to being that man. I love our lazy mornings and late nights. Watching you do yoga and dance. You're an amazing mom to our son, and you're my best friend. I crave you and want you and desire you, and I know I'll never stop."

He lifts my hand, and I spot the shiny diamond that's now resting on my finger. It's simple yet elegant, and I love it.

"Marry me, Kitten, and I promise to spend our lives proving to you that the risk you took on me was totally worth the reward."

I throw my head back with a laugh, remembering when I told him that. "I don't need you to prove anything to me, Lincoln. You already do...Every single day...Through your actions, with your love. Yes, I'll marry you, but I was wrong...You were never a risk...Because you've always been my safe place."

About the Author

Reading is like breathing in, writing is like breathing out.
– Pam Allyn

Nikki Ash resides in South Florida where she is an English teacher by day and a writer by night. When she's not writing, you can find her with a book in her hand.

From the Boxcar Children, to Wuthering Heights, to the latest single parent romance, she has lived and breathed every type of book. While reading and writing are her passions, her two children are her entire world. You can probably find them at a Disney park before you would find them at home on the weekends!